The

PROTECTOR

The

PROTECTOR

JODI ELLEN MALPAS

FOREVER

New York   Boston

Copyright © 2016 by Jodi Ellen Malpas
Cover design by Elizabeth Turner
Cover photograph by George Kerrigan
Cover copyright © 2016 by Hachette Book Group, Inc.

Forever
Hachette Book Group
1290 Avenue of the Americas
New York, NY 10104
forever-romance.com
twitter.com/foreverromance

Printed in the United States of America

First Edition: September 2016

RRD-C

10 9 8 7 6 5 4 3 2 1

Forever is an imprint of Grand Central Publishing.
The Forever name and logo are trademarks of Hachette Book Group, Inc.

The Hachette Speakers Bureau provides a wide range of authors for speaking events. To find out more, go to www.hachettespeakersbureau.com or call (866) 376-6591.

Library of Congress Cataloging-in-Publication Data is available upon request.

ISBN 978-1-4555-6819-2 (trade paperback edition)
ISBN 978-1-4555-6820-8 (ebook edition)

For my dad—my forever protector

Acknowledgments

There are just so many people to thank, and I always wonder if you all get fed up of hearing it. But just in case you don't, to my teams here in the UK and across the water in America, thank you for continuing to be a constant support in my career. I'm a very lucky girl to have you all behind me.

There is one person who I must single out—someone who means so much to me, and not just in a professional capacity. My agent, Andrea Barzvi. It's been over three years since she and I met—when I was clueless on all things publishing and caught up in the whirlwind of *This Man*. I'm still pretty clueless, but knowing I have Andrea by my side makes this roller coaster ride more thrilling than frightening. She's a pure gem, and I still count my lucky stars every day that she found me. Thank you, Andy, for everything you do, professionally *and* beyond.

And finally, to all of you amazing bloggers and readers across the globe. Thank you for welcoming me into your online world and sticking around to see where my writing journey takes me. I hope you enjoy my new man, Jake.

The
PROTECTOR

CHAPTER 1

JAKE

His eyes, *wide and terrified, stare up at me, his body frozen beneath mine. The heat, the dust, the sounds of screams around me—it's all making it nearly impossible to focus. But I must focus. I blink rapidly, shifting to keep him secure, pushing him into the gravel and grit under me. I'm not supposed to be here. I should be out of sight in the surrounding hills, invisible amid the overgrowth and rocks. The unknown, unseen threat.*

The man I'm holding prisoner is thin and malnourished, and the whites of his eyes are tinged by yellow. This brainwashed fucker has taken out two of my comrades. The intense ache in my shoulder reminds me that he nearly took me out, too. I should have stayed in position. I've fucked up. A reckless, selfish need to rain holy hell on these fucked-up arseholes has resulted in the deaths of two soldiers. It should be me lying dead in the dirt a few meters away. I deserve it.

His heart is beating frantically behind the thin material of his filthy T-shirt. I can feel the thuds punching into my chest, even through the layers of my clothing and bulletproof vest. But that evil glint in his glazed eyes is still there as he mumbles a jumble of foreign words up at me.

He's praying.

He should be.

"See you in hell." I pull the trigger and put a bullet in his skull.

* * *

I bolt up in bed, sweating and heaving, the thin sheets sticking to every part of me they touch.

"Motherfucker," I breathe, allowing my eyes to adjust to the early morning glow until I can see the inky skyline of London from the panoramic window in my bedroom. It's 6 a.m. I know that without even looking at the clock on my bedside cabinet, and it isn't only the rising sun that tells me so. The alarm in my head that explodes at the same time every morning is both a burden and a blessing.

Throwing my legs off the side of the bed, I grab my phone, not surprised when I find no messages or missed calls.

"Morning, world," I mutter, tossing it back onto the nightstand before extending my arms toward the ceiling, stretching my tight muscles. I roll my shoulders, breathing some air into my lungs before letting it stream out calmly through my nose. Leaning forward, I rest my forearms on my knees and stare out across the city, pushing back the nightmare to a safe corner of my mind as I breathe slowly through it. In and out. In and out. In and out. I close my eyes and thank the power of forged serenity. I'm a master at it.

But then my muscles tense all over again when the bed shifts beneath me. My hand slips straight under the mattress to pull out my VP9 before my mind has even voiced its command.

Impulse.

The gun is aimed at my waking target before my eyes have even focused.

Instinct.

I'm on my feet, naked as the day I was born, arms steady and stretched at full length in front of me. The 9mm handgun fits too well in my grasp.

"Hmmmmm." The soft purr sinks into my mind, and I take in the tangle of long, naked limbs stretching out on my bed. My mind plays catch up, taking me back to the bar that I landed in last night, and I immediately shove the gun out of sight, just in time for her eyes to flutter open. She smiles lazily and lengthens her slim, tight body on a stretch, a calculated move designed to have my mouth watering and my cock twitching with want.

Too bad for her. There's only one thing on my mind. And she isn't it.

"Come back to bed," she whispers, lustfully gazing over all 6 feet, 4 inches of my body as she props herself up on her slender elbow, her chin resting in her hand, long fingers drumming the smooth skin of her cheek.

I don't give her the attention she's demanding. I'm anticipating a very disappointed woman on the horizon. Same scene, different day.

I walk away, feeling the stabs of a filthy look being thrown at my back. "Sorry, I have things to do," I say bluntly over my shoulder, without giving her the privilege of my attention while I speak. I haven't got time for this. "Feel free to help yourself to a banana on the way out." I round the corner into my bathroom.

The floor-to-ceiling windows on two walls give me a 180-degree view of the city, but all I can see is my haggard face in the mirror. I sigh and brace my hand on the side of my sink as I flip on the tap and stare at my pitiful reflection. I look as shit as I feel. Damn fucking Jack Daniel's. My palm comes up and runs over the roughness of my jaw, just as I hear "You're a fucking asshole!" followed by the telltale signs of a naked woman falling into my bathroom. I can't disagree with her. I *am* an arsehole. An uptight, vengeful arsehole. I wish I could let the peace and quiet settle over me, but in *my* life there is no peace. I see their faces every time I close my eyes. Danny. Mike. They were like brothers, and even four years later, I know it's because of me they're dead. My stupidity. My selfishness. There's no escape. Only distraction. Work, drink, and sex are all I have. And without an assignment at the moment, I'm down to two.

I cast tired eyes past my reflection and find her looking as outraged as I knew she would be. But there's desire there, too. Her pert breasts are tipped with solid nipples and her angry eyes are still getting their fill of me. Turning my head to the side, I wait for her greedy gaze to fall to mine. Her lips part. My cock remains soft. Not even morning wood.

"Shut the door on your way out," I say flatly, giving her nothing more than a straight face to accompany my blunt order. And then I see it. The intent.

"Here we go," I muse to myself, pushing away from the sink and straightening, bracing myself.

She steams toward me, her hand locking and loading on her way. "You bastard!" She slaps me clean across my cheek. And I let her, gritting my teeth and waiting for the sting to fade before cricking my neck and opening my eyes. "The door's that way," I say, extending my arm past her.

We fall into a staring deadlock for a few moments—her stunned, probably reflecting back to the good fucking I gave her last night, and me impassive, wishing she'd hurry the hell up and get out so I can get on with my day.

"Thanks for the hospitality," she snipes, finally pivoting on her bare feet and stomping away.

Moments later, the door slams, making the walls around me vibrate from the force, and I return to the mirror, grabbing my toothbrush. I clean my teeth, then pull on some shorts and running shoes and hit the streets.

* * *

The morning air feels good. I head to the parks, hearing the settling sounds of London by dawn, the sparse traffic, the birds, the sound of other running feet pounding the pavement. It all has the calming effect that I need to get my day off to a good start. The dew is still lingering on the grass, and a damp mist sticks to my naked torso as I sprint down the path. My legs are starting to go numb. It's how I like it.

My focus remains forward, my direction automatic, like I've run the route a million times. I probably have. The same faces, mostly women's, all smile hopefully when they see me pelting toward them, their backs straightening, their breathing suddenly forced into something close to consistent. Today might be the day I stop and say hi, or maybe even toss them a quick smile as I race past. Like I said, huge disappointment. They're each just another face among a sea of meaningless faces, humans in my way. I round every one of them stealthily, my body working automatically to avoid any collisions.

Half an hour in, my mind's starting to feel clearer, and the sweat is purging the alcohol from my system. All of it seeps from my body over the last mile stretch of my run until my lungs start burning with need.

Done.

I break down my pace and come to a slow stop outside Nero's café, looking up to the sky. I nod to myself, satisfied. 7:20 on the dot. Pushing my way through the door, I grab a napkin and wipe my forehead as I stride toward the counter. I scoop up a bottle of water as I pass the fridge and crack it open, glugging down the whole thing before I make it to the server. She's rung it through the till before I have a chance to reach into my pocket and retrieve a note.

"Your black coffee is on the way," she says, having a quick check over her shoulder as she speaks.

"Thanks," I mutter, tossing the empty water bottle across the café. It lands with accuracy in the bin. My black coffee is on the counter by the time I return my attention to the server.

Every day, the same. I scoop up my coffee and leave.

The traffic is building as I walk down Berkeley Street, collecting a newspaper from my usual vendor. He's holding it out to me as I approach, his face smiley. "Early this morning, mister."

I nod and take the paper, flipping him a quid before scanning the front page. The anger rises from my toes the second I catch a glimpse of the headline.

19 DEAD IN TURKEY AFTER HOLIDAY SHOOTING

"Bastards." I swallow down the fury, as well as the helplessness, and read on. Evacuations being made, tourists warned not to travel there. Turkey has been added to the list of other red zones. The whole fucking world is a red zone these days. I fold the paper and toss it in the bin as I pass. I don't know why I do it to myself. There's nothing I can do to help. Not now. I'm not needed. Or wanted. My destructive rampage in Afghanistan took care of that. The faces of my comrades, my friends, start to break down the wall of defense in my mind. Happy faces. Dead faces. I blink back the flashback, forcing it away before it can take hold. I need another fucking ten-mile run.

* * *

I flip on the shower and leave the temperature exactly where it is. Freezing fucking cold. Bullets of icy water hit me from all four directions, ensuring my whole body gets a punishing. It feels good. Real. My head tilts back on my neck and gives the spray access to my face, while I mull over my workload for the day. Clean my gun…for the fourth time this week. Check my e-mails. Maybe call Abbie.

The last one has been on my list each day for the past four years. It remains unfulfilled. Just call her. Let her know I'm alive. That's all she needs. All I can give. Yet I can't bring myself to return to the past. My breathing slows, my head dropping. Gunfire, explosions, screams.

E-mails!

I scrub at my cheeks, pulling myself back from the brink of an anxiety attack, and grab the shower gel. I need to get on with my day. After I wash down and wrap a towel around my waist, I grab my pills and pop one as I pad into the open space of my apartment, over to the foot of the panoramic windows where my desk dominates the space. I lower to the huge black leather chair and fire up my laptop, looking out across the city as my computer loads, resting back in silent thought.

Just text her. Let her know I'm still alive. I laugh coldly under my breath at my pathetic reality. Abbie is the only person on this planet who probably cares if I'm dead or alive. Or maybe she doesn't anymore. It's just me. No family. No friends. No parents.

From the moment my mother and father were killed on Pan Am flight 103, I had one purpose. War. I was seven years old. I didn't even really understand what had happened, but I knew there were bad people out there and they needed to be stopped. The burning need to fight the evil grew as I got older. My grandmother took care of me until old age took her. Then there was no one to worry about me anymore. I could join the forces and do my bit. Anything to help.

My sharpshooting ability was soon noticed and I was pulled from the cadets. They handed me a rifle. I never looked back. I aimed, I fired, I hit. Over and over again, and each time I felt a sense of achievement. No guilt. Just achievement. Because there was one less dangerous bastard in the world to be worried about.

Ding!

The ping of an e-mail pulls me from my thoughts. "Hello, gorgeous," I say to myself when I see her name on my screen. I'm suddenly hopeful of some respite. It's been two weeks with no assignment, and I've been losing my fucking mind. Two weeks with nothing to do but drink, screw, and fight to keep my mind away from haunting memories.

As always, and typical of Lucinda, her note is simple and straight to the point... which is undoubtedly why she's the only woman I actually like.

But my contented smile soon drops away the more I read.

CLIENT: Trevor Logan—business tycoon and property owner.
SUBJECT: Camille Logan—Youngest child of client and only daughter.
MISSION: Shadow
DURATION: Indefinitely
VALUE: £100K p/w

I lean back in my chair, my fingers forming a steeple in front of my mouth. One hundred grand a week? There must be some kind of catch. A shadow mission? I haven't undertaken one for a long time, and I'm not sure if it is such a good idea now, for no other reason than that the subject is the daughter of Trevor Logan—a ruthless business-man who has stomped on anyone and everyone on his way to the top. I've seen him in the papers, more recently in a court battle when he was accused of suppressing a minority shareholder of a firm he bought in to. Of course, he won. He always wins, and the press always backs the prick. The man is unbearably sanctimonious, and I can't imagine that his precious daughter is any different. Lucinda must have considered this.

She should know better. She knows my past. The horrors, every dirty little detail. This kind of job would require constant surveillance, a full shadow. And for a woman like that? No way. I'd end up strangling her... or, worse: the constant reminders of another woman who had the same qualities could accelerate my flashbacks.

I snap my thoughts back into line before they run away with me.

No. I can't, not even for that kind of money.

"I was beginning to like you, Lucinda," I say quietly under my breath as I bash out a reply.

She'll know I'll be struggling without anything to focus on. Drinking and fucking just aren't cutting it after weeks of indulging in both with a lack of an assignment, but sending me this offer is plain stupid. Is she trying to kill me off? I'm about to click send when the Google search bar beckons.

"Fuck," I mutter, typing a few words into the empty space that's begging to be filled.

I immediately hate what I see. A woman—mid-twenties perhaps, with slender legs and a dangerously tempting smile. Her long blond hair is tousled and braided haphazardly over her shoulder as she sips champagne at a garden party, surrounded by drooling men.

I was spot-on. This right here is the worst kind of woman, and I definitely shouldn't get involved for any longer than it takes me to fuck her brains out. Yet when I should be closing down the window and returning to my reply to Lucinda and clicking send, I find myself mindlessly clicking on *more images*, instead. I sift through dozens of photographs, some of her leaving clubs, some of her at parties, some of her strolling down a London street with piles of shopping bags weighing her down. Then there are the professional shots, mostly for fashion brands and designers. I frown when Wikipedia comes up on the screen. She has a fucking Wikipedia page? I sigh, but still find myself clicking on the link and reading on.

Camille Logan, youngest child of business tycoon Trevor Logan and renowned party girl. Born June 29, 1991, Camille studied fashion at London College briefly before being headhunted by Elite Models. She lives in central London and is a regular face on the social circuit. Romantic links include Sebastian Peters, heir to Peters Communications. Camille boosts typical model stats: 5'8" tall, 34" inseam, 30C bra size, and 25" waist. Blond hair, blue eyes. After a rough breakup with Peters last year, Camille admitted herself to The Priory Clinic to overcome a cocaine addiction. She's since picked up her modeling career and represents brands such as Karl Lagerfeld, Gucci, and Boss.

I slump back in my chair, shocked. "They give her fucking stats?" My mind twists in disbelief as I return to my e-mail and add a *P.S.*

Not even for a million! It's a pass.

I don't add a *thanks*. Lucinda must have lost her fucking mind. And with that, I slam my laptop shut.

* * *

I swirl the amber liquid in the glass, watching the smooth swish of my drink as it coats the inside of the glass. How many is this tonight? Ten? Eleven? I breathe out and knock it back, slamming my empty on the bar. The bartender immediately refills my glass, and I nod my thanks, resting my elbows on the bar. I'm aware of the looks being pointed in my direction by the women here, all of them willing me to glance up so they can catch my eye. But if I give any one of them even a hint of my attention, the night will end up how most of them have recently. A fuck, a good-bye, and a slap. And repeat. Just a drink tonight. Just a drink.

My knuckles wedge themselves in my eye sockets and rub harshly. With a lack of a distraction, whether it be an assignment or a woman to fuck, the fight to stop my mind from wandering to past, dark places is a battle like no other. Faces start to flicker through my mind, faces that haunt me daily. Explosions rattle my brain, and my resting heart starts to crank up in speed.

"Motherfucker," I breathe, looking up and finding a woman batting her eyelashes at me from across the bar. She's a respite from my personal torture that I'm going to take, but just as I'm rising from my stool to go over, the deafening sound of smashing glass has me reaching for the bar to steady myself. My heart is in my fucking throat, my mind whizzing frantically through familiar scenes. Shattering windows, explosions from enemy fire, screams of fear. I try to talk myself down, my eyes darting around the bar in an attempt to remind myself where I am. The bartender curses, and I glance over to find him looking at the mess of broken glass at his feet.

"Hey, handsome."

My eyes shoot to my side and find the woman from across the bar, smiling seductively. The notion that I could grab her, drag her back to my apartment, and fuck her until my heart is hammering for another reason doesn't settle me like it should.

I can't see her face. I can only see my past. This isn't going to work.

I reach for the inside pocket of my jacket and pull out my pills, unscrewing the cap as I stalk out of the bar. I need something to focus on and I need it quickly. The flashbacks are becoming more frequent and my pills less effective.

If I keep going at this rate, I'll be taking Camille Logan's room at The Priory Clinic. I'll be back to where I was four years ago—lost, wasted and with nothing to do but constantly torture myself and relive my nightmares. They'll never leave me, but I can limit them. I just need to force my personal shit to the side and see Camille Logan for what she is.

A job. Focus on the mission. That's it. That's all I have.

I pull out my phone and dial my lifeline.

"I was just about to call you," Lucinda says in greeting.

"The Logan job. I'll take it." I don't give a shit who the client is. A woman, a kid, a fucking monkey. I just need to work. Nothing could be worse than this.

"Good," she replies simply, not making a big deal of it. "Glad you've saved me from having to kick your arse into shape."

My heart starts to ease up a little. "Someone needs to," I mutter.

"Where are you?"

"Chelsea."

"In a bar?"

"Just leaving."

"With?"

"No one."

She laughs, like she doesn't believe me. Which she undoubtedly doesn't. "Get a good night's sleep, Jake. And be at Logan Tower tomorrow at three. One hundred grand will be deposited into your account in the morning." She hangs up and I head home, my mind now centered on the job ahead and that alone. I'm the best at the security firm I work for. I'm not blowing smoke up my own arse. It's a cold, hard fact.

You want to keep someone safe, you hire me. I have a clean sheet. I plan on keeping it that way.

My head is in the game.

CHAPTER 2

CAMI

Camille!"

I spin around, my bags whirling with me, creating what I know will be the illusion of a huge elaborate paper tutu. I smile when I see Heather hurrying toward me, her eyes bright and excited. Wrestling my hand up to my face, my bags bashing against my side as they lift, I pull off my sunglasses before the weight of my shopping forces my arm back down.

"Hey!" I sing, matching her excitement. "No work today?"

Heather's happy face takes on an edge of repulsion, just before she throws her arms around me. I'm unable to return her hug due to the obscene amount of shopping bags in my grasp, and I'm not in the slightest bit sorry. She'll love what I have to show her. "They fired me," she spits resentfully, squeezing me to her.

"Oh, shit! What happened?" I ask as she releases me, flicks her glossy auburn hair over her shoulder, and rearranges her Chanel purse.

"Tuesday night. That's what happened." She links arms with me and starts leading us down Bond Street.

"Ohhh." Tuesday night comes flooding back to me. Or what I can remember of Tuesday night. Champagne. Lots of it, and some questionable dance moves at our favorite bar.

"Yes, oh," she counters, giving me a sideways smile. "I got to work on time yesterday, but I couldn't for the life of me read the autocue. It was all blurred."

I laugh, picturing her squinting at the monitors beyond the camera. "Being on form is kind of necessary when you're live on TV."

We cross the road and head toward a café like homing pigeons. I need an iced lemon tea pronto. "So what now?" I ask, letting all of my bags drop like lead from my aching hands when we reach a table.

Heather rests her neat arse on a chair. "Now I get to focus on our dream, Camille!" Her eyes dance excitedly. "Any developments?"

"We have another investor interested," I tell her, trying to sound casual. I've not allowed myself to get excited about the potential of getting our clothing line off the ground. Not until we have a firm deal on the table. We've made that mistake already. We virtually had the pen on the dotted line when I noticed a clause that wasn't mentioned in the negotiations. Something about making clothes up to a certain size, which basically meant that any woman with even the slightest curve or hint of an arse wouldn't be wearing our fashion line. It was a deal breaker, and something Heather and I feel strongly about. We made it clear that our clothes should be available to every woman of every shape and size. The investors wouldn't budge, and neither would we. "They sound keen."

"Really?" She gives me a big, toothy grin.

"Really," I confirm, unable to stop myself from matching Heather's smile, but I'm so nervous. At the moment we're just two pretty faces with bodies that look good in clothes. I love my job modeling, but the urge is fierce to prove to everyone, including my father, that I can be more than just a mannequin. I know Heather feels the same. Neither of us is willing to compromise on our dream, and on top of that, neither are we prepared to accept any funding from our fathers. Heather's dad is minted, too. Not as minted as mine—granted, not many are, if *any* in London—but he's obscenely wealthy, nevertheless. "We have a meeting with my agent tomorrow. She has a few things to run over with us."

"I'll be there!" She smirks and points at my bags. "What have you been buying, since the Camille Logan and Heather Porter fashion range isn't yet available? You do realize that we'll only ever be able to wear our own label when it's available."

The thought thrills me. Picking out fabrics, coming up with designs, creating good-quality, affordable pieces. Fashion moves too fast for women to spend a fortune on the latest trend. "Just a dress for Saffron's twenty-fifth-birthday party." I grab my purse from my bag. "And some fabric I picked up in Camden that I want you to look at. It'll make an amazing dress." I have the design in my head already, and I just know Heather's dress-making skills will do it justice. "Iced tea?"

"Please." She's riffling through my bags before I make it into the café. Still feeling the strain of my overindulgence on Tuesday night, my skin less radiant and soft, I grab a bottle of water to accompany my iced tea and chug it down before I make it to the counter. I need hydration and maybe a facial. Jesus, I'm twenty-five, and I already feel like I'm past it where the social life in London is concerned. "I'll have a regular iced tea and a regular lemon iced tea. Thank you," I say to the girl across the counter as I go to my purse and pull out a tenner. "Oh, and the water."

"Oh my God!" she gasps, knocking me back a few paces. "You're Camille Logan, aren't you?"

I feel my cheeks flush, and I cast my eyes up to her, seeing a face riddled with awe. It's both flattering and embarrassing. "Yes," I confirm, hoping she doesn't go on to make a big deal of it.

"You're even more perfect in the flesh!"

"Thank you."

"I'm so jealous! Your life is perfect! I love you!"

My smile now is forced. Perfect. Yes, of course it is. She must be seventeen, if that. She has no idea. No one has any idea about the constant battle to keep my mind focused on my future and not my past, the overbearing father who tries to control my life, or the challenge I face almost daily in London's social scene that's driven by cocaine and champagne. These are private battles that will remain private. Too many of my struggles have already been broadcast to the world...and my father. "You're very sweet." I strain my sincerity, despite the fact that she is, actually, very sweet. Naive, but sweet. "I have a friend waiting outside. Would you mind?" I nod to the machine behind her, hoping my subtle hint will snap her out of her starstruck moment.

"Oh God, yes!" She flies into action, all in a fluster, and has my order ready in record time. Handing my drinks over, her face proud, she leans in a little. "I'm going to pay for these. Then I can say I bought Camille Logan a drink!"

"Oh, no, you really shouldn't." I shake my head, point blank refusing to accept her kind gesture. "I'm paying for the drinks, but thank you anyway."

"No!" She places them down and steps back, out of reach so my tenner just floats in the middle of us over the counter. She adamantly folds her arms over her chest, a cheeky glint in her eye.

I'm not going to win this one with convincing words, so I take the only other option. I go to my purse and pull out another tenner, then place them both on the counter, before scooping up my drinks and making a run for it. "Now you can tell people that Camille Logan bought *you* a drink!" I just hear her squeal of delight as I land on the pavement outside, only just upright in my wedges. Heather has the reams of the fabulous material I found in her grasp, her hand paused mid-stroke of the velvety fabric as she watches me drop into my chair.

"All right?" she asks, folding it back up.

"A lively one." I hand over her iced tea as she laughs, craning her neck to see inside the café.

"Bless!" Heather coos, taking a long slurp of her tea. "Love the material!"

"Fab, isn't it?" I poke the ice down with my straw and rest back in the metal chair, my skin soaking up the sunrays. "I'm thinking clinched-in waist—"

"Full skirt." Heather finishes for me, grinning.

"Yes!" This is why I love her and why we're such perfect business partners. We're so in sync with our thoughts and ideas. "I'll have a drawing to you by the end of the week."

"I'll get straight to it."

"Perfect. And we need to make arrangements to visit that fabric supplier you were telling me about." I grab my diary and flick through the pages. "Next week?"

"Sure. It's not like I'm busy in a day job anymore."

I laugh. She sounds devastated. "I'll let you arrange that, then." Glancing down at my tea, I note the ice melting rapidly. I take a long draw on the straw before slipping on my glasses. "What are you wearing for Saffron's party?"

She leans in, encouraging me to do the same. Anyone watching would think she's about to divulge something juicy in the gossip department. "I was thinking red dress and gold heels."

"Good plan," I assert quickly.

"You?"

"You haven't helped yourself to *that* bag, then?" I ask, reaching down and pulling out my new dress.

"That would be rude," she sniffs, eyes widening as she takes in the lovely black piece. "Wow, I love it!"

"Me too," I agree.

"It's short." She waggles a brow at me, and I get the gist straight-away.

Paps.

With photographers on the prowl on most of our nights out, we're all fully aware of the potential damage a wrong photo could do if it were to turn up in a magazine the next week. Like your dress riding up and revealing that little bit too much leg, and, God forbid, a bit of cellulite. That's a mild example in the grand scheme of things, however annoying it is. There's a nastier side to the press, a more damaging side, and, regretfully, I've been on the receiving end of it during that particularly hard time last year when Seb and I split up. I know Dad paid many of the newspapers off to stop them printing the pictures. Whether with money or promises. But his connections and relationships didn't stretch to the glossy mags. And there were far too many pictures of me out there.

I shudder, remembering how hopeless I felt, how black my world was, and how disappointed in myself I was. Sebastian did that to me. Dragged me into his drug-induced haze and nearly ruined me. He took my money when he'd squandered his own and his parents turned their back on him; he got arrested on more than one occasion for violent, drink- and drug-induced outbursts; and when he had no one to lash out on, I was always to hand. I hope he never comes back to London. I hope he's never released from rehab. I never want to see him again.

"Camille?" Heather's soft voice startles me, and I jump in my chair, trying to focus on my best friend. "Where were you?"

"Nowhere." I look down at my cup and find I've drunk my way through it while I was lost in the land of regret. I can feel Heather watching me, probably with a sad smile on her face, undoubtedly after reaching the right conclusion.

I look up and paste on a strained smile, and she smiles right back, reaching over for my hand. "He's gone," she whispers, tightening her hold.

I nod and breathe out slowly, gathering myself. Heather was there through it all with me, loyal to a fault. Thanks to the media, the world knew about my tangle with cocaine, but they didn't know about Seb's habit of venting his anger on me. That happened behind closed doors. Heather pieced it together and after I begged her, she didn't tell a soul. The press reports already had my controlling father going into overdrive, chipping away at the independence I'd fought so hard for. Heather helped pull me back onto the right path. We're kindred spirits. Childhood best friends. Every step of our life has been taken side by side. I hope that never changes. Heather is the only person on earth who knows the explicit details of mine and Sebastian's relationship. I plan on keeping it that way.

"Anyway!" she releases my hand and claps her own. "Fancy a trip to Harvey Nic's?"

My shoulders drop despondently. I would love nothing more, but I can't. And I'm pissed off about it, because what I have to do is far less exhilarating. Far, *far* less. "I've been summoned by my father." I give Heather my Elvis lip, which is more commonly known as a curled lip. "Actually, I've been summoned by his personal assistant, but who cares how I received the order. It came, so I'm going."

Her face screws up. "Is he going to try to force you into dating some boring business associate again?"

My face matches Heather's at the thought of Dad's idea of a match made in heaven for me. Rich. They're always rich. And deadly boring.

I stand and collect my bags, leaning down to give Heather a kiss on the cheek. "I'd rather push hot pokers into my eyes. Want a lift anywhere?"

She pushes her cheek into my lips. "No, Saffron's meeting me. She needs to find an outfit for her birthday."

I grumble my annoyance, wishing I could join them, and head off toward the NCP down the street to collect my C63. The entire journey to Logan Tower is spent trying desperately to conjure up some strength to get me through my "meeting" with my father.

Which basically means that my strong head is screwed on tightly.

CHAPTER 3

JAKE

Breaching the glass doors of Logan Tower, I'm not surprised to find an X-ray machine and baggage scanner in the lobby. But if they think that's going to stop me from getting a weapon in the place, they're stupid.

I fall into stride beside a stunning Hispanic woman, keeping my eyes set firmly forward on the security guard. Seriously? All this high-tech detection equipment and this old boy is employed to monitor it? I shake my head in dismay. He must be ready for retirement, and he's ogling the woman beside me rather than watching me—the 6' 4", towering, suited guy with a Heckler VP9 tucked away.

Okay, I'll cut the dribbling security guard some slack. He doesn't know that I have a concealed weapon, but I'm definitely more of a threat than the petite beauty who's now brushing against my arm, oblivious to the security guard's lust-filled gaze. Because her eyes are staring dreamily up at me.

I make a point of pressing our arms just a bit closer, winding her in. I hear her catch a breath. Then I make my move, stopping abruptly and turning, as if I've forgotten something, being sure to knock her bag from her shoulder.

It happens perfectly.

She yelps, dropping her bag and staggering back. I just catch her arm and steady her before releasing my grip. The contents of her bag scatter at her feet, and I bend to be the gentleman she will soon believe I am.

"Apologies," I say robotically, gathering up some of her things. She's soon on the floor with me, as planned, taking more time to straighten out her fitted shirt than help me collect her belongings. I mildly note the thin material hugging what I can see will be pretty tasty tits.

"No problem," she gushes, just as the security guard joins us, willing to crack his bones so he can crouch to help and hopefully lap up some praise from the dark-haired beauty. Fuck me, I couldn't have written this any better. I reach behind my back and pull out my gun, having a quick scan before I slide it with just the right force and accuracy across the marble floor on the outside of the X-ray machine. It comes to a smooth stop just under the baggage scanner on the other side.

"Here." I hand the lady her bag and do the decent thing. I help Old Bones up before he actually cracks a bone. "Okay there?"

"All grand!" He laughs, his chest puffing out as he shakes off my helping hand. I smile on the inside. I actually smile, and it's a genuine one. He sees me as competition. The mid-seventies, overweight old boy sees me—the thirty-five-year-old, ripped, renowned bodyguard—as a threat. Gotta love his pride.

"After you." I sweep my arm out in gesture for the woman to lead on once the security guard has taken up his position.

Her smile. I swear, if I had twenty Jacks in me and it was the early hours, I might have taken her up on the blatant offer. I slip my hands into my pockets as she wanders over to the baggage scanner, adopting a shameless, seductive sway of her ample arse as she goes.

I laugh under my breath, but enjoy the show while it lasts, as I step up and empty my pockets of my phone, keys, and wallet, placing them neatly in a tray on the baggage scanner. Then I wander casually through the X-ray machine behind her. The old boy barely even looks at me, probably wouldn't even hear the sharp chime if I were to set off the alarm. He's too rapt by that curvy arse heading toward the elevator.

"You're clear," he mutters, giving me a brief moment of his eyes before he strolls back to his stool and grunts as he plonks himself on the seat.

Clear? He has no idea. I collect my things, and then dip to tie my shoelace, scooping up my handgun and tucking it back into its rightful place as I rise. Then I make my way to the elevator and join the beauty, glancing up at the floor indicators and joining my hands behind my back.

"Nice tie," she muses, reaching over and stroking the silk that's draping the length of my torso.

I fail to hold back my smile at her brashness, my eyes dropping to watch her fingers caress the material. "A lady who knows what she wants," I say quietly, meeting her eyes. "Some men find that attractive."

She bites her lip, pushing her chest out discreetly as she drops my tie. "They do?"

I laugh under my breath at her feigned innocence. "Apparently." The doors to the left-hand elevator slide open, and I stroll in before her. No need for gentlemanly manners now. She's served her purpose. I turn and press the button for the fiftieth floor. "Shame I'm not one of them. It's been a pleasure." I wink cheekily, just catching her look of incredulity before the mirrored doors meet in the middle. For yet another woman who's encountered me, I'm a fucking bastard. Story of my life. Or, at least, for the past four years.

I'm carried quickly to the top of Logan Tower and exit into a minimal space, with white at every turn. I feel instantly cold. White marble floors, white walls—broken up only by a few abstract canvases that are equally as cold—and a huge white reception desk.

"Sir." A high-pitched, delighted tone yanks my attention to a woman behind the desk. "How can I help you?"

"I have a three o'clock with Mr. Logan." I scan the area, noting cameras at every corner. I'd put my life on the fact that he's watching me now. My spine lengthens, my hands linking behind me as I return my eyes to the receptionist.

She straightens her shoulders and picks up the receiver. "Mr. Logan, I have a Mr...." Her words fade to nothing as her slip registers. She looks mortified, and it only increases when I hear the booming demand of a man down the line. She visibly cringes, covering up the speaker piece of the receiver. "I didn't catch your name."

"That's because I didn't tell you my name." I leave it there and watch as she dies on the spot.

"Your name?"

I flick a finger to the back of her computer. "Didn't that thing tell you?"

"You're not on the system." She's losing her patience, and I'm lost in my land of amusement once again, for, what? The second time today?

"Jake Sharp." I put her out of her misery and she quickly removes her hand from the receiver, her body relaxing with relief.

"Mr. Sharp, sir. Jake Sharp." She jumps in her chair, dropping the receiver. Logan's reputation precedes him, it seems. I'd feel sorry for her... if I were the compassionate type. Which I'm not. She scrambles to retrieve the phone. "Yes, sir!" Slamming it down, she slumps in her chair and swallows, closing her eyes. "Last door on the left." She points down the corridor.

I browse the few scattered canvases on my way, my nose turning up at the notorious businessman's poor taste. They all look like a wishwash of colors, splattered haphazardly. I'm sure my perception would be gasped at by art lovers, but I say what I see. And I see a mess.

As I raise my fist to knock on the solid mahogany door, I hear the curt demand, "Enter!" I pull my hand back and cast a look over my shoulder, seeing a camera mounted on the wall adjacent to his office door.

"Like Big fucking Brother," I mutter, taking the handle and pushing my way in. I don't know whether to be insulted or impressed to find him flanked by two apelike men.

"Afternoon," I say pleasantly, flicking a trained eye to the huge beasts eyeing me warily.

Logan motions to a chair in front of his desk. "Take a seat, Sharp."

Shutting the door softly, a calculated move to give his ape-men a false sense of security, I wander casually over, keeping my focus on Mr. Logan but capturing every detail of his office to memory.

Unfastening my suit jacket, I pull my trousers up a little at the knees and lower calmly into the chair. I don't entertain the ape-boys with even a fleeting look. That would tell them I'm threatened by them. I'm not. All brawn and no brains. I bet neither could keep up a sprint for longer than five seconds.

"Pleasure," I lie, relaxing back in my chair. The animosity that emanates from the two bruisers pierces my skin. They don't like me. Good. I'm not here to be liked.

"Your reputation is impressive." Logan picks up a file and flicks through, pretending to peruse what he expects me to believe is a pile of intel on me. I'm embarrassed on his behalf. There's nothing in that file, but pointing it out to this idiot would be foolish. He's paying me too well.

Play his game, Jake.

"I never fail." There's little point in being humble. My reputation really is impressive, and everyone worth their salt in security knows it. But that's one of only a few limited details anyone knows about me. Everything else is classified.

He casts the useless file aside, standing from his chair. His photos do him no justice. He's even uglier in the flesh. Camille Logan gets her looks from her mother, Logan's second estranged wife, something I quickly discovered after a detailed search on her. Camille's mother is a stunner, probably twenty years Logan's junior. Wife number one, a modest ten years younger than him and mother to his son—Camille's half-brother, TJ—was tossed aside for Camille's mother. She fled the country for her native Russia after losing custody of TJ in a nasty court battle, leaving their son in the hands of his ruthless father.

I looked up TJ, too. Unlike Camille, he's been unfortunate enough to inherit his father's looks, rather than his beautiful Russian mother's.

Now Trevor Logan, who is turning sixty later this month, is on wife number three, the woman he left Camille's mother for. She's even younger than Camille and TJ.

"You received the down payment?" Logan asks, strolling over to the window, his back to me.

"Yes," I answer simply, avoiding thanking him for it. We need to establish an even working ground, and me expressing any gratitude doesn't feature in that. "When do you want me to start?"

"Immediately." He turns and motions an instruction to one of his men, who swiftly collects a file from Logan's desk and brings it to me. "Everything you need to know about Camille is contained in that file."

Ape Boy #1 holds it out, looming over me threateningly. Any normal man would stand to avoid being towered over. I'm no normal man. I reach for the file and rest my fingertips on the end, waiting for any sign that he's going to release it. There's no sign, no hint that he intends to hand it over willingly. He wants me to tug, just so I can feel his resistance. I lock eyes with him, but I don't feed his ego. I keep my fingers poised where they are and wait. I'm not backing down, and it doesn't look like he will either. We could be here a long time.

"Grant!" Logan barks, obviously detecting the animosity. "Give him the flaming file, for crying out loud!"

Grant relinquishes his hold in a flash, like a scared cat, letting me have the file. I don't relish in my victory. That would put me at a level equal to these two idiots. I rest the file on my lap and have a brief flick through.

"My daughter is very precious to me," Logan says.

I don't look at him, not because I'm absorbing the information before me, but because Logan has taken it upon himself to include a wealth of family photographs of his daughter, ranging from when she was a baby to now, and none of which I've already seen on the Internet. She's always been a stunner. My eyes freeze on a shot of her exiting a club. The date displays October 2015, and she looks totally wasted. The ex. This is a paparazzi shot. How much did Logan pay to keep it out of the press? Whatever, it was wasted money. There are plenty more like these on the Web, all showing his daughter looking wasted and all in the company of her drug addict ex-boyfriend. On a grimace, I snap the file shut and give Logan my attention.

"So why exactly are you hiring me?" I ask. I know why I'm here, but the information was sketchy. I need to know more.

"To protect my daughter."

"What does she need protecting from, Mr. Logan? Has there been a threat?"

"Your services are a precautionary measure."

Precautionary? I don't believe him. I'm a very expensive precaution. "You're going to have to give me a little more than that," I say flatly, tossing the file back on his desk, ignoring his shocked look. I'm guessing not many people tell this man how things are going to be.

"I've hired you as private security. Your job is to protect my daughter."

"From what, Mr. Logan?" I grate, rare frustration creeping up on me. The man's a dick. "The more information I have, the better I'll be at my job."

He huffs and waves a hand in the air to one of the giants flanking his desk. "Show him."

I watch as one of the men takes a white envelope from the desk and passes it over, this time with no signs of resistance. He's a fast learner. I take it and slide out the unfolded paper, finding a picture of Camille with four letters typed beneath her face.

D.E.A.D.

Short and to the point.

"That came via courier yesterday," Logan says. "It's probably just some fool who's come out on the bad side of a deal. Threats are part of the job. I upset a lot of people." He indicates his security men. "But never has a threat been directed at my daughter. Like I said, you're a precautionary measure. You're the best."

I nod, dubious, running a thumb over the paper thoughtfully. "Yesterday, you say?" I ask casually as I chuck the paper on the desk with the file. That paper is too crisp and clean to have been handled much. There are no creases, no folded edges, no crumpling. It's pristine. You'd expect *something* somewhere, even if it's a tiny curl of a corner, given that it's been stuffed in an envelope, delivered, and removed. God knows how many people must have handled it on its journey to the fiftieth floor of Logan Tower. Nothing?

"Yes, yesterday."

I play it cool. "The name of the courier?"

He waves a dismissive hand in the air. "We have endless couriers delivering here. We don't keep records. They come, someone signs, and it gets sent up to the right floor."

I accept his answer. At least, I appear to. "No demand for any money?"

"No."

"No demand for anything?"

"Nothing."

"So they just want to scare you?"

"Many people want to scare me, Mr. Sharp."

"I'd rather take your money." I shrug nonchalantly, getting more suspicious by the second. Something definitely isn't sitting right.

"Everyone's motivation is different." He gives me a knowing look that I don't like at all. "I guess yours right now is the handsome fee I'm paying you."

I force my eyes not to narrow and smile instead. Logan doesn't need to know what my motivation is. "I'll look into it. I'm sure you want to know who's making these threats on your daughter's life." I revert back to the reason I'm here.

"Of course." Logan's face twists a bit in anger, throwing me a little. He looks genuinely disturbed. Could even be mentally plotting the demise of whoever's threatening his daughter. "I've given your colleague access to my e-mail and records."

"Good." I make a note to call Lucinda at my first opportunity as I pick up the file on Camille Logan and flick through it briefly again. "There's nothing in the file about a boyfriend. Does she have one?"

"Not at the moment." He looks relieved about that. "Camille's choice in men is historically bad. Though I plan on rectifying that."

"Oh, really?"

"My friend has a son. It's time for Camille to start settling down, and she *will* marry sensibly. The union of the two families would be . . . beneficial to all of us."

"Except Camille," I point out. What is this, an arranged marriage out of the 1800s?

"Mr. Sharp, you are not here to question my business decisions." He glances down at his watch, and I growl on the inside. His daughter is a business decision? The fucking prick. "She's due momentarily. Probably best you're not here when I tell her what's happening. She can be fiery." He looks up at me, almost fondly. "Has her own mind. You know young girls."

Actually, no, I don't know young girls. "You haven't told her about any of this?" I'm shocked and I sound it. "She's out there unprotected?"

"I want everything in place first."

I'm not surprised very often. It takes a lot to throw me after all the shit I've dealt with. But I'm thrown now. "The girl's life could be at risk and she doesn't even know? She's out there now, running around the streets of London in that flash Mercedes cabriolet, and you allowed that?"

"She's headstrong," Logan mutters, almost regretfully. "I tried to get her to stay with her mother, but she was having none of it. And I can tell you right now that she's not going to be happy about *you* shadowing her."

I blow out a long stream of air. "I'm hardly concealable," I mumble under my breath as I stand. You can only protect someone if they want to be protected. I thought she *wanted* to be protected.

I wander away from the three men, astounded, my gun burning a hole in my back, itching for me to draw, aim, and fire at Trevor Logan's forehead—punishment for being such a narcissistic prick and producing such a brat of a woman. "You have a half hour before I leave," I say over my shoulder as I let myself out. I'll keep the upfront 100K. Payment for my inconvenience and for misleading me. I'll have to get Lucinda to source me another contract pronto. Anywhere in the world. I don't care. Just keep me busy.

As I wander down the corridor, I pull my phone from my pocket and set the stopwatch. "Time starts now, Logan," I say under my breath.

CHAPTER 4

CAMI

Logan Tower. The place fills me with dread, because when I'm summoned to Dad's office it usually means that I'm not going to like what he's going to tell me. Whatever it is, I will see it as an intrusion. Dad, however, will see it as business. That's why I'm at his headquarters. His workplace. The center of his business dealings. If the call this morning was regarding genuine father/daughter quality time, I'd be at his sprawling country mansion on the outskirts of the city, gritting my teeth while I endure his overbearing current wife, Chloe, and listening while he fills my head with details of men suitable by his standards. Not mine. His. Which means they're rich, but also insanely boring and lacking a personality beyond business.

I hate that I still find a need to work up some bravery each time I'm here. I'll never bow down to his unreasonable demands and insistences, whatever they may be—like when he tried to force me into studying law instead of fashion, or when he tried to sign me up for The University of London and I defied him and signed myself up for London College. Or like his attempt to fix me up with an associate when I started dating Sebastian. All of his wives have fallen into line, no questions asked, including my mother. I won't, and he can't divorce me for it either. He's my dad, and I love him, but he's a bully, too.

I push my way into his office and spy Pete and Grant holding position either side of his desk. They're not here for show. My father is a ruthless businessman who's upset a lot of people on his way to the top, like the time he muscled out the ninety-year-old chairman of a chain of retirement homes he bought in a hostile takeover. The man died a week later, and a week after that, one of Dad's buildings was set alight. Or the time Dad's rival bidder in the fight to secure the sale of a hotel chain was arrested for sexual harassment of a staff member, resulting in him having to pull his bid. It was suggested Dad paid the woman to make the accusations. The suspicions went unfounded, though I believe to this day that my father had something to do with it. I have no rose-tinted glasses on. He's callous and ruthless.

I flip his security a forced smile, which they return through habit, and then I focus my attention on the man sitting between them at his desk, holding court.

"My little star!" For a man of his girth, he's up and coming at me surprisingly fast before I make it to the chair. "Give me a hug!"

I indulge him, suspicious of his overenthusiasm. I'm getting more worried by the second. "What's up?" I ask, eyeing Pete and Grant. Both evade my eyes. That doesn't bode well.

"Nothing, sweetheart." He releases me and holds me by the tops of my arms, smiling fondly. He's dyed his hair black again. I wish he would just admit defeat and embrace the silver. He'd look far more distinguished and less like he's trying to keep up with his latest wife. And that's pretty impossible, since he's really pulled out the stops this time and wed a woman a year younger than me.

I shudder as mental images of Chloe, wife number three and the woman he ditched my mother for, engulf my mind like wildfire. She's a stunning beauty, but she's not the brightest. Bless her, she just wants to be my friend. Personally, I'd rather shove nails in my eyes.

"Take a seat." He virtually pushes me down into the chair. Then he worries me further, because he doesn't take up his usual position behind his huge over-the-top desk, where he's the king of his castle. He pulls up a chair next to me instead and takes a seat, faffing with the solid-gold clip of his tie. "You look particularly beautiful today." He takes a lock of my hair and tilts his head thoughtfully. "I'm so proud of you, sweetheart."

"You are?" I question warily. What's going on? I chance a glance over to Pete and Grant again. They give me nothing.

"And I'd do anything to ensure your safety."

Oh, fuck, has a bastard photographer snapped me stumbling out of a bar? Was I flashing my knickers, very unladylike, as I got in a cab? It doesn't matter if it's perfectly innocent. Thousands of young women go out partying every night of the year. Unfortunately for me, the paparazzi can make it seem so uncouth. Since my spell in rehab, I only have to sniff a bottle of vodka or be captured blinking and it's reported that I'm on the road to self-destruction again. Those days are gone, and although I still struggle from time to time, Dad doesn't need to know that. He's unbearable enough.

"Dad." I lean forward, ready to plead my innocence and once again reassure him that I never plan on going back to those dark places. "I'm not—"

"Just listen to me for a moment."

Much to my own surprise, and undoubtedly to my father's, I do. I shut up and let him say whatever's on his mind, because my Spidey senses are telling me it's serious. "I received something yesterday," he says.

"What?"

He sighs, taking my hands, like a show of support. I don't like it. Not one little bit. I've seen my father's many dispositions, but I haven't seen this one. He's worried. "A message."

"A message?" I question. "What kind of message?"

"A threatening one."

I could laugh. My dad is threatened daily, which is why he has

Pete and Grant flanking him constantly. Why is it such a worry now?
"And?" I ask nonchalantly.

"And they've threatened *you*."

I recoil, my mouth snapping shut. I don't need to ask anything
more. His words, plus his potent stress right now as he holds my hand,
looking at me with apologetic eyes, tells me he thinks this one is
serious.

I can feel resentment stirring in my gut, and he knows it. I try
to disconnect myself from my father's business as much as possible.
I work hard, make my own money, and strive to make my own way.
The only hold I allow him to have, and, granted, it's a big one, is my
apartment. Or *his* apartment. It's his, but I insist on paying rent. The
fact that it goes out of my bank account and falls into another of my
accounts, along with the fifty thousand he deposits monthly, is inconsequential. I haven't touched a penny of it, and I don't plan to.

My half-brother, TJ, on the other hand, works for our father. He's
involved in all the business dealings, and is following in Dad's footsteps as a hardcore businessman, though he's far more likeable than my
father. Everyone says it. And I love him dearly, but he thrives on being
the son of one of the richest, most powerful men in London. He *wants*
to be a part of it all. He's our father's son, that's for sure. Why isn't he
the one being threatened? Not that I would wish it, not ever, but it
would make more sense.

"Now listen to me, sweetheart." My father proceeds with caution,
probably expecting the proverbial bomb of expletives to explode from
my mouth at any moment. If I could form a sentence, I would, but I
can't. My mind is a muddle of nothing. What does this mean? "It's just
idle threats, I'm sure," he goes on. "But I've taken precautionary measures, nevertheless." His hand comes up and cups my cheek, his pudgy
thumb stroking my cheek soothingly. "I can't be too careful with my
little star, can I?"

I just stare at him, and through the fog of confusion and shock,

I manage to comprehend one thing. He doesn't think this is an idle threat at all. "Okay," I say.

He can't hide his astonishment. His daughter, the one who he refers to openly as a "defiant live wire," has just bowed to him and his precautionary measures. Past the astonishment I see relief, though, and that only emphasizes how serious he thinks this is.

"Good girl." He leans in and kisses my forehead affectionately before standing and flicking a demanding finger to Pete. "Get him in."

I throw a frown across to Pete, catching him executing a sharp nod of his big head on his thick neck, before he strides out of the room.

Him? Get *him* in? "What's going on?" I ask, sitting up in my seat as my father slumps in his.

He says nothing, and instead starts tapping away on his iMac, looking intently at the screen. "Grant, have my car ready in a half hour."

"Yes, sir." Grant makes tracks, passing me without a word or look and exiting swiftly, leaving me and Dad alone in his office. I can't remember the last time I was alone with my father. He always has either his minders or his dumb new wife stuck to his side.

Resting back in my chair, I look at the man across the desk, my father, and try to read him. Now, I can't. All of his worry and stress seems to have slipped away. "Dad, will you—"

The door to his office swings open, and my head swings around. Pete is practically filling the doorway, his face not quite there, but very close to a scowl. What's got his beef?

He steps in. "Sir," he mutters, moving to the side, revealing...

A man.

All the moisture in my mouth evaporates. Gone. Dry as a bone, making it impossible to speak the words that are stuck on my tongue.

Who the hell is that?

Him?

My eyes are burning with a mixture of delight and curiosity. Oh my days, he's stunning—so tall, solid under that grey suit, but not bulky, and his long legs are spread a little, his stance wide. He looks power-ful. Strong. Fucking delicious.

I open my mouth, willing some moisture there, swallowing contin-uously while my eyes remain locked on his handsome face. His jaw is sprinkled evenly with dark stubble, his short, un-styled hair matching but with flecks of grey at the temples. And his eyes. Dark, *dark* brown, and they're watching me with equal intensity. I shift in my chair, my mind screaming at me to say something. But nothing's working ex-cept my ability to appreciate the ridiculously fine man standing on the threshold of my father's office.

He takes just a few long strides with those long legs and makes it to me. My head lifts as he comes closer, the magnetism of his eyes holding me in place, until he's standing over me, straight-faced and so serious. A big palm extends toward me, and my eyes fall to it. "Jake Sharp," he says, those two single words licking the entire length of my spine and having it snap piece by piece until it's stretched straight and I'm sitting bolt upright. It's fucking hot in here.

I seize his hand, seeing my slender fingers surrounded by his large capable ones, and the strangest feeling comes over me. My hand. It feels so safe held in his—a stupid notion, of course.

But it's not there for long. He drops it, his arm retracting speedily. My eyes lift to his, and I just catch a frown and a dazed shake of his head before he turns toward my father. "We're good to go?" he asks flatly.

This strange man's presence is tangible. It makes Pete and Grant and all their brawny muscle seem laughable.

"Look after her," my father says.

"She's in safe hands." Sharp flicks a strange look down to his big hands and turns them over.

I'm compelled to grab them and trace every single one of the many lines on his palms. In safe hands. One of his hands felt *very* safe wrapped around mine, so I can only imagine how safe I'd feel with his whole body enveloped around me.

Who is this Jake Sharp? I find my muscles going lax, my body melting into the chair. I might stop by Dad's office more often if this man is now on his payroll.

Maybe Dad's replacing Pete or Grant. Maybe he's realized that he needs speed and agility rather than pumped-up muscle. Maybe...

My train of thought drifts to nothing as Dad's words come back to me. *Look after her.*

I'm standing before I know it, but my legs don't seem quite ready to support my weight. I stagger right into Sharp, colliding with his tall frame. He doesn't budge, remaining tall and stable. His only detectable movements are stealthy arms that come up fast and catch me.

"Careful now," he murmurs softly, handling me with ease until I'm steady on my own two feet again. "Okay?" He looks at me, but gives me nothing.

I immediately miss the warmth of his broad chest. He is just about the most perfect man I've ever seen, and that's an achievement, given I've had shoots with more beautiful men than I care to remember. But he's a man. A proper man—big, strong, mature. The crisp, stark-white collar of his shirt and perfectly knotted grey tie can't conceal the primal energy practically thrumming from him.

Oh God!

I fight some composure and turn to my father. "What do you mean, *look after her?*" I ask.

"I've hired Sharp to watch you," he explains. Sharp coughs next to me, and Dad rushes to rephrase that. "He's your bodyguard for the foreseeable future. The best protection money can buy."

"Excuse me?" I splutter. "He—" I throw an arm out in the general direction of Sharp, and my hand collides with his solid bicep, having me retract in shock. Fucking hell, he's like Action Man. "He's my bodyguard?"

"Yes." My father nods decisively.

"No." I laugh, looking up at Sharp. "No offense intended."

"None taken," he replies, completely unfazed, like he fully expected to be subjected to this little family drama. I look away, unable to focus on him for too long for fear of bursting into lusty flames.

Dad's face is tight with the frustration that's been absent since I arrived. "Camille Logan, this isn't up for debate. I've hired Sharp to protect you, and you will not be difficult about it!"

"I'm a grown woman," I say calmly, holding onto the temper that's dying to be unleashed. "I have a busy schedule—modeling contracts to fulfill, meetings to attend."

The dismissive huff that my father releases does what it always does when he shows such disregard for my career. "You mean looking pretty for the camera?"

"And negotiating a deal on my new fashion line," I add, reining my temper in. "And getting it off the ground, and building my profile outside of my modeling career."

"Camille, how many times have I got to tell you?" My father sighs. "You and that silly friend of yours are wasting your time. There are plenty of fashion brands out there already."

I grit my teeth. He just doesn't get it. "Then one more won't hurt, will it?" I flick my eyes to the hulking man standing next to me. "I doubt Mr. Sharp will appreciate having to endure the simplicities of my pointless career."

Sharp looks out the corner of his eye to me. "I endure what I need to."

"How's your runway walk?" I ask seriously. Let's see if he's aware of what he'll be subjected to. "Maybe I could use you in a campaign." I can tell by the slight hitch of his eyebrow what he thinks of that. Good.

"Maybe you can give me a tutorial." His face is suddenly as serious as mine. "Since you're the expert."

"Are you offering?"

"Are you asking?"

I only just hold back my gawk. He's being sarcastic. I huff to myself. Two can play that game. "Strike a pose."

"If you're lucky," he says quietly, straightening his shoulders.

I clamp my lips shut, rummaging through the corners of my muddled mind for a smart retort. "I think you'd look good in a skirt."

"I'm told I have great legs."

My damn eyes plummet to his legs. Long, powerful legs with thick thighs. I drop my gaze to the floor quickly. How did this happen? Why am I engaging with him?

I shoot a glare back to my dad. "I don't want or need a bodyguard following me around randomly."

Sharp shifts next to me, clearing his throat. "It won't be random," he states evenly, looking down at me again. "It'll be constant."

If I didn't know better, I'd think he's relishing in this. "Constant?"

"Twenty-four/seven." There's an evil glint in his dark eyes that I suddenly want to knock out. "I'll be shadowing your every move."

I feign nonchalance and return my attention to my father, furiously ignoring the thrilling rush of desire that nearly veers me off course. "You will not invade my privacy," I say calmly, retrieving my bag from the floor. "And no way are you telling me what to do."

"I will not stand for this!" Dad shouts. I don't even flinch. His patience is wearing thin. I don't care. So is mine.

I have no idea what I expected when my father told me that he'd taken precautionary measures in light of the threat, but this creature *wasn't* it. Maybe a driver, or a curfew. I could live with a curfew. Give me a curfew!

But *him*? I take a quick peek out the corner of my eye, seeing Sharp's doing the same to me. I quickly look away. No, it's not happening. To have him near twenty-four/seven? All of the men I've ever worked alongside have to work hard to portray intensity in a photograph. Sharp exudes it naturally. It's beyond masculine. It's almost too much to stand. And it's... *so* fucking hot.

"I refuse to be shadowed by one of your minions." I turn and walk away, hearing my phone chime in my bag, as well as an audible grunt of frustration from my father. Rooting through my huge bag as I continue on my way, I pull out my phone and see a message from Heather.

Sebastian is back in town.

My heart stops in my chest, and my feet skid to a halt by the door. I stare down at the message, hoping the words might shift and form another message. But after reading it for the fifth time, I'm still going over the same horrific words. This can't be happening.

My ex is back? This is bad. So, *so* bad.

I've finally gotten back on my feet. It's taken everything out of me to find myself again, and now he's back in London and all of my stability that I fight daily to maintain is suddenly rickety. I damn the traitorous tears that pinch the back of my eyes and start to breathe deeply, but as I begin reasoning with myself, telling myself over and over that I'm stronger now than I've ever been before, something starts to seep into my mind.

I turn to confront my father as it all slots into place. He already knows that Sebastian Peters is back in town. Of course he knows. This bodyguard business is all just an elaborate plan to keep me away from Sebastian.

I laugh on the inside for his creativity, but his underhandedness isn't such a surprise. Having me shadowed by a bodyguard, having that bodyguard reporting back to him, will certainly keep him abreast of my life—something that he strives to do daily.

I grit my teeth and fix my formidable father in place with a pissed-off glare. Has he no faith in me? Does he think I'll run straight back into Seb's arms and let him ram a gram of coke up my nose?

"You really don't know me at all, do you?" I spit as I turn and leave.

CHAPTER 5

JAKE

My hand comes up and rubs my jaw as I watch her disappear out of her father's office door, and one thing that springs to mind, surprising me, is that I didn't see a brat. There were no signs of a self-indulgent, selfish female. What I saw, in fact, was a fiercely independent, bright young woman.

It's not what I expected, and the revelation should be a relief, except my strumming heart, my racing mind...and my annoyingly aching cock are telling me not to get ahead of myself. My feet are suddenly moving of their own volition, taking me out of Logan's office and in pursuit of his daughter. Protect her. It's simple and it's going to keep me busy for a while.

I'm on autopilot, my strides long and fast, as I make my way down the corridor toward the elevators. But then I catch a flash of Camille disappearing around a corner, and not in the direction of the elevators.

"The little fucking..." My legs are sprinting, powering after her, before my quick-thinking brain delivers the instruction.

Impulse.

Instinct.

Get to her.

I charge through the door to the stairwell, the heavy wood smacking the brickwork behind it and creating a deafening echo that bounces off the contained walls. I halt, fighting the urge to pull my gun.

She's just doing a bunk, I reason with myself. That's all. The last thing I need to do is scare her half to death with my Heckler. I force my breathing down a notch, listening, and I hear the light clicking of her heels.

"Ready or not, here I come," I mutter under my breath, throwing myself down the stairs after her. My long lunges eat the steps up in no time, and it's only a few seconds before I spot her dainty hand holding the rail. Those ridiculous things she had on her feet are suddenly all I see in my mind's eye. Stupid high-heeled things. She'll break her fucking neck.

No subject has ever been injured under my watch, accidental or not. Damn her!

My pace increases, my urgency growing, and the relief when she comes into full view as I round a flight of stairs nearly suffocates me. It's a silly reaction to a silly situation, but I've never had a subject try to escape me. Or a woman, for that matter. I fly past her, landing at the bottom of the staircase she's tottering down, and swing around to face her. Fuck, I'm sweating. A few flights of stairs and I'm fucking sweating. What's up with me?

She doesn't get time to figure out what's just flown past her like a raging bull. Her feet fail to stop and she collides with my chest on a yelp. My arms are around her fast, holding her to me.

I gasp, too. I don't know why, but her slight frame compressed to my chest has sparked a bolt of heat, streaking straight down to…my cock.

Fuck!

I release her before I'm certain she's gathered herself and take a few very cautious and wise steps back. My jaw is tense. My fucking heart is going loopy. What the fuck is that?

The ball of my palm comes up and presses into my forehead, my eyes clenching shut.

Walk away, Jake. Just walk the fuck away.

I don't know how long I'm standing here repeating the firm mantra, but when I finally open my eyes, she's still standing before me, looking stable and composed. It's more than I can say for myself, but her clear self-control forces me to bully my thoughts back into line.

Her cute little chin lifts confidently, her face determined. For a second, I let myself admire her poise, thinking it's quite a turn-on. Then she speaks and all thoughts of how sexy she looks vanish with the reminder of why I'm here. "I'm not agreeing to you tailing me. I have a life, and I want to get on with it."

"Agree or not, you and I are going to be very close." I regret my choice of words immediately when her mouth drops open... because I can see the tip of her pink tongue, and it's all I can do not to slam my mouth to hers and taste it. I move back again, putting space between us, as does she. I use her need to distance herself to my advantage, disregarding the fact that I moved away, too. "Don't worry, I don't bite." That's a blatant lie. I'd happily sink my teeth into her...

"Maybe I do."

My eyebrows jump up in surprise before I can stop them. She's quick. I'll give her that. "Well," I deadpan. "I'm told I taste good."

She scowls a little. "You look a little meaty for my liking."

"Of course. You prefer the pretty-boy type, don't you?" I stand tall and clear my throat, as if to enhance the fact that I'm the furthest she could get from the preened, streamlined men she gets pictured with.

She steps forward, confident, but her eyes definitely struggle not to get a quick fill of me. "And what type are you?" She cocks her head, waiting for my answer.

That single question has me swallowing a cough. "You don't want to know," I answer honestly, getting no thrill from the slight widening of her eyes. I quickly remind myself why I'm here, and it isn't to goad her. I step back again, giving us both space.

Camille pulls herself together quickly and tugs her bag onto her shoulder. "There is no threat, is there? My ex-boyfriend is back in town, and that's the only reason my dear father has hired you."

My first thought is: *The drug addict of an ex-boyfriend is back? Why didn't I know this?* My second thought is: *If he comes close, I'll put a fucking bullet in his brain.*

The latter thought is purely professional. Because it's my duty to protect her. "The threat is very real, Miss Logan." I turn on my professional switch. The one that's always on. Why it's malfunctioned now is something I plan on fixing very quickly. "I've not been employed to keep you away from your ex-boyfriend," I say mechanically, adding in my head that I'll go out of my way to do exactly that, anyway. I saw the pictures of Camille during that brief meltdown. She was a shadow of the woman standing before me—this beautiful, bright, enticing woman.

Enticing?

The irony doesn't escape me. I encounter women daily who go to shameful lengths to catch my eye. This woman is doing it without even trying. And damn, if it isn't the most attractive, *enticing* thing in the fucking world. I shake my head mildly and those unprofessional thoughts away. Again.

"Right," she huffs and pushes past me, catching me off guard.

I have her pinned to the wall in a nanosecond.

And a nanosecond after that, I'm wondering what the fuck just happened.

"Oh my God," she breathes, pressing her back into the bricks behind her, her fresh breath hitting my neck in short, panting bursts.

I consider, only for a second, that I've frightened her. Then I feel her hardened nipples pressing into my chest through my suit. I breathe in, swallow and repeat. Over and over, bending my knees to get her face in line with mine.

What am I doing? This is stupid. Release her. Step away!

Her eyes are wide, unsure and ... flickering with desire. This usually wouldn't be such a surprise to me, but I know, frighteningly, that mine are mirroring hers.

She gulps, blinks, and looks away. "I'm pretty sure physically restraining me isn't in your list of duties." She swallows.

"Don't make any sudden movements," I snap, battling away all of the obscene thoughts her statement has spiked, right to the deepest, safest depths of my mind. "I thought you were going to do a runner again." I step back, and she straightens, hitting me with shimmering topaz eyes.

"Since it seems I'm stuck with you, let's get a few things straight."

I nod my agreement, short and sharp, thinking this is a great idea. Set the ground rules. The boundaries. "Go for it," I prompt curtly.

"Don't talk to me," she says, looking away from me. "And don't touch me."

Again, I nod, easily agreeing. It's probably safest all round.

Camille pauses for a few moments. What is she thinking? "Fine," she mutters, taking a tentative step toward me. "I'm going to pass you now. Just want to make sure you're not going to rugby tackle me again."

I keep my mouth firmly shut and gesture for her to lead the way. She passes swiftly and I follow, but I center my focus past her, locating my discipline and locking it down.

Tightly.

Before I do something insanely stupid.

CHAPTER 6

CAMI

I'm still trembling on the inside when I make it out to the fresh air, not remembering one stagger or step that it has taken me to get here. My breathing is all over the place. He's behind me, keeping his distance, but still way too close for comfort...or my stability.

I stop and glance over my shoulder, finding him stationary behind me, his hands linked behind his back. He looks like a typical bodyguard, and I'm mortified that he's guarding *me*. Heather is going to fall apart. Or be jealous. I'm not sure.

Frowning to myself, I take two steps forward, then stop again, taking another peek over my shoulder. Sharp takes two steps, too, bringing the distance between us back to a level that he obviously deems comfortable. One hundred miles away from this man still wouldn't be comfortable. In fact, as long as this man is on the same planet as me, I won't ever relax again. I feel violated. My freedom, my life, my happiness...my senses. They're all under attack.

I take two more steps and watch as Sharp does the very same thing. "This is ridiculous!" I mutter, marching on my way, dialing Heather as I do.

"Thought you'd call pronto," she says, definite concern in her words. "What happened with your dad?" Oh, she should be concerned, because if Jake Sharp is shadowing me, then he'll also be shadowing my best friend, since we're practically stuck together. Sebastian's back. A threatening message. My new bodyguard. In the last half hour, I've had more shocks than is fair.

"He hired a bodyguard for me. Apparently there's been some threat against me."

She coughs and splutters down the line. "You serious?"

"Unfortunately, yes." Resentment churns in the pit of my stomach. "At least that's what I'm told. Now that you've told me Seb's out of rehab, I'm suspicious."

"Hmmm."

I open my car and throw my bag onto the passenger seat before getting into the driver's. I put the key in the ignition and start my car, waiting for the Bluetooth to kick in before I toss my phone on the seat with my bag, while also waiting for something else from my best mate.

"Hello?" I prompt.

"I'm here."

"Then say something!"

"Well, either is a possibility, I guess. Seb *or* the threat. So what's the deal with your bodyguard?" she asks, confused.

"He's basically shadowing me at all times."

"Well, that's your sex life down the plug hole." She laughs and I scowl at my windscreen. I hadn't thought of that. I was more concerned about my freedom. Not that I put it about or anything, but if the opportunity arises, I don't want Sharp standing at the end of the bed, observing. I shudder.

"Cunny funt," I mutter indignantly.

"You know, if you're going to say it, just say it," she scorns as she always does when I utilize my insult of choice.

"I need to see you."

"I'm outside Picasso's. Glass of fizz?"

"Yes," I breathe, only just stopping myself from telling her to order a bottle, even though there's nothing much to celebrate. "I'm just leaving Logan Tower."

"See you in a jiffy." She hangs up, and I slide my Merc into drive, but I'm interrupted from speeding off when the door flies open and Sharp's head appears.

"This should be locked," he points out curtly, indicating the passenger door. I'd almost forgotten about him.

Almost.

Not at all.

"You're not coming in my car." I look away before I have a chance to indulge in his gorgeous masculinity. In my car? That's way too close.

"Not today, no, but once we've sorted the logistics, you'll be travelling with *me* in *my* car."

I scoff my thoughts on that one. "We'll see," I say to myself, knowing damn well he caught it. Maybe if I'm as difficult as possible, he'll quit. Worth a try.

"Yes, we will." He points to a Range Rover parked in front of me. "That's me. I'll follow you home."

"I'm not . . ." I let my words trail off, my conniving mind quickly hatching a plan. "Fine."

He nods and shuts the door, and I watch with narrowed eyes as his long legs eat up the short distance to his huge car. He removes his suit jacket on the way. I hiss, slamming my eyes closed to avoid the god-gorgeous sight of his tight arse beneath his trousers, and the god-*damn*-gorgeous sight of his broad back beneath the white cotton of his crisp shirt. "Bastard," I mutter, cautiously peeling my lids open. His arm appears out of the window and motions for me to pull out and pass. Damn. I was hoping he'd take the lead and let me follow him.

I sigh and check my mirrors before indicating and pulling out of my space, driving at a sensible 20 mph down the road, constantly checking my rearview mirror. He's close behind, the chunky hood of his Range

Rover practically sniffing the arse of my car. Tempting as it is, I don't slam on my brakes so he rams me from behind and I can sue his irritating arse.

Rams me from behind...

My foot goes all heavy, my prized Mercedes coasting off down the road, yet he still remains tucked up closely behind me. I take a right, then a left, then a right again, and even overtake a few cars to gain some distance from him. None of it loses him, and my frustration builds and builds as my car gets faster and faster. "Fuck you, Sharp."

I take a sudden hard left, cutting across a black cab, getting honked and cursed at as I do. Glancing up at my mirror, I laugh when I see the taxi has come to an abrupt stop across the junction, blocking anything from coming down the road after me.

"Take that!" I sing, feeling way too pleased with myself. The best bodyguard my father could buy? Yeah, right! I flip my music on and jig in my seat, pleased as punch as I make my way to meet Heather.

* * *

I pull up down a side street, seeing Heather sitting outside Picasso's under a parasol, two glasses of champagne in front of her. Her neck lengthens like a meerkat's when she spots me, and she waves me urgently over. I bet she's dying to hear the lowdown. I might leave my car exactly where it is all night and order that bottle I so desperately need.

I hurry toward her, but come to a quick stop when I hear the sound of screeching tires cornering up ahead.

"Oh..." I breathe, my smugness dropping down a nearby drain into the sewers.

His Range Rover speeds toward me, the roar of the engine thunderous, almost like it's angry. Or could that be the driver inside? He skids to a stop, and I flip a glimpse to Heather. She's riveted.

The slam of a door makes me jump a little, and I swear I feel the ground shake under my wedges as he strides toward me. I muster up a hard front to face him.

His finger rises and points at me accusingly as he comes closer, his face twisting. "You ever pull a stunt like that again, then I'll... I'll...I'll..."

"You'll what?" I ask, adopting my Elvis sneer. Who the hell does he think he's talking to?

He comes right in close, nose to nose with me. The safe distance doesn't seem to be applying now. The pulse in his tense jaw is detectable, even though I'm staring his hard gaze down. "I'll put you over my knee," he whispers menacingly. "And spank your fucking arse bright red."

My arse muscles stiffen, and once again I'm struggling to contain this bizarre cocktail of disgust and lust. "Excuse me?" I breathe, taking one step back to escape his closeness.

He straightens to full height and rolls his shoulders, like he could be trying to rid a weight resting there. "Just don't try to give me the slip again."

"Or you'll spank me?"

"It was a figure of speech."

"An inappropriate one, don't you think?" *Please say no. Please say no. Please say no.* I don't know what I'm thinking.

"Yes," he mutters, looking around us, high and low, scoping every space there is. He has a fixed glower in place as he does it. "Why are you here?" he asks.

I look across to Heather, seeing her mouth lax and her champagne flute poised at her lips. "I'm meeting a friend."

Sharp follows my line of sight and sighs. "Heather Porter."

"How'd you know...?" My words disintegrate. Of course he knows. Pulling my braid over my shoulder and landing him with a contemptuous glare, I leave him on the pavement and make my way over to a dumbstruck Heather.

"Give me that drink," I say, throwing myself into a chair. She either doesn't hear me or totally ignores me, so I reach across the table and grab it myself. *Swig!* "Hello!"

She looks at me, all *what the fuck?*

"Don't," I say, shaking my head. *Swig!*

"Is that him?" she mumbles, not averse to pointing her glass at him. "The bodyguard?"

"Yes." *Swig!*

"Oh, fucking hell."

"I know." *Swig!*

"Where's the billboard?"

I swallow. "Huh?"

"The billboard." Her eyes dart, genuinely looking around.

"What billboard?"

"The one he's just fallen out of?"

I snort my repulsion and swig yet again. "He's a twat."

"A fit twat."

"Heather, this is not an appropriate conversation to be having about my bodyguard."

"Give me a break!" she laughs, properly amused. "Don't tell me you haven't thought about him in bed. He's solid. Tall. Gorgeous."

I look over my shoulder when Heather's delighted stare starts to move, clearly following Sharp. He'd better not be coming over here! He's not. He sits down a few tables up, looking huge in the small chair. And he might look relaxed, but I can see every muscle strung under his shirt and trousers. He's like a giant tiger, poised and waiting for an attack. "Not at all," I mumble quietly, more for myself than Heather. "Anyway, he's greying at the temples."

"Oh!" Heather chuckles, and I return my attention to her, swiping up more champagne. "And now she's searching desperately for reasons to find him unattractive."

"I don't need to search. There are plenty to choose from."

"Like?"

"Like he's bully, for a start. Heavy-handed and forceful." I know deep down there was no intent to hurt me or scare me, and he didn't. What's actually scared me each time he's come close, spoken, or touched me, is my reaction. The internal battle I'm having while fighting to maintain a strong front is exhausting me already.

And he's been with me for less than an hour.

Twenty-four/seven? And for how long?

I shrink in my chair and have another sip of my fizz. "Change the subject," I plead, and instantly regret it when Heather's lips straighten. There's only one other subject that should be addressed right now, and I can't decide if it's more of a situation than the man sitting behind me and *why* he's sitting behind me.

"Saffron saw him. Said he looked well," Heather says tentatively, and wisely, too. Or maybe she shouldn't have said it at all. I don't need to hear that. Saffron doesn't know the nasty details.

As far as she and everyone else is concerned, Sebastian led me onto his dark, cocaine-lined path. That's bad enough, and all anyone needs to know. Sebastian is a model, too, chiseled in the face as well as in the body. He makes girls drool...but he's troubled. Terribly troubled, and he got me into trouble, too. He has an addictive personality, as well as an addictive nature. But he's a lost cause. Even his parents have given up on him.

"Is he clean?" I ask.

Heather shrugs. "Saffron said his eyes were clear and his body not as strung as it always used to be. But who knows?"

"Hmmm." I look off into the distance, reflecting on those dark times.

"So, where's he sleeping?" Heather cuts into my thoughts before they take hold, and I'm grateful. But her question confuses me...until she nods past me.

I find myself peeking behind me again. He's watching me like a hawk, intensely. The shaky breath that escapes me is barely evident, yet my instinct tells me he detected it all the same. Then our eyes meet and he shifts on his chair. Conjuring up a filthy look, a stupid defense mechanism, I aim and fire.

"Good question," I mutter, watching his eyes fall to my mouth. I don't mean to, really I don't, but my betraying tongue slips out and slides across my bottom lip. Sharp shifts in his seat again, his nostrils flaring as he looks away.

"Then you need to clarify, because if Mr. Gorgeous-Pants over there is staying at your place, then I might, too."

"He's not," I say clearly, resolutely, as I find my friend again. She isn't helping. Not one bit. "Tell me the plan for Saffron's birthday," I order, wondering how we veered back onto Sharp.

"Well, it's at The Picturedrome." She grins. "Flashy cow hired the whole place out. Bet Daddy's paid for it."

I roll my eyes. Unlike Heather and I, our friend Saffron doesn't think twice about squandering her father's money for such luxuries. "And she claims to be independent?" I could laugh.

"I know," she agrees. "But you're not so independent now, either, are you?" She nods past me again, but this time I refuse to look. I just need to pretend he isn't there.

He's not there. He's not there.

I fight the urge to turn and get a fill of his lovely face, wondering how we managed to veer off subject to Sharp again.

My wondering is silly.

It's not like he can be ignored.

Chapter 7

JAKE

You can't protect someone who doesn't want to be protected. You need compliance and cooperation. She's giving me neither. And it makes me want to wring her beautiful, obstinate neck.

After she hugs her friend good-bye and sashays to her car, she leads me on another merry dance around London, all the way to her apartment in Mayfair.

I pull down into the underground car park, only to find no available spaces. I see the smug look in her eyes as she collects her shopping bags from the trunk of her Merc...so I dump my Range Rover behind it. She can't go anywhere if I'm blocking her in.

Once she has rounded up all her bags and heaps of files, she pivots and her smug smile drops like a rock. I slide out of my car, pulling out my bag behind me. I came prepared. I answer her question before she can ask. "I'm sleeping here, in case you were wondering. It's part of the contract and your father has insisted."

Her lovely lips straighten. "This is a violation of my human rights."

"Take it up with your father. I have my orders."

"Well, I'm ordering you to leave me alone."

"You're not paying me, Miss Logan."

"How much?"

I raise interested eyebrows at her. "That's confidential."

"So you will literally do anything my father tells you?"

"Within reason," I reply.

"Is running me a bath within reason?" She smiles sarcastically while I fight off the mental images that cute quip spikes.

"Depends if you want me to get in it with you." I cock my head, looking to be waiting for a serious answer.

She snorts. It's so cute, I almost crack a smile. Then she gives me a filthy look before she pivots haughtily and hustles away. "You wouldn't fit."

Not so cute.

I barely stop myself from rolling my eyes and start to follow her through a solid steel door and into a lobby, where big, elaborate gold mirrors hang at every turn. I have a good look around, confirming what I already know from my background checks. Card entry, three cameras, two elevators, one concierge. Daddy owns this building, and I'd put my last pound on the fact that Camille Logan doesn't pay the going rate. I nod politely at an intrigued doorman, who nods right back. Then I wait for the elevator to come, standing a safe four feet from Camille. The doors are mirrored. Avoiding her reflection is a killer, so I divert my gaze and continue scoping out the building. Revolving doors, not very secure, despite the card entry, and a doorman who looks like he could be the twin of the old boy who protects Logan Tower.

A faint ding indicates the arrival of an elevator, and I do the gentlemanly thing and allow Camille to enter first when the doors slide open. Then, just as I'm about to breach the threshold myself, the doors close in my face.

I swear, I only narrowly miss head-butting the glass, but I manage to catch the satisfied smirk on Camille's face before I lose sight of her. "For fuck's sake," I mutter, dropping my bag to the ground and clenching my fists. Breathing in some patience, I crick my neck on my shoulders and close my eyes, repeating a calming mantra.

Don't strangle her. Don't strangle her. Don't fucking strangle her.

I'm tempted to put a bullet in my own head and put myself out of my misery. What the fuck have I signed up for? The other elevator arrives and I collect my bag and step in, pressing the button for the top floor. The lift travels way too slowly for my liking. She's out of sight. She should never be out of sight.

"Pain in my fucking arse," I mutter. But she's a pain in my arse for oh so many different reasons than I imagined—irritating, annoying, *painful* fucking reasons.

I step out when the elevator finally reaches the top floor, finding what I knew I would when I round the corner in the corridor. Apartment 30's door is firmly shut. I can guarantee the bolts, chain, and dead bolt are all engaged, too. Two minutes and I could be in, but I decide against utilizing my skills and instead rap the wood calmly. I'm not surprised when I get no answer, so I knock again, ensuring I maintain a calm, controlled persona. It's hard when on the inside I want to kick the door in and wrap my palms around her slender, lovely neck.

She remains quiet on the other side. "Fuck's sake." I pull my gun out and aim it at the lock, thinking this will be far quicker than trying to reason with the silly woman. Then a scrap of lost reason muscles past my building frustration and advises me against it.

I sigh and tuck my gun in the back of my trousers. "Camille, this door is really pretty," I say quietly, knowing she's on the other side, probably with her ear pressed to the wood. "Would be a shame to damage it." I notice a looking hole and smile to myself. Then I slowly lean forward, bringing my eye closer and closer until it's pressed up against the small cylinder of magnifying glass that runs through the wood. There's a scuffle and a burst of activity directly behind the door. I chuckle to myself. The girl is impossible. "We can do this the easy way or the hard way."

"Fuck you!"

My head drops on my shoulders, jarring my neck as I weigh up my options. I can either break this door down, and lower myself to her childish approach to this situation, or I can show her that this situation isn't going anywhere, no matter how difficult she is. And I mean the threatening, anonymous-message situation. Not the potent chemistry that's bitten me on the arse and chewed until it hurts. Women have served one purpose to me and one purpose alone. Neither frustration nor fury is that purpose. In fact, those two exact emotions are why women and I are best kept on limited time spans. Camille Logan has already overstayed her welcome in my life.

Looking down at the carpet, I decide against any further sparks tonight and sit my tired arse down, ready for a long fucking night. With my back resting against the door, I pull my phone out and send a quick update to Logan, only just stopping myself from tagging on the end that his daughter is a headstrong little madam. I do, however, tell him that the ex-boyfriend is back in town.

Then I pull up my contact list. And my heart jumps. Abbie's name stares up at me, and my finger hovers over the dial icon, lowering and lifting time and time again. Contact will serve one purpose. Spiking memories. I don't need those. I laugh out loud, a cold, chilling laugh. The memories are always there, torturing me daily, but I don't need to fuel them. I don't need to go back to places that are only going to enhance the agony and the hatred for a woman who tore me apart and sent my life into a downward spiral.

I chuck my phone to the side and press my head into the wood behind me, looking up at the ceiling as I fight to clear my mind. My phone starts ringing, a welcome distraction from one of my regular internal battles, and I look to see Logan's name. I'm not surprised. Before I connect the call, I put my ear to the door, hearing distant movement. She's not listening.

"Thought you'd call snappily," I say in greeting.

"Sebastian Peters." There's pure venom in Logan's tone that I can fully appreciate. I've read all the shit on the Internet. "He nearly broke her."

"Is this why you've hired me?" I ask outright, thinking maybe Camille was onto something.

"No, you know why I've hired you. You've seen the message, but it won't hurt for you to look out for Sebastian Peters." There's an edge to his tone that reeks disgust. Yes, I've *seen* the message, but why do I get the feeling I haven't *heard* everything? "He has a fondness for cocaine. I don't want that shit anywhere near my daughter again."

"Right," I breathe, thinking protection against ex-boyfriends isn't what I signed up for. I'm a bodyguard. Not a counselor or a therapist. It's not my job to stop Camille Logan shoving cocaine up her nose if that's what she wants to do. But I fucking will.

"I'll call you if I have anything to report. You should extend the same courtesy to me." I hang up before he can confirm that he will, and shift one way, and then the other, trying to get comfortable, my legs extended at full length in front of me.

After ten minutes in that position, my knees come up, my forearms resting on them. Ten minutes later, my gun is stabbing at my lower back and my arse is starting to go numb. I'm being paid, I remind myself. A lot. I can endure this shit. I've been in worse places in worse conditions.

I close my eyes and imagine thorns from overgrowth severing my cheeks as I crawl on my elbows through wild terrain, and before I can stop my mind from spiraling, it moves on to the vision of my comrades, Danny and Mike, lying dead in the dirt. I feel the deep ache of a bullet buried in my shoulder. The smell of death invades my nose, and the screams of innocent civilians fill my ears. Then a clear mental image of *her* face reminds me of how I came to be amid the anarchy. The anarchy that I caused.

I snap my eyes open and catch a labored breath, wiping away a bead of sweat from my forehead. "Damn." So much for being distracted. I curse Camille Logan for not allowing me to do my job as I reach to my back, pulling my gun out and laying it next to my thigh. Resting my head back again, I try to distract myself by sprinting through all of the information I have. Which isn't very much.

There are a pile of wronged businessmen who have fallen into financial ruin after hostile takeovers by Logan. Any one of those could be looking for revenge. Quite simply, Trevor Logan has a lot of fucking enemies. I feel like I'm diving into a pot of possibilities with not a clue of where to dive deeper. Add to the situation that I have a gut feeling Logan is withholding information, and I'm in all kinds of a mind tangle. Then there's the ex-boyfriend. Technically not a suspect but definitely a threat. Threat? Yes, a threat. He's a threat to Camille's health, possibly her life if he gets his hands on her again. Which makes him as equal a threat as the potential threat. So I'll treat him as such. The message Logan showed me. That paper was too perfect. On that thought, I grab my phone and send Lucinda a quick message.

I don't think Logan is giving us all the relevant information. The threat was printed on paper that looked like it had come fresh out of a ream. He said it arrived yesterday by courier. Check the CCTV at Logan Tower.

I click send, and as expected, I get a reply within seconds.

Interesting. I'm on it. On another note, I've been through Logan's e-mails with a fine-toothed comb. Nothing suspicious. No one suspicious. Everything clean as a whistle. How's it going?

I laugh at my phone.

Don't ask. You women are difficult. While you're at it, get me everything on the system for Sebastian Peters.

Her reply is speedy.

The ex? May I ask why?

My answer is simple and sweet.

No.

Dropping my phone, I resume my position, forearms resting on raised knees, my head dropped back as I start to chew things over. None of it sits particularly well. Speaking of which...

I shift again, scowling, but my silent annihilation of the uncomfortable floor is interrupted when I hear the click of a lock. I freeze.

And then I'm suddenly falling back, my stomach muscles engaging too late to hold me up. I'm on my back, staring up at the most amazing legs I've ever seen. They go on forever, starting with pretty pink tipped toes and perfectly narrow ankles that drift into slender calves. They're just about the most perfect calves. And her thighs. I can feel my hands twitching by my sides, begging for a little stroke. Her pink lacy knickers are peeking out the bottom of her oversized white T-shirt. The slogan on the front makes my lips twitch.

I AM NOT TO BE IGNORED.

Has she worn that on purpose? *No, Miss Logan, you most certainly are not.* Especially now. What the hell is she trying to do to me?

Shit, I need to pull myself together before I get us both killed. Distraction. It's still the best tactic to nail a target, and whoever wants to potentially nail Camille Logan is at a massive advantage right now. Because I'm stupidly distracted. Her blond hair is tumbling over her shoulder, splaying over a perfect breast beneath her T-shirt, and when I reach her face, I find she's removed her makeup. My cock jolts behind my trousers. Jesus Christ, she's a masterpiece. I feel compelled to tell her not to bother with the rigmarole of applying makeup anymore. She doesn't need it.

Her upside-down face moves in, hovering over mine. She folds her arms, pressing the material of the T-shirt into her curves. My jolting cock is instantly solid.

"Why do you have a gun?" She flicks her chin to my Heckler, reminding me where it is. Her question also reminds me of why I'm here.

I shoot up, collecting my gun on my way, and tuck it into the back of my trousers. "To shoot you when you piss me off again."

She scowls, her button nose wrinkling in disgust. Good. Hate me. It'll make this situation a whole lot easier. "You're a real charmer, aren't you?" she sniffs, turning on her bare heels and punishing me with a rear view of those bare legs. "You'd better come in."

My eyebrows jump up in surprise. What's changed? I don't know, but I'm not about to argue. My arse is still tingling its way back to life. I pick up my bag and stroll slowly into...hell.

I gaze around, alarmed, though I keep it contained. For a woman so immaculately turned out, she's a messy fucker. Shoes, handbags, clothes, makeup, every imaginable girlie thing scattered over chairs and on the sofa. And then there are the drawings, scraps of material, and piles of papers all over the place, too, including the floor. How does she live like this? Surely she has a cleaner? I'm unable to confirm exactly what look she's gone for in her apartment, except a fucking mess, but judging by the clear walls, which are the only areas free from some kind of fashion crap, I'm guessing it's minimal. Minimal? I inwardly snort. Camille Logan soon took care of that. I can feel myself twitch, my regimented military past racing to the surface. I kick my way through a sea of clothes and drop my bag on a table that's cluttered with every color nail polish under the sun. I immediately spot the one she currently has on her toes. Soft pink. Subtle and girlie.

"You can sleep here."

I look up and see her bending over the couch, brushing more clutter from the seats. I nearly go cross-eyed. Fucking hell, she's killing me! "I'll clear it," I offer, anything to stop her bending over like that. "Let me." I muscle past her, literally bumping her out of the way with my hip to avoid extended contact.

"Fine." She sounds slighted as she wanders to her bedroom. "Such a fucking gentleman."

I ignore her insolence and take my gun from my trousers, resting it on the arm of the sofa. Then I kick my shoes off as I unfasten my fly, noticing Camille hasn't closed her bedroom door completely. Her innocent move, leaving a small gap, makes me feel a little better about being in another room.

I yank my tie loose and unbutton my shirt, then spend five minutes looking for a clear space to put them. I give up and place my neatly folded pile on top of some clothes strewn on a chair. Making my way back to the sofa, I fall to my arse and rub my palms over my face, sighing. It's still going to be a long night.

"Woman has a death wish," I mumble.

She catches my eye through the gap in the door as she moves around her room. I need to look away. I need to close my eyes and pretend she's not there. God damn her, she trashes that plan when she stops right in front of the door, her back to me. Slowly, too slowly to be innocent, she draws her T-shirt up over her head and tosses it to the side.

My breath catches in my throat. The exposure of that vast expanse of her creamy skin is a vision that will never leave me. Good God, I'm shifting again, and my hand rests over my cock, which has developed its own heartbeat. I'm underestimating this woman. There was nothing innocent about her leaving that door open. Nothing innocent at all.

She's playing me like a fucking fiddle. Maybe I'm the one who has the death wish.

She disappears from view and all the stored air I was keeping locked in my burning lungs gushes out, my heart dancing in my chest. I grab my pills from my bag and swallow on a hard gulp, hoping they'll not only keep the nightmares at bay, but also give me some resistance from my new client.

CHAPTER 8

CAMI

It's still dark, but I can hear the birds tweeting the arrival of morning. I haven't slept a wink. I couldn't switch off and go to sleep knowing he was in the next room. With a gun. I've never seen a gun, not in real life. He looks good with a gun. It suits him too well. He looks good, full stop.

My eyes feel puffy and will undoubtedly be red. Not a good look when I have a meeting with my agent today. Most of my night was spent on my iPhone searching for information on Jake Sharp. I felt compelled to find out everything I could, since he has a detailed knowledge of me and my life. I found nothing, though a search on Google Images threw up a few photographs of various celebrities with him in the background, looking impassive and cool. Other than that, nothing. The dead end has frustrated me more than I care to admit.

What's his story?

It would be easier to hate him if I wasn't so insanely attracted to him. He must be, what? Mid-thirties? I don't really have anything to go on where his age is concerned, except the dusting of grey at his temples and his obvious experience in the job.

Rolling onto my side, I stare at the gap in my door. I know he saw me last night when I shamelessly stripped before crawling into bed. I'm still at a loss as to why I did that. Self-satisfaction? I don't know. Maybe the unreasonable urge to have it confirmed that he's as attracted to me as I am to him got the better of me.

I crane my neck, looking into the lounge until something comes into view. His leg. His naked leg, still and stretched down the couch. I breathe in, my eyes nailed to it. I can see the dark hairs from his ankle to just above the knee, and compelled to get his thigh in my sights, I place my palms into the mattress at the side of my bed and start leaning out a bit. Disappointment fills me when he shifts, taking his long, lean limb out of view. I throw a filthy look at the door and lean some more, edging out slowly and carefully until his foot is back in my sights.

"Fuck!" My hands slip off the side of the mattress, and my body follows them down to the floor.

Thud!

"Ouch!" I whisper-hiss, my cheek squished into the fibers of the carpet, my legs still on the bed, my torso hanging off the edge. I cringe and hold my breath, waiting for him to come bursting into my room and locate the threat. The only threat here are my greedy eyes.

"Idiot," I mutter to myself, starting to unfold my tangled body and push back up onto the bed. He's supposed to be the best security an individual could wish for. What a load of shit. He hasn't even come to check up on me. I could be pinned to my bed with a gun pointed at my head.

"Idiot," I whisper again, this time my insult pointed at the sinfully delicious man currently sprawled on my couch, possibly naked.

Sprawled on my couch.

Possibly naked.

"Oh God." I'm suddenly not on the bed anymore but moving toward the door as though drawn by some unseen force. The soft pile on my bedroom carpet is pushing between my tippy-toes as I pull on my T-shirt, and the door is getting closer and closer, until the full length of his body is in perfect view. Lord, have mercy. He *is* sprawled, on his back, arms extended above his head, his face resting inward on his right bicep. He's asleep.

Hard.

It's the first word that comes to mind, followed by *dangerous*. And then followed quickly by *masterpiece*. I've developed a tremble, and my blood is pulsing in my ears, making it impossible to register the voice in my head that's telling me to shut the door, rather than open it wider so I can pass through quietly.

I'm in the living space of my apartment, taking light, tentative steps toward my shadow, hungry for a more detailed, close-up look of his perfection. I make it to his side without instigating a murmur or stir from him. He looks serene and even more handsome without the hardness in his eyes that's present when he's awake. His face alone could hold my attention for all of eternity, his dark mussed hair all askew, his stubble rough, his jaw sharp. Absolutely gorgeous. Manly. Primal. Rough.

Allowing my eyes to start drifting away from the tranquil beauty of his face, I let them linger on his torso. His muscles are relaxed but still prominent, every ridge defined under a sprinkling of dark hair. I'm only mildly grateful that he has boxers on when I reach his groin. The black material hugs his hips and wraps around his thick thighs too well. There isn't an ounce of fat on him. He's like a freak show, he's so perfect. He has the art of *less is more* down to a tee where his body is concerned.

I'm close enough to appreciate it all, but I still dip a little, holding my breath, certain that if I breathe, it will touch his skin and wake him. I have to force my hands to remain at my sides and not feel him. Then I notice a small scar on the taut flesh of his shoulder. It's faint, a silvery mar on his perfect skin. I lean in a little more, intrigued.

He moves.

It happens so quickly I don't even have the chance to yelp in shock. It's only when my back meets the floor and I've blinked my vision clear that I realize where I am.

Beneath him.

His naked skin pressed into my thin T-shirt.

Sensibility is telling me to protest, to wriggle and free myself, yet he feels so good touching me, firm and strong, warm and safe.

He's looking down at me, expressionless, his dark eyes singeing my skin until I can feel a flush working its way up my neck to my cheeks. Despite my inability to move, my erratic breathing is making my body heave under him, causing our skin to press…everywhere. Oh God, his cock is solid and pushing into my thigh, and my nipples are buzzing, probably injecting his chest with electric shocks. He has my wrists pinned to the floor above my head. I'm a prisoner, locked in place, anticipating his next move. What will it be?

Kiss me!

Oh my God, did I think that? The words are suddenly screaming in my head repeatedly. I want him to kiss me, ravish me, pound into me with his powerful body. I've never experienced instant attraction before. Not on this level. This is new, something wild and dangerous, and it's got me all desperate and pent-up. He must be able to see it, and judging by the large, hard length of flesh wedged into my thigh, I'm guessing he feels it, too.

I search his eyes for any sign of his thoughts, becoming frustrated and irritated when I find nothing. Just dark pits of emptiness staring down at me. But then something shifts and a wave of frustration furrows his forehead, slowly forming a deep frown. I suddenly register a lack of heaving from him. He's holding his breath.

Swallowing down all the air he was storing, he shifts and winces when he rubs into my thigh with his cock. He quickly pulls himself back around, though, obviously locating a force of will that has abandoned me. Releasing my wrists, he pushes himself off of me, leaving me feeling stupidly deserted.

"Get a good look, did you?" he says, moving away.

I feel like I've just been slapped in the face, all desire and want tumbling away at his curtness. I fly into defense mode. "Do you always sleep half-naked on a client's couch?" I ask shortly as I stand and wrap my arms around my torso, backing away to my room, feeling so bloody stupid. What was I thinking?

"Do you always make a habit of falling out of bed?" he retorts over his shoulder.

I cringe and curse myself to hell and back at the realization that he was awake the whole time. Of course he was. If he was asleep and thought I was an intruder, that gun would have been pointing at my head, both in my room when I fell off the bed and just now when he tackled me to the floor. He didn't even grab his gun. He just grabbed me instead. He was dazed...and then he was mad. With me. The notion pulls at my gut for reasons I may never know. Shutting my bedroom door, I let my back fall against it and look up to the ceiling in despair, feeling like a fool. "Stupid!" I force myself to sit on the end of my bed and spend a good half hour talking some sense into myself. Jake Sharp shadowing me is proving more of a problem than I ever imagined.

* * *

After showering and getting myself ready, I emerge from my bedroom tentatively, wearing some denim shorts and an oversized gypsy top, my Havaianas on my feet. I'm braiding my rough-dried hair as I wander through my living space to the kitchen, my eyes darting, looking for Sharp.

I find him leaning against the worktop, showered and looking obscenely fresh and handsome in some worn jeans and a round-neck black

T-shirt. So he found the other bedroom and bathroom, then? He looks up at me as I enter, his mobile poised at his ear. I quickly look away and head for the fridge, pulling out a bottle of grapefruit juice and glugging down half the bottle in one go.

"Appreciated," he says, not sounding appreciative at all. "Good-bye."

I keep my back to him, still hugely embarrassed, dying on the inside that I practically offered myself on a plate and he didn't take it. If he didn't think I was a stupid little girl before, then he most definitely does now.

I hear a shift of movement behind me, followed by a light cough. I start to screw the cap of my bottle on, mentally locating the where-abouts of everything I need before I leave.

"You didn't mention there was a spare room with a bathroom," he says clearly, with no accusation, but I sense it's there. "It's actually tidy in there."

He's having a dig. The only reason my apartment is such a mess is because Heather and I have been busy perfecting our designs, scruti-nizing fabrics and brainstorming marketing ideas. Not that I owe him an explanation. So I say nothing and go in search of my bag. I find it and head for the door, looping the strap over my shoulder as I go. Making a grab for the handle, I pull the door open, but his palm slams forward over my head, keeping the door from swinging open. I curse myself for jumping.

"Since I accepted your ground rules, you can do me the decency of following one of mine." He speaks from behind me, holding the door shut over my shoulder. I scowl at the wood before me, keeping my mouth firmly shut and my back to him. "Don't ever creep up on me again." He pulls his hand away and I waste no time reaching for the handle again and letting myself out, shrugging off the tingles spiked by his closeness.

"Are you forgetting who is working for who?" I snipe as I bypass the elevator and push my way into the stairwell, not prepared to stand and wait for the lift. I need to keep moving. Away from him.

He doesn't answer my question; neither does he acknowledge it, choosing to follow quietly. Good. He's respecting my boundary. No talking.

I break into the underground car park and aim my keyfob at my Mercedes, striding over. "Can you move your car, please?" I call over my shoulder.

"We're going in my car," he says flatly.

"I can drive myself." I pull my door open and throw my bag in before dropping into the driver's seat. I start the engine and yank my belt on, looking in the rearview mirror. Sharp gets in his Range Rover, and I hum to myself, satisfied. Maybe he's decided he can't bear being so close either and has decided to retract his rule of traveling with him. Good.

I wait, my hands on the wheel, for him to move his huge car, but two minutes later, he's still stationary and my patience is beginning to fray. I start to grind my teeth, and a few minutes later, I'm smashing my horn. It has no effect. Sharp sits in the driver's seat of his car, busy on his phone, calm as can be.

"Arsehole," I mutter, swinging my door open and marching over. I rap on his window and it begins to lower, though he keeps his eyes on the screen of his phone. "Move," I order curtly.

"No," he retorts simply. The window starts to rise, and I gape at him, not that he takes much notice of my affronted state.

I beat the side of my fist on his window, and the glass comes down again, his attention still on his phone. "I have an eleven o'clock meeting with my agent," I inform him as calm as can be. "I haven't got time for this."

"Then I suggest you stop being difficult and get in." The window lifts again, denying me the opportunity to reach in and strangle the bastard.

I let out a frustrated yell and stomp over to my car, swiping my bag from the seat and slamming the door. I've never met such an infuriating man!

Getting in his car, steam virtually bursting from my ears, I slam my back into the seat and grab my phone from my bag. Sharp pulls off without a word, and I dial my father. I can't deal with this. It isn't fair.

"Camille." Dad's straight voice does nothing to settle me. It simply reminds me who he is and that my protests are going to get me nowhere on this occasion. But I still try.

"Dad." I aim for sweetness, locking back the sass that I'm sure he's expecting. "As much as I appreciate your concern, I can't have this bloke following me around. I have work to do. Meetings to go to. He's getting in my way."

"Camille, I already told you that this is not up for discussion."

"Is this about Sebastian?" I ask. "Because I can assure you I won't be seeing him ever again."

"This is not about Sebastian. This is about a threat I'm not comfortable with. Sharp stays until we find out who sent it."

"But—"

"Camille, I haven't got time for this." He cuts me off, and my Elvis lip takes shape. "I'm in the middle of an important meeting. Sharp is staying. I'll hear no more of it." He hangs up, and I throw my phone into my bag, so fucking wound up!

I've always defied my control-freak father. Always done what I want instead of what *he* wants. This is the first time ever that I really don't have any choice, because unless I kill Sharp off, I'm not getting rid of him. I'm powerless. And I hate it.

Glimpsing out the corner of my eye discreetly, I see his profile, his eyes trained on the road. He hasn't even flinched while I've been talking about him like he isn't here. That's what I need to do. Pretend he isn't here. No more lapsing from stable to annoyingly admiring him.

No more sneak peeks at his broad chest or the evident power of his muscles. No more wondering about him. Not in *any* capacity. He looks across to me, and I quickly avert my eyes, mortified that I was doing all of those things just then and he caught me doing it. I definitely hear him chuckle lightly under his breath, and I flip him a scowl, the salt-and-pepper fleck at his temple holding my attention. "How old are you, anyway?" It just falls right out of my mouth without warning, mortifying me.

"Thirty-five." He turns an amused half-smile toward me. "You?"

My scowl deepens. Yes, because he wouldn't know that after reading up on me. I turn away, ignoring him.

"Where's your agent's office?" he asks, as he turns out of my street the correct way, telling me he already knows exactly where he's going. He's trying to get me talking. So I keep my mouth shut, ignoring him again. He's making my life miserable, and I intend on reciprocating. He'll quit by the end of the day.

* * *

We pull up outside my agent Kerry's office in Hatton Garden and I jump out, shutting the door behind me without a word. I spot Heather waiting outside for me and hurry over, ignoring her small smile when she obviously spots Sharp. She embraces me. "So how's—"

"Don't ask," I warn, breaking away and opening the door. I know he's a few paces behind us as we take the stairs to the first floor, and when we walk into my agent's office and her eyes widen, looking past us, I know I'm going to have to explain. Like I said before, it's not like he can be ignored. "Short-term arrangement," I say, approaching my agent's desk and taking a seat.

Heather lowers to the chair beside me. "Daddy's been upsetting people again," she quips.

My agent laughs a little, not in the least bit surprised. "Good old Daddy."

"What do you have for us?" I ask, trying to focus on work—something I love and that will distract me from Sharp, who's lingering somewhere behind.

Kerry takes a seat and slides a file across the table. "You don't mind if I go over a few other bits with Camille, do you?" she asks Heather.

"Don't mind me." My friend waves a casual hand in the air and looks over her shoulder. "Sure I can find something to pass the time."

I smack Heather's knee, and she shrugs, begrudgingly returning her attention to Kerry, who is transfixed past us again. I cough to snap her out of it. "Right!" Kerry shakes herself back into the meeting. "Levi's is launching a new line, and want *your* legs in their jeans."

"Ohhh," I muse, opening the file and browsing through, ignoring Heather, who's turning again to ogle my bodyguard.

"And Dior is launching a new miracle cream. You're top of their list of blondes to do it." Kerry winks, pointing to my face. "Clearest complexion in the industry."

Heather laughs, turning back around. "Does that matter? They'll still airbrush the shit out of her."

Kerry pushes her fingers through her severe crop, shrugging off my friend's comment. "Interested?"

"Of course," I chime. "What are the themes?" I place the file on her desk and watch as her eyes constantly flick past me, making me wonder what Jake's doing behind me. Is Kerry blushing? My hardball agent who never displays a hint of emotion? I frown and crane my neck, peeking over my shoulder. He's standing by the door, hands joined in front of him...looking fucking sinfully gorgeous. I swing back around to Kerry before I can let my greedy eyes relish the sight any longer. "Themes?" I prompt.

Kerry's eyes whip to mine. "Oh, yes, themes!" She's all a-fluster, grappling at papers on her desk as Heather giggles beside me. This is a first. Kerry doesn't get flustered either. I suppose the sight should be a comfort. It isn't just me who finds the arrogant wanker attractive. "Here." She picks up a piece of paper and reels off the brief. "Levi's is going back to its roots. Ranch-theme, cowboy, hats and boots, that type of thing. Dior is a minimal headshot. Minimal makeup, expressionless; you know the score."

"Sounds good!" My mood is lifting, some new projects giving me the nudge I need.

"Great. I'll start the negotiations. Any requests?"

"Yes," Heather pipes up. "She wants a bowl full of orange Smarties and the room temperature at 19 degrees. Not a sniff over," she deadpans, and I burst out laughing.

Kerry looks up as she writes something down—something I know won't be a record of what Heather's just demanded. "You know I'd get it for you, right?"

I smile, amused. "I know. But I don't like Smarties and there will be robes to keep me warm."

"God, I love how easy you are to deal with." Kerry goes back to her scribbling. "I'll call you with the finer details."

"Perfect. Now tell us about the new potential investor," I ask, not liking the cautious flick of Kerry's eyes to mine at the mention. "What?"

"Yes, what?" Heather sits forward.

"Well." Kerry coughs, stalling.

"Kerry, just come out with it."

"They want to work with you, Camille. They really do. They love the idea of you fronting the campaign, and have even championed the idea of extending the range for all women of all shapes and sizes."

"But?" Heather and I ask in unison.

"But you don't get a say in the designs." She bites her lip. "Or the fabrics. Or the accessories."

I deflate in my chair. "So basically they just want my face and body to sell a new line of clothes that'll have our names on, but we have no input on...anything?"

"Where do I feature in this arrangement?" Heather asks indignantly.

"You don't," Kerry answers, to the point, leaving my friend wilting in her chair, hurt invading her pretty face. "Sorry, but it's still a great opportunity, Camille. And they're offering great money." She pushes a file across her desk to me.

I reach over and rub my friend's arm as I give my agent a tired look. Does she really think I'll go for this? "Kerry, it'll be no different from the modeling I do day in, day out. And they want me to ditch my best friend and partner? We have hundreds of drawings, some great designs!"

Her lips straighten, a little sympathy making its way onto her face. "Take a look at their offer." She taps the file, and I take it on a roll of my eyes. "They're keen."

I stand and collect my bag, stuffing the file inside carelessly before nudging my dazed friend from her injured trance. She gets up slowly. "Call me when you have the details on Levi's and Dior." I swivel, and my despondency deepens when I'm forced to confront Sharp. Our eyes lock for a few moments, but he's the first to break our stare, opening the door for me. I mutter my thanks as I push Heather past him.

"They don't want me," Heather mumbles, plodding down the stairs on heavy feet. "They want you, but they don't want me."

"We're a package deal," I remind her. "This isn't happening unless we're both involved. I'm not doing this without you."

She turns and looks at me through glassy eyes. "Do you really mean that?"

"Yes! Heather, you're a genius dressmaker, and your eye for detail, textures, and contrasts are immense! I wouldn't want to work with anyone else but you."

Not to mention that this girl has been with me through thick and thin. She was there, holding my hand through my darkest days. She never gave up on me. I owe her everything. The reason I'm standing here now is because Heather didn't give up on me. I'll never forget that. We're a team, and no one will change that. No matter how much money they throw this way.

I see her doubts drain from her body, and she launches herself into me. "Thank you."

I let her squeeze me, smiling. "What are you doing now?"

"Having lunch with my mum. Want to join us?" She releases me and straightens herself out.

I ponder her offer for a few moments, wondering if making Sharp endure that will be awful enough for him to want to quit. "No, but thanks for the offer." I need something painstaking. Not for me. For Jake. I smile to myself. "Free tonight?"

"You want to go out?"

"I was thinking a girlie night? Wine, maybe a manicure while we eat crap and watch something girlie on TV?" Sharp will hate it. I'll make sure of it. "We could draft more ideas, too."

"Love it!"

"Be at mine for six?"

"Fab!" She jumps into the road and flags a taxi. "See ya then!"

I wave my good-bye and turn to see Sharp scowling, but not at me. He's staring across the road. Wondering what has his acute attention, I follow his line of sight, but all I see are rows of vehicles parked on the street.

"Wait there," he orders curtly, striding into the road. He's all tense, coiled and focused.

"Jake, what's..." My words fade when he breaks out into a light jog. I feel my brow bunch, perplexed. Then I see a white van pull out of a space and take off down the road fast.

Jake's jog breaks down until he comes to a stop, the van

disappearing around a corner. He reaches for his pocket and turns back toward me, pacing over. "White van," he says down the line. "Didn't catch the plates or a face. Could be nothing." He hangs up, and I stare up at him, bemused. "What?" he asks, tucking his phone back in his pocket.

"It was just parked on the street."

"It made a pretty speedy getaway."

"So would I if I saw *you* prowling toward me." I shake my head and round him, walking off. He's being paranoid.

I can feel him tracking me as I cross the road toward his Range Rover, but before I have the chance to pick up speed and put a more comfortable distance between us, I spot a familiar face and pull to a sharp stop. Sharp bumps into my back on a curse and I jolt forward. "Watch it!" I snap, tossing a scowl over my shoulder while vehemently ignoring the sizzle of electricity from our contact.

He immediately backs up, his jaw twitching. But his eyes remain on mine. "Sorry."

I shoot my stare away, locating what had me stuttering to a halt in the first place. "TJ!" I yell, breaking into a run toward my brother.

"Hey, little star!" He laughs as I crash into him, embracing my fierce hug. Funny, the nickname doesn't annoy me as much when TJ uses it. It's so good to see him! Our catch-ups are rare, mainly because Dad works him to the bone. Not that TJ is bothered too much by it. He relishes the trust my father puts in him, as well as the responsibility. He's been nurtured by Father to succeed him in all things where business is concerned, but TJ isn't nearly as ruthless with it.

"What are you doing around here?"

He peels me off him and gives my cheek a cheeky squeeze. "Just picked up my suit from the dry cleaners." He holds up a suit bag. "Now I'm heading to meet Dad at his lawyer's office."

I'm not surprised. That's a weekly event for my brother and Dad. "Who's suing him now?"

"The fucking world!" He laughs. "How's tricks, kiddo?"

"Fine," I answer quickly. TJ will know what's going down. Dad shares everything with him. "Has he got a killing machine tailing you, too?"

He jabs my shoulder lightly, then gets me in a headlock, roughing up my hair. "All right, Miss Funny Knickers."

"Hey!" I wriggle free, and as soon as I brush some escaped strands of hair from my face, I find I can no longer see my brother.

Because Sharp has put his big body between us.

He's so close I have to tilt my head way back to look up at the back of his head. I catch the signs of muscles bunching beneath his black T-shirt on my way.

"You are...?" he asks, full of suspicion and hostility.

Seriously? Can this man be civil and warm toward anyone? And come to think of it, he should know damn well who TJ is. He must have seen pictures of him in the extensive background checks he's likely done. And, come to think of it, he's the spitting image of my father. Sharp's being pathetic. He's still worked up. Because of that van?

Placing my hand on Sharp's arm, I put some weight behind me and push him to the side. Or I try to. He doesn't budge. Not even a miniuscule jolt from my effort. "This is my *brother*." I sigh, moving to the side so I can see TJ again, since Sharp isn't showing willingness to move.

As expected, TJ's eyes are quite alarmed. "So this is the killing machine, eh?" He lifts his hand. "Nice to meet you, Mr. Sharp."

I'm pretty sure I hear a growl emanate from my bodyguard as he raises his hand. He has a death stare locked on my brother, who, being even shorter than me, has to step back or break his neck in order to see Sharp's snarling face.

"And you," Sharp replies, short, sharp and with no sincerity behind it.

TJ virtually yanks his hand free from Sharp's fierce grip and tosses me a questioning look. I step forward, taking my brother's arm. Him, I can move. TJ laughs nervously. "Dad wasn't kidding when he said he didn't hire him because he liked him. What an arsehole!"

We come to a stop and I hum, thoughtful, as I cast an eye over my shoulder. Jake's scoping everywhere. It's beginning to make me nervous.

"Anyway," TJ goes on, pulling me back round. His face is serious. I know what's coming. "I've heard a certain someone is of out of rehab."

"Funny, I heard that, too."

"Camille," he warns, drawing out my name tiredly. "We're just..."

I hold my hand up to stop him. "I'm done with him." I strain to say the words, not because they're hard, but because I'm pissed off with having to repeat myself for the millionth time. My initial worry when Heather told me that Seb is back in town has been replaced with a ton of resolve. I don't plan on bumping into him. Anyway, from what I've heard, he'll be back in rehab before long.

"Funny how the day Sebastian is released, Sharp's hired to protect me." I give TJ a high arch of my eyebrow. It's an accusing arch.

TJ mirrors it, except his is a warning arch. "I saw the threat, kiddo. We can't be too careful with our little star."

"What did it say, anyway? And who sent it?"

"What it said doesn't matter. And if we knew who sent it, don't you think something would be done about it?"

I sigh, admitting defeat. I know I have no place in *business*, even if the business involves me. "You want a coffee?" I indicate the café across the road.

"Maybe another time. I've got to get to this meeting." On cue, his phone starts ringing and he smiles, holding it up to me. I see "Dad" flashing on the screen. "I'm thirty seconds late." Dropping a kiss on my forehead, TJ backs away toward his car, being sure to give my hulking guard a wide berth. "Look after our girl," he says to Sharp, being all brotherly. It makes me warm on the inside...until I see Sharp notice-ably rigid again. The man needs to lighten up, for the love of God!

TJ jumps in his Maserati and screams off down the street, and I start toward Sharp's car, knowing he won't be far behind. It's like if he gets a certain distance from me, an invisible rope starts winding in to bring him closer.

* * *

At six o'clock, Heather virtually bangs the door down. I run to answer, but Jake beats me to it, looking through the peek hole with his hand resting on his lower back, where I know he keeps his gun. So fucking paranoid.

"It's Heather," I mutter, watching as he turns and wanders away from the door, not bothering to open it for my friend.

My lip curls as he passes and I reach to open the door, matching Heather's grin when she holds up two bottles of wine.

"I'm here!" she sings, pushing her way past me. I know the second she finds Sharp because she stutters to a stop and shuts up. I close the door and push her on, into the kitchen. "He is divine," she whisper-hisses, plunking the bottles on the side while I fetch glasses.

I scoff to myself. "If you like the moody type."

"Oh, I do." Heather pours while I rummage through the cupboards for anything to snack on. Once I've loaded up the tray, I head back to the lounge, Heather in tow. Sharp is on the couch, his laptop on his thick thighs. I come to a stop in front of him and wait for him to rip his eyes from the screen and look at me.

"Excuse me," I say politely, smiling sweetly.

He looks across the room to the single chair, then to Heather. His face is perfectly straight, and just when I think he might refuse, be dif-ficult, he rises from his seat. All of his muscles unfold painfully slowly, forcing me to cast my eyes away before I'm captured dribbling over it all. I catch Heather out the corner of my eye. She's not holding back, getting her fill, her eyes delighted as Sharp strides to the chair across the room and settles again, his face in his laptop.

I fall on the couch and cough, getting my transfixed friend's attention. She shakes her head in wonder and joins me. I can tell there are all kinds of things she wants to say to me, but Jake's presence is preventing her. It's probably a good thing. I place the bowl of crisps between us and clink her glass with mine.

"What are we toasting?" she asks.

Her question gives me pause, and since I don't know, I don't answer, instead asking a question of my own. "What color?" I grab my box of nail polishes and shove them under Heather's nose. Let's get the girlie shit on the road.

"Red!" She dives in and grabs a bottle. "You can do my toes for me." Kicking her shoes off, she gets comfy and rests them on my lap

I get to work separating her toes with cotton wool pads. "I have that sketch for you. Of the dress," I tell her.

"I already know what it looks like," she replies, and I smile, getting to work on her toes as she goes on. "I arranged a meeting with the fabric supplier. And I've had an idea for a lingerie range. Oh my God, you'll look fab in it!"

An abrupt cough makes me startle a little, and I look across to Sharp, finding him staring at me. He quickly diverts his eyes back to his laptop, though, avoiding my questioning look. Frowning on a shake of my head, I return my attention to Heather, finding her pursing her lips, assessing my bodyguard. So I knock her foot to get her attention.

She smiles at me. I ignore it.

After I've painted Heather's final toe, we settle down and spend the next few hours chatting, laughing, brainstorming and getting a little tipsy. Once *Dirty Dancing* is finished, I jump up and drag Heather behind me, forcing her to play Patrick Swayze while I pivot and prance around her. She sings. Badly. And I laugh when she braces herself for me to dive at her. "Seriously?" I laugh.

"I'm stronger than I look." She gives me flappy, impatient hands.

My amusement increases as I turn, catching Sharp watching us larking around. Or, at least, watching me. Is he grinning? I narrow my eyes a little, curious. Then he seems to jolt in his chair, darting his eyes away quickly.

"Come on, Baby!" Heather shouts, pulling me back to face her. My smile is back, and I run at her, watching as she shifts her feet, trying to anchor herself to the floor. We collide messily on high-pitched yelps and collapse to the couch, both laughing like idiots.

"Not that strong," I giggle, so relaxed in the privacy of my apartment goofing around with my bestie. There's no need to be on my guard, waiting for the flash of a camera to catch me on an off day. No controlling father to keep at bay. It's just me and my best friend.

"I bet *he* could lift you up like a feather." Heather nods at Sharp, grinning, and I'm reminded that it's not just us. Yet the stress Jake's caused me this past day doesn't re-surface with the reminder that he's here.

My palm rests on my heaving tummy as I glance over to him, seeing him shifting on the seat. I spend way longer than is acceptable admiring his gorgeous form slumped in the chair. I study his stubbled face and dark brown eyes for a moment, while they study me. His eyes are smiling.

I cock my head, just as he cocks his. He doesn't look at all exasperated having been forced to endure me and Heather being total girls. Why? I purse my lips, thinking.

And then Sharp quickly looks away, as if he's just realized he's staring. I bite my lip and look at the box of nail polish sitting next to me. I grin, collecting the most garish pink I can find in the box, and rise, wandering slowly over, trying not to stagger after too much wine. I'm standing at his feet for a good few seconds before he decides to look at me. I hold the polish up. "Want me to paint your toes?"

His eyes definitely widen a touch. "No," he answers flatly, looking back at his laptop, dismissing me.

My grin stretches as I drop to my knees at his feet. His bare feet. He has nice feet. I reach for his foot and try to pull it onto my lap. "I think this color will suit you."

He fights my hold, pulling away. "Camille," he warns, but I ignore him, wrestling with his foot. "Camille, what the hell are you doing?"

"Let me!" I insist, laughing, my amusement increasing when Heather joins me on the floor, helping me get Jake's foot where I want it. Even with both of us, we're no match for him. He shakes us both off and stands, leaving us falling to our arses.

I look up at him looming above me, my body shaking with amusement. I can see him gathering patience, breathing in deeply. *Now* he's exasperated and I can't help delighting in it. I expect him to stomp off at any moment to escape me and my annoying friend. But then he surprises me, rolling his eyes on a tiny huff of air and dipping, taking the tops of my arms and hauling me up. My laughter dries up in a second as he lifts me like I'm nothing. And he doesn't release me once I'm on my feet. Probably a good thing, since I can't *feel* my feet. Or my muscles. I can feel my heart, though. It's going bonkers in my chest, and it only gets worse when he leans in, putting his lips to my ear. I freeze in his hold.

"I've told you, Camille," he breathes, holding his mouth close. "I endure what I have to." He drops his grip, leaving me trembling on the spot, and strides away. "I'll be in the shower."

"Oh...goodness." Heather is next to me in a heartbeat, her hand on my arm. "Notice he didn't help *me* up. And he'll be in the shower? Was that an invite?"

I pull myself together and straighten my thoughts into line. "Don't be stupid," I mutter, making tracks to the kitchen to get more wine.

"Maybe, but can you imagine him naked? And wet?"

I silently beg for my best friend to shut the hell up and not fuel my already inappropriate thoughts. My plans to piss off Sharp have backfired. It's me who's pissed off. With myself.

* * *

After Heather has left, I stand with my back to the front door, my teeth sunken into my bottom lip. He didn't return after showering. He left us to it, probably deciding he'd stomached enough of the girlie stuff. The thought should make me smile, but it doesn't. All I can think about are the endless times I captured him watching me. He didn't look pained. He looked content. The complete opposite of what I wanted or expected.

A yawn creeps up on me. I need to sleep, and, more importantly, turn off my whirling mind. I collect some of my designs from the table and make my way to my room, set on making a few notes on my sketches in bed. But just when I'm about to shut the door behind me, I hear him. I'm unable to stop myself from peeking out of the door in search of him, jumping when I find him right in front of me, freshly showered but fully dressed. My eyes cement themselves to his chest, imagining the flesh beneath his grey T-shirt as I toy with the sketches in my grasp.

"Camille?"

My eyes fly up to meet his. "Yes?"

He's quiet for a few moments, thinking before he speaks. Then he reaches forward and takes one of my sketches. I remain quiet, silently amused as he scans the drawing. I bet he doesn't even know what he's looking at. "It's good," he muses, tilting his head a little. "What is it?"

"It's a belt. Part of the accessory line I've designed." I take the drawing back, laughing to myself. Why's he being all friendly all of a sudden? "Want to model it for me?"

Unamused eyes get narrowed onto me. "I don't wear belts." He reaches to the hem of his T-shirt and pulls it up. I expect he's showing me what will be empty belt hoops in his jeans, but all I can see is the taut stomach on display. My mouth dries up on me, and I reach for the door frame for support. Fucking hell. I could slice a finger on any one of the defined lines. "The only accessory I wear is a gun." He turns on his bare feet and strolls away. "I can't shoot you with a fucking belt."

Just like that, my lust vanishes and my face contorts with rage. And with no words coming to me, I resort to slamming the door in a temper.

CHAPTER 9

JAKE

She's doing this on purpose. I swear, all this girlie shit is turning my brain pink. All in all, I'm feeling pretty fucking pussy-ish right now.

I stand behind Camille Logan at the beauty department in Harvey Nichols, watching the lady behind the counter produce product after product for Camille to try, giving gushing, positive opinions on every shade of lipstick she applies to Camille's lips. Personally, I think her lips look the loveliest in their natural state, but I'm guessing my opinion isn't needed or wanted. I resort to closing my eyes when Camille bends over in front of me, leaning into a mirror to check the latest shade staining her lips. She's doing that on purpose, too. In my blackness, I force my thoughts straight, wiping the mental image of her tight arse within grabbing distance, and only open my eyes again once I'm sure I've got ahold of my composure.

I should have kept them closed. She's looking at me in the reflection of the mirror, rolling her lips together slowly for a few teasing seconds before she smacks them and pouts. My cock twitches, and I cough, quickly looking away and taking the opportunity to scope the joint. She definitely did *that* on purpose.

I'm not playing her silly games. I don't know what the fuck she was thinking yesterday morning, creeping up on me like that. One ill-judged move on my part and she could have been dead in my arms. When I had her pinned to the floor, I saw none of the fright that should have been there. There was something else, and I didn't like the look of it. It was tempting. Annoyingly tempting. I only just stopped myself from attacking her mouth with mine.

And then last night, making me endure her and that silly friend of hers. God, I've never struggled so much, and it had nothing to do with the girlie shit she was inflicting on me. My damn eyes refused to stay trained on my laptop. They kept taking on a mind of their own and searching her out. Her face, so beautiful anyway, is beyond stunning when she's smiling. She doesn't smile much in the pictures that are taken of her. It's all moody and mostly expressionless. It's a fucking waste.

I look at Camille and my heart slows. Her presence, though challenging, is settling. I can't for the life of me figure it out.

This a fucking problem, because I shouldn't be looking at her like I do, and I definitely shouldn't be having these damn stupid thoughts. But it hasn't escaped my attention that I didn't have one black thought yesterday, and last night while I was trying to get comfy on that damn couch, I was thinking of Camille, and Camille alone. It's a relief and a worry in equal measure.

I cast my eyes around the hall, avoiding Camille and that mirror. My phone chiming is perfect timing. After meeting Camille's half-brother, TJ, I immediately texted Lucinda and had her dig deeper on him. I didn't like him. He's shifty and has a smarmy face that begs to be punched . . . a bit like their father's. I can't tell you how hard it was to resist doing exactly that. Camille's brother, the cheeky fucker, had the nerve to tell me to look after her. Idiot! Having something interesting pulled up on him would have given me the excuse I was looking for to rip him apart.

I open Lucinda's message. It tells me her digging has brought up nothing. Clean as a fucking whistle. Of course he is. I sigh and bash out a reply.

The courier? Who delivered that threat?

There was no courier. Not that day, anyway.

I frown down at the screen, not knowing what it means to have my suspicions confirmed. I abandon texting and call her, wandering a few feet away from Camille, but keeping my eyes trained on her. "No courier?" I say when she picks up.

"Nope. Nothing."

"He's hiding something," I muse, dropping my eyes to the floor, thinking.

"Then let's ask him."

"No, don't give him any reason to believe we're on his case."

"Then what now?"

I look up to Camille. She's still bent over that damn mirror. "He wouldn't hire me for nothing," I say, concluding Logan must genuinely fear for his daughter's safety. I'm no precautionary measure. "Keep digging." I hang up, slipping my phone back into my pocket. I'm frustrated. Every angle is a dead end, and that white van outside Camille's agent's office was definitely suspicious. I've been in the job long enough to know when something is suspect.

I glance around. It's obscenely busy, women flooding the counters, credit cards being thrown about willy-nilly. It's hell.

After Camille has forced me to suffer an hour of the god-awful beauty department, she wanders off, leaving me to follow. The mix of a million scents begins to irritate my nose, forcing me to rub the itch away before I break out in a sneezing fit.

As we round a corner, I see a security guard up ahead, his body bowling toward us fast. A swift assessment of the situation tells me why. I quickly search out Camille and find her heading straight for his path, engrossed on her phone.

"Whoa!" I make a grab for her, pulling her back. Her startled yelp doesn't dent my focus, and I pull her off the walkway just as a young lad sprints past, followed quickly by the security guard. I watch them go, not fancying the guard's chances. The little crook is speedy, despite clearly having some goodies stuffed up his hoodie.

I shake my head and turn to Camille, not realizing I still have my arm slipped around her waist. The moment I register it, I'm hit with heat. Lots of it. I drop her and move back, giving her shocked form some space. Her topaz eyes are huge round balls of...Oh fuck, it's that look again, the same one she's had every time I've touched her.

I clear my throat and my head, ripping my eyes from hers. She's in a daze. "Your phone," I say, noticing it on the floor at her feet. I dip and collect it, handing it to her. It takes a few uncomfortable seconds for her to snap out of her trance, her arm lifting timidly and taking her iPhone.

"Thanks," she mumbles and turns, looking as unsteady as my heartbeat is feeling. Fucking hell, her no-touching boundary is probably the best idea she's ever had, but not effective if I physically *need* to touch her. Every time I look into this woman's eyes, I see want, desire, need, but more frighteningly, I fucking *feel* it.

I need a drink. And a good screw. Anything to rid my head of these stupid, pussy thoughts. There's only one woman who has even remotely had this effect on me before, and she's the fucking reason I'm a fucked-up, ex-SAS sniper. *Ex* being the operative word. *Sort it out, Sharp!*

Catching up to Camille, I fall into line behind her, wondering what shit she's going to inflict on me next. Nothing can be worse than an hour at the makeup counter, I'm sure.

Wrong.

The lingerie department.

Is she fucking kidding me? I keep my focus forward as she leads me through a maze of sexy underwear, collecting various pieces as she passes on through. I refuse to look. I keep my eyes on something safe, and, right now, the only safe place for me to look is at the back of Camille's head. Until she turns around. Her blue eyes sparkle, and I see mischief in them. A hand loaded with lacy bras and knickers comes up between us, and I face the dilemma of what's best to look at now: Camille, or the pile of underwear in her grasp.

The little...

She smiles, just a hint, and nods across the way. "I need to try these on."

I widen my stance and join my hands in front of me, nodding. "Take your time," I say evenly, my eyes betraying me and dropping to the mass of luxury material in her hand. I swallow and mentally shoot my brain out. If I was shadowing a bloke, I'd probably be standing at the end of a bar in some pub right now, or, better still, be half-enjoying some live sport. Fucking shopping! And for underwear? Lucinda must fucking hate me.

"This way," she sing-songs, wandering off to the changing rooms.

I follow obediently and overtake her, having a quick check of the area before wandering back out and positioning myself at the entrance. "Use the cubicle closest and you'll be good." It's ten feet away. I can live with that.

She gives me a dubious look. "You're going to stand there?"

"It's as much space as you're going to get," I tell her straight.

I see her crane her neck around the corner to the corridor of cubicles. "The first cubicle?" she questions.

"Yes."

"I prefer the ones at the back," she replies offhandedly, going on her way.

I try to hold back my tired sigh. Really, I do. "Camille, don't think I won't come in there." She's underestimating me.

"Don't think I care," she retorts.

My eyebrows jump up in surprise. She's not suggesting...?

I laugh to myself, but I'm not amused. "Camille, just use this one."

I step into the corridor and rap my knuckles on the wood to confirm it's empty before pushing the door open. She reaches the end of the changing rooms and tosses a cunning smile over her shoulder before disappearing into the cubicle of her choice. I stand like a twat for a few disbelieving moments, staring at nothing. It would seem that *I* am underestimating *her*. I look over my shoulder, seeing the assistants busy, and slowly accept my fate.

I want to kill her. Slowly.

As soon as I arrive outside her door, I hear shuffling from beyond. Camille Logan stripping. I look to the heavens for help. The door opens a smidgen, her arm appearing from behind. I scowl at her hand, where a pair of the smallest red lacy knickers I've ever seen are hanging from the tip of her index finger.

"These are a yes," she calls smugly.

I breathe in and close my eyes, gathering patience, and blindly snatch them off her finger. There's two minutes of more shuffling and puffing from behind the door before it opens again, this time the matching bra coming toward me.

"Another yes."

I leave her hand hovering in midair, thinking what a great gag that bra would make. I surprise myself. My thought isn't sexual at all. I want to ram that sexy underwear into her obstinate mouth so she can't talk. Then she opens the door a little more and peeks out. Our eyes meet, and that thought turns into an image. A sexual image. An image of Camille Logan on all fours, that bra shoved under her tits, and me smashing into her.

"Sharp!"

I jump, snatching the bra from her dainty hand on reflex. Fuck me, I need to sort myself out.

"I'll be outside." I stomp off, sweating, feeling so damn claustrophobic. When I reach the entrance of the changing rooms, I rest my back against the wall and breathe deeply, fighting away that image with all I have.

"Sir?" An assistant appears, pointing to the red matching set in my hand. I look down and immediately regret it, that mental image popping into my head again.

"They're a yes!" I thrust them forward and brush off my hands, like the action might brush my inappropriate mind clean, too. This is fucking torture. I make a mental note to e-mail Lucinda to reinforce the point that I *never* want a female client again.

The sales assistant takes the underwear on an unsure smile. "I'll get them wrapped."

"Thank you."

She leaves me to finish unraveling my tight muscles, but Camille appears, halting my task. They all coil back up again.

"Done?" I ask, praying the answer is yes. She has a knowing smile on her face that I wish I could wipe off. With my mouth, maybe?

She holds up both hands and more sexy lace sucker punches me in the face. "I like these, too." She sashays off and places the sets on the counter, looking over her shoulder on a small smile. I keep my curled lip at bay and look away from her. Yes, I hate her. With a vengeance.

Ten minutes later, I can smell freedom as the exit comes into sight. I just need to make it through the beauty department again and hope Camille isn't distracted by something shiny. I need air. My trained eyes split their attention between Camille and the door up ahead that'll get me out of this god-awful place, my hand twitching at my side, wanting to push it into Camille's back and hurry her along. No touching, I remind myself. Do not touch her.

I spot a woman up ahead armed with a bottle of perfume, spritzing lengths of cards and handing them to people as they pass. With the sunlight streaming into the store from the glass doors, I can see the air before her is a mist of dancing scented particles.

"Poison, madam?" she asks Camille as we pass, taking the liberty of squirting a card ready to hand to her. Except she misses the card and the spray hits Camille's arm, startling her. I look down to see her rubbing at her arm, smiling at the woman. "No, thank you. It's not my scent."

"I'm so sorry!" The woman, mortified, brushes at Camille's arm, too. "The atomizer must have turned!"

"It's fine, honestly." Camille pacifies the assistant. "It's a bit strong for me."

Forgetting my boundary, I push Camille on, through the haze of perfume-sprayed air. The particles drift up my nose, and I sniff, wincing. Then I cough, and the scent overwhelms me. I drop Camille, my feet grinding to a halt.

That smell.

My heart rate drops, my skin turning cold.

That smell.

I swallow and blink, seeing floating specks of torture closing in on me.

That smell.

I feel a flashback taking hold, nailing me into position, locking down all my muscles. I can't move. Can't escape it. I need to breathe, and when I gasp for a breath, my nose is invaded by a huge dose of the heavy scent, going straight to my brain. Poison. I haven't smelled it in four years.

She used to wear Poison. My surroundings blacken, leaving room for only one image. Her face. Her face followed by the bloodbath in Afghanistan. Screams, gunfire, my out-of-control rage. I bend over and brace my hands on my knees, starting to hyperventilate. Fuck, I need to get out of here.

"Jake?" Camille's voice is a distant hum. "Jake, are you okay?"

I draw in air through my nose, unable to control where I get my oxygen from. I get another potent hit of perfume and start to wretch, my heart smashing in my chest. "I need to get out," I say tightly.

I steam forward aimlessly, bumping into people as I go, knocking aside anyone who's in my way. The doors, so close but so far away. I fall out of the store, perspiring like I just ran a marathon, and fall against the wall in a heap of anxiety.

My shaky hand goes to my inside pocket as I drink in clean air, fumbling for my pills. It's stupid; there won't be any miracle effect from swallowing one now, but the psychological need is there. I pull them free and fiddle with the stupid small twist-top, the bottle slipping from my grip. They hit the floor at my feet.

"Fuck," I curse, dipping, trying to straighten out my vision to locate the small bottle. I'm seeing ten of everything. Breathing ten times faster than I should. My hands feel the floor as I desperately try to home in on my target.

"Here." The blur of another hand appears in my hazy vision, claiming the bottle and holding it out to me. My vision clears in an instant, and I look up to find concerned topaz eyes staring at me.

I swallow and take the pills, trying to unscrew the top as I rise and slump against the wall again. Camille puts me out of my misery and claims the bottle, opening it with ease and tipping a pill out into her palm. She holds it out to me, and I stare at the little tablet for a few seconds before taking it and knocking it back.

I close my eyes and force some deep breaths, hating myself for exposing the weak side of me to my subject. This has never happened before. Not to this extent, perhaps only in my dreams. But that perfume. It was a trigger. Fuck.

"Beta-blockers," Camille says quietly. "They control adrenaline. Stop anxiety attacks."

I drop my head, finding her screwing the lid back on, chewing her bottom lip. I can't lie. But what the fuck would I say?

I reach forward and take the bottle from her, slipping it back into my inside pocket before assessing the stability of my legs. A quick tense of my thighs confirms they're good enough. I push myself away from the wall, feeling her watching my every move.

"Where to next?" I ask, evading her eyes.

"I have some paperwork to go over at home this evening," she replies quietly.

"Home, then," I declare, gesturing for her to lead on.

But after a few uncomfortable seconds, she still hasn't moved and I'm forced to search her out, set on giving her an expectant look. The expectant look doesn't happen. She's looking at me, not in interest and not in curiosity. It's compassion, and as much as I know it shouldn't be, it's comforting.

"Don't feel sorry for me," I say quietly, our eyes glued, neither of us breaking the connection.

"Why?"

"Because I don't deserve it." I find myself falling victim to the intensity of her beautiful eyes, hauling me in, enhancing the comfort that I don't deserve.

"What happened to you?" she whispers.

"War," I say simply, surprising myself with my easy, if not detailed, offer. I see understanding surface on her flawless face, and I finally yank my eyes from hers before I spill any more shit on her.

"Home." I sweep my arm out and hope she follows this time. She does. Quietly and pensively, she passes me.

Camille Logan has exhausted her sass for today. She'll never know how grateful I am.

* * *

As I tail Camille into the lobby of her apartment block, my mind is still reeling, my nose still full of the scent. I press the call button for the elevator, turning when I hear footsteps approaching. The concierge is holding up an envelope, smiling. "Miss Logan, your mail."

Camille takes the envelope just as the elevator pings its arrival and the doors slide open. "Thanks," she says, pulling the seal open as she wanders into the lift. Her steps stutter and I frown, following her in.

"What's up?" I ask, not liking the visible goose bumps that have jumped onto her bare arms. She gazes up at me, a little vacant, forcing me to take the envelope that's held in her limp hand.

An image hits me square between my eyes. "Fuck," I curse, staring down at the photo of Camille wandering down a street with bags hanging from her hands. I flip the picture and am immediately confronted with another, this time her getting into her red Merc. There's text at the bottom of this one, and I get tenser with each word I read.

YOUR FATHER HAS 3 DAYS TO COMPLY.

The elevator doors start sliding shut, and my hand shoots out to stop them. "Hey!" I shout to the concierge as he wanders away. He turns, still smiling. "Who delivered this?" I hold up the envelope.

"Royal Mail," he answers, making me turn the envelope over and search out the postmark. There's nothing, just Camille's name and address on a typed label. I let the doors close this time, getting my phone from my pocket. Logan answers after the first ring.

"Camille's had some photographs delivered." I cut straight to the chase. "Whoever this is has been following her. I saw a white van outside her agent's office yesterday morning. I approached and they drove off rather hastily."

Logan lets out an audible gasp. "What are the photographs of?"

"Camille," I snap. What the fuck does he think they're of? "There's a note. They say you have three days to comply. Comply with what?"

"I don't know! How can I comply if I don't know what they want?"

I resist punching the wall of the elevator, glancing down at Camille. She still looks vacant. "You've had no further threats?" I ask.

"No, damn it! Don't you let her out of your sight, Sharp!"

"I don't plan on it," I grate, hanging up and immediately calling Lucinda. She answers with silence. "I'm sending you something by courier within the hour. Have it checked for fingerprints." The doors to the elevator open and I make quick work of guiding Camille out.

"Got it."

Stuffing my phone back in my pocket, I come to a stop at Camille's apartment door and look down at her. "Keys?" I ask, knocking her from her trance.

She looks up at me, making no attempt to get her keys out. "How serious is this?" she asks quietly. The fear I'd expect to be riddling her expression isn't there. There's still that compassion instead.

"Threats are usually exactly that," I say robotically. "Just a form of scaremongering. Besides, nothing can happen to you while I'm around. Open the door." I force my eyes away from hers. It's harder than it should be, when she's looking at me with a million questions in her eyes. But I know they're not questions about the threat and what it means. They're questions about me.

Chapter 10

CAMI

I spent the night lying awake, but the photographs that showed up weren't the cause for my insomnia. It was my curiousity about Sharp. Once I'd let us into my apartment, he only spoke to me when he absolutely needed to, giving one-word answers. The tension was thick. Horrible. And I know it had nothing to do with the photos that arrived. I knew what I was doing in Harvey Nic's, baiting him, making him suffer, forcing him into a man's hell. I loved every moment of it, seeing him squirm and sweat.

Yet every time our eyes connected, my amusement was stripped away and replaced with something I didn't love so much. But I can't deny it was there. I tried my best to disregard it, but I couldn't deny it. A sizzling electricity that I concluded wasn't my imagination. Not that it matters now.

Since Sharp had that shocking episode in the store, he's shut down. Hardly even looks at me. I should be grateful. It's removed the awkwardness of us constantly catching each other's eye, but unfortunately that awkwardness has been replaced with something else. Tension. Intrigue. At least it has on my part. He's here but not here. He's like a robot, and I can't help wondering if it's because he let his defenses down. Let me see deeper into him. Not that he looked like he had much choice. He wasn't in control. It was pretty agonizing to see his big, strong body reduced to such a mess. I can imagine how he felt. So strong, but so vulnerable. It reminds me of someone else. Me. Much of me is a front. Privately, I feel like I'm constantly battling my demons. Sharp and I are more alike than I'm comfortable with. Because whatever his internal battle is, I understand. I get it. And it's humanized him a bit more, made me see him a little differently.

As I enter the lounge, pulling my hair up as I go, I find the space empty. Sharp isn't in his usual spot on the couch. It looks odd without his big body reclined on it. I hear sounds from the kitchen and follow my ears, entering to find him by the sink, just finishing a glass of water. I momentarily wonder if he's had to take another pill. Betablockers. One thing I have figured out about Jake Sharp is that he's definitely suffering from post-traumatic stress disorder. I know, since he told me indirectly, that he's a war veteran. He also has what I know now must be a bullet wound.

But it's not my place to pry further, and after the state he was in at Harvey Nic's, I dare not. It was painful to witness. I wouldn't want to expose him to that again.

I make my way to the fridge to grab a detox juice. "I'm meeting Heather for coffee," I say, unscrewing the cap of my juice as I turn.

Sharp hasn't moved and he doesn't seem to have heard me. He's in a daydream.

I assess him as I wander away, sipping my juice. Then I notice a bag at his feet. "You going somewhere?"

He looks across to me, still appearing a bit spaced out. "I've been assigned to another job," he says mechanically.

My heart sinks, which is daft. Him leaving is undoubtedly the best thing that could have happened.

"Someone else is on their way to take over," he adds. "You'll be safe."

My heart receives a sharp shot of pain. It baffles me beyond measure, yet I carry on my way, my grip of the bottle in my hand tightening until the plastic starts to crunch loudly. What's most fucked up here is that I'm disappointed he's going instead of worried about the photographs that were delivered. It's crazy.

"Fine." I force the word through my clenched jaw, spotting my handbag across the living room as I enter.

Just get it and go. Don't look at him.

I throw my phone inside and turn, finding Jake standing in the kitchen doorway, watching me closely. His deep eyes when they study me this closely always render me incapable of movement.

"What?" I ask, sounding harsh and stroppy.

He picks up his bag from the floor, shaking his head. "You'll wait here until they arrive."

"I have things to do!" I argue as he throws his bag over his shoulder and heads for the door.

"Five minutes, Camille. You can wait for five minutes. Then you'll never have to do a thing I tell you to do ever again." He takes the door handle and looks over his shoulder, almost smiling at me, expecting my retort. Which is why I don't give him one.

I don't need to prove myself to anyone, except myself. I have my integrity and independence. I also have an unbearable pain in my heart as I watch him pull the door open. I try to reason with myself, tell myself that I'm being stupid and the only thing that's making me feel this way is the comfort I *don't* want to feel from his presence. That he can protect me. But that isn't just it.

Jake takes one last long, hard look at me, then turns to leave, but he gets no farther than two paces, coming to a sudden, abrupt halt. The muscles of his back bunch under his T-shirt, his shoulders high and tense. His bag falls to the floor, and his hand comes round to his back quickly, resting on something. His gun?

I step back, cautious...and then I hear someone speak. "Is Camille home?"

My stomach bottoms out.

Sebastian.

I start to back away, frightened, but then I panic for a different reason. Shit, Sharp's going to shoot him!

I fly toward the door and grab Sharp's hand, which is halfway to pulling his gun from the back of his jeans. He expertly yanks himself free and swings around, eyes full of dangerous intent, his forehead displaying a sheen of sweat.

The moment he realizes it's me, I see his face soften. "It's my ex-boyfriend!" I rush to explain.

He freezes, and once I can be sure the information I've just given him has sunk into his robot mind, I start to move in front of him, slowly and cautiously, watching him closely. He looks dangerous. Volatile. Good Lord, he looks murderous.

"Jesus." Seb's startled curse pulls my attention away from Sharp. My ex is standing in the corridor, his back pressed to the wall on the far side. His blue eyes are wide and wary, but they are perfectly clear, too.

It's been nine months since I've seen him. Nine months of sorting myself out. He knows we're done, that there's no going back for me. "Why are you here?" I ask, flicking a glance over my shoulder, not liking what I find. Sharp looks positively deadly, his hand still behind his back, ready to pull his gun.

"How are you, Cam?" Sebastian asks. The super-shorted version of my name, the one only *he* ever used, brings on an onslaught of flashbacks. My only saving grace is that the flashbacks are of the dark times. It's the best reminder.

"I'm good." I give Sebastian an even face to match my even answer. *I'm good, without you!* While in rehab, he gave me regular updates in long, detailed e-mails. I chose not to respond, and after the first two weeks, I stopped reading them altogether. They only hindered my own recovery. He was full of remorse. He always was. He will not make me weak again. He won't have that hold over me.

Flicking a look past me, Seb weighs up the mountain of lean muscle still looming behind me.

I choose to answer his silent question, if only to move things along. This is awkward.

"He works for my dad," I tell him. "He's driving me today." It's not a lie, but it isn't the truth either. It's of no consequence who Jake Sharp is because, apparently, he'll be gone soon.

Once again, a nasty shot of regret pinches my heart, but more significantly, it completely overshadows any fear of facing Seb. I realize in this moment how thankful I am that Sharp is here. Especially now.

Sebastian steps forward and smiles. "Coffee?" he asks.

"I don't think so," I answer.

"No?" He looks shocked by my refusal, and it seriously astounds me. What did he think I'd do? Leap into his arms and tell him how much I've missed him? I nod my confirmation and watch as a familiar wave of anger flickers across his face. He tries to hide it, and maybe to the outside world he'd succeed, but I've seen this forced calmness before. He isn't fooling me. "Come on," he croons, stepping forward with a smile in place. "Haven't you missed me?"

I don't get a chance to answer this time. I yelp as I'm swiped from my feet and placed to the side. Sharp takes the door handle and moves toward Seb, who wisely backs up. "Your contact with Miss Logan stops here." And with that, he slams the door and stalks toward the kitchen, pulling his phone from his pocket.

I look at my closed front door, then to the entrance of the kitchen, just catching Sharp's back, still heaving, disappearing through the door.

What the hell just happened?

I follow him to the kitchen and find him at the sink splashing his face with water.

"I thought you were leaving," I say, frowning at his heaving back.

"There's been a change of plan," he declares.

CHAPTER 11

JAKE

I slowly stir my coffee as I sit a few tables away from Camille and Heather outside a small Italian café off Kensington High Street while they slurp iced teas and chat like girls do. It's all I can do not to moan when I hear Heather mention their social event tonight. Saffron's twenty-fifth-birthday party. Great. More torture in the form of Camille Logan wearing something shit-hot and strutting around a bar while endless men drool all over her. Perfect. Can't fucking wait.

She has been noticeably more receptive to my protection since my meltdown in Harvey Nichols yesterday. Her new approach is a surprise, and I can't figure out if it's a welcome one.

The way she looked at me after she'd relieved me of my slippery pill bottle and gave me what I needed did things to me that I'm struggling to comprehend. There was no judgment in her eyes when she helped me. There was nothing but compassion. I'm still questioning whether it was the psychological impact of swallowing that tablet that calmed me, or the peace I siphoned off of her. I tried to figure it out and found myself growing more and more distressed and perplexed by the sense of comfort I got from *her* comfort. I can't stop myself from looking at her. I can try to kid myself that it's my job to watch her, but I'd be lying. I'm not watching her. I'm admiring her—her work ethic, how she's pulled herself back from the brink of self-destruction, and her determination to chase her dream rather than take the easy path. Like her father's money, or these investors with other ideas that I've listened to her talk about. She's so fucking strong. Just being around her offers a sense of calm that I know I shouldn't be taking. She's not a distraction. She's a comfort, and I don't deserve any comfort.

I lay on the couch last night and came to the solid conclusion that all those factors meant my head wasn't in the game. So this morning I called Lucinda and told her to find me another job. I was all set to leave Camille Logan behind, along with the confusing feelings she spikes in me, and find another distraction.

But that all changed the moment I opened the door to her ex-boyfriend. I knew who he was the second I laid eyes on him. I nearly put a bullet in his posh head. The natural instinct to protect her was more primal than duty-driven. I couldn't ignore it. And I suddenly couldn't walk away. I've seen pictures of Sebastian Peters since his release from rehab, falling out of nightclubs with watery eyes and his jaw tight—all evidence that he's using again. It seems reading girlie magazines has become part of my job. If I were a lesser man, I'd feel like a pussy.

His unexpected visit to Camille's apartment changed my decision to hand her safety over to a replacement in a heartbeat. I saw a flash of menace in his eyes when Camille refused his offer of coffee. He seems like more of a danger to Camille than any threats. But I *will* protect her from both.

It's imperative that I train my mind into submission and avoid all situations that have the potential to veer me off the course of professionalism. I'm not going to try and plead that this will be easy. It won't be. Camille Logan is a beautiful, tempting young woman, and she also has an air of determination and independence that I can't help but find fascinating. And attractive. My initial conclusions are completely unfounded. She's no brat. She's a woman fighting for her independence.

She repels her father's insistence to feed her cash and clearly finds the suppression attached to being his daughter a burden.

I've also silently concluded that there's a heavy amount of resentment weighing her down. Her life is watched, not only by paparazzi, but now by me, too, though she's accepted that compliance will make this situation go away a lot faster if she plays ball. There's no denying she's attracted to me, and for once I'm not smug about it. I'm also not being an arsehole about it.

I watch, rapt, as she laughs, so carefree, her cheeks pink, her eyes sparkling. Damn. I quickly avert my gaze, and I'm about to wave the waiter for some ice water when a sharp movement across the road snatches my attention. My mind clears and my muscles engage. I'm immediately on high alert. Narrowing my eyes, I watch, searching the empty space at the alley entrance. There's nothing now, but there was definitely something.

I hear the faint chatter of Camille and her friend a few feet away as I shift in my chair, feeling my gun press against my back. My mind's eye captures snapshots of the surroundings and stores them. My leg muscles flex, ready to engage if they have to. I wait patiently, keeping my attention divided between the girls and the alley.

Then I see movement again: the head of a man popping out quickly and taking in the scene outside the café before retreating. It's a brief second, but I file a wealth of information in that brief second. His face, his slight frame, his beady eyes. He's spying. I'm up and across the road like lightning, my legs feeling good under the strain that's been absent for too long. I reach the wall adjacent to the café and wait. It's only a few seconds before his head appears again.

I grab the collar of his shirt, yanking him from the concealed darkness of the alleyway and slamming him into the wall front forward. Holding him in place with my body, his arms pushed up his back, I ignore the whimpers and yelps.

"What the fuck do you want?" I hiss in his ear, releasing him a little, then slamming him into the wall again. He stutters and stammers all over the place, trembling under my hold. "Tell me!" I roar, hearing the clicking of a few pairs of heels getting louder and louder behind me.

Camille.

My heart speeds up and I turn to find her running across the road toward me. "Stay back!" I bellow, making her skid to a frightened stop. "Stay where you are!"

The man in my clutches keeps whimpering and whining. The fucking pussy. "I'm sorry," he chokes.

"You fucking will be." I quickly check Camille is doing what she's told, then whirl him around, keeping his arms restrained behind his back, now pressed into the bricks of the wall. His wide eyes look like they could burst from his head at any moment. Good. "Tell me who the fuck you're working for, and I'll let them know why you won't be reporting back to them."

"Jake!" Camille yells, her voice urgent and worried.

"Just stay where you are!" I shout, not taking my eyes off the scum in my hold.

"He's paparazzi!" she yells, coming closer. I take a moment to allow that information to sink in. Paparazzi? I keep my hold, not convinced, and look down, seeing a camera smashed to smithereens on the ground. "He just wants a picture," Camille says soothingly, her hand coming up and resting on my bicep. I glimpse down, seeing her slender, manicured fingers resting on my bare arm.

"Paparazzi?" I mumble to her hand, feeling a delicious heat sinking into my flesh.

"Yes," she assures me, and I look up to find her smiling a little, trying to pacify me. "He won't hurt me." She looks to the terrified man, who I still have pinned to the wall. "Hi, Stan."

"Hey, Camille." His voice is trembling as much as his puny body. "Mind asking this nice gentleman if he'll let me go?"

I hear her chuckle under her breath. It's the sweetest fucking sound. "Sure." She looks at me. "Would you mind freeing him?"

"Yes, I would mind," I snap, thinking of the pictures that were delivered to Camille yesterday. When she moves in a little, looking up at me, I realize she's cottoned onto my train of thought.

"I've known Stan for years," she says. "He's one of the good guys."

I assess him again, running suspicious eyes all over his alarmed face. He looks truly terrified. "Who do you work for?" I ask.

"Freelance. My I.D. is...is...it's...in my breast pocket." He stutters and stammers all over the place.

I help myself to his pocket and pull out his wallet, flipping it open and checking while holding him in place. "Stan Walters?"

He forces a nervous smile. "That's me."

I pull away, satisfied that he's no threat, and he flops against the wall, taking his wallet back when I hand it over. I turn toward Camille. "You're on first-name terms with the fucking paparazzi?" I ask incredulously.

"Sure." Camille shrugs and starts collecting the many pieces of broken camera littering the ground. Stan finds it in himself to crouch down and help, constantly darting wary eyes to me. "Stan and I have an arrangement, don't we, Stan?"

"We did!" He laughs sarcastically. "I think we need to renegotiate the terms."

What the fuck? "I'm sorry." My hand comes up and rakes through my hair. "What?"

Camille stands, followed by Stan, and hands all the broken pieces over to him. "He gets his pictures, but only so many a month."

"Then why the fuck is he loitering in an alleyway spying on you?"

"Because he's had his quota this month. Right, Stan?" Camille fires him an accusing but forgiving look.

"Right," he admits guiltily. "Sorry. Bit short of excitement this month."

"I'm drinking tea!" She laughs, head thrown back and all. That neck. I blink and suck in air.

Stan sidesteps that comment and looks at me. I read his mind in an instant. "Don't even think about it," I warn with all the threat I mean.

"But you're so handsome!" he whines, and then pouts. He fucking pouts at me.

"No." I point a finger at his protruding lip. "I swear, if my face appears in any magazine, posed or not, then I'll hunt you down and kill you. Understand?"

"But the handsome bodyguard is the most prized accessory these days! And, boy, do you top them."

"Fuck off!" I spit, incensed. Accessory? He's making a fucking mockery of it. "Get out of here." I dismiss him with a shove to his shoulder and a curled lip.

Wisely, he dumps all the broken pieces of his camera into his bag and saunters off, flipping an indignant wave over his shoulder as he goes.

"I'll replace the camera, Stan!" Camille calls, guilt rife on her lovely face.

"No, you fucking won't," I retort. She's got nothing to feel guilty about, and neither have I, even after roughing up the little twerp.

"Are you done?" I ask Camille, turning to find she's been joined by Heather. She has a miffed look on her face, while Heather is grinning. "What?" I ask, truly flummoxed by Camille's filthy glare.

"You could have just ruined my relationship with the press!" She pushes past me and makes her way back to the café, collecting her bag from Heather as she goes. I grit my teeth as the lasting effect of her touch, angry or not, fades.

I feel Heather's smirk still pointed at me, so I face her, ready for whatever she might chuck at me, too. "I love how protective of her you are," she muses.

I wasn't expecting *that*. "Of course I am. I'm paid to protect her."

She scoffs as she turns, shaking her head as she walks away from me. "Open your fucking eyes, big man."

What the hell does she mean by that? I'd ask, but she's out of talking distance too quickly. I wander over, seeing some serious words exchanged as I approach, before both women shut up and Camille gives Heather a quick peck on the cheek. "I'll see you later," she says to her friend, tossing a note on the table for the bill, at the same time tossing me yet another filthy look.

I sigh. What does she want me to do? Wait until someone tries to bundle her in the back of a van before I make my move? I can't fucking win.

Camille sashays off and Heather heads the other way, leaving me standing like an idiot between them. My head drops back, my eyes rolling to the heavens. Then I expel a long, fucking annoyed sigh. What I can't decide, though, is whether I'm annoyed with myself for shooting from the hip, or whether I'm annoyed about the outcome. She's pissed off with me, and I fucking detest myself for being bothered by that.

Following Camille to my car, I jump in and find her sitting in the passenger seat, focus rooted firmly forward. I start up the Range Rover and pull out, peeking at her out the corner of my eye as we head off down the road. It's awkward, the tension palpable.

"Home?" I ask, taking a left at the top of the street.

She keeps her mouth shut and her attention forward.

"Home?" I repeat, this time clearer and louder. Again, nothing. Great. So I'm being punished with the silent treatment now? I hate that it bothers me. "Camille," I say, loading my voice with authority as we come to a stop at some lights. "Would you like me to take you home?"

The light changes to green, but I stay exactly where I am. I'm not moving until she answers me. I could take her straight home, regardless of where she wants to go, but something silly inside of me wants her to acknowledge me. Speak to me. Stupid? Yes. Proud? Most definitely. She's rubbing off on me, for fuck's sake.

Car horns start blaring around us, drivers cursing out of windows and throwing hand gestures. I ignore them all. I'm not bothered. I'll stay here all day if I have to. Camille, however, is looking increasingly embarrassed by the whole noisy spectacle, shifting in her seat uncomfortably. "The light's green," she mutters, refusing to look at me when she knows I'm turned in my seat, facing her.

"Very observant of you." I shouldn't be sarcastic. That won't help. I should have known her compliant behavior wouldn't last long.

Her face twists as she turns toward me, her jaw tight. "Why are you being difficult?" she asks seriously, car horns still going loopy around us.

I gawp at her in disbelief. Me? "Camille," I laugh lightly, trying to rein myself in before it breaks into a belly laugh. She's a case! "I'm asking you a simple question."

"Yes," she grates. "I want to go home."

"See, that wasn't so hard, was it?" I pull away swiftly and leave the noise behind.

"Don't patronize me," she spits, and I smile on the inside. I fully expect a *fuck you* at any moment.

But weirdly, and quite surprisingly, I don't want her to hate me. It's a revelation. Most women hate me after only a few hours in my company, usually after I've kicked them out of my bed. They've never cost me a thought. Camille, however, is costing me lots of thoughts. Inappropriate thoughts. Painful thoughts. Annoying thoughts. I quietly groan. What I wouldn't do for a drink right now. I haven't had a drop for days. Drinking helps me relax. And I haven't run for too long. Running soothes me.

I haven't fucked for what feels like forever.

Fucking helps with...well, fucking is fucking. It's a means to an end. I shift in my seat, my cock beginning to swell no matter how hard

I try to talk it down. I'm just one big fat bag of pent-up man. None of this has ever been a problem on any previous jobs, but I wasn't shadowing Camille Logan on those jobs. It wasn't a daily battle to control my...

I shake my head furiously, flicking her a glance, just to check that she hasn't caught sight of my awkward shifting. I find her gazing out of the passenger window, deep in thought. Part of me wants to leave her be, to let her have her quiet time, but a selfish part of me—a misplaced instinct—wants to know every tiny detail currently whizzing through that smart mind of hers.

Because I need to know if any of her thoughts are matching mine. Thoughts that are wrong. Thoughts that I shouldn't be having. And maybe then I won't feel like I'm going slowly crazy.

Chapter 12

CAMI

After Jake's driven me home, I spend the rest of the afternoon in my room going over the offer from the investor, hoping to find some redeeming clause that will make it more appealing. It's wasted time, I already know that, but it's a great ploy to avoid Sharp. I feel guilty, like I'm betraying Heather by even touching the offer. When I left her outside the café, after Jake had very nearly put Stan in the hospital, she commented on the way Jake looked at me. I brushed it off, yet obsessed about it the entire journey home. I've seen the way he looks at me, too. I'm trying not to think about it. And I'm failing.

Once I've tossed the offer aside, I call my agent to confirm my decline. Then I lose myself for a little while longer updating my portfolio. Anything to avoid him.

And then I'm out of things to do. And I'm thirsty. It takes too long for me to muster the courage to leave my room to fetch some water, but once I have, I scurry across the lounge toward the kitchen like a rat up a drainpipe. I feel his eyes on me the entire time.

After filling my glass, I make quick work of getting back to my room without searching him out. I nearly make it before my treacherous eyes betray me and flick to my sofa. Our eyes meet. My heart jumps. My hand pauses on the handle of the door into my room. And the water in my glass definitely swishes a little from my trembles.

All from just one dash of eye contact. He quickly returns his attention to his laptop. The atmosphere is thick. Horrible. He knows I'm annoyed, but what he doesn't know is why. He thinks he knows, but he's wrong. I'm not angry because he could have ruined my relationship with the press. I'm angry because I like having him around. I've quickly become used to him. Always there, shadowing me. I feel safe. Safe from Sebastian, safe from the paps, and safe from the stupid threats because of my father.

I push my way into my room and immediately start pacing up and down, looking at the door constantly. I feel like a prisoner in my own home. Scared to roam free for fear of catching his eye or, worse, accidently brushing past him. I sigh and pluck up the courage to confront him, prepared to voice my fake grievance just to clear the air.

Heading out of my room again, determined, I find him nowhere to be seen. I check the kitchen, finding no life, and finally conclude that he must be in the spare room where he keeps his things and showers. But he still insists on sleeping on the couch. I look down the corridor and force my feet to move, knocking lightly on the door when I reach it. I wait for any kind of indication to enter, but hear nothing, not a peep from beyond the door. So I knock again, this time a little more firmly. Nothing.

"Jake?" I call, bringing my ear closer to the door. "You in there?"

I get no reply.

Taking the handle, I turn and push the door open a fraction, peeking through the gap. There are no signs of life. I glance over to the bathroom. I can't hear the shower or movement coming from there.

"Where is he?" I ask myself, pushing my way into the room until the whole space comes into view. The bed is still perfectly made and on the end are a few piles of his clothes, folded and placed with precision. His bag rests next to them, the zipper gaping open. There's something silver lying on top, catching the setting sun shining in from the window.

What is that? I glance over my shoulder as I creep forward, unable to stop myself. I should get out. I'm invading his privacy. But the knowledge that this might shed some light on the mystery and darkness that surrounds my shadow is far too tempting to resist. Besides, he knows so much about me. It seems only fair I have the same advantage.

As I get closer to the bed and the open bag lying atop of it, I can tell the silver is from a picture frame. A picture frame? My breath catches in my throat. A photo?

Another quick check to the doorway tells me I'm still alone. I stand in front of the bag, a good ten feet away, oddly scared to go any farther. The sensible side of me, telling me to walk away, is being hampered by the compulsion to see the picture in that frame.

I crane my neck as far as I can, one side of the picture coming into view. I'm holding my breath when I see a happy face appear. Jake's face. My teeth clamp down on my bottom lip to stop any tiny gasp of surprise. He's smiling brightly, his eyes twinkling, his perfect teeth on full display. I've never seen him smile like that, and his eyes are always so dark and serious. He looks so happy in the picture, and wondering who is on the other side of the photograph creating that happiness, I take the step needed to bring the whole frame into view. A beautiful woman with long, glossy black hair is cuddled into Jake's side, laughing. My heart squeezes as I pick up the frame. Jake's in combat trousers and a khaki T-shirt. He looks lethal behind his happy smile, his arms solid, the material of his T-shirt stretched across his biceps.

"What the fuck!" Jake's loud boom sends my nervous strumming heartbeats into heart attack territory, and the picture falls from my grip. I jump and swing around, my palm on my chest, my eyes wide and frightened.

He's standing in the doorway, annoyed, his chest heaving.

"I'm sorry," I sputter, my cheeks heating under his fierce glare. "I thought—"

"You thought you'd snoop through my private belongings?" He strides forward and snatches up the picture, stuffing it in his bag and zipping it closed.

"Who is she?" The question I have no right to ask just tumbles right out, surprising me.

"None of your business," he snaps and stomps into the bathroom. "Get out."

I flinch at his harshness, swallowing down the unreasonable hurt that it's spiked. I would love for shame to overshadow my curiosity about the photograph, but it hasn't. That woman made him happy, and she's clearly not in his life anymore. Who is she? And, more interestingly, what happened to make him react so violently to my inquiry about her? My tangle of thoughts is interrupted when he appears in the bathroom doorway. I can't look him in the face. My eyes plummet down his body so all I see are his perfect feet. His perfect bare feet.

"You're still here," he says, gruff but calm, those feet bringing him closer to me.

"I'm going." As I step back, finally convincing my body to move, I reluctantly raise my eyes to his. I don't find the anger I expected. I find remorse. But I can't fathom whether it's remorse for that woman, his past and the fact that I've seen a hint of it, or whether it's remorse for yelling at me.

When Sharp closes his eyes and swallows, I conclude that it's all of those things. "I'm sorry," he breathes.

"Don't be. I shouldn't have pried." I wholeheartedly mean it, but my regret goes deeper than my disregard for his privacy. I'm more regretful because I've spiked questions about my shadow that I don't expect will be answered. His past has nothing to do with me, yet the burning need to know is there and I can't help it.

"She's an ex." He says the words quickly, and I recoil, surprised.

"She..." His words fade to nothing, and he recoils now, too, evidently shocked by his semi-offer of an insight into his past. He seems to shake himself back to life, looking a little lost in the moment. "She's nothing." He glances away.

She's nothing, but he still carries her picture around with him? I offer a forced smile and move to leave, but his hand shoots out and clasps my arm, stopping me. I don't mean to, but I flinch. It's hard not to react when a simple touch sends a warmth so intense to your heart.

Looking down at his hold of me, he falls into a trance, virtually burning holes in my flesh from the hardness of his gaze. Then his fingers flex a little around my arm, and every nerve ending I possess fizzles, my breathing becoming shallow. It brings back memories of him holding my hand in Dad's office, how amazing and calming it felt. I want to know how it would feel to have his whole body wrapped around me. I got a hint when he pinned me to the floor the other morning. And when he seized me and moved me from the path of the security guard in Harvey Nic's. And when he picked me up off the floor when I tried to paint his toenails. I want more of a hint.

We both look up at each other at the exact same time, our stares meeting and holding. Then his face starts to come slowly toward mine, his eyes flicking down to my lips. I hold my breath, arrested by anticipation. He's going to kiss me.

I'm about to move forward, too, but the sound of my phone ringing in the background breaks the moment. My muscles lock, and Sharp withdraws quickly.

"You should get that," he says quietly, looking away. The difficult atmosphere returns full force.

I move quickly, keen to escape the awkwardness, mentally cursing my arse off as I walk away. So fucking stupid! Oh my God, what was that? What have I done? I mentally beat myself around the head a few times as I scurry away.

Finding my phone, I see Mum's name flashing up at me. I fold a little on the inside. I've avoided her all week, knowing she'll be unaware that Dad's having me shadowed, and the reason why. She doesn't exactly hold my father in high esteem since he dumped her for a younger model. The knowledge of anything untoward, especially where I'm concerned, will not be taken well. I don't need an earache over this. I don't need her to rant on about my father and his questionable business activities. Anyway, she turned a blind eye for the twenty-two years they were together, when she was living the life she was accustomed to. She's still managing to live that life, thanks to a good investment after a less than satisfying settlement in her divorce, but now she's living the life with a shitload of bitterness attached.

"Mum." I try to sound as chirpy as I can, waiting for the scorn I deserve for being missing in action this past week.

"There's my girl." Her soft, well-spoken English accent makes me feel a little better. "I was beginning to think you'd left me for your father."

I smile, just as Sharp breaches the entrance to the lounge, looking no less emotionally detached than when I left him a moment ago. Though I can see faint curiosity in his expression, wondering who's on the other end of the line. "Never, Mum," I say, telling him without actually having to tell him.

"How are you, sweetie pie?"

"Been checking the magazines?" I ask, knowing she's a sucker for all the gossip, even if it's sensationalized by the media. She's asking because she's spotted Sebastian crawling out of a bar.

"I know you'll be wise." She has true belief in her tone. It actually helps. Unlike my father, she has faith in me. "I have a free evening," she goes on, making me smile. That's a rarity. She's a social butterfly, spreading her time far and wide between women's clubs, tennis clubs, bowling clubs, and endless ladies lunches. I've been on one of those ladies lunches. Only once, and I swore never to again. A table full of bitter and twisted women slamming their ex-husbands over cute sandwiches and champagne isn't my idea of time well spent. "Meet me for a spot of dinner."

"I have Saffron's birthday party to go to." I reel off my excuse easily, since it's true, yet I hold no hope that it'll make any difference.

"Then meet me before. Line your stomach."

I cringe as I search Jake out, finding he's now taken up position on the couch, laptop resting on his long legs. I'm trying to figure out who will be easier to brush off. I know my mother won't hang up until I agree. Plus, I haven't seen her for over a week. Yet I can't very well take Sharp along. That'll raise all kinds of questions that I don't want to answer. He's hardly unnoticeable, with his powerful presence and 6'4" lean frame.

How can I convince him that dinner with my mother doesn't require him to chaperone? I'll sit on that one for a few minutes and work out the best approach. I can't deny I need some space from him right now. All this awkwardness is becoming unbearable. I can't seem to say or do the right thing.

"TJ is coming," she adds, sealing it for me. I love that my mum treats him as her own, even though he's a carbon copy image of the ex-husband she hates. She sees the endearing quality in TJ, just like I do, probably because she worked hard to install it into him from when he was a toddler.

"What time and where?" I definitely see Sharp's ear cock up as I speak.

"Marvelous! I'll have my driver collect you at seven. Look pretty, sweetie pie!" She hangs up and I start chewing my lip, thinking how best to approach this.

"That was my mother," I say casually, wandering into the kitchen to get a glass of water. As expected, I get no answer, not only because I've not told him anything that he didn't already know. "She wants to have dinner with me tonight," I call, pulling a glass down from a cupboard. "Her driver's picking me up at seven."

Again, not a murmur of acknowledgment.

I scowl at the tap as I fill my glass before wandering back into the living space. Jake's not there. His laptop is closed and now sitting on the seat where his arse was looking comfortable a moment ago. I take a gulp of water, as well as a gulp of confidence, then go on my way to find him and tell him how it's going to be. With every step, I get more and more confident, and I'm not ignoring the fact that I'm less worried about Mum and her questions about who Jake is, and more determined to gain some breathing space from him. I feel suffocated by...I don't know what, but I know it is not good.

I'm so wrapped up in my mental pep talk that I forget to knock and walk straight into the spare room. My glass slips straight through my hand and hits the carpet with a thud, splashing water up my legs. "Oh fuck!" I choke, coming face to face with Sharp, naked and with a towel held limply in his hand. He doesn't move. I don't move. We're just staring at each other, my eyes undoubtedly matching Sharp's. Bugged. Shocked. Useless.

Cover yourself up!

I scream the order in my head, trying to shift the command from my brain to my mouth so I can voice it. My mouth isn't playing ball. But something else is working, and it's not to be ignored. I bring my legs closer together to try and stop the pulse from breaking out into a full, hard throb, my eyes dropping down his chest. Every tiny bit of air I was storing tumbles past my lips on a lusty gasp. His cock. It's long, solid, and twitching.

"Camille." His soft call of my name barely registers. I'm too rapt by what I'm faced with. Someone save me before I drop to my knees and start worshipping it. "Camille!"

I jump, so much that my back hits the edge of the door, sending a shot of pain shooting through my shoulder. "Fuck!" I reach up and grasp the top of my arm, dazed and confused.

"Are you okay?"

I shake some clearness into my vision, seeing Jake approaching, now with that small towel wrapped low around his tight hips. The definition of his stomach, drifting down into perfect hollows past his lower abdomen, makes me all fuzzy again. "Yes!" I move back, escaping, colliding with the damn door again. "Fuck!" I rub my shoulder. "I'm fine," I say as I stagger into the corridor. Jake comes to a stop just before the door, a frown marring his face. "I'm going to dinner with my mum," I blurt, moving away some more.

"I know." He runs a quick scan of me, from top to toe, probably checking I'm okay. I'm not. My shoulder might ache, but I'm aching more elsewhere. I need to get away pronto.

"Her driver's collecting me. TJ will be there, too. You don't need to come." I can tell by his sudden disgusted expression that he thinks otherwise.

"Don't even think about it." He turns and walks away from me, letting the towel fall away without a scrap of shyness, exposing everything to me. I slam my eyes shut to hide from the obscene flawlessness.

"I'll be with my mum and brother," I protest to my darkness. "I'll be fine."

"I'm not having this conversation with you, Camille."

I want to open my eyes and hit him with my filthiest look, but that would be a stupid move. "Are you dressed yet?" I ask, unable to hide my irritation.

"Yes."

My eyes open and immediately find him with some trousers on, hanging open at the waist, his chest still bare and fucking divine. I gasp my annoyance. "Jake!"

"Then turn around, Camille." His motions falter as he pulls his shirt on.

I hate how difficult I find it to turn away from him. But I do, begrudgingly, still seeing all those fine lines riddling his stomach. "There's really no need for you to come with me."

"Your father wants me to shadow your every move. You saw the pictures. You are lucky you're even allowed to leave this place, and you should note that the only reason you are is because I'm with you. I'm not averse to enforcing this." He virtually spits the words, his frustration growing.

"Enforce how?" My ears prick up for the wrong reasons as I imagine him pinning me down. Like he did when he captured me studying him when he was pretending to be asleep. My body springs to life.

"Try me," he says simply.

A lick of desire mixed with curiosity beats its way up my spine, straightening it. I want to try him. I want to see what lengths he'll go to in order for me to comply. I want him to tie me to him so we're connected and I can relish in that lovely warmth that sinks so deeply into me. I want...

"I'm coming." His breath in my ear startles me, yanking me from my inappropriate fantasies, as he moves past me, fastening his tie as he walks away. "Call your mother and tell her there's no need to send her driver."

I find a wall and let my forehead meet it with a little too much force, hoping the shockwave the bang creates will chase away my building desire for a man who should not be desired. And, more significantly, doesn't want to be.

CHAPTER 13

JAKE

I can still feel the dull pulsing in my cock, an aftereffect of an erection that has long outstayed its welcome.

I don't know what I was thinking, but Camille's face when I barked at her nearly broke me. I hated myself in that moment. I've been an arsehole with many women and never felt even a smidgen of guilt about it. Kept them at a distance. Simple.

With Camille, it's different. I crave her closeness, and I felt like a first-class bastard when I snapped at her. Then I hated myself even more when I stopped her from leaving after telling her to. I could see the wonder in her eyes, her thoughts going into overdrive. I can guess what those thoughts were. Fucking hell, for a moment there, while I was holding on to her, I very nearly caved in. I nearly kissed her. I couldn't fucking stop myself.

Thank God for her mother. Eye on the ball, Jake, and the ball isn't a face worthy of a goddess and a body made to be worshipped.

I groan, fighting to ignore the dull pulse in my dick. It's not my only frustration. Camille's ludicrous idea—the one that involved her out in public without me—both angered and frustrated me. Logan's still heard nothing and Lucinda is keeping track of his e-mails. What the hell do they want? Money is the obvious answer, yet Logan has stacks of the stuff and they aren't asking for it. He's hiding something. I'm convinced he is.

I park down a side street after being advised, quite curtly by Camille, where we were headed. She jumps out and is on her way to the main road before I cut the engine. I fall into pace a few steps behind her, following quietly. She looks effortlessly lovely, having thrown on a little black dress, but those red-soled things on her feet look like death traps. The black material of her dress made her topaz eyes pop for the brief moment she met my gaze before we left her apartment. She hasn't looked at me since.

When we arrive at the entrance of the plush hotel where she's meeting her mother and brother, the doorman is busy loading some flashy luggage onto a trolley, so it's left to Camille to open the door. I watch as she wrestles with it, pushing her slim frame into the polished metal surround.

I reach over and take the handle, brushing her hand innocently. I freeze, as does she, before she pulls her hand into her chest on a little gasp. We both remain motionless, my hand poised on the door, my spine tingling. Jesus, this is getting worse—the atmosphere, the innocent touches . . . my reaction to them.

I peek down at Camille, finding her eyes darting wildly. I quickly pull the door open for her, standing back to eliminate the risk of us touching again. She rushes through without any thank you or acknowledgment, and breezes into the lobby like I'm not even there.

I breathe in deeply and follow behind, but come to a stop when Camille does, a few feet in front of me. She turns to face me, but refuses to look at me. "Keep me in sight if you must, but can you do it at a distance so my mother doesn't interrogate me?"

"She doesn't know?" I ask.

"No, and I don't want her to. She'll only worry and proceed to annihilate my father. She does that enough already."

I run a quick scan of the area, assessing every nook and cranny, every person in the vicinity, storing it all to memory. "Where will you be sitting?"

"She has the same table at the back of the restaurant every time." She's still refusing to look at me, but indicates the restaurant entrance.

"Looks like I'm eating alone." I gesture for her to lead on, which she does, ignoring my cynicism.

I allow her to get a few feet away from me before I follow, holding back while the maître d' greets her before leading her to a table. Camille's mother looks exactly like she has in every picture I've seen. A well-turned-out woman in her mid-forties, with blond hair that matches Camille's and topaz eyes that are a little less bright than her daughter's. Apart from the uncanny likeness, I sense no other similarities. She looks overbearing and self-important. A diva, in fact. The same table every time? A driver? All that's missing is a Chihuahua in a frilly pink jumper and a diamond-encrusted collar.

They greet each other with hugs and double kisses as I make my way to an empty table a few feet away from Camille and her mother. It's about as far as I'm prepared to be. I sit on an angle, the whole room in view, turned away enough to look inconspicuous, but just right to see her.

"Sir?"

I look up and find a smart waiter hovering at the edge of my table for two, a questioning look on his face. "I'll have a water, please." I resist ordering the Jack that I so desperately need.

"I'm sorry." He looks nervous. I've hardly said a word, *and* I was polite. What's his problem? "Do you have a reservation?"

That's his problem. This place doesn't look like the kind of joint you just breeze right into and expect to be fed. "Yes," I answer smoothly, taking a menu from his hand on a smile that suggests he should accept my answer and hurry on his way.

"Your name, sir?" he asks.

I sigh. "Check your little book on that stand up front." I wave a finger toward the entrance of the restaurant. "Whatever name you have down for this table, that's me."

"I'm sorry, sir. This table is reserved."

I sense Camille watching me warily, aware of the potential upset I might cause. And that's the only reason I begrudgingly relent. "Do you have another table?" I ask politely.

"Yes, sir." He smiles and indicates across the restaurant. "If you'll just come this way."

I follow his pointed finger and spot the empty table he must be referring to. Then I scoff. Too far. "I'll be staying here, thank you."

"But, sir, I'm——" His words cut dead when I look at him. I can only imagine the threat in my eyes. *Don't make me get mad*, I say to myself. "Sir." He nods and backs away. "I'll get your water."

"You do that." I have a quick peek across to Camille and find her watching me, her mother chewing her ear off. I see her mouth murmuring the odd agreement here and there, her lips soft and inviting, moving slowly.

I'm unable to stop my line of sight drifting up from her mouth when I feel her eyes burning into me. She quickly looks away, shifting in her chair and sipping some champagne, focusing on her mother instead of me. The loss does things to me beyond my comprehension. I mentally slap myself as a jug of water, laced with slices of lemons and limes, lands in front of me.

"Sir, have you made a decision from the menu?"

"Whatever you recommend," I say, pulling my phone from my pocket, finding no calls or messages.

"The Lobster Thermidor is famous, sir."

"Then I'll have that." I pull up my contacts list and Abbie's name flashes up at me. I frown, waiting for the inevitable twisting of my stomach. It doesn't come, and I find myself glancing across to Camille as my frown deepens. I try to think of what I'd even say to Abbie if I did call. *Hi, did you miss me?* I laugh.

Dropping my phone to the table, I scrub my palms over my face before removing my jacket and hanging it on the back of the chair. I don't know why I torture myself with this same dilemma day in and day out. She doesn't want to hear from me. She'll be happier if I stay away. She's probably forgotten about me completely by now. Best not to upset that. Nothing good will come of it.

A giggle hits me from the side, shocking me from my straying thoughts, and I turn to see Camille with her head tossed back, her mother laughing, too. My past is suddenly forgotten when my present smacks me in the face, making me smile. No woman has made me smile since . . .

I grab my phone and call Logan. He answers promptly, as normal. "Sharp," he says as I sit back, casting a quick eye over to Camille. She's lost in conversation.

"Anything?" I ask.

"Nothing."

My teeth grind in frustration. "We checked the courier deliveries to Logan Tower the day you told us the threat arrived." I pause to give him the opportunity to speak, and to listen for any unspoken reaction, like a hitch of breath, anything to tell me I'm onto something. I get nothing, so go on. "There's no sign of a courier on the afternoon it arrived."

"There must be," he claims. "Did you check the CCTV?"

"Yes."

"The records?"

"Yes."

"Then maybe it was delivered by someone else. Not a courier."

His claim gives me a moment's pause. "You were quite clear that it was a courier," I point out.

"I . . . assumed. Maybe . . . I could be wrong." He trips over his words, only heightening my suspicions.

"I understand." I brush it off, make his remark sound like it's of no consequence, when on the inside I'm raging with frustrating curiosity.

I get the feeling that if I push this, my services will no longer be required. He'll get someone else in to protect his daughter. Someone who won't ask questions. I don't trust anyone else to do the job. Besides, it's keeping me busy and distracted from my nightmares. "I'll call with an update as soon as I have one." I hang up, thoughtful, until the sweet sound of Camille laughing knocks me from my pondering. She looks happy. Relaxed.

TJ arrives a few minutes later and greets both women affectionately. Camille's mother, TJ's stepmother, embraces TJ like he could be her own. The sweet scene makes me see something in Camille's mother that I never would have expected. She's stuffy, but she clearly has a fondness for her stepchild. Before TJ settles in his seat, he casts an eye over to me, nodding his hello discreetly. I nod in return and realign my focus on Camille.

* * *

Camille picked her way through a measly salad, hardly touching it. The laughs have been constant from their table. It's actually been quite a pleasure to see her so happy in the company of her mother and brother. The whole few hours we've been here have been uneventful otherwise. No suspicious activity or characters, and no paparazzi.

I settle my bill, anticipating Camille will be wrapping up very soon, and wait for her to stand. I watch her like a hawk, searching for any signs of drunkenness. There's none, though her mother is a little unstable on her gold heels as she rises from the table, knocking back the last drops of her fizz as she does. TJ catches his stepmum's elbow to steady her, and Camille links arms with her as they wander from the restaurant, me close behind.

When we make it to the pavement outside, I hold back as they say their good-byes, not liking our distance, trying to be discreet. It's hard to look casual and unassuming when you're as tall as me.

A Bentley pulls up and a driver gets out, rounding the car and opening the back door for her mother. "Sweetie pie, it's been wonderful to see you." She embraces her daughter and hugs her, before she moves onto TJ. "You take care," she orders. "Let's not leave it so long next time."

TJ laughs. "You're the one with the hectic social life!"

"Just keeping my finger on the pulse." She winks and kisses his cheek. "Bye-bye, sweetie pies." She lowers gracefully into the backseat and the driver shuts the door.

TJ's flash car pulls up behind and a driver passes him his keys. "Thanks," he says as he slips him a twenty. "Be good tonight."

Camille rolls her eyes. "I'm always good. Why don't you come?"

He laughs, thoroughly amused. "I'll leave the partying to you." Leaning in, he kisses her cheek and flicks a look across to me. "Looks like you're in good hands, but be safe, yeah?"

Be safe? I realize he's not trying to insult my ability to watch her. What he's doing is gently reminding her of the shit she's gotten into before. And judging by the soft, almost pleading expression in TJ's eyes, he's reminding me, too. He has nothing to worry about. She's safe. From *everything*.

Camille casts a fleeting look over her shoulder, biting her lip. "Yeah," she says.

I wait for the cars to pull away before I join her on the roadside. All that's running through my mind right now, unjustified and inappropriate, is how relieved I am that Camille shares none of her parents' traits. She's molded herself into the person she wants to be, and despite a few blips along the way, she should be proud of herself.

"Interesting woman, your mother," I muse, coming to a stop next to her.

"You mean pretentious, right?" She turns to look up at me. "You don't need to be polite. She's okay in small doses." She takes her phone out, punches out a text, and clicks send. "The Picturedrome is a few streets away. Let's go," she declares decisively, strolling off toward my car. I deflate as I follow, reminded that the night is far from over.

* * *

The noise. Jesus, it's unbearable. The speakers are booming out some hard, throbbing beats, and hundreds of kids in their mid-twenties fill the place, all drinking champagne. The seedy darkness bothers me as I scope the place. A few young women descend from every direction when Camille enters, with squeals of delight.

A glass of champagne is thrust into Camille's hand, courtesy of Heather, and hugs are thrown all round. I growl when the hugs start coming from men. A few looks are tossed in my direction—the women interested, the men wary—as I watch Camille hovering a few feet away. She's relaxed, still happy, and it makes me loosen up somewhat as I take position by the bar a few feet away and settle in, preparing for a long night.

An hour later, I'm at my wits' end. I've endured some pretty torturous situations in my thirty-five years of life, but I can safely say, hand on my black heart, that the past hour has been the worst. Watching her shimmy around that dance floor is causing me physical pain. Every now and again, I fleetingly wonder if she's purposely making this as hard as possible for me. Regardless, I'm a professional and I can withstand it. But I'm also a man, a man who hasn't had any for too long.

I groan under my breath, trying not to look at her. It's hard when she's my client. A job. But damn, she's perfect, effortlessly gorgeous and understated in her beauty and disposition. Not one man in this bar is immune to the attention she demands without actually demanding it. The other women, all beautiful, pale into insignificance with her in the room. I smile a secret smile, feeling an odd sense of pride.

Then I mentally knock myself out, flicking my eyes up to the top shelf of the bar. I need a drink.

"Hey!" Camille appears at my side, bubbly and smiley. "I need a wee," she says, starting to shift from one foot to the other. "Wanna watch?"

She's drunk. Her cheeky declaration doesn't faze me. If anything, I'm pleased she's advised me instead of dancing off to the loo and leaving me to follow.

"Come." I place my hand in the small of her back, vehemently refusing to acknowledge how good it feels spanning nearly the entire width of it.

She moves with ease, but has me faltering in my steps when she reaches behind me and detaches my touch. Given the chance, I might have mourned the loss, or possibly scorned her for it, but she takes a firm hold of my hand instead and I lose all cognitive thought. My legs are still working, but everything else ceases to function. The softness of her delicate hand in mine feels too good to be safe. My heart bucks in my chest as I try to reason with myself. Her blond hair sways across her dainty back as she bumps and shimmies in front of me, taking the levels of torture I've endured all night to new heights. I can behave as professionally as I like, but my cock and all other vital organs aren't playing along. Resistance is key. Being sensible is paramount.

I fall into a haze of conflict, unable to fathom what it is about this girl that has unearthed all of these feelings in me—feelings that have been dead for years. Since I took this assignment, I've tried to be strong, fought to find reason through the confusing feelings—to keep things in perspective. Now I fear the feelings are becoming stronger than my ability to fight.

Camille swings around to face me as we reach a long corridor, her hair wafting in slow motion. She's still smiling. I've never shed a tear in my adult life. Toughness was trained into me and emotion was something I forgot long ago. I was happy that way. This girl is fucking all that up. She's dangerous to me. I could cry with fucking frustration.

"Are you coming in?" she teases, flexing her fingers for me to release. I look down, thinking how perfect our two hands look entwined together, and squeeze a little, frowning as I do. What the fuck is happening to me? I drop her fast and step back, just as Saffron joins us.

She gives me the once-over before she speaks. "I might need to get me one of these."

"Saffron!" Camille says scornfully, nudging her giggling friend.

"I'm not sorry." She flips me a wink before taking Camille's hand. "You going toilet?"

"If I'm allowed." Cami looks at me seriously, and I find the strength to pull on my poker face.

"I'm coming in." I'm not being a sicko. I'm just not comfortable with Camille out of my sight.

"You can't!" she gasps, truly horrified. It goes way over my head. "You'll be arrested!"

"Camille, do I look like a man who would get a sick thrill from a few women peeing behind cubicle doors?"

"No, but the other women might not agree!" She looks to Saffron as she commences dancing from one foot to another again. "Come on."

I move forward. "Ca—"

Her whole palm slaps over my mouth, and I freeze, watching as her drunk eyes glaze over. What is that? Desire? She quickly backs off, her blues clearing somewhat as they drop like stones to the floor. "There's no danger in there," she murmurs quietly.

I force my heart to even out its beats. I can't bear this. "Then you won't mind if I check, will you?" I say clearly, evenly, watching as her head starts to nod jerkily. No objection? No fight? And, more significantly, no sass?

This is too much. I'm a sexually frustrated mess. I move past her and push the door to the ladies' open, going to step inside...until the screams start. It takes a lot to make me jump, but it seems a gaggle of alarmed women does the trick.

"Fuck!" I release the door, just catching the looks of the few ladies at the mirror. Understandably, they aren't happy. "Just go," I snap impatiently at Camille, waving a pissed-off arm to the door. "And be quick!"

Both girls disappear into the ladies' quickly, and I plant myself opposite the door, my back to the wall. Tonight has taken everything out of me. I'm fucking exhausted. Mentally *and* physically. When this assignment is over, I'm going to drink a crate of Jack, sleep for a year, and fuck for two.

The door opens and two ladies exit, tossing looks somewhere between attraction and disgust at me. It's nothing I'm not used to.

"Ladies," I say for the sake of it as they flounce away.

I crane my neck, spotting Camille in the mirror brushing at her cheeks, just before the door closes again. She looked flustered. A lot how I'm feeling. My arms come up and fold across my chest, my foot beginning to tap impatiently. A few moments later, another two girls exit. Camille's still there, faffing with her hair. I roll my eyes and silently promise her one more minute before I go in and remove her.

It's the longest minute of my fucking life. I realize she won't be best impressed if I go charging in there, but my fucking heart is beginning to throb uncomfortably. Fuck it. She'll get over it. I push my back from the wall and slam my palms into the wood, shoving the door open. It hits the tiles behind, but I'm not sure whether the noise is a result of that, or whether it's a result of my head exploding.

My stomach drops into my feet, taking my heart and lungs with it. How the fuck did Sebastian Peters get in here without me noticing?

His hand flies forward and connects with Camille's cheek on a sharp slap. "You stupid bitch!" he yells, shoving her to the floor. Her cheek hits the edge of the sink on a deafening crack. "Do you think I'm not good enough for you? You're mine!"

I snap. My palm is squeezing his throat before I realize I've moved, and I'm walking him the rest of the way across the ladies in that hold. The force of his back hitting the wall sends vibrations up my arms and into my chest. And before I've even registered it, I've delivered two sharp, accurate cross hooks—one to his eye and one to his cheek. The sensations feel good. So fucking good. I draw my gun and yank the slide back, then ram it into his temple. He doesn't know what's hit him. Literally. He's gasping for breath, his fingers grappling at my hold on his throat.

"Let me help you out," I snarl, forcing the gun into his flesh some more. "There's currently a Heckler VP9 aimed at your pretty little head. It's going to make a mess when I blow your fucking brains out, and I'm probably going to be locked up for the rest of my fucking life, but I'll go happily with the comfort that you'll be dead." I raise my knee and slam it into his balls, making the little runt squeal in agony. "Does that hurt, Sebastian?" I deliver another blow, sadistically relishing in his pain.

"Please," he sobs, drool and snot dribbling down his chin pathetically. He's sniffing constantly, his eye puffing up and his nose displaying hints of red around his nostrils. I know the deal. I bet he feels invincible when he's loaded up to his eyeballs on coke. Not so invincible now.

I blink. I shouldn't have, because my fleeting darkness gives me a swift replay of his hand connecting with Camille's cheek. Rage consumes me. I've killed many men. I've done what's needed to be done. I was detached, hidden far away out of sight and feared by thousands. I was the sniper. I was the unknown. I was calm, cool, and collected. Dangerous for all of the right reasons.

That all changed when *she* fucked me over.

I made sure everyone in my path saw the hatred in me. It didn't matter that my vengeance was misdirected. Raining holy hell on the enemy felt like my only available outlet. I *needed* an outlet for the anger and hurt. The hurt she'd caused me.

So I took myself out of the concealed darkness on the edge of the danger zone and put myself in the field. That day, I looked into the eyes of a man and saw fear before I killed him. I didn't care. I became reckless. Stupid. I was so stupid. My selfish need to lash out resulted in the deaths of two of my own men. Two faces that'll haunt me forever. Two men who left behind wives and children. Two *good* men. I wasn't a good man. It should have been me. Self-loathing and guilt—it's plagued me. Has done so ever since.

That's not going to be an issue today. My meltdown back then was because a woman fucked with my head. I can feel a similar rage rising in me now, except I'm perfectly lucid with it. I know exactly what I'm doing.

I holster my gun and release Sebastian's neck, and with one more crushing kidney punch, he crumples to the ground like a sack of shit, whining and whimpering on his way.

"You're not going to be working for a very long time, pretty boy." My foot comes out and delivers a precise kick to his ribs.

Holding back from killing the fucker is the hardest challenge I've faced.

CHAPTER 14

CAMI

I've never seen violence so raw and damaging. And yet something deep and scary inside me knows he's holding back. He could finish this in a second. He's making Sebastian suffer. The power of his fist is clarified with each ear-piercing crack.

Time stops, the sounds blurring into nothing. If it wasn't for the furious burn of my cheek and pounding of my head, I would think I was dead. I feel dead. Defeated. Shocked and weak.

Sebastian appeared from one of the cubicles as if from nowhere. Just one refusal to entertain his pleas for a second chance made him flip. Just one attempt to push past his threatening stance spiked the flash of anger in his eyes that I've seen before when he's been high. But his violence pales in comparison to what I'm seeing now.

I really do believe that Jake Sharp could kill any man with his bare hands. The precision of each hit, the punishing blows.

"Jake." I push his name past my thick tongue and watch as he releases Seb and lets him crumple to the ground as he searches me out, as if he's just realized I'm here. When he lays his eyes on me, he straightens to his full height, seeming taller than ever before, and gives me a stare full of resolve.

Then he stalks forward, bending when he reaches me, and lifts me into his arms silently. He pulls me into his chest and looks down at me, his dark eyes glazed and haunted.

The lump that's settled in my throat expands and bursts, because through my shell shock, I manage to conclude that what's just happened wasn't only Jake doing his job.

His nostrils flare before he centers his attention forward and stalks out of the club with me cradled in his arms. The music is still loud, but I can see people whispering to each other as I'm carried through the crowd, Jake's grip becoming firmer with every stride he takes. My eyes are heavy, and my heart is full of hope.

Hope that I never encounter Sebastian Peters again. And hope that Jake Sharp stays with me forever to ensure it. To protect me from him. From everything.

* * *

The bright lights of my foyer make me squint, the harsh glare too much for my tired vision to tolerate. My body is rising and falling in flow with Jake's long paces, and my arms are back around his neck. There are many thoughts tangling my mind right now, but the loudest one is telling me to hold on tighter. To never let him go. I've had a lot to drink, but the delivery of a stinger of a whack and a crack to my cheekbone from my fall have done a great job of sobering me up. I'm tired but with it, foggy but clear.

After getting us into my apartment, Jake takes me straight to my bedroom and places me on the end of the bed. Then he turns and starts to walk away.

"How did you get that bullet wound?" I blurt, desperate to know more that will clue me in to what just happened in that bathroom. He was there but wasn't.

He stops but keeps his back to me. "I was shot in combat."

War. "You were in the army." I state it as a fact, since it is, but I feel it's a good starting point to try and coax more from him.

He nods, turning around to face me. "SAS."

I feel my eyes widen. "Like a spy or something?"

"I was a sniper."

My mind goes into overdrive. "Is that why you're not in the services anymore, because you were wounded?"

"Something like that," he mutters, looking past me, like too many bad memories are invading his mind.

"How did it happen?" I ask, hungry for more information.

"Bad judgment."

I bite my lip, my mind racing. I'm taking in all of his uncomfortable vibes right now and concluding that however that wound occurred, it haunts him. I can see a shimmer of sweat forming on his brow and he seems to be in a little bit of a trance, just the mention of his wound affecting him severely. And then he flinches as if shaking off a memory. It confirms my thoughts. He has flashbacks. I've heard of it, men coming home from war with post-traumatic stress syndrome. I've heard how they battle demons and nightmares and lose sleep. Jake's had those moments. I've seen him take the pills.

The silence becomes uncomfortable, but before I can't think to remedy it, Jake turns and walks away.

"It only happened a few times when we were together." My quiet declaration comes from nowhere and with no further explanation.

He doesn't need one. The tensing of his shoulders as he comes to a stop and the tangible simmering rage speak for themselves. I don't know what's come over me; I swore I'd never tell a soul, but a deep-seated need within me wants to tell Jake.

"I wouldn't care if it happened once and he sacrificed his life in apology." He growls the words. "I'd find a way to bring him back to life just so I could kill him again. Once is one time too many. Don't try to defend him."

"I'm not telling you because I'm defending him. I'm telling you so you don't think I'm a pathetic walkover."

"I don't think that!" he snaps as he paces to the door, his fury obvious.

"Then what do you think of me?" I ask, and he stops. "How do you see me, Jake? A weak little woman who needs looking after? A spoiled little brat? A materialistic, self-centered female with no appreciation of what it's like to go without?"

He swings around, outraged by my accusations. "No! Exactly the fucking opposite, actually!"

I jump off the bed, squaring my shoulders in an attempt to look as imposing as possible. It's laughable when I'm faced with Jake's stats. "What happened in that bathroom?" I ask, hitting below the belt. I don't care. I want to know.

"What happened?" he asks, looking at me like I'm stupid. I want to punch him for it. "I beat the shit out of a man who was assaulting you! What do you think I'm going to do? Hold you in place so he gets his aim right?"

"That's not the only reason!" I yell. "You were somewhere else! What happened to you?"

"It's none of your damn business!" he roars, signs of him losing it again vibrating before me. "You are my client! I am your bodyguard! That's it! Stop trying to delve deeper! Stop trying to figure me out!"

I start to shake with fury, unreasonably hurt. Something happened in his past and it's none of my business. Of course he's right, but given the fact that I've spilled my secrets so willingly to him makes his rejection hurt all the more. I'm not the only one who's overstepped the mark. I've seen him struggle with the chemistry, too! Damn it, I know he's struggled, too!

Without warning, my hand sails out toward his face. He sees it coming a mile away, moving fast and catching my wrist.

We stand in front of each other, staring... and our rage changes into something else. I breathe out shakily and shrug off the goose bumps, watching as his eyes fall to my lips before quickly flicking back up to meet my gaze. Fire crackles between our bodies.

I try to straighten my thoughts, but I don't get the time that I need to analyze it all. Jake's coming at me fast, grabbing me and slamming his lips to mine. I feel like all the pressure bursts out of me, the stress and confusion going with it. His kiss is primal and unforgiving, his hard body forcing itself against my front. I whimper, accepting his power, grabbing at his shoulders while we explore each other's mouths, hungry and desperate. My hands move to his hair, the pleasure wracking me, making my knees weak. I start to wobble, holding onto him to keep from falling out of his strong arms.

Oh God, I've imagined this for so long. I've silently begged to experience it. And now it's happening, and it's happening, mad and frenzied, backed by a pile of frustration and desperation.

"Fuck!" Jake curses and drops me, shooting back, leaving me heaving uncontrollably before him, my lips swollen and raw. He rakes a hand through his hair, pulls a little, turns, and starts stalking around the room. "We can't do this," he says harshly. His resolution pierces my heart like a dagger. "It's wrong. I'm your bodyguard." He turns to face me, revealing more determination in the form of a cut, even expression. "Your father will make sure that I never work again." He mumbles the words, clenching his eyes shut. "And I need a purpose, Camille. I need to work."

I feel wretched tears stab at the backs of my eyes, and not for the first time in my life, I damn my father to hell. Jake needs a purpose. He needs to keep his head in the game so it doesn't wander to other places. Like his past. Like war. Like that woman.

It kills me, but I say what needs to be said. Not just because Jake needs me to say it, but because I know that he is right. My dad would destroy him if he found out Jake overstepped his professional mark. He's my bodyguard.

"I understand." My heart constricts in my chest as I back away a few paces, before turning to make a hasty escape, desperate to get away from him. I make it to the door on my unsteady legs and grab the handle, pulling it open, but that's as far as I get.

A palm comes over my shoulder and lands on the wood with a slap, pushing it closed again. My squeezing heart beats up to my throat, and I swallow, staring at his hand before me, feeling his torso close to my back.

"I don't want you to understand," he breathes in my ear. I close my eyes when his hands rest on my shoulders and slowly turn me around on my shaking legs. "Open your eyes," he orders. I do.

My lids peel open, showing him the chaos in my head, the water pooling in my eyes as I try to gather my tattered mind. "I know this is wrong," I murmur, trying to keep my tears at bay. "I know I shouldn't be attracted to you like this."

He nods mildly, agreeing. "I get it. Trust me; I fucking get it," he murmurs. "But I can't think of anything right now but you."

He searches my eyes before dropping his gaze down my body, like now he can dedicate as much time as he likes to absorb me in my entirety. And he does. There's not a piece of me that he doesn't take in, not a hair on my head that he doesn't feel or stroke.

Tenderly, more tenderly than I ever imagined he was capable of, he brushes a wayward lock from my forehead, watching as he pushes it back. I'm so still, he could probably shoot an apple off my head. His hands feel so good wherever they roam, and his face, etched in concentration, looks awestruck.

"So fucking beautiful," he whispers softly, snaking his forearm around my waist and pulling me close.

My hands come up between our torsos on a little gasp, resting on his shoulders, and he dips and brings his forehead down to mine, having to bend his knees a little to do it. His spare hand wraps around my neck gently and he closes his eyes. I feel so small in his arms. So safe.

Yet all of the ease and perfection isn't slowing my thumping heart. I can hear the whoosh of my pulse in my ears, my veins simmering with a want so intoxicating it's making me wobbly.

But I'm going nowhere, his hold keeping me steady. His tactic seems to have changed. The wild, chaotic meeting of our mouths a moment ago is almost forgotten as he breathes steady and deeply while I watch him, so close I could kiss him. But I refrain—not that I'm not desperate to feel his lips on mine again, but because his sheer rugged beauty is so gratifying, and I'm fascinated by his silence and sudden mellow disposition. I've never seen him so peaceful. Completely passive. Like he's surrendered to an inner need.

"Are you okay?" he asks, his eyes slowly revealing themselves to me. The light I see in them is dazzling. It's hopeful. It's everything I feel myself.

I swallow on a little nod and run my hands down the sleeves of his jacket to his elbows, thinking how wonderful his skin will feel beneath. He pulls his head away from mine, and the sea of stubble blanketing his face holds my attention around his mouth.

His lips part slowly and his tongue traces a path across his bottom lip.

I look into his eyes, ensuring he sees the certainty and desperation I feel. I've never felt so certain or so desperate in my life. I want him— this cryptic, unfathomable man. I want him with every fiber of my being.

He starts lowering his mouth to mine, taking his time, as if preparing himself for the onslaught of pleasure that he knows is on the horizon. I'm doing the same. Closer, closer, closer, our eyes nailed to one another's, until his lips brush mine. I jolt in his hold, my shallow breaths almost strangling me. The sensations that little contact creates blow my mind, more so than the animalistic kiss of a moment ago, which leaves me wondering with impatient longing what's to come.

He moans, low and ragged, opening his mouth to me. My tongue darts out and catches his. I'm instantly consumed, hands reaching for his neck and pushing him to me, our tongues lapping delicately but purposefully.

"Fucking hell, Camille," he says into my mouth, forcing our bodies apart and my hands from his neck, but maintaining the dance of our tongues.

His fingers brush my thighs as he takes the hem of my dress, pulling up until I have to free his mouth so he can get it over my head. It's discarded quickly before his hands are at his throat, yanking his tie loose. Matching his sudden urgency, I reach for his jacket and start pushing it from his shoulders. He wrestles his arms from the sleeves as his mouth finds mine again, tackling it with force.

"Shirt," he mumbles, finding my bra fastening and releasing the hook with one flick. I feel the material cupping my breasts loosen as my fingers fiddle with the buttons of his shirt, frantic and clumsy. He realizes my struggle and relieves me of my task, ripping the front of his shirt apart, sending buttons flying in every direction. Then he reaches for the front of my bra and pulls it from my chest, leaving me no choice but to extend my arms or have it ripped from my body with the force.

I gasp, getting a glimpse of his chest peeking through his white shirt. While I'd love to spend a few moments admiring it, Jake has other ideas. He reaches behind his back and collects his gun, dropping it to the floor on his suit jacket. The button of his fly is tackled with deft fingers, his shoes and socks kicked off and his trousers discarded. All so quickly. He's not messing around. His boxer shorts come last, but he removes these carefully and slowly, watching me watch him as he does.

And now he's naked.

And I'm rapt by the sight once again, yet this time he's closer. This time it's not an accident. This time there's no awkwardness... just acceptance and understanding.

"Take it all," he commands hoarsely, motioning down his tall body. "Please, just fucking take it all."

I gulp, I swallow, I start to shake like I've never shaken before. I want it. All of it. All of *him*.

But I'm suddenly incapable of following through and claiming what I've silently begged for. He's so tall and strong. He looks like he could break me in two with a flick of his finger. Probably could. His erection is protruding proudly from his groin, the tip glistening with his arousal. My nipples zing with craving, and the silver scar marring his shoulder catches my eye. He glances down, knowing what's holding my attention. And then he reaches up and circles the scar slowly and lightly with his fingertip for a few reflective moments before he swoops in and seizes me in his arms, lifting me like a feather and carrying me to my bed.

I'm laid down gently and feel my knickers drawn down my legs with care as he kneels by the side of my bed, his chest expanding as he pulls air into his lungs, his head shaking mildly. I feel like a gift laid upon a stone slab waiting to be worshipped. My head, dropped to the side, rests on my shoulder. Jake takes my hands gently and guides them to the pillow above my head, placing them tenderly before softly tracing a path down the length of them to my chest. I moan, unable to avoid expressing my indulgence, and he smiles in response. I'm stretched out, naked and exposed, my breaths coming faster while he caresses me, taking his time to stroke and feel me. When he reaches my nipple, my back bows subtly, arching and pushing my breasts upward, silently begging for more.

His eyes flick to mine as he starts to gently trail the edge. "Do you want my mouth here?" he asks, pausing with his delicate circling.

Again I nod, silently willing him on, but his finger remains unmoving on my buzzing nub of nerves.

"Talk to me, Camille," he says, watching me closely. "Tell me what you need from me."

"Please," I murmur, not averse to begging for his attention and touch. Anything. His finger starts moving again, but it drifts south, following a straight path across my tummy and onto my thigh. A low, broken cry escapes me, my body tensing with anticipation.

"And here?" His finger slips between my thighs and skims the pulsing lips at my entrance.

I lose control, my eyes slamming shut and my bowed spine arching some more on a scream of despair. "Jake, please!" I beg, my arms twitching above my head, ready to grab him and pull him close.

"It's coming." He pushes two fingers inside of me, filling me, dowsing down the burn of desire. "I feel it." His voice shakes as he circles far and wide, exploring me inside. "So ready and desperate."

"Oh God," I sigh, settling a little with the welcome feeling of him inside, massaging me deeply. All of my muscles constrict, doubling the pleasure. I'm building already.

"Don't come," he orders, prompting me to open my eyes in alarm. I find his face, still studying me closely as he tortures me with precise, talented fingers. "Not yet," he adds in reassurance, but then also adds his thumb to my swollen clitoris, magnifying the difficulty of following his order.

I can no longer keep my arms where they are, pulling them down and sliding them across my tummy, relishing in the feel of my own touch. The heady cocktail of sensations being inflicted on me is new. It could also become very addictive. Jake is already addictive. What he can do to me, how he can make me feel. He's been devoting his attention to me for a few moments and I'm already tinkering on the edge of eternal want. Of eternal safety.

"Do you feel good, Camille?" he asks, low and rough, watching my hands gliding all over my tummy as he pumps his fingers into me methodically.

"Yes!" I'm losing my mind, and he's enjoying it.

"I'm jealous." He uses his spare hand to take both my wrists in his grip and pulls them away, devastating me.

He releases my hands gently and slowly above my head, fixing me with a telling stare. I'm not allowed to move them, and when he's certain I'll comply, he rises and looms over me. "Are you on birth control?"

I nod.

"Are you clean?"

I nod again speedily, unoffended. There's no room for insult amid the bombardment of longing and want. There's also no room to think, which is why I don't return the question. Not that I need to.

"Me too." He comes down over me, planting his fists into the mattress on either side of my head.

"My arms?" I whisper, asking for instruction of what to do with them.

"Just keep them where they are."

His chest meets mine, heavy and firm, his arms bending at the elbows to bring his face closer to mine. Then his groin meets my hips and I feel the hot head of his cock nudge lightly at my opening. My heart kicks, and he hisses, freezing and closing his eyes. He's searching for restraint. He's dragging this out, making me dizzy with impatience, but I have to let him go slowly.

"I've tried not to imagine how good this would feel." He exhales, opening his eyes and letting them sink into my gaze. "I tried so fucking hard."

Another brush of contact from his arousal physically burns, and then I hold my breath, almost scared of the pleasure I'm about to experience. For no other reason than I know I'll want more.

Jake lifts and angles his hips, then glides smoothly forward, entering me unhurriedly, gradually filling and stretching me. I groan, sighing, my legs linking around his lower back and pulling him in, my arms draping around his shoulders.

"Oh, fucking hell," he whispers. Dropping his head, he begins to breathe through his single stroke, his body trembling in my arms. "I knew it," he says hoarsely. "I knew I'd fit you so fucking right."

He does. He's long and broad, but my internal muscles hug him inside of me so perfectly. "Move," I beg, flexing my hips a little, encouraging him on.

"Just give me a second." He drops to his forearms and raises his head, letting the tip of his nose meet mine. "I need a second."

I want to hurry him along, but seeing him so in awe of how we feel connected so deeply is keeping that want at bay. So I let his eyes caress mine and wait for him to gain some stability. I use the time to draw delicate lines across his back, my ghosting finger instigating shudders from him.

"You're not helping, Camille," he gently scorns, rubbing his nose with mine and withdrawing, sliding free until the tip of his cock is tickling my entrance again.

I hold my breath. And he holds his. Then he dips his hips and dives deep again, both of us gasping into each other's faces, our broken breaths colliding and mingling. When he's fully submerged again, he grinds hard but slow, circling and eliciting all kinds of intoxicating sensations.

I'm done for. My head is thrown back, my arms clinging to his shoulders as he finds his pace, hitting me constantly with stroke after stroke, each one delivered meticulously. I'm lost in a world of raw abandon with my strong protector, praying that I never find my way out. Our moans of pleasure drown the quiet air around us, our wet skin slipping, our bodies moving together in harmony. It's all so perfect—the sounds, the feel, the rightness of this moment.

Jake's maintaining his rhythm and extending the bliss for as long as he can. The feel of him swelling within me is a sign that he won't last much longer. I feel my own release start to creep forward.

"Put your legs down," he rumbles, reaching down to his lower back and pushing my legs away. "Straighten them."

I'm a little taken aback, but I follow through and straighten my legs to full length.

The reason for his demand hits me between my thighs like a wrecking ball. "Oh my God!" I cry, but the sound is soon swallowed when he crashes his mouth down onto mine, kissing me firmly and fervently. My pleasure has just hit new heights, my new position sending me there.

"You feel that?" he asks into my mouth, pumping on, rubbing me in just the right place as he fills me.

I whimper and start grappling at his back, the slow-building orgasm now powering forward fast.

"Claim it, Camille," he orders, biting my bottom lip before attacking my mouth again.

I feel my world starting to tumble away from beneath me.

CHAPTER 15

JAKE

I've never felt a connection so intense that I can *physically* feel it. It's no distraction. It's no means to an end. It's tangible. It's pulling at every one of my muscles and stabbing at every inch of my naked skin. I've never felt so absorbed by a woman that she makes me want to sacrifice my soul in her honor.

I've never felt this. Never.

Many words are trying to wrestle their way into my twisted mind, but only one is making it through.

Mine.

Holding her willowy body against me is beyond any realms of pleasure I've experienced in my time. It's a feeling that is so very easy for me to accept, but so very hard for me to understand. All of it. I'm not tender with women. I don't take my time to extend their enjoyment or wish that it never ends.

This woman has changed all of that. I never want this to end.

She's panting shallowly into my face, straining to keep her eyes open. She's almost there, and I need to be with her when she climaxes. I push myself up onto my fists, digging them into the mattress to get better leverage.

"Hold it," I order, unable to ignore the frantic flash on panic on her face. "I'm nearly there." I pick up my pace and realign my position and control. It's there. It's coming. "Oh fuck!" I bellow and pump on, swiftly entering and retreating from the luscious warmth of her tight pussy, each drive ramping up the urgency.

"Jake!" Her scream of my name as she shakes violently beneath me tips me over the edge. My cock explodes, and I roar through the crippling pleasure, feeling her vibrating around me as I find release in long, pulsing spurts. My climax knocks me out, making me fall to my forearms, trapping her beneath me as I battle my way through. It goes on forever, Cami's sleepy groans muffled in my ear by the rush of blood to my head. My body feels relieved, sated, but my mind and heart are more twisted than ever. I feel settled but apprehensive. Then she sighs, long and satisfied, and the apprehension begins to cloud everything— all of the peace, calm, and rightness of this moment.

Fuck me, I feel like I'm under attack from the enemy, my mind sprinting through my options and analyzing my safest and quickest route out of the danger zone. This time, there feels like no way out.

It's the oddest feeling of tranquility and terror. She's a young, bright woman with a shining future. Me? I'm a disturbed, twisted arsehole with a black soul and a hard heart. I shouldn't risk infecting her with my demons. Yet at the same time, I'm full of hope that she could be the cure that I *haven't* been looking for. It's always just been me, my memories and my bitterness. That was fine by me. But since I've met Camille, all of my burdens have been diluted by a want so powerful it's made it difficult to focus on anything else. The irony of my situation is fucking brutal. My duty is to protect her from a potential threat. An unknown danger.

I'm the biggest, most real threat to this woman. She needs protecting from *me*.

It's guaranteed I'll hurt her. I'm a danger to her. Her father won't be happy about this, and Lucinda might wring my fucking neck. No emotional connection with your subject. It's rule number-fucking-one.

It distorts your purpose and hampers your duty. It also gets you swiftly ejected from the agency. But shit, there's a whole lot of emotion running rampant through me right now, and I'm powerless to stop it. Feeling powerless isn't something I deal with well. I need my purpose. My purpose is my job. What I've just done could lose me that. I'll be in an empty, black pit once again. No purpose. Just nightmares.

I clench my eyes shut and lift my hips, pulling myself free of her warmth, all the time ignoring the sense of loss that fills me with every inch I withdraw. Her sleepy mumbles of protest would be like sweet music to my ears...if I wasn't currently in mental turmoil.

What the fuck have I done?

I roll off her to my back and stare up at the ceiling, my palm resting on my pumping chest. The urge to pick up my gun and sink a bullet into my skull is tempting. So is my urge to get dressed, get my bag, and walk out.

But then she'll be unprotected.

Who the fuck is going to protect her from me? Who's going to warn her off, tell her I'm no good for her? I know exactly who. Me. I should.

My head falls to the side as she shifts next to me, and I find her sprawled on her back, her blond hair fanning the pillow and her arms flopped limply above her head. She's snoozing, her face nuzzled into the crook of her upper arm. She looks like a fucking angel. Sweet, innocent, and vulnerable.

Mine.

"Motherfucker," I breathe, pushing myself up urgently before I give in to my instinct and pull her into my side. I sit on the edge of the bed, my elbows resting on my knees, and let my face fall into my palms.

"Jake." Her sweet voice is sleepy and broken, but the velvet edge still licks across my naked skin, making me shudder. I look over my shoulder and find those gorgeous eyes half-open, watching me.

"Go to sleep, Cami." My response is automatic, and so is my need to touch her. I turn a little and reach for her face, pushing some golden wisps of hair from her creamy cheeks. She hums and nuzzles into my touch, her eyes closing.

And my fucking heart shatters on me. Screwing up my face in agony and despair, I rip my hand away from her face and rise to my feet, battling the rampant impulse to climb into bed and hold her all night.

Distance.

I need distance. Or as much distance as I can get when I'm shadowing someone. I sit in the chair by the window, my big body arguing with my brain's decision to put it there. It's a small chair, more for decorative purposes than for a big, meaty bloke like me to try to get comfortable in. Which isn't fucking likely. I shift one way and then the other, until I'm somewhere close to comfy, my arse on the edge of the seat to allow me to recline as much as possible, my legs extended and crossed at the ankles. It'll do. I've endured a lot worse.

Planting an elbow on the arm, I fist my hand and wedge it under my jaw.

And I watch her.

All night long.

And with each minute that passes, my regret intensifies.

* * *

I've always survived on little sleep. I'm just wired that way. Exhaustion isn't a term I'm familiar with, so how I'm feeling right now is alien. I feel fucking drained. Wiped out completely. I also have a bastard of a headache. All in all, I feel like shit. Not even my good friend Jack Daniel's has the ability to make me feel this weary.

I've been sitting here for six hours watching her sleep. It's been the most pleasurable and confusing time in my existence. I've cursed more times under my breath than I care to admit. Fuck, no, I will admit it. It can't make matters any worse than they already are.

And matters are bad. Fucking awful, in fact. My conscience is telling me to leave before she wakes and hope she thinks it was all a dream, and a deep-rooted possessiveness I never knew existed is telling me to wrap her up tightly in cotton wool and keep her forever.

The conflict is fucking with my head, making it impossible to align my thoughts and reason. I've skipped through my possible replacements, anyone I trust to take over the assignment and guard her like I can. There are a few possibilities—all experienced and renowned bodyguards. But none as good as me, though I fear my own judgment is being challenged. I think back over the past few days, in particular to the bloodbath I created in the ladies' restroom last night.

And I don't regret a thing. No, that's not true. I regret one thing.

Camille's face when I snapped out of my blind rage. She saw the darkness in me. A darkness I need to hide, especially from her. Her eyes were full of questions. The instinct and urge to answer them, to share my burden, is there. This woman is doing things to me that I loathe and love in equal measure. I read up on her. I fell into the camp of idiots who think they have this young woman nailed. With parents like hers and the media's ability to twist innocent scenarios to create gossip, plus the influence of a toxic boyfriend, everyone in London thinks they have Camille Logan all figured out. I was in her company for a few minutes and concluded what I'd read was grossly inaccurate. Those who know her well will know it's a load of bollocks, too, but this world is full of cynics. This world is full of people who thrive on others' misfortune.

A soft murmur and stir has my heart shouting its presence in my chest and my vertebrae uncoiling from my slouched position. I let all my conflicting thoughts fall away and watch in silence as her exposed naked body stretches lazily atop the sheets.

My cock wakes up, too.

I groan as I reach down and lay a palm over my groin, forcing it to remain flat against my thigh. My attempts are in vain. The pink tips of her perfect breasts are calling to me, making my bare feet twitch on the carpet. I'm rigid in the chair, frantically trying to summon some restraint. It's the most challenging task I've ever undertaken. Everything inside me is willing me to her, telling me my place is next to her in that bed, holding her, protecting her. I'm not going to insult my instinct and tell myself it's the professional protector in me. It's more than that. I buried myself in her body and fucked her with a delicacy that I didn't know I was capable of.

My need to protect this woman isn't duty. It's instinct.

Her eyes flutter open, and I study her as she gathers her bearings. I can see her mind playing catch up, reminding her of the events of last night. I know when she's remembering dinner with her overbearing mother. It makes me smile, recalling her laughter. I see when she remembers the scene in the bar toilets, her eyes going round and her hand coming up to the mark on her creamy cheek. And I see when she mentally finds herself back here with me, her body stilling as if trying to figure out whether it was a dream or not. I find my body stilling, too, my heart slowing to a dull kick in my chest. Her small hitch of breath that comes next triggers my own, and she bolts upright in bed and frantically scans the room.

Over here, angel.

I only just block the mental command from voicing itself, but it doesn't matter. She doesn't need me to call her.

She finds me in a heartbeat, her sparkling blues landing on me with a bang, before she drops them, scanning her lap. She shakes her head, as if trying to reason with herself, and then slowly lifts her gaze to mine. The fire inside of me continues to rage.

"Come back to bed," she whispers, as if unsure whether that's a good idea. I know I should refuse her— I've said the words a thousand times to many women.

But the words don't come.

I can't find them.

And I'm searching really hard.

I study her sitting on the bed, her hair an adorable mess around her gorgeous face, her long, slim limbs a tangle of trembling uncertainty. I stop trying to find my rejection. I don't want to find it.

I free my cock from the constraints of my palm, letting it do as it damn well pleases. And it wants to jut from my groin, like it's pointing the way. It doesn't escape Camille's notice, her eyes—mixed with hope and nerves—dropping to my lap, her lips parting to reveal her glistening tongue. Slowly standing from the chair, I use each second it takes me to rise to my full height to accept my fate.

I'm going nowhere. She is my fate.

It isn't something I'm prepared to fight. All of my doubts and self-hatred dull at the sight of her big, round eyes looking up at me. Because by the look of her quivering, looking scared and unsure and...hopeful, she wants me as badly as I want her.

I might not understand it, but I'm also not prepared to ignore it. My past isn't the only challenge I'll face to be with her. There's also her father, the agency, her ex. There are a pile of issues in my way, and they all need dealing with. I'm not going to pretend it will be easy. But for her...

I answer her silent pleading and go to her, taking sure, even strides.

I let my eyes caress her, storing every inch of her skin to memory as I go. I fight off the notion that my subconscious is doing that for a reason. Like it's preparing for the inevitable. Like maybe I won't get the privilege of her in the flesh for long.

When I'm standing at the edge of the bed, her chin lifts so she can look at me. Our eyes meet and I pray she doesn't see the way my body has started to shake. I'm panicking about the damage I can do to her, the hatred I can poison her with. The darkness I can drown her light in.

"I'm no good for you, Camille," I warn her. The details don't matter. I won't burden her with them more than I have already. I'm doing this out of duty—warning her because I feel I should. Gallant, maybe, but I don't know what I'll do if she listens to me.

When I expect her to recoil, hurt, she moves in closer instead, shifting her bum forward on the bed. She takes my hand and tugs, bringing me down to my knees before her. I go willingly. Her legs wrap around my waist, the strength of her thighs constricting around me defying reason. Then, sliding her palms up my stomach to my shoulders, she pulls me in and crushes our chests together, her face hiding in the crook of my neck. The feeling of belonging overshadows that panic, and I calm instantly, following her lead. I coil my arms around her back and once again marvel at her strength and determination. She's so damn strong. I stand, her body attached to mine, the weight of her feeling so right on me, and walk to the bathroom, flipping the shower on. I keep her held snugly to my chest, blanketing her with my body while allowing peace to blanket *me*. My efforts to frighten her away are feeble. Because I don't want her to go.

I sink into her clinch while the shower warms and try to clear my mind of everything except the fulfilment I'm feeling in this tender moment. Tender. Something, again, that is new and alien to me. Last night, after ripping that scumbag to shreds, my priority was making her feel safe. I'm not skirting the fact that my cock ached with need, but I'm aware that I had a stronger need to rain devotion on her. I didn't want to just fuck her. I stopped that manic kiss before I could do what's instinctual to me—screw her with nothing but the purpose of release. I wanted to relish in her unraveling under my gentle attention. And I did, enjoying every second more than I should have allowed myself to.

Once steam surrounds us, I walk us into the shower and lower her to her feet. Camille drops to her knees, surprising me, and looks up at me with heavy, searching eyes. I see her intent and drop my head back, bracing myself.

She grabs my hips and hauls them forward, my cock finding her mouth like there's a radar attached.

"Holy shit!" My palms cup the back of her head, my thigh muscles wobble.

The warmth of her mouth around my pulsing dick is incomparable to anything I've experienced. My head drops down, finding her hair, a waterfall of blonde caging her in. I want to see her. I want to see her mouth work me into a haze of ecstasy. I reach around and pull a handful of hair away from her face.

The sight is something that'll never leave me. Exquisite. Her mouth glides like it's on rails, up and down, slowly and carefully, her eyes closed in bliss. Freeing my strung muscles, I relax and accept the pleasure she's inflicting. My plan to reject her was destined to fail whether she tempted me or not. She's one huge force of temptation.

My hand slides onto her cheek, and she moans around her mouth full of cock, grazing her teeth down my flesh teasingly. My balls go tight and my knees weak, my palm skating from her cheek to the back of her head, my hips starting to flex in time with her mouth's advances. "Oh Jesus Christ," I gasp.

She moans again, this time more deeply, the vibrations tickling the tip of my cock when it meets the back of her throat. Then she retreats and slides her hand around the base, holding firmly as she licks and laps at my wet tip, pulling a long draw up my shaft that pushes a bead of pre-cum from the tip. I drop my head and watch as she laps it up like it could be the sweetest thing she's ever tasted, groaning her pleasure as she does.

And though I'm savoring each lick, lap, and suck she delivers, thriving on the incredible sensations she's inducing, I have an urge to take more from her. I clench my fist in her hair and gently tug her from my groin, smiling a little when she looks up at me, slighted. I don't give her time to ask what's up with me. I could never explain, anyway. I pull her up my body with a forceful yank of her arm and walk her back until I have her held prisoner against the slippery tiles. She gasps, looking up at me in shock.

"Thank you," I say, truly grateful for her attention. But it's my job to lavish her with the time and attention she deserves. I reach down to the back of her thigh and pull it up to my waist. "You're good, Camille, but nothing will match the feel of your tight, warm pussy wrapped around my cock."

Satisfaction reflects in her topaz eyes, a contented grin stretching across her face. Then she lifts her other leg and captures me in her hold, constricting tightly before releasing to allow me to guide myself to her. I can smell me all over her, the intoxicating mix of my clean sweat and her feminine floral scent a heady combination.

I push in a little, breaching the initial tightness. It steals my breath. Her lips, wet and inviting, pull me in and I kiss her as I advance the rest of the way, filling her completely. The hot softness of her passage is comparable only to a fleece blanket wrapping around my entire body and warming me through. The rightness. The gratification. The comfort. The tranquility. It's a quick reality check. It's an indication that I've just wasted too many hours beating myself up over something that feels so incredibly natural, it can't possibly be wrong. I won't waste any more time trying to make sense of this, or trying to talk my way out of it.

Mine. And not even *I* will take that away from me.

CHAPTER 16

CAMI

He's being as careful and delicate with me as he was last night, despite having me pinned to a wall. My relief is only doubling my pleasure. He might be able to fool himself, but he can't fool me. Every word he said to me last night is engraved on my brain. He can't scratch it away with feigned grit or a pathetic attempt to be professional. He can't half-heartedly warn me off. I'm not stupid, and he knows it. He knows *me*. Not the person the media perceives or what my heritage dictates I should be.

He sees *me*.

I'm not about to let him forget that.

His back is slippery, but it feels good under my palms, my mouth working in perfect sync with his, our tongues rolling, our moans mingling. He's pumping into me with precision, pushing me up the wall a little each time. I let my palms slide over his wet skin and into his damp hair, weaving and feeling, putting weight behind my touch to push his lips harder to mine.

His cock feels like the softest of velvet as it glides in and out of me, each advance pushing me closer to release, each retreat making me moan with despair. For such a big, sometimes menacing man, his way with me, how tender and caring he's being, only makes me want him more.

I'm totally taken by him.

He bites my lip gently and pulls away, dragging my lip through his teeth until he's staring at me, his eyes full of wonder. "You feel amazing," he says, taking his hands to the back of my thighs and jerking me up, deepening our connection.

I cry out, feeling him all the way to my womb.

He just smiles, clearly loving the effect he's having. "Did you feel that?" His voice adopts an edge of harshness.

I nod and breathe through the intoxicating mix of pleasure and pain.

"Good." He digs his fingers into my thighs and hits me with another well-thought-out smash of his powerful body.

This time I scream.

"You're mine, Camille Logan!" He releases his hands and slams them into the wall either side of my head. *Bang!* "Can you accept that?"

I scream again, throwing my head back. Does he actually want me to answer that? Thinking straight when he's inflicting this level of decadent pleasure on me isn't fair! "Jake!" I cry, tossing my head from side to side as he continues to punish me with hard hits.

He's not being so gentle anymore. He's being brutal, but once I convince my head to fall back down and my vision clears, I still see tenderness in his dark eyes. His instinct to pound into me is nothing more than desperate hope. He's getting carried away, and I realize that telling him what he needs to hear is actually very easy. "I can accept that," I pant, cupping his cheeks and thriving on the instant relief that washes across his stubbled face.

His pace slows in an instant, telling me that his edge of ruthlessness was induced by a fear he was unable to control. Fear that I might say no. I've mastered part of his complicated mind. And I'm making it my mission to master the rest. I want to know him inside out. Like I feel *he* knows *me*. He knows everything now, including Sebastian's physical abuse. There's a very simple reason why I kept it to myself. Some people see weakness in a woman who stands for that. Some people would be unbearably sympathetic. I'm comfortable with neither. Jake knows that. He knows me.

We're back to a steady rhythm, and now that we've clarified where we stand, we're both climbing to a release that I know is going to knock us out.

His face plummets into my neck, his teeth grazing my flesh as I throw my head back and let my climax claim me. His thick cock is rolling on long pulses each time he pushes into me, swiveling his hips and circling deeply.

"Oh God!" It comes fast and furiously, blowing my world into a haze of bliss with its intensity. "Oh! Oh! Oh my God!" I sink my nails into Jake's back, and he roars into my neck, bucking and jerking against me.

I know the second he finds his own release, not only because the hot essence of him floods me. His knees give out and take us to the shower floor, and Jake rolls to his back, taking me with him. His breathing is strained and loud.

"Fucking hell." He releases me and throws his arms over his head as I ride the waves of his heaving body.

I'm inclined to agree.

My world has spun off its axis and is barreling into the unknown.

* * *

I come to in a haze of peace and darkness in my bed, Jake swathing me completely, his arms wrapped around me where I lay on his chest. It must be the middle of the day, but my drawn curtains are keeping the light at bay. I feel so sated. So peaceful. Like an invisible weight has been lifted from my shoulders. Looking up at his serene face, I smile. Then I slowly start to peel my body away, smiling more when he opens one eye and frowns at me.

"I have a call to make," I tell him. "My agent has some details on some new campaigns I'm fronting and a shoot I have tomorrow."

"Be quick," he murmurs, relinquishing his hold of me and rolling onto his front.

I plan on being quick. Pulling on my T-shirt, I find my phone, noting a few missed calls from Heather, and call my agent, listening as she reels off the finer details before listing some suggested changes to my portfolio. I'm hearing it all, but my mind is still in the bedroom with Jake, reliving every second from last night and early this morning. I'm itching to get back to him.

When I hang up, I start to make my way back to the bedroom, but my phone in my hand vibrates and for a fleeting moment, I worry that my father has found out about me and Jake. Then I laugh, because how could he know?

I see Heather's name and take the call. "Hey."

"Oh my God, Camille!"

I back up into the kitchen and rest my arse on the worktop. "What?" I ask nonchalantly. Call me a terrible friend, but I can't tell her what's happened. I don't want anyone to know. I trust her, of course, but it's...complicated.

"Are you serious? I saw your face last night when he carried you out. And I saw his!"

"He was doing his job, Heather."

"Fuck off, Camille!" She sounds truly annoyed. I can't blame her, but my guilt doesn't prompt me to confirm what she thinks she knows. "Where's Jake?"

"On his laptop," I lie, avoiding the fact that he's still in bed. My bed. Where I plan on being the moment Heather stops interrogating me and gets off the phone.

"Right." She sighs. "I can tell I'm going to get nowhere here."

"There's nowhere to go."

"Sebas—"

"Please don't," I blurt, cutting her off. "I don't ever want to talk about him again."

She's silent for a few seconds before she breathes out tiredly. She can't possibly argue with that. "For the record, Cami, I'm glad Jake was there."

"Me too," I answer quietly.

"What are you up to?"

"Going over my portfolio."

"Want some help?"

My guilt intensifies as I glance toward my bedroom door. "I'm good, thanks. I'll call you tomorrow, okay?"

"Okay." Heather relents after a loud sigh, before she hangs up. I waste no time tearing myself up for lying. I run back to my room and climb into bed, smiling when Jake seizes me and tugs me into his front, spooning me deliciously.

"We're staying here until tomorrow," he says in my ear, rough and sleepily.

My answer is a sigh as I push myself further into his warm chest.

* * *

Tomorrow comes too quickly. The director of the shoot is less than delighted when I turn up at the studio with a bruise on my cheek. Jake's eyes each time he's looked at me have flashed with danger, making my instinct to cover the reminder of the awful night instinctive. But each time I've laid my palm over my cheek, he's pulled it away and dipped to kiss the blemish.

Heather called me again last night to check up on me. Jake was still in my bed. She slipped into the conversation that Seb refused a trip to the hospital, and I know why. Any trace of Seb's habit being detected by his parents or professionals and he'll be carted back to rehab faster than Jake can draw his gun. Which is fucking fast. I've seen it only once and I never want to see it again. He looks formidable enough *without* a loaded weapon in his grasp.

I smile, thinking about how Jake couldn't keep his hands off me for the rest of yesterday. He meant what he'd said. We didn't leave my bed all day. Then the moment we left my apartment this morning, he was emotionless and professional. Almost hard and cold. His edginess was palpable, his body close to mine the entire journey here. His eyes were watchful on the drive, his attention trained on every bit of our surroundings. I've no doubt that it's because today is three days since that threat was delivered. He's hyperalert.

I drop my bag to the floor and keep still while Lawrence, the shoot director, fusses over my bruised cheek, wincing and mumbling under his breath. He doesn't ask me how I came to have the corker of a mark, nor does he ask if I'm okay. His only concern is how to arrange the lighting and figure out how I can keep that side of my face angled away from the camera. I suspect makeup will take considerably longer this morning.

"We'll airbrush if worse comes to worst," he declares, clicking his fingers. A young brunette scurries over with a pallet of foundations and a brush. "Honestly, Camille," he says, scornfully, letting the makeup artist at me. "This shoot has been scheduled for weeks. Fancy getting yourself all scuffed up."

I roll my eyes to myself, clocking Jake by the doorway scowling at Lawrence. He doesn't look happy, and when he strides over, I fear the worst. Lawrence gives Jake the once-over with wary eyes, while Jake accepts, coming to a stop beside us. I look at him while the makeup artist pats at my cheek with a brush loaded with concealer.

"Okay?" I ask, feeling tension building.

Jake grunts his reply, staring Lawrence down until the director backs off and twirls, barking some orders at his staff.

"Prick," Jake spits, turning toward me. His eyes soften and he watches for a few moments as I'm poked at with a brush.

"It's not so bad," the makeup artist says, moving away from me and inspecting her handiwork. "Let's get you into makeup so I can work my magic."

"Thanks." I smile. "Be there in a tick."

She leaves us, and I find myself reaching for my cheek again when Jake's eyes darken. He steps forward to do what he's done every time I've tried to hide the bruise. He goes to take my hand, but doesn't make it any farther than midway between our bodies. He looks around, remembering we're in public, before withdrawing. "What's the shoot for?" he asks.

"Perfume ad," I tell him, pointing to the corner where an expanse of white screens are set up. "Clean and minimal scent by a new designer that complements her fashion line. The theme is clean and minimal, too. Silver on white." I see interest creep onto his face as he takes in what I've said.

"Minimal theme?" he asks, homing in on that one little detail. "What does that mean?"

I laugh and collect my bag. "It means I won't be wearing a lot."

He stiffens from top to toe. "How much is not a lot?"

"A pair of knickers."

His dark eyes go all round and worried as his hand comes up and gestures at my chest area. "And here?"

"Nothing." I'm taking far too much pleasure from his evident alarm. It doesn't matter that the camera angles will be manipulated to give a hint of full nudity without actually showing any of my bits. Jake doesn't know that, and I'm enjoying playing with him.

"Nothing?" he asks, having a quick peek around to check no one is in close proximity. He's safe. Everyone is too busy setting up. "Cami." He steps forward, bringing his head down a little so he can whisper. "You've never posed nude and I'm not sure it's a step your career will thank you for. The design stuff. That's your thing. Don't give up on it."

I keep my amusement contained. It's tricky. He's trying to be diplomatic, when what he actually means and won't say is that he's not happy about me flashing my breasts to the world. His possessiveness is deeply satisfying. "I will keep focused on the design *thing*," I assure him. "But this is a huge campaign with a massive backing from investors. Trust me, my career will thank me for it."

He scowls. It's the most endearing expression. Then he unbends his tall body, back to full height, clearly thinking hard about what he should say. "I can't sit here and look at you virtually naked. It'll drive me mad." He walks past me and my smile breaks out, watching as he tries to discreetly adjust his groin area, muttering as he goes.

"Camille!"

The familiar, excited voice pulls my attention away from my brooding bodyguard and to the dressing room entrance across the studio.

"Shaun!" I race over to give him a hug. He and I have been in the industry for the same number of years, both of us having been headhunted by the same agency around the same time. He's a dish—tall, dark, and handsome, with a cheeky single dimple that's his trademark. Women fall at his feet, but he's happily engaged to Cynthia, a TV presenter on a morning show. He literally doesn't see the attention he gets. He's modest and humble. I love him.

"How are you?" I throw my arms around him, unperturbed by the fact that he's sporting only a skimpy pair of silver trunks.

He laughs and squeezes me. "I'm great." Releasing me, he holds me at arm's length, his happy face transforming into a frown the second he claps eyes on my cheek. "What happened here?"

"Oh, nothing." I brush his inquiry aside, ignoring the question on his face. "Nice trunks!" I look down at the dull silver scrap of material covering his manhood.

He laughs. "Don't get too cocky. Yours are smaller."

I giggle and jab him in the shoulder, noticing him looking past me with interest. "I've heard you've got yourself a bodyguard," he says quietly. "And don't you just."

I give him a tired look before glimpsing over my shoulder, finding Jake hasn't yet left the studio. He's now watching me from across the room like a hawk, standing looking professional and hyperalert. "I certainly do."

"I'm as straight as they come, Camille, but even *I* would."

"Shaun!" I gasp, giving him another smack. "Stop it and tell me how Cynthia is."

"Gorgeous as ever," he replies quickly, making me smile. "She was pissed she had to work and couldn't come and say hi."

"We'll have to catch up soon," I say, seeing the makeup artist poke her head around the door, looking for me. "Hey, I'm wanted." I reach up and kiss his cheek. "See you on set."

"Yeah, see you in a bit."

I leave Shaun and make my way over to my dressing room, but I don't get much more than three paces before my path is blocked. Jake is looking down at me, worried. "Everything okay?" I ask, not liking his pent-up disposition. He looks nervous.

"Who was that?"

I frown. "Shaun?"

"Is that his name? The ponce in the sparkly knickers?"

"You mean the silver trunks?"

He waves an indifferent hand in the air. "Whatever. Who is he?"

"He's a model. We're shooting together." I see my makeup artist appear again, tapping at her watch face. "I have to get ready." I go to pass him but get blocked.

"Camille." Jake comes in close, trying to be inconspicuous again. He's a six-foot, four-inch, brooding bodyguard. It's not possible for him to be inconspicuous. "You've just told me that you're going to be wearing next to nothing on this shoot, and now you're telling me Mr. Sparkly Knickers is going to be rubbing up against you?"

I clamp my lips together and think how best to ease his concern. Something tells me nothing will work, and if it does, Jake isn't going to hold on to that comfort for long, especially when we start the shoot and Lawrence instructs me and Shaun into what I know are going to be some interesting poses. "It's work," I say quietly.

"It'll be fucking torture, that's what it'll be." He sucks in air, already preparing himself.

I study him for a few moments, very aware that Shaun being on set isn't the only thing that's making Jake tense. He's been edgy all morning. "You're twitchy today."

His eyes shoot to mine. "Is it any wonder?" he asks, flicking his head to Shaun's dressing room. He's trying to avoid the real issue, which needs far more attention than my semi-naked model friend.

"It's day three." I bite my lip nervously, but when Jake doesn't acknowledge my observation, I sigh. "You should wait for me outside."

"I'd rather wait in here," he mutters, moving to the side to let me pass. "Have fun." There is zero sincerity in his light order, his scowl pointing to Shaun's dressing room again. I move past him with caution and a little worry.

This is going to be horrendous.

CHAPTER 17

JAKE

It's official. I've gone off my fucking rocker. I must have. Why else would I put myself through this? I've dumped myself on a black leather couch across the studio and I'm not moving. Not for nothing or no one. Not even for the toilet. I'll piss my pants if I have to. Talking of pants, I've never seen anything so fucking ridiculous in my life. Silver trunks? He might be giving me a run for my money in the definition department, but he lost all hopes of a win the second he slipped into those sparkly knickers. What a twat! I try to relax in my chair, struggling to shake off the tension. My edginess isn't just because of Mr. Sparkly Knickers, though he's certainly adding a new dimension to my bad mood. It's day three. The proverbial ticking time bomb could explode at any moment, and the unknown danger is making me twitch. I'm tense, snappy, and suspicious of everyone and everything. I should have kept her in bed all day.

Camille appears from her dressing room, a thin white robe tied loosely around her, a woman following behind spraying at her hair with a can of something. I sit up straight and my cock comes to life.

Holy...fuck...

Her hair is wet and brushed off her face, showing every perfect piece of her skin. Wet blond locks are splayed over her shoulders, and her makeup appears barely there, though judging by how long she's been in that room and the fact that there's no trace of her bruised cheek, I suspect there's plenty caked onto her skin. Her cheekbones look sharper, her eyes bluer and her lips fuller. She looks fucking divine.

I cross my legs tactically, catching her flick a glance over to me. Her eyes are popping madly, the intensity of the topaz the only color on her face. This was a huge mistake, and my conclusion is only confirmed when someone pulls the robe from her back and she slips free, allowing them to attack her entire body with yet another can of something. I cough and look away, beginning to sweat. Good fucking Christ, it's hot in here. Naked. She's practically naked, and though I knew she would be and thought I was prepared, the reality is very different. I'm no more prepared now than I was the day I walked into Trevor Logan's office.

She never fails to knock me sideways.

I got only a peek of her naked, willowy body before I forced myself to look away, but that glimpse has welded itself at the front of my mind, dancing teasingly. Her skin looked smooth and shimmery, and that tiny silver string bikini only just covers her special place, the place I could lose myself in forever. *My* special place. I groan under my breath as I frantically search for something to distract myself with. There aren't any of those annoying girlie mags, not even a fucking newspaper. I should leave before I embarrass myself, but just when I've made that sensible decision and begin to get up from the couch, the ponce in his silver knickers appears on set. I freeze in my semi-raised position.

Fuck!

I'm going nowhere. I release my tense muscles, let my arse fall back to the sofa, and watch as they're all gathered into a circle. The ignorant idiot who greeted Camille when we arrived looks like he's performing ballet, his arms waving around dramatically as everyone nods their understanding. Then someone puts a robe around Camille's shoulder as they're talking, and I sag a little, relieved. She could get chilly.

My girl listens carefully when she's pulled to one side by the director, nodding and smiling, and once everyone appears to be clear on what's happening, they all disperse, scattering around the room. I watch on, disturbed by the pandemonium. It's like organized fucking chaos. Then Camille pads onto the blanket of white that covers the floor and two walls, and powerful lights point on her from every direction, lighting her up, making her glow. She's standing deathly still while people poke and pull at her, listening as people continue to bark urgent orders around her. I start to prepare myself, knowing it won't be long before I'm forced to endure the sight of her naked again. Forced? Not true at all. I could get up and walk out, if the caveman inside of me wasn't waving his club and snarling at the idiot in the sparkly knickers.

I swallow when her robe is removed again, resting my elbow on the arm of the couch and propping my chin on my hand. Enjoy it, I tell myself. Enjoy watching her do something she loves, with passion in her eyes as she does it. That look is something I have firsthand experience of. That glistening and shimmering of her blue eyes was there when I was buried inside of her. It's fire and passion. It's consuming.

I'm lost in my daydreams, frozen by my wonder and awe.

Then *he* appears, shimmering like a fucking god, snatching me from my happy place. The urge to go over and physically remove him from the area nearly gets the better of me. I breathe in deeply and reason with myself. She's working. It's just a job. I'm stronger than this. More controlled and calm.

I watch with narrowed eyes as the guy in the sparkly knickers rounds Camille and comes in behind her. Close. Too fucking close. He laughs, she laughs. The whole fucking studio is laughing.

Except me. There's nothing funny about this. I'm hot again.

His hands; they appear from behind Camille, and I watch with bated breath for where they might be heading.

Please, no. Don't you dare fucking touch her!

They fall neatly over her breasts.

Oh, fuck!

I fly up from the couch and catch my big foot on the leg of the coffee table, tripping and stumbling my way from the area. "Motherfucker!" I yell, catching my balance in the nick of time before I fall flat on my face. I swing around and find my performance hasn't gone without notice. Everyone is looking at me—Camille with shocked eyes and Mr. Sparkly Knickers with his hands still on *my* breasts.

I look away before I stalk over and yank them away. "Excuse me," I mutter, backing up, waving my phone in the air. "Call." I turn...and collide with the coffee table again, my shin cracking on the edge. I hiss and spit through the stab of pain, then make a swift exit, just avoiding breaking out into a sprint to the door.

His hands on her fucking tits! I slam the door behind me and find the nearest flat surface to whack my forehead on. That was totally uncalled for, and I don't mean my peculiar behavior. What the fuck? I sag into the wall, battling away the flashbacks of another man with his hands on Cami, trying to reason with myself. So much for keeping it professional.

"Handled with class, Jake," I mutter. My phone starts ringing, and I laugh under my breath. "A minute too late, Lucinda," I say, taking her call. "What do you have?"

"Nothing," she answers flatly, to the point as always. "Honestly, I'm at a loss. I've just spoken to Logan. He's probably going to pull you."

"What?" That three-day warning is all I see. Today is day three. He's pulling me on day three? He can't be serious! "He's hiding something, Luce," I grate.

"We don't know that for sure. If he's going to pull you there's nothing we can do." She sighs, and I look at my phone incredulously. "I have another job for you, anyway. Not as handsome on the fees, but not to be sniffed at."

I look at the blank wall in front of me, feeling my stomach drop like a rock. Pulling me off the job? Nothing we can do? Another shadow job? "Who?"

"Greek diplomat. Got himself in a spot of bother involving money laundering."

Greek. Greece. Like another fucking country? My heart follows my stomach to the floor. No Camille.

"What with the state of the Greek economy, death threats seem reasonable." Lucinda goes on while I continue to stare blankly at the wall. "I reckon a year in the sun will do you good."

A year? I balk, feeling numb, my head spinning, as I turn toward the door that I've just fallen out of. My lungs squeeze, making my breathing come short, fast, and panicked.

"Jake?" Lucinda says. "You there?"

The sweet sound of Camille's laugh seeps into my ears, intensifying my panic. Leaving her is out of the question. I refuse. "It's a pass," I breathe down the line, aware that I'm about to endure a string of expletives.

But they don't come. "Can I ask why?" Lucinda asks.

"Nope." I cut her off and hang up, unprepared and unwilling to explain myself. But the news I've just received has made me think seriously about what comes next.

Protecting Camille is essential. Her ex-boyfriend is a *very* real threat, and I still don't know what the fuck is going on with her father. I can't leave her vulnerable. I can't let her wicked ex-boyfriend get his nasty claws back into her. The thought makes me sweat. Leaving her makes me sweat. This job hasn't been about my need to bury myself in work to stop myself from being buried by my self-loathing. This job isn't about duty or maintaining my reputation as the best.

This job has been different from day one, and the reason is currently standing naked on the other side of that door with another man's palms cupping her breasts. And as for my reputation? Well, that just burst into pathetic flames as I staggered out of the studio like a newborn fawn. But none of it matters. Only Camille matters. Her and how she makes me feel.

For the first time in four years, I have a personal purpose. I want to be here, if only to look at her every day.

I drop to a nearby chair and stare at the door. This isn't just about her needing me. This is more me needing her. Young, strong-minded, determined, and brave.

I'm mad for her. I need to keep her. I need to protect her.

* * *

It's the longest few hours of my fucking life, waiting for them to wrap up on the shoot. But strangely, my torture has nothing to do with what initially put me on this side of the door and everything to do with my mind whizzing with how best to approach my imminent situation.

Camille appears, her hair still wet, but now bundled in a messy knot atop her head, her makeup still in place, but, thank God, she's back in her baggy trousers and oversized T-shirt. The fact that she insists on wearing clothes that are ten times too big for her just makes me admire her all the more. She has a body to die for, yet doesn't flash it. I stand as she pulls the door shut behind her, looking pensive. It takes my mind a few moments to catch up. The last time she saw me I was tripping up all over my big feet.

"Go well?" I ask as I take her bag.

She narrows her bright eyes onto me accusingly. "What was that?"

"What?"

"Your funny little turn in there." She waves over her shoulder.

"Like I said, a call." I avoid her eyes, certain she'll nail me and my white lie.

"Your phone wasn't ringing," she points out, scuppering my coolness.

"It was on silent." I mentally cheer to myself for my smart thinking.

"And who was it?" she presses, obviously still suspicious.

This one is easy, because I did actually take a call. Just not when she thinks I took it. "A colleague."

Now would be the perfect time to give Camille the heads-up on what might be on the horizon. No more shadow. But I don't, and I have no idea why. Because I don't want to accept it? Because I don't want to upset her? Will she even be upset? "Just updating me on a few details."

"And is there anything?" she asks, walking on when I motion for her to lead the way. She sounds casual, yet I can hear her uncertainty. Has she thought about what comes next, too?

"Nothing," I say, passing up on another opportunity to share the news.

"That's funny, because Dad just called and mentioned that he's getting to the bottom of the threats. Said they'll probably have it all sorted by the end of the day." She says this all very quietly, peeking up at me discreetly.

I force my eyes not to widen. He did, did he? "Nothing's certain," I say robotically before going for subject change swiftly. "Are you hungry?" She must be. I didn't see her eat any breakfast this morning, and it's way past lunchtime. I'm not all too fond of her eating habits at the best of times, but her tradition to starve herself for twenty-four hours before a shoot is a massive bugbear. It's not healthy.

"No, I'm good," she answers thoughtfully, pushing her way through the doors into the reception area. "Dad also reminded me that it's Chloe's birthday garden party this evening." She sounds less than enthused. "I need to be at his place in the country by seven."

"A garden party?" I muse. Sounds fucking awful. "Sounds exciting."

She throws a tired look up at me. "Don't be sarcastic. You've got to be there, too, remember?"

I hum to myself. I'd like to see anyone try to stop me.

Like her father. Kind of convenient that Logan's *probably* going to pull my protection after I casually pointed out that there was no courier on the day he claims the threat was received.

"Let's go get some iced tea," Camille suggests, carrying on her way.

I close my eyes briefly and follow. I'm trying not to let my edginess show. I want to take her home and lock her up, not go for fucking iced tea.

* * *

"Sit," I say, pulling a chair out for her and instinctively scanning the surrounding area. For the first time since I started shadowing her, I take a seat at the same table as Camille, my move not costing me a thought. Then I pick up the menu and wave the waiter over. "One of those iced lemon teas, a black coffee, and a tuna salad." The waiter nods and goes on his way, and I settle in my chair, looking up to find Camille with raised eyebrows. "What?"

"I thought you were my bodyguard, not my personal caregiver."

My elbows meet the table and I lean in. "That changed the moment you let me inside you." I take the best of pleasure from her creamy cheeks heating under my fiery stare. "Anything more to say?"

She shakes her head and dives on the glass of water the waiter just poured. "Why aren't you eating?"

I avoid telling her that my appetite was sucked up as a result of the call I took from Lucinda. Not that I had much of an appetite in the first place. "Not hungry." I accept my coffee and load it with sugar.

"I've been thinking." She takes the straw in her drink and fiddles with the tip.

The stirring of my coffee slows as I look up at her. "About?" I prompt, uncomfortable with her hesitance.

"About how little I know about you." She glances up at me, gauging my reaction. I don't disappoint her. I've gone rigid in my chair, the reminder that there's so much more for her to know biting me on the arse.

"Nothing much to tell," I say quietly and instinctively. It's not pretty and I'm less than comfortable with sharing it.

Hurt invades her face, and I hate myself for it, but before I can attempt to make it right, however that might be, she goes on. "Your bullet wound."

I feel my teeth grind. "What about it?" I'm being a dick, but my own mood isn't great on day three and after Lucinda's call. Dragging up a past I try to rein in isn't going to lighten it. My attacks have been minimal these past few days and I'm mad that Camille's toying with my stability.

"I wondered—"

"No, Camille." I cut her off harshly, and she snaps her mouth shut.

Silence falls and I stir my coffee until it could disappear, my hand working on autopilot, giving me something to do. It's awkward, but not as awkward as I'll be if I have to talk. Voices in my head yell at me, tell me not to be such a spineless coward, but until I can be sure that she won't be as disgusted as I am with myself, then my mouth shall remain firmly closed on all things concerning me and my history. I have to stop hating myself and my past before I can move forward.

I laugh to myself. That day may never come. I loathe myself today as much as I loathed myself back then, and I've had *years* to try and wrap my mind around what happened. Camille could never be expected to understand. I'm a bastard. Plain and simple. She'll hate me, and that's about as painful a thought as any.

"Tuna salad?"

I look up and find the waiter hovering, a plate in his hand. Camille is lost in thought, gazing into the distance. I indicate for him to place it down in front of her and reach over, placing my hand on hers. She snaps from her daydream and smiles a forced smile, trying to convince me that my abruptness hasn't upset her. That she understands. I should be so lucky. I retract my touch so she can eat, trying to return her strained gesture.

She starts poking at the leaves, still semi-lost in thought. "Do you have any family?" she asks quietly, throwing me a curveball. I thought we were done with questions.

I fight not to shrink in my chair. "No." I don't mean to sound so clipped and final. Not that she pays much attention to my obvious need to avert this conversation.

"What about your parents?" Her teeth sink into her lip, nervous.

I sigh, closing my eyes for a brief second. But I bite the bullet and relieve her of her wondering. Give her something. Not everything, just something to pacify her. "They died when I was seven. I was raised by my grandmother. She died when I was sixteen. As soon as I was old enough to sign up for the forces, I did." I put it out there in a verbal vomit of words and pray she won't press me further.

My prayers go unanswered. "How did your parents die?" Her quiet question is drenched in sympathy that I can't bear.

"Lockerbie disaster." I swallow and look away, hearing her quiet hitch of soft breath. She wasn't even born in 1988, but she's obviously aware of the horrific terrorist attack. Who isn't?

"I'm so sorry."

"Me too." I return my eyes to her and read her thoughts, knowing she's reached the right conclusion. I joined the forces because of my loss. To do my bit. It was my own personal peace mission. Then I fucked it all up with the help of a woman.

"And what about that woman?" she asks tentatively, like she's heard my thoughts. My discomfort spirals.

"She's irrelevant."

"Irrelevant enough for you to carry her picture around?"

I feel my lips straighten, the dormant resentment inside of me showing dangerous signs of surfacing and tipping me. I'd never be able to explain my reasons for keeping that photograph. It's fucking backward, a sick reminder, a personal torture.

"Eat your salad," I say, pointing to her fork, telling her without saying so that that's one thing I'm *really* not ready to talk about.

But I will have to. One day I'll have to face that piece of my history head-on. The lame excuses that Abbie won't want to hear from me, the ones I tell myself constantly, are weakening by the day. Every time I use my phone, I find myself pulling up her name and staring down at it, wondering if today will be the day that I finally find the strength to do what I should have done years ago. I'm a coward. A bastard. But I need to be in the best frame of mind to venture down the road to redemption, and I haven't been in that frame of mind since I left.

I breathe in deeply. "We need to get you home so you can get ready for this party."

"Can't wait." She sighs, taking a mouthful of tuna and chewing, looking past me thoughtfully. I sigh myself, feeling hopeless, watching as she chews slowly.

But then her eyes suddenly widen.

"Hey, what's . . . ?" My words fade when she visibly starts to shake, her frightened stare rooted past me. I swing around to find out what has her panicked attention, my heart leaping, my hand ready to find my gun.

I jump up from my chair.

"Jake!" Camille's scream is distant, foggy behind my instant cloud of fury.

The motherfucker!

Seb's hovering a few meters away, his face black and blue, a small army of beefy dudes flanking him. Oh, here we go. How much has he paid them? There are five of the steroid-hyped twats, all trying to look menacing. Fucking insult. The rage that creeps up my spine might make me feel unhinged . . . if I wasn't perfectly lucid. I'm lucid. Perfectly sane.

"Still walking, then?" I ask, pushing my chair out of the way. "Let me remedy that for you." I stride forward, planning my moves as I go, my brain telling me which chimp to take out first and how.

"Jake, stop!"

I can hear Camille through my controlled rage, screaming for me to stop, but there's only one instruction hammering at my brain.

Eliminate the enemy. Kill the fucker who dared lay a hand on her.

The first guy goes down like a sack of shit with one blow to the face, the second just as easy. I duck, my mind noting the positions of Sebastian's three remaining minions as I swing around and throw my elbow out, cracking one clean on the jaw. He's on his arse a second later, rolling around groaning.

"Shit!" The random curse is a signal that one has jumped ship and legged it, and a bellow from behind tells me the last is coming at my back. Fucking amateurs.

I look up to the shop window in front of me, seeing the prick charging like a fucking rhino. I have plenty of time to figure out what to do with this one. Roughly three seconds. It's even enough time to catch my breath.

I see his arm come wide, and I duck at the last second, sending him staggering past me, straight into the window of the shop. It surprises me when it doesn't shatter. He recovers quickly, shaking away the proverbial birds fluttering around his meaty head, then he comes at me again.

I remain where I am and wait for the move that I know is coming. He doesn't disappoint. After a lack of accuracy from his failing punch, he goes for a good old-fashioned tackle instead, charging at my waist and taking me from my feet. I let him, my back hitting the concrete with force. I grunt and circle my legs around his waist, then flip him onto his back, straddling him. His dazed eyes take a few moments to clear before he realizes where he is. I smirk wickedly, then put him out of his misery, launching my fist into his face, the blood from his broken nose splattering a meter in every direction.

Job. Done.

"You're a fucking psycho, man!"

I pause, flexing my fist. Not so done.

I look up and find Camille's ex backing away, his eyes darting across the carnage I've caused with my bare hands. I feel my lip curling as I rise to my feet. This little prick thought he could outnumber me with a few oversized thick idiots? I want to kill him even more. Painfully. Slowly. Until he begs me to finish it. I take long strides toward him as he retreats, holding his hands up. "I'm going."

"Only where I'm planning on sending you."

His back slams into a car before he turns and jumps in, firing up the engine of the black Porsche. He screeches off fast, wheels spinning, the back end of his car swaying all over the road, looking as panicked as its driver.

Allowing the fog of purpose to clear, I take in the damage I've done, seeing four of the five men rolling around, groaning. The fifth meaty fucker—the sensible one—is nowhere to be seen. If I were the compassionate type, I'd feel a little sorry for them. They should have had a little more information on who they were apparently going to do over.

I straighten my jacket and turn, set on getting Camille in my car and out of here before the police turn up.

I locate the table where I left her.

And my knees give.

She's gone.

* * *

I've never felt a panic like this. I've been so numb for so many years; the barrage of emotions striking me relentlessly now are enough to make me go on a killing spree until she's safe in my care again.

What have I done?

I turn on the spot, frantically searching the surrounding area. "Camille!" I roar.

This is my fault. I've failed her.

"Camille!" I run over to where we were sitting, finding her phone still on the table and her bag where I left it on the seat next to us. "Fuck!" I snatch up her bag and phone and pelt toward my car, throwing them onto the passenger seat and racing off down the road like a madman.

I drive up and down the street—scan every person, look down every alley, zoom in on every car.

Nothing.

I grab my phone and call Lucinda, not even giving her time to greet me before I bark my instructions down the line. "Camille's gone. Call Logan, call the police. I have her phone and bag. There's a CCTV camera on the building opposite the café on Stretton Street. Get me the footage from the last hour."

"Got it," Lucinda answers, cool and collected. "Where are you?"

"Looking for her." I hang up and punch the steering wheel, taking a hard right and racing to the main road. I don't know where I'm heading, just driving randomly, up and down road after road, searching for her. I'll kill myself. I swear, if anything happens to her, I'll slice myself to pieces. This will be a mistake I'll never forgive myself for. This will be the nail in the coffin for me and my black soul.

The small light I've found in my blackness is fading by the second.

* * *

It could be one hour, could be two, three, or a whole fucking day. I don't know. I lost all concept of time the moment I noticed she was gone. I pull into the underground car park of her apartment block and screech to a stop by her car. Something immediately catches my eye. An envelope on the windscreen of Camille's Merc. I'm at the foot of the shiny red convertible in a heartbeat, and a second later, I'm staring down at more pictures of Camille. There are two words printed on one of the pictures.

Time's up.

"Fuck, no!" My fear and worry multiply by a million, and so does my anger. The photos in my grasp crumple under the force of my clenched fist, my teeth ready to crack from the force of my bite as I stomp my way through to the lobby and into the elevator, dialing Lucinda as I do. "I found a note on Camille's car. It says time's up."

"Shit," she curses. "The camera opposite the café has been out of order for over a month."

"Fuck!" As the doors open, I step out and pace in a haze of ruin down the hall. "Logan? The police?"

"On their way to her apartment."

"Good." I round the corner, Camille's door coming into view, and I jolt to a screaming halt.

Because slumped against the wood on her arse is my angel.

I grab the nearby wall to steady myself, relief making me dizzy.

She looks up, eyes overflowing with tears, her face red and blotchy. But she's still the most beautiful thing I've ever seen. "I couldn't get in," she chokes, sniffling uncontrollably. "My keys are in my bag. And my mobile." She sniffs. "I was going to use my neighbor's phone." She points across the hall. "But he's not home. And I don't know your number."

Relieved air pours from my mouth and I let my back meet the wall opposite her, my legs finally giving up on me. My arse hits the carpet with a thud as I vaguely hear Lucinda calling my name. I bring my phone to my ear. "I've got her. Call off the police. And Logan."

"What?"

"Just do it, Luce. She's safe. I'll call you soon." I hang up and drop my phone to the floor by my thigh, along with Camille's bag and the envelope. I can't hide my emotion and I don't want to. I allow a tear of relief to trickle down my cheek and drop onto my suit jacket. It's too much. All of these feelings and need and the fucking fear.

"I thought you'd been taken." I swallow around the lump in my throat. "I thought I'd lost you, Camille."

"I couldn't watch." She sniffs and coughs over her words. "I don't like seeing you like that. You frighten me."

I shake my head, feeling so remorseful, but only for putting her at risk, for making her feel like this. I was so lost in my mission to wipe out the ex-boyfriend and his posse, I lost sight of my true mission. I struggle to my feet and walk over to her, dropping to my knees before her slumped body. I take her hands and find her eyes, hoping she sees the regret and guilt that are blinding me. "I'm so sorry. I saw red, Cami. What he did to you, I can't..." I clench my eyes shut, struggling to finish. "I can't bear it."

She uses my hands as an anchor, pulling against them to haul herself into me. I catch her and squeeze her warm body against my chest, hoping to fuse us together, whispering my apologies in her ear and vowing to never let her leave my sight again.

CHAPTER 18

CAMI

I didn't mean to send him to hell and back. I didn't mean to scare the ever-loving shit out of him. I just needed to get away from the fight, and in my desperation I didn't consider the risks. I didn't consider Jake's worry.

I staggered to the roadside and threw myself into a cab, blubbering my address as the cabbie drove away. I didn't consider the fact that I had no money until he pulled up outside my building. He took pity on me. I was grateful, insisting on taking his details so I could forward the fare. He refused, passing me a tissue before demanding softly that I vacate his cab.

The violence in Jake is potent. It defies the control he usually exudes. Yet it's like he's planned each and every one of his moves without needing time to think. He's like a machine.

I didn't run away because Seb was there, or because I couldn't watch Jake potentially get hurt. There were five of them after all, excluding Sebastian, all big and menacing, and I knew what was going to happen. I knew Jake would cut through them like a hot knife through butter. I ran away because I couldn't watch it. He's ex-SAS. A trained soldier. A trained killer. Why he joined the forces is understandable, given what happened to his parents. But he's a natural warrior, even if his fight was personal.

What I can't figure out, though, is why he's no longer serving. He's only thirty-five, so definitely not old enough to be retired. His gunshot wound hasn't hampered his ability to fight, therefore I can't imagine his aim has been compromised. There's more to it; I just know there is. I know he has no family. But friends? I don't even know where he lives.

I need to find out what makes Jake Sharp tick. The woman in that picture. The anxiety attack. The deep-seated hurt that he can't hide. The mystery is growing each day. I pull away and he cups my cheeks with his palms, looking so relieved. "Come," he says, standing and pulling me to my feet.

"What's that?" I ask, watching as he collects a crumpled envelope with my bag and his phone.

"Nothing. Just some paperwork from the agency." He scoops me up and lets us into my apartment. Carrying me into my bathroom, he sits me on the edge of the bath, fetches a cloth, and damps it under the hot tap. He kneels before me and starts to gently wipe at my tear-stained face, watching each of his light swipes as he does.

"How long have you been a bodyguard?" I ask quietly, starting with an easy question and one I hope will break him in gently before I try to delve further into that mind. Now that he's given me something, I want more. I want everything that's weighing him down.

He answers quickly and easily, still cleaning the dried tears from my face. "Four years."

A quick mental calculation makes me more curious, because I know for sure no one would retire from the forces at thirty-one. Maybe they'd get promoted or move regiments, but not retire. There would have to be a reason, and a bullet wound that he seems fully recovered from couldn't be it. "Why do you do it?"

He's not so quick to answer this time, his hand definitely faltering as he glides the washcloth across my cheek. He seems to be thinking hard about how he should answer. "To feel useful." He frowns, looking a little bewildered.

"Like you did when you served your country?" I ask.

He smiles a little, his eyes flicking to mine. "I guess so."

I purse my lips, studying him, trying to keep the suspicion from my face. He's agreeing with me, and my instinct is telling me he's doing that because it's easier than disagreeing and risking having me press him.

He once told me that he needs a purpose. His purpose was war, fighting the evils of the world. Something stopped him from being able to do that, something major, and now he finds his purpose in personal protection. It all makes me suspect that he would still be serving if he could. So why can't he?

Whatever demons Jake has, he isn't going to be free of them unless he wants to be. He'll be held prisoner by them forever, and it's infuriating that he seems okay with that. I've been in the deepest depths of hopelessness. I thought there was no way out. It was hard, but I found my way out. So can Jake.

"Tell me why you stopped serving."

His motions falter briefly before he quickly gathers himself and continues to clean me up. It was just a split second, but I caught it, and I also saw the flash of pain in his eyes. "I'd served my country. Time to move on."

I don't believe him, and he'd be a fool to expect me to. That pain is still lingering deeply in his dark eyes, no matter how hard he's trying to conceal it behind his tough front. His evasion angers me, and I push his hand away from my cheek, ignoring his worried look.

"I need to get ready," I say, standing and leaving him crouched before me, looking up at me. I pass him and make my way into my room, hoping he takes the initiative to vacate my bathroom so I can shower.

"Camille?" he calls, his footsteps padding on the carpet as he follows me. "Why are you walking away from me?"

"You've made it perfectly clear that the conversation isn't going anywhere. I'm not stupid, Jake. There are things you're not telling me. I need to get dressed for the party."

I pull a floral oversized T-shirt dress down and lay it on my bed before heading to the shower, leaving Jake standing like a spare part in the middle of my bedroom. Shutting the door behind me, I flip the shower on, strip down and step in. The hot water feels divine, and as I absentmindedly soap down, staring at the tiles, my mind starts running away with me.

He's so complicated yet so simple. I'm perplexed by him, but I'm even more perplexed by my need to get beneath the cold, hard front he keeps in place. He's shown me a soft side. He's demonstrated that he isn't heartless and unfeeling, and I've seen him spiral into a meltdown. He's given me scraps of his history. Tiny pieces. But it all feels worthless without his trust. It feels one-sided as long as he decides what I should and shouldn't know.

And then I ask myself something. Something important.

Why do I need to know?

My hands pause on my stomach as my eyes drop to the shower floor, hating the conclusion that I'm reaching. It has nothing to do with curiosity. I haven't a burning need to unravel the puzzle that is Jacob Sharp. I want to know so I can help him.

Because I love him.

A single tear falls and mixes with the hot water spraying my face. I can't help him if he doesn't want to be helped. I can't bring him into the light when he's content residing in darkness. And I can't let him drag me into that darkness.

I can't fix him if he doesn't want to be fixed.

I can feel myself breaking under the pressure I'm putting on myself. I don't know when this became more emotional than physical, but I do know that I need to disconnect myself before I'm too far into his darkness to find my way out. I've been there before and I never plan

on going back. Different circumstances, yes, but it'll be the same outcome.

Hurt. Though I fear the hurt Jake is capable of inflicting on me
would be excruciating, and I know I would never recover from it.

* * *

The drive to my father's sprawling mansion in the countryside is long
and painful, both Jake and me quiet and pensive.

The gates to Dad's estate creak open slowly, and we're greeted by
a sea of luxury cars parked up the driveway. Jake drives unhurriedly
toward the house, and the sounds of chatter and laughter get louder
as we draw closer. It's sunny and warm and I'm dreading the evening
ahead. There will be dozens of insanely rich men who rub shoulders
with my father, in either business or pleasure—all as materialistic and
ruthless as he is. And their wives—as shallow as they are glamorous,
most just waiting for the younger model to muscle in on their privi-
leged lives and snatch the rug from under their feet.

If Dad even tries to push any potential boyfriend on me, I might
scream. It's hard enough to keep a smile fixed at the best of times.
Now, when I'm feeling as hopeless and empty as I do, enduring my father's intentions will be a challenge I'm not confident of overcoming.

I hop out of Jake's Range Rover and take the path that leads to the
extensive grounds at the back of my father's home, walking through
endless pavilions with honeysuckle waterfalls. When I pass the final
archway into the garden, I'm faced with hundreds of people, all sipping Pimm's or champagne, and I scan the faces, spotting TJ by the
pool. I make my way over, smiling when he sees me.

"Little star!" he croons, swiping a glass from a passing waiter and
placing it in my hand before kissing my cheek. "Last to arrive, and I
bet you'll be the first to leave."

I don't correct him. He knows me too well. "Thank you." I raise my glass and let him chink it before taking a swig. "Is Heather here yet?"

"Yes, over there." He points to the other side of the pool, where I spot my best friend with her parents. TJ returns his attention to me. "Still being tailed?" he asks, obviously spotting Jake somewhere behind me.

I don't look to see where my shadow has taken up position. "Dad said they may have gotten to the bottom of the threats. Do you know anything?" I ask, moving in closer to TJ. He lives in Dad's pocket. If anyone knows anything, he will.

TJ dips his head, giving me a warning look. "You know I don't discuss anything I hear within his office walls."

"Even when it's about me?"

"*Especially* when it's about you." He laughs as he leans in closer and kisses my cheek. "You'll be free as a bird again very soon, kiddo," he tells me, reinforcing Dad's claim.

He wanders off, shaking hands and kissing cheeks as he goes. I turn and see Jake a few meters away, his eyes fixed firmly on me. I immediately kick myself for searching him out. I've managed to evade direct contact since we had words earlier, knowing that refreshing my memory and attraction will serve no purpose at all. He's kitted out in a dark grey suit, looking perfect but formidable and obscenely handsome. As I glance around, I see the attention he's stirring with the females in close proximity. My eyes drop to my glass and I level out my thoughts and quash the urge to tell them all to keep their eyes to themselves.

"Cami!"

I look up and see Heather waving me over, and keen to find any type of distraction, I make my way around the pool to her and her parents, being accosted by various people on my way.

"Hey." I reach them and greet them each with a kiss.

"How are you, Camille?" Heather's father asks, pointing over my shoulder. "Got company, I see."

I should have made my excuses and stayed away from here. I'm sure the whole of the party must know about my bodyguard, and if they didn't, it's not like I can hide him here. He'll be the talk of the party for more reasons than his official capacity. I spot Heather's mother eyeing Jake discreetly, an approving smile on her face. Then she looks at Heather and nods. What was that? I look to my best friend, who casually shrugs off her mother's move.

"I'm fine, Henry, thank you," I reply to Heather's father. "How are you?"

"I'll be better when your father stops playing hardball and accepts my offer on his boatyard in Belfast."

"You know he likes to play the game," I laugh, taking Heather's arm lightly by the elbow. "Excuse us for a second." I pull her away and lead her over to a couple of empty lounge chairs.

"What's up?" she asks, following my lead and taking a seat, slipping her shades on.

"That look your mother gave you. What was that?" I don't beat around the bush. What's she been telling them?

Heather feigns innocence, an act I've grown to recognize. "What look?"

"Really?"

"I might have mentioned the stunt Jake pulled at Saffron's party."

"You mean when he leathered my scumbag of an ex after the bastard whacked me?"

Her lip curls in disdain, matching my own loathing for the lowlife. "No, you know I'd never tell a soul about that. I told her about Jake carrying you out of the bar like a knight in shining armor."

"He was doing his job."

She laughs. It's condescending and should be. "Camille, don't treat me like I'm stupid. You've fallen for him."

Her words hit me like a boulder in the face. Is it that obvious? "I haven't fallen for him," I argue meagerly as I glance over toward Jake.

He looks like a solid marble statue, just a few paces away. I'm not worried about him hearing us; the surrounding noise is too loud. He's got me firmly in his sights. It's no different than any other time, yet today I really don't like it. I feel like he's reading my mind, figuring me out. His bristled jaw is sharp and tight, the hollows of his cheeks evident, and his handsome face is etched with annoyance.

It's ridiculous that he's here. I'm surrounded by family and friends, and apparently I'm to expect the all clear very soon. Nothing could happen here, anyway.

"I haven't fallen for him," I murmur quietly again, ripping my eyes from Jake.

Heather's palm meets my thigh. "Why won't you admit it?" she asks.

I take a deep breath and choose to end the conversation right there. "There's nothing to admit," I say resolutely, disregarding my screaming heart and my best friend's incredulous face.

She sighs and relaxes back on the lounger, putting her feet up. "Do you remember when we used to lay here every day in the summer holidays, planning our fairy-tale lives while sipping fruit punch and telling your brother and his mates to stop splashing us?"

I smile and reflect back to the days when it was really that simple. Just us, plotting our perfect world without the burden of real life getting in the way. There was no debilitating sense of hopelessness or fear. There were no challenges like temptation and wrong decisions. There was no father trying to make choices for me and telling me who my prince should be. There were no threats. There was no Jake Sharp. "If only it were still that easy."

"It can be." Heather slips off her glasses and looks at me, a thousand reassuring words in her eyes. "Most of the time we make it complicated ourselves." She swings her legs off the lounger and stands. "I don't know what's stopping you, apart from your father, and I *know* you don't care what he thinks. You so obviously mean more to Jake than a contract." She dips and kisses my cheek. "You should go see your father and that wonderful stepmother of yours. She wants a birthday kiss from her favorite little girl. Catch you in a bit."

I watch as Heather strolls off, giving Jake a shake of her head as she goes. He doesn't react to it, doesn't frown or even raise his eyebrows in question, but he does look across to me. I avert my eyes and stand, set on finding my father when all I want to do is go home and hide under my bedcovers.

As I make my way up the garden, I conjure up the fortitude I need to face my dad and my unbearable stepmother. Ten paces in, no fortitude to be found. In fact, I grow more despondent by the second. I know I'm going to find my father holding court in his elaborate bar in the orangery, and I just know that there will be some boring associate of his, ready to please my father and displease me.

"Oh!" I yelp as a result of an abrupt tug on my arm, pulling me into a nearby recess at the entrance of the orangery. A palm covers my mouth and a hard body holds me against the wall. I blink rapidly, trying to focus on Jake's dark eyes, his lips almost touching the back of his hand where it's lain upon my mouth, keeping me quiet.

"I let my personal emotion compromise my judgment once when I was in the service," he whispers quietly, searching my eyes. "Two of my friends died. I got shot. And then I was deemed too volatile and unstable to continue my duties."

I still, but my heart pumps faster. Jake's dark eyes shut, robbing me of the comfort they're offering while he spills his story, rushed but clear. His nostrils flare. This is taking everything he has. "The only thing that mattered to me was stripped away after one bad decision because I let my personal life affect my duty. I swore I'd never let that happen again in any element of my life, Camille. I've always upheld that promise." I can hear the pain in his words, and he breathes in deeply. "Until you," he finishes softly, giving me his eyes.

I choke on a sob, making him lift his palm a little, his face blurring as tears threaten. His face is straight, but his eyes are swimming with emotion.

Then he swallows before he goes on. "I can't make another wrong move again."

I'm instantly fearful of what he means by that. His face is still expressionless. Why now? In the middle of my father's garden party, why is he telling me this now? That woman. That woman in the picture is the personal emotion he's talking about—the emotion that made him question his judgment. Am I making him question his judgment?

He goes to speak again, but hesitates for a moment, gathering strength. Then he squeezes his eyes shut, and my heart slows in my chest. He looks beaten, ready to give up. A treacherous tear slips down my cheek and hits his hand, and he opens his eyes. The conflict in them floors me. "My need to protect you goes a lot fucking deeper than a well-paid job, Camille." He whispers the words so softly, defying the hulk of a man that he is.

I breathe deeply in relief, trying to see past the tears welling in my eyes, and Jake drops his hand from my mouth and steps back, out of the recess into public view. He shrugs, like he's apologizing, and my heart finally kick-starts again, skipping all of the lower gears and roaring straight into a thundering rush. The activity of the party is a distant hum, and the people are a blur of lethargic movements in the distance. All there, but not there. The world is happening around us, oblivious to Jake and me trapped in our bubble, and I realize in this moment as I stare into his eyes that he won't pull me into his darkness. He wants me to help him find his way out. He feels trapped. I've felt like that. I know how it feels to see no way to the light. I had Heather to help me. Jake has no one. Except me. I can't walk away from him. I have to help him.

I don't know what to do. My instinct is telling me to go to him, but my barely functioning brain is reminding me that my father is nearby.

He won't approve of this. In fact, he'll do anything to stop it. I know and dread he will.

I move out of the recess and watch Jake watch me as I back into the orangery, a silent understanding passing between us. I'm preparing my excuses to Dad as I go.

Jake's need to protect me goes deeper than a well-paid job?

How deep?

Chapter 19

JAKE

I follow as Camille weaves through the crowds, ignoring anyone who tries to stop her for a chat on the way. Her urgency is calming. I'm not at all comfortable with her being here, whether it's her father's home or not. It's still day three. I'm still edgy. And Logan's intention to pull my protection isn't easing it.

I had no intention of seizing her and spilling the details of my darkness to her, but as the evening passed, I could see her falling further away from me, and I can't bear the thought of letting her go. I'll do *anything* to keep her in my life. Even if that means laying myself bare to her. Even if it means losing my sanity. It's too late. I already feel certifiably crazy.

I have nothing to lose. I've more or less just thrown myself down for her, despite my better judgment. I've been torn apart before at the hands of a woman. I never expected to put myself in that position again. I feel vulnerable and scared. Yet more hopeful than ever before.

Camille Logan can damage me far more than anything else I've encountered in my past. She has a stronger hold. She has the ability to destroy me. But she's my only hope of happiness again, of freeing myself from the clutches of my past.

A sniff of my history is all I'm prepared to give her right now. It's all I'm capable of, and telling myself that she has enough to deal with at the moment, without my shit, is easy. And a cop out. Part of me is riddled with guilt for letting her step into my darkness without being armed with all the information she needs to decide if she's making the right decision. But the other part of me is too desperate to cling onto her—I'm not prepared to jeopardize what we have before we really have it. I saw no disgust in her eyes when I told her a part of my story. I saw only sorrow. But there's the problem. It was only *part* of my past, and I need to find the strength from somewhere to share the rest. To face that part of my old life. To do the right thing and put it to rest, to finally move on.

Camille wastes no time muscling in on her father's group, smiling her apologies when she brings the conversation to a halt. Trevor Logan casts his eyes across the room to me, checking my presence and narrowing his eyes briefly before giving his daughter the attention she wants. His look tells me everything I need to know. I'm not the kind of man that he wants for his daughter. I'm not even the kind of man that *I* want for his daughter. I'm not ignorant of his power and influence. He could destroy me. Have me booted out of the agency. I need to figure out the best way to approach this.

Logan's minions are hovering across the way, keeping watch on me as he indulges his daughter. His current wife, Chloe, is also lingering close by, but her attention is elsewhere while her husband's distracted by Camille. I watch closely as Chloe talks to a man. She's being coy, her eyes constantly flicking to Logan and Camille, wary and watchful. Then the man's hand comes up and brushes her arm subtly, and she jerks nervously, moving away and shooting him a warning look. It prompts him to check for any attention that might be pointed their way, but he seems to relax when he sees Logan and everyone else in the group are focused on Camille. Shame he missed me. I get my phone from my pocket and tap out a message, taking a discreet picture and attaching it to the e-mail.

I think Logan's wife is having an affair. Picture attached.
Who is he?

I click send and get an immediate reply.

On it. Just found out Trevor Logan funded Sebastian Peters's
rehab. I also checked the kid's bank statements. 100K landed
in his account the day he was admitted. Kind of convenient.

I hold on to my composure. Just.

Logan paid the little fucker off? Yeah, 'cause that clearly worked.
The bastard achieved nothing but feeding the lowlife's drug habit for a
year or two. Logan should have just done what I plan on doing: killing
him. He doesn't even know that the prick has hit his daughter. Logan
will do anything to keep Sebastian Peters away from his daughter, and
on this occasion I'll give him credit, even if his plan was shit. It also
confirms what I should expect when he finds out about me.

I slip my phone back into my pocket, seeing Chloe rejoin her husband. Her smile is fake as she approaches and slips an arm around
Camille's shoulders, hugging her, and I can see from here that Camille
stiffens in response. Then another man approaches the group and the
Neanderthal in me screams like a demon to be let loose when he leans
in and kisses Cami's cheek. Logan smiles fondly and Camille grimaces,
jerking away. A suitor? The son of a friend that Logan plans on marrying Camille off to? I growl deep in my throat. He makes her skin
crawl. He makes *my* skin crawl. Camille backs away from the group
and her father's face drops in disappointment, but she doesn't give him
the opportunity to keep her there.

She's passing me quickly, looking as eager to escape the confines of
the extensive mansion as I am. I fall in behind her and quicken my
pace to pass so I can open the door for her. I use the opportunity to
look back as I hold the door, seeing Logan watching us leave, his face

thoughtful as his stare falls to mine. I lock eyes with him for longer than I should, unable to stop myself from narrowing them. It's a stupid move; I shouldn't be spiking any suspicion, but seeing him trying to throw his daughter at that prick rattles me dangerously.

"I need to say good-bye to Heather," Camille says, heading down toward the pool. I have no choice but to follow when all I want to do is gather her up, take her home, and keep her safe from her father's debasing world.

She finds Heather quickly, whispering something in her ear, and Camille's best friend's eyes smile, but her mouth remains straight as she nods her agreement to whatever Camille has said. I know I'm under close inspection from elsewhere, and I look to my side, seeing an older woman looking at me knowingly. Heather's mother. I don't give any indication that may confirm what she may or may not be thinking, ensuring I maintain my professional front.

"Ready?" Camille asks, approaching me.

"Just keep walking," I say under my breath, spotting Logan's personal security exiting the orangery and scanning the pool area.

Cami continues past me as ordered, and I discreetly scan the crowds as I walk behind her, taking in all the faces, hyper-aware. Reaching behind my back, I feel my gun, reminding myself that it's there and waiting to blow out the brains of anyone who tries to stop us from leaving. That look I gave Logan—I shouldn't have challenged him like that.

Once we're out of the garden area and rounding the house, I move to Camille's side and slip my palm onto her lower back, pushing her along.

"You're twitchy." She looks up at me as I gauge the distance to my Range Rover. "Why?"

"I just want to get you home." I pull the door open and physically lift her into the seat before rounding the front quickly and hopping in. As I start the engine, I see Logan's apes come barreling around the corner.

"Hey, what do Pete and Grant want?" Camille asks, throwing me a questioning look. I pull off down the drive, faster than I planned, my head whizzing. "Jake!"

"I don't know, Cami," I grate, picking up speed.

"It could be some news," she says innocently. "Maybe Dad's found out who's been sending the threats."

"I don't think they want to talk about the threats." I'm only half-lying, but what can I tell her? That I think her father's hiding something? I don't feel in the least bit guilty for hiding the most recent photographs from her—the ones that I found on the windscreen of her car. She has enough on her plate.

"Then what?" she asks.

"What do you think your father would do if he found out about us?" I glance across the car and find horror etched all over her face.

"He'd say no one is good enough for me. Only some idiot business associate's son."

"I know that, angel. But you haven't answered my question."

"He'd do anything to keep you away." She looks pained as she openly admits what we both know. "But you are good enough," she says quietly.

"I don't think your father will agree, angel." I reach over and take her hand, squeezing some reassurance into it, choosing to keep the tiny detail that he paid Seb off to the tune of 100K to myself. It's irrelevant, since it hasn't worked, and it'll only upset Camille, for no other reason than it's her father taking her life into his hands again. There's nothing unreasonable about Logan's motives. Camille's fierce desire to be independent isn't always a good thing, especially where abusive ex-boyfriends are concerned. Stubborn little thing.

"I don't care what he thinks, Jake," she spits out shortly. "He's obsessed with controlling everything around him. He will *not* control me. I'm not marrying a man so Dad can make a few more millions!"

"He cares about you. He wants to look after you," I say quietly, for reasons I don't know.

She looks at me, that fierce passion burning bright in her eyes. "But I have you to look after me now."

My breath catches in my throat. Never has anything sounded so good. So right. "You have me now," I confirm in a hushed whisper, returning my attention to the road.

* * *

I don't take Cami back to her apartment. I take her to mine. I don't want Trevor Logan to know where we are, and the only way his goons would find me is if they hacked into the agency database. That isn't going to happen.

I pull into the factory unit down by the Docklands, smiling on the inside at Cami's evident concern. "Where are we?" she asks, looking around with a half-concealed, appalled expression on her face.

"My home." I exit the vehicle and circle to get her out, trying not to laugh at her obvious revulsion. She's plain horrified.

She takes my hand and lets me help her down. "You live here?"

"That's right, angel." I walk on, waiting for the sound of her heels clicking against the concrete to kick in, but when I reach the old industrial elevator and stop, there's no sound. I punch in my code and turn to find her gazing around the huge open space, up to the steel rafters and corrugated iron roof. The low evening sunlight hits her face, seeping in from one of the broken panels. I smile, expecting nothing less. Not because it's Cami standing in the derelict space, but because it really is that bad. "You coming, or shall I bring your coffee down here?"

She drops her eyes from the rafters and gives me a disdainful glare. "It's not what I expected; that's all."

"A bit like you didn't expect me?" I waggle an eyebrow, loving the sight of her trying to stop her button nose from wrinkling.

"Exactly like that," she admits, making her way to me. "Why have you brought me here?"

"Because I think Daddy might try to have us followed."

"By Pete and Grant?"

"Yes." I usher her into the elevator and make a racket as I yank the rusty iron bars across, slamming them into position. "Not exactly inconspicuous, are they?"

"Neither are you." She laughs, waving a finger up and down my tall frame.

I give her a cheeky wink and wrap my arm around her shoulders as we rise to the factory floor, hauling her in, relishing the feel of her close to me. "The point of my job is to be a presence, Camille. A visible warning."

"I didn't get that warning."

Her phone rings, and she looks down at it, as do I. Her father. She rejects the call and turns it off, doing what I would have done had she not beaten me to it. Then she snuggles happily into my side and hums her contentment as the lift jolts, declaring our arrival to my apartment. She grumbles when I release her to drag the doors open, but the grumble soon transforms into gasps of awe as my living space comes into view.

"More like it?" I ask, hanging back as she takes tentative steps forward, gazing around.

"Wow." She swings around to face me, eyes full of shock. "Just... wow."

I smile and take her shoulders, walking her back, all the way across the vast space until she's in my bedroom. The urge to throw her on my bed and rip her clothes off is nearly too strong to resist, but I have a few things to do. So I force myself to push her on, grinning down at her, finding that telltale lust building in her gorgeous eyes.

The panorama of the city comes into sight, and I know she catches the beautiful view, but she refuses to drop her eyes from mine. It's a massive compliment. That view is fucking immense.

"Take a shower," I order, reaching to the back of her head and pulling her hair tie free, leaving her locks tumbling across her shoulders. The urge gets the better of me. My face drops to the masses of blonde at her neck and I inhale, giving myself a hint of what I've got to look forward to once I've seen to business.

"On my own?" she asks, bringing her hands to my shoulders and digging her nails in. I groan, blood rushing to my cock.

"Be waiting in my bed in ten minutes," I demand, ripping myself away. "The towels are on the shelf." I back away and she pouts, her big eyes full of disappointment. "Ten minutes," I reiterate, turning and walking away from her. It's a challenge, but I won't relax and enjoy her until I've cleared a few things up.

Striding through to my living space, I yank my tie from my neck and shrug my jacket off, throwing them on the couch as I pass. I drop into my chair and pull my phone from my pocket, dialing Lucinda as I unfasten my top button.

"I was just going to call you," she greets me.

"Why?"

"We hacked Logan's e-mail."

"We had his e-mails," I point out, frowning down the line. "He gave us access."

"Not to this one. He chose not to give us this one. Any clues why?"

"I fucking knew it." My lip curls. "He *is* hiding something."

"Yes. He received an e-mail two days ago. Unknown IP address and account untraceable. The e-mail was deleted from the server, but I can tell you that it had an attachment."

I sit up a little in my chair. "What was attached?"

"I can't confirm that, but the untraceable IP address is ringing alarm bells, as well as the swift deletion from the server. Logan called and confirmed your contract is terminated. I pointed out the photos that arrived by Royal Mail and the ones you found on Camille's car earlier. He said his personal security team is closing in on the source of the threats. I don't believe him."

"Neither do I." I take a deep breath and recline in my chair, the side of my finger brushing across the stubble of my chin. "The threat's not gone, but he wants *me* gone?" I muse, hearing Lucinda hum down the line.

"Seems so. Now why would that be, Jake?"

"No idea." I cut off her intended line of conversation in its tracks. "Anything on the current wife?"

"Why are you asking me to look into his wife?"

"She's shifty. I don't like her."

"You think everyone is shifty!" She laughs. "But why you think his wife would threaten to harm her stepdaughter is beyond me."

"Just tell me what you have," I groan, my frustration building. All these dead ends we keep hitting. There has to be something somewhere that tells me something!

"I have a name for the guy you sent me a picture of. Simon Sanders. He's Logan's lawyer. His *divorce* lawyer."

"Logan's wife is having an affair with his divorce lawyer?" I ask, stunned. You couldn't write this shit.

"Yep. And by the looks of it, it's been going on for months. E-mails flying between them at a rapid rate. I won't make you blush and read them to you."

I laugh, amused. "Keep looking. I'll call you in the morning."

I hang up and dial another number. Logan answers swiftly, despite the fact that he's still undoubtedly entertaining guests at his cheating wife's birthday garden party. He must have been expecting my call. "Your security guys were quite keen to catch up with me when we left earlier." I cut straight to the chase.

"Yes, I wanted a private word with you, but you seemed in a bit of a hurry." There's an undercurrent of mistrust in his tone, telling me we're on the same page.

"You pay me to protect your daughter. I didn't like the intent on their faces."

"Their intent was to ask you to return for a few moments, so we could have a private conversation. Camille is in no danger from my security team."

Team? His security is a fucking joke. There could be an army of the fat fuckers. One man with half a brain could outwit them. "Everyone is a danger," I growl. "What did you want to talk about?"

"Your services are no longer required."

He says what I knew he would, but rather than hit him with what *I* know, namely an e-mail account that he has chosen not to share with us, I take a different angle. There's a reason why he's keeping that to himself, and I plan on getting to the bottom of it. "So I hear. May I ask why?"

"We're dealing with it," he says matter-of-factly, making my skin tingle with anger. The lying bastard. "As I expected, just rivals with a beef. All mouth, no trousers."

"Names?"

"Probably best I deal with it."

"Are you willing to risk Cami's safety based on *probably*?" I pray he says no, or so help me God, I'll run back to that fancy fucking mansion of his and gun him down.

"'Cami'?" He misses everything and homes in on my one mistake. *Shit!*

"Since when have you earned the privilege of calling my daughter by a nickname?"

His tone says it all. His impression of me, his disapproval. *Bring it on, Logan.*

I'm aware I'm talking to her father, but everything I know isn't making me want to shower him with respect. "Since *she* asked me to." I grind the words out. "As long as my subjects' requests don't put their life in danger, I'm all for accommodation, Mr. Logan." I can't fucking help myself, letting him read between the lines. "I don't think a simple wish for me to call her by her shortened name is a risk to her life, do you?" I want to add that her name sounds even better when it's falling from my mouth on a moan of pleasure. When I'm driving my cock into her, firm and deep. I want to. But I don't. Because that would be vindictive and serve no purpose other than confirming what he thinks he knows.

I realize the importance of knocking him off the scent. It's hard when I'm seething on the inside, knowing that he's not being honest about his daughter's protection. I need to rein myself in. He's willing to put Cami at risk in an attempt to keep me away from her? I fear that's the crux of it. Does he realize who he is dealing with? I'm no pathetic prep boy with a drug habit. Nor will I be paid off, not for all the money in the world. For the first time in his life, I'm going to make Trevor Logan feel weak and powerless. And I'm going to fucking enjoy it.

"Whatever my daughter wants," he mumbles quietly, making my lip curl.

"Whatever Camille wants," I reply. "I'll relieve *myself* of duty when I have concrete evidence that Cami's no longer at risk. I have a clean sheet, Logan. It's why you hired me, remember?" I hang up, resisting adding on the end that I'm about to go and give his daughter what she *really* wants.

Me.

I've also resisted advising the pompous arsehole that his wife is getting what *she* wants from his divorce lawyer. Information is pouring in now, but it takes me a nanosecond to decide it'd be safer not to tell Cami what I've learned, and while it goes against my instinct, I'm not going to beat myself up with guilt. Logan's bribe of Cami's ex, his wife's infidelity, the secret e-mail account—it's all ammo I can use in a war that I don't plan on losing.

Chucking my phone onto my desk, I kick my feet up and rest my head on the back of my chair. For the first time today, I feel relaxed, despite all of the revelations. Because she's here. With me. It's been a long, draining day. I can think of a wonderful way to end it on a high.

I stand and walk over to my drinks cabinet, catching a whiff of the long-lost scent of Jack on my way. I haven't had a drink in weeks, and I would never usually while on the job. But my job isn't usually within the safe confines of my apartment. I grab a glass, pour a healthy dose, and bring it to my lips, inhaling. Oh, that smells good. I knock it back and slam the glass down, letting the burn of the liquor heat me through on its way to my stomach.

Then I start unbuttoning my shirt as I prowl toward my bathroom, hearing the sound of water pouring over her naked body. I shrug off my shirt and let it fall from my hands before starting on the fly of my trousers, stopping at my bedroom door to push them from my legs and remove my shoes. Once I'm naked, I pad on bare feet toward the bathroom, the rush of water sounding louder until I'm on the edge of the steam-ridden room. I walk quietly to the shower, searching through the fog, until I'm a foot away from the glass door.

Her back is to me, her willowy body drenched and calling. I'm certain I could just stand here all night and watch her quietly as she runs her hands all over her skin, her head dropped back, accepting the water beating down on her face. Her blond hair is sopping and stuck to her back, skimming her gorgeous, pert arse, and her hands come up, bracing on the tiles before her. My erection lunges, desperate for me to take her.

I open the door and watch as her shoulders jump a little. She knows I'm here. My lips part, and I psych myself up for the pleasure I'm about to take. I scan her back as she removes her hands from the wall, her delicate chin coming to her shoulder, giving me her profile. She doesn't give me her eyes, though. She doesn't need to. Her body is singing to me, calling me to take her as much as my dripping cock is.

Her fragility should render me petrified of touching her. But I can't break her. She's too strong, and when we connect, I feel that strength growing for reasons I can't fathom. She feeds off me as much as I feed off her. She wants me. Maybe a little naively, but I've forbidden myself to question my motives for holding back on information that might change her mind. Here and now, there's a very real danger in the form of her corrupt father, and protecting Cami from him is my priority. It's not only my paid duty to protect this woman. It's my life's mission.

I reach forward and take her hair, gently gathering it into my fist and moving it to the side so I can see the full length of her perfect spine. She keeps her profile in my view, her mouth falling open as she takes what I've gathered and pulls it down her front, helping me. My fingertips drift through the air and come to rest at the base of her neck, the light pressure causing her to push her breasts forward, bowing her back.

The animal in me shouts for me to slam her into the wall and take what she's willing to give, but the growing softness of my heart forbids it. Every woman I've had in this apartment has been fucked. Hard, fast, and with no consideration for their pleasure. Cami isn't going to be one of those faceless women.

Lightly and slowly, knowing what it will do to her, I draw a perfect straight line down her back, licking my lips as I go, hearing the increased rate of her breathing. It's like a drug. An addictive drug. The tip of one finger reaches the tiny indentation at the top of her arse and circles, before I spread my palm and cup a cheek possessively. She jerks and slams her hands back into the wall, a small cry permeating the air.

I move in, unable to keep my distance any longer, my wet chest merging with her back. Her soft skin slips teasingly against mine as my hardness wedges itself into her lower back, forcing us closer, making me relinquish my hold of her arse. It's no great loss when we're touching everywhere. The flesh of her neck glistens up at me, and I dip down, licking across it, my palms finding her breasts and blanketing them.

"What would you like me to do to you, Camille?" I murmur against her skin, forcing her forward into the wall until she's trapped under my body.

She cranes her neck, nuzzling into my face until she finds my lips. The force of her kiss is mind-blanking. "Do what you want. Take what you want." Her tongue rolls over the words perfectly, pushing them deep down into my chest. I feel them sear my heart and bring another small part of me back to life.

My rapacious growl rumbles from the pit of my stomach and erupts, echoing through the confines of my shower. I spin her to face me and reach behind her thighs, yanking her up my body and slamming her back into the wall. She gasps and squirms, wriggling against the tiles as she grapples at my shoulders. The slippery movements do nothing more than increase my hunger for her, and I'm thinking she knows that. If I were in a teasing mood, I'd prolong the whole episode, make her beg, just to get a thrill out of knowing how much she wants me. But my own desperation to rid today of the trials we've faced is too powerful for me to hold back. I jack her up, level myself, and let her sink onto my cock.

The sensation of her wet pussy surrounding me does exactly what I knew it would. My mind is wiped of everything except Cami. She is all I see, all I feel. She belongs to me, every piece of her spirit, her body, and her heart. I'll cherish it all with everything I have. Let it be known, as God is my witness, I'll tear apart anyone who tries to take her away from me, be it her ex-boyfriend, her father, or an unknown threat. Blood will be shed, and I will show no remorse for the carnage I create along the way.

Amen.

I withdraw, savoring every second, and then slowly and precisely drive back into her, pushing her up the wall on a disjointed cry. I have every intention of extending our pleasure long into the night, until she's physically exhausted and I can carry her to my bed and lay her down. Knowing she wants that, too, is making it all very easy to take my time with her. I find her swollen lips and kiss her gently, rolling my tongue slowly, exploring her mouth deliberately. Her moans feed my purpose, her hands skating my shoulders, working their way to my neck and holding on as she returns my kiss with equal passion and intent. My hips are rolling, grinding, searching for the innermost part of her, and with each plunge, it becomes more difficult to resist release. With each retreat, my cock pulses harder. Holding onto my control is easy when I see that she's as lost in the moment as I am.

I'm not ready for this to end yet.

I surprise myself when I pull free of her on another retreat, my hips trembling, telling me to find her warmth again. Yet I don't. Instead, I push her legs down and let her find her feet, steadying her, before I crouch and look up at her, kissing the inside of her thigh.

"Oh God!" She grabs my hair and tugs, wrestling with me as I work my mouth up to her core. Her entrance is wide open, exposed and swollen.

"Hmmm." I lick a firm stroke up her center, nibbling on her twitching clit as I pass. Shit, she tastes divine.

"Jake!" She starts to shake before me, vibrating against the tiles.

I could make her come in a second if I keep my mouth here, yet knowing how much satisfaction I'll win by doing that isn't enough. So I continue the hard lash of my tongue, up to her stomach, her torso, and onto her breasts, the sweet tips like dark pebbles, each vying for my attention. I indulge them both, dividing my time, the water pounding my back as Cami continues to tug my hair.

"You want me back inside, angel?" I ask, lightly biting down on one erect nub, dragging it through my teeth until it pops free. "Tell me, Cami. Tell me where you want me."

Her head drops and she pants, desperation rampant on her gorgeous, fresh face. "I want this." She reaches down and grabs my cock. I gasp. "I want this inside me."

I have no clue how the fuck she manages it, but she pushes me to my arse. Then she's on my lap, pressing into my shoulders a second later, forcing me to my back. I follow her lead, smiling like crazy on the inside, and lay down on the shower floor, immune to the hardness beneath me. She lifts on her knees and watches me as she reaches between her legs and reclaims my dick.

Fuck me, she's going to ride me, and while that strips some of my control, I'm more than happy with my new view. My arms come up over my head as she takes her sweet time guiding me to her, her mouth lax, her eyes hooded. This right here has just taken first position in my most favorite views of all time. Her breasts, her face, and if I look down, my cock entering her, are all within sight. Holy shit, I'm in heaven.

She sinks down, forcing sharp breaths from me and a need to resist throwing my hips up and slamming into her. Let her have her way. Let her possess my body like she does my mind.

"Oh fuck!" I look down and see myself half-submerged, tinkering on the edge of full penetration. She's not without a powerful reaction herself. Her legs are trembling, trying to hold herself above me, extending my torturous delight. "All the way, angel. Take me all the way."

She gasps, telling me the position is making it harder for her to take me fully. "One second," she pants, clenching her eyes shut just as she releases her muscles and drops the rest of the way.

I buck on a roar, and Cami screams, the noise overwhelming the hammering of the water. My hands shoot up and grab the tops of her thighs, holding her still. She's not moved yet and this is already too much to cope with. One stroke and I might explode. I'm not done yet!

"Easy, angel," I say, the sheer wonderful sensations making me drowsy. "Take your time."

She groans, slapping her hands into my abs, her head dropping. "I can do it," she says, rounding her small hips, sucking in air. I force myself to remain still. It takes every fucking scrap of strength I have and more. Then she circles again, and I choke, digging my fingers into her thighs. "Oh God, yes!" she cries, hitting me with another rotation.

My world tumbles into a decadent bliss that will never be rivaled. She finds strength from somewhere and drives on, her head tossed back, her screams constant. Never before have I experienced anything like it, and never again am I likely to, unless it's with this heaven-sent angel connected to me, looking like she's on the cusp of explosion.

Just as her arms stiffen, forcing her palms into me, the blood swirling in my cock rushes to the very tip, making my hips jerk, taking on a mind of their own.

"Cami." I try to warn her, try to tell her that I've reached the point of no return, but then she wails, landing me with wide, hungry eyes. She's nearly there, too. "Oh, yeah," I choke, starting to work her motions by shoving her thighs back and forth, pushing us both on, stimulating more feeling.

"Jake!"

I see her mouth open and lip-read her yelling my name, but all I can hear is my blood rushing through my veins as my arousal swells, jerks and bursts within her, the rolls of release coming and coming until the intensity of it renders me incapable of admiring her fighting her way through her own climax.

I close my eyes, feeling her fall onto my chest in an exhausted heap. My arms find some energy to encase her, my heart beats wildly against her chest.

I'll pick her up soon and take her to my bed. But until then, she's good held tightly in my arms. It's where I plan on keeping her.

CHAPTER 20

CAMI

My last memory is the feel of Jake's chest against my cheek and the water hitting my back. Somewhere between then and now, he's moved us to his bed. I don't remember when. I must have been unconscious, knocked out by exhaustion and pure contentment. Sex with Jake has been overwhelming every single time, but last night in the shower was on another level. I've never been taken to those heights before. I've never been made to feel so needed and wanted. It was all-consuming.

I stare across the planes of Jake's chest, tucked into his side, our legs a tangle of limbs, half-covered by the sheets. His arm is holding me in place, his head slightly dropped to the side. His heart is throbbing an even, steady beat under my ear. He's asleep. Not snoozing lightly like always; half-awake and aware. He's deep in sleep. It's the first time I've seen him looking so at ease.

I walk my fingers up his chest, unable to resist feeling him. His jaw is shaded with his usual stubble, his lips full and parted as my fingertips drift onto them lightly. He doesn't flinch, his eyes still closed. I just watch him, wondering what today might bring.

Should I brave a visit to my father and tell him about me and Jake? Or should I just call him? Or maybe I just don't tell him at all and run away with Jake? When I decided to make my excuses so I could leave my father's party, I knew that if I did, it was going to change my life forever.

Jake is probably the only man on earth not intimidated by my father. It's both a comfort and a worry. Dad sees my purpose as just another business transaction. And Jake has dared to get in his way. Whatever the fallout, it's going to be immense.

But the comfort of having Jake by my side offers some security.

I sigh, snuggling back into his chest.

"That was a weary sigh." His sleepy voice breaks into my thoughts, and his lids flutter open, revealing dark, concerned eyes.

"Just wondering about a few things."

He moves lethargically, pulling himself down the bed and onto his side so our faces are level and close. His hand on my hip, he leans forward and kisses the tip of my nose. "You look inconceivably gorgeous this morning," he says, and I smile. "Tell me what you're wondering."

"About my father. Do you really think he had Pete and Grant follow us?"

He watches me for a few moments, a fond smile on his lips. "Yes, I do."

My lips purse. Since my dad has told me that he's gotten to the bottom of the threats, there could be only one other reason for him to send them after us. "Because he thinks we're..." I drift off, letting my eyes fall to his chin. I'm not sure how to word it. I can't tell him I've fallen in love with him. Mostly because I still haven't figured out how Jake sees *us*. How he feels. Apart from having a need to protect me that goes beyond his call of duty, what else does he feel? How deep is this for him?

Grabbing my arm, he hauls me up, manipulating my body to where he wants me, straddling his stomach. I go without protest, my mind a fuzz of thoughts. He brings my hands to his mouth and kisses my knuckles. It's a loving gesture, and my thoughts distort further. The last time he let his personal emotions compromise his judgment, he said the consequences were grave. But I'm too scared to ask what happened. Or how it's all connected to the woman in the photo. It's obviously a painful story, but I've figured out one thing. He must have loved her. I feel terrible for hating that thought.

"Like it or not, angel, your father isn't going to be happy. I'm prepared for that, and you should be, too."

"I am," I murmur, a little relieved that Jake and I seem to be thinking along the same lines. "Though when you say you're *prepared*, what do you mean?" That's a worry, too. I couldn't allow or accept Jake going maniac on my father. I shudder, flashbacks of yesterday popping into my mind when he annihilated a crowd of grown men.

"He's going to try to stop me from seeing you. I won't let that happen."

"How?" He's being too vague. I need details to fully prepare.

His lip tips at the corner a little, as if he knows what I'm thinking. "I won't hurt your father."

"Promise me."

"I promise."

"Thank you." Massively relieved, I lower my chest onto his and snuggle into him, feeling the softness of his bristle rub into my temple.

Jake sighs, a long smooth sigh, his hand cupping the back of my head and holding me to him.

We relax into a lovely cuddle, and it's all so very peaceful, until a subtle bang from beyond his bedroom door makes Jake's relaxed body tense beneath mine. He stills and seems to stop breathing, and I start to push my way out of his embrace, but get tugged back down and held prisoner in his arms. His sudden alertness and the wary vibes make it impossible not to panic a little.

"Jake, what's the matter?"

More sounds ring out, this time a collection of bangs, and this time louder. I'm removed from Jake's body in a heartbeat. "Stay here," he orders harshly, bolting up from the bed.

I fly back against the headboard, pulling the covers up my body, like the pathetic thin sheets can protect me from whatever's gotten him so agitated. His whole body is shaking with tension, and his jaw is tight. I've seen him behave like this before. When he saw a threat. He reaches under the mattress, keeping his eyes on the door in his bedroom, and pulls out a gun.

"Holy shit!" I scramble back some more, my eyes rooted to the weapon that always looks so comfortable in his grasp. Like an extension of his arm. "Jake—"

"Quiet, Cami!" he hisses, slowly pulling back a section on the gun. It clicks as he paces toward the bedroom door.

Even completely naked he looks lethal, every muscle on his back and in his legs poised to strike. He's holding the gun steady by his thigh, his finger on the trigger. He takes a quick peek around the door frame, then disappears from view, and I'm left on the bed, shaking and struggling for breath.

Part of me is demanding I go after him. Part of me is telling me I need to stay put. Part of me is ordering me to run away. I feel small and useless, huddled on the bed, the silence killing me as I wait for...I don't know. What am I waiting for? Shouts? Gunshots?

"Fuck!" Jake roars. My heart leaps into my throat and bursts, choking me. But I can't move. Fear has frozen me in place. I hear a collection of curses and a few thuds...and then it goes silent.

"Jake!" I scream, my body coming to life and catapulting itself to the end of the bed, the sheets left behind in my haste. There's no reply, and I hover on the brink of total meltdown, not knowing what to do for the best. "Jake!"

The door flies open and I jump back. It takes me a few seconds to focus, and a few more to see that the silhouette in the doorway isn't Jake's.

It's a woman.

"Oh, this is just fucking perfect!" she yells, waving an accusing hand up and down in front of me.

Cautiously I move back, collecting the sheets to cover myself and assessing what I'm faced with. She's short but looks formidable, and her black hair's cut into a severe pixie style. She's wearing a grey skirt-suit, a white shirt beneath the blazer. Who is this?

Jake appears behind her, towering above, his shoulders and head clearing her tiny frame. He looks pensive. I don't like it. "I nearly blew your fucking head off, Lucinda," he grumbles, flicking me a worried stare.

Lucinda? Who the hell is Lucinda?

"I wish you had!" she snaps, swinging around and coming face to face with Jake's nipples. She huffs, steps back, and looks up, while Jake looks at her a little tiredly. "Because *that*"—she throws an arm back in the general direction of the bed, or in the general direction of *me*— "makes me want to shoot my own brains out!"

I gawk, offended, and Jake rolls his eyes. "Don't let me stop you," he mutters, turning and wandering across to a chair. He's still totally naked and completely unbothered by it. And this Lucinda person, whoever she is, isn't fazed by the mass of naked muscle, either. He pulls on some boxers and strides out of the room.

She starts stomping after him, her anger tangible. "Heads will roll, Jake! The whole fucking agency will suffer!"

Ooohhh . . .

I'm beginning to understand what her issue is. She's a colleague, and she's worried about the repercussions of mine and Jake's involvement. My father's wrath is something I'm well aware could cause problems for Jake and the agency he works for.

"And just because you couldn't keep your cock out of a hole!" she rants on. "Any fucking hole! If it has a pulse and a fucking hole, it's good to go, right?"

I recoil, disgusted, as I remain on the bed listening to Lucinda's tirade about Jake's stupidity, but Jake doesn't argue, doesn't breathe a word. Then it falls quiet, and I wonder, probably reasonably, whether he might have strangled her. I get off the bed with the sheets wrapped around me and creep toward the door, listening carefully for any signs of choking. But when I reach the threshold of Jake's colossal living space, I see them both hunched over a desk that's sitting in front of the floor-to-ceiling window, looking at a computer screen. Lucinda is very much alive.

I cough lightly, indicating my presence, and they both swing round. Jake gives me a little smile, while Lucinda shakes her head in despair.

"Have you met Lucinda, Cami?" Jake asks dryly, indicating the woman next to him. "She's dead friendly."

I'm halfway between smiling and trembling, unsure whether I should be teasing her like Jake seems so comfortable doing. "Hi." I hold up an awkward hand, and she sighs, wandering over.

"Pleasure," she says, taking my hand and shaking lightly, before pausing and looking down at our joined palms. She frowns and pulls away, looking at her hand before wiping it on her skirt.

Jake laughs loudly, while I'm a bit put out. Cheeky cow!

Lucinda ignores Jake's amusement and holds up a magazine in front of my face, too closely for me to focus. "If Daddy suspects anything, then I guess he'll have it confirmed soon."

I step back and home in on the top left-hand corner of the page. There's a picture of me draped across Jake's arms. As he carried me out of the bar like a hero, my face buried against his big chest. I shoot a look to where he's standing at his desk, finding him lost in thought.

"Let me read you a section, shall I?" Lucinda says, glancing down at the print. "'London socialite Camille Logan, daughter of business tycoon Trevor Logan, is always a step ahead. The leggy blonde, who models for the likes of Karl Lagerfeld and Christian Dior, might have just taken job perks to a new level with her tall, dark, handsome body-guard.'" She looks at Jake. "That's you, by the way." She coughs and goes on. "'The pair were spotted—'"

"Okay!" I snap, getting worked up on Jake's behalf. "I get it."

Lucinda drops the magazine and looks at me as if she could be my father. I could slap her for it. "Do you really?"

I scowl at her. I know what she's thinking. She's thinking the same thing everyone thinks when they read the shit that's printed about me. They have that preconception of what sort of person I should be based on the bollocks they read. This woman thinks I'm just a stupid little girl who's fallen in love with her bodyguard. Only one part of that statement is true, but I have no desire to waste my breath on putting her straight on the other. Like the rest of the world who think they know me, she can go fuck herself. I'm tired of trying to justify myself. "Excuse me, I need to go file my nails." I swivel and walk away, boiling on the inside.

I toss the sheets on the bed and head for the shower, resisting punching the door frame on my way through it. I could burst with fury.

How fucking dare she?

Slamming the shower on, I stamp my way in and viciously scrub at my skin, trying to scrub away the anger and resentment at the same time. He puts his dick in holes. Any holes. She thinks I'm just another hole for him. My teeth clench.

I must be the cleanest I've ever been by the time I'm done, but I feel no better. Snatching a towel, I scrub at my body some more until I'm bone dry and my skin is tingling sore. Then I stare out the window across the docklands, my stomach sinking further and further by the second. Damn my father. Damn everything.

"Angel?" His soft call drifts into the room and swirls around in my head. But I don't look at him, choosing to pull my towel up and tuck it in under my arms instead, busying myself.

"Has Cruella gone?" I ask curtly.

"Yes." He's pensive. "Why are you so mad?"

I give up the landscape of London and face him, but I'm unable to appreciate my new view. "I don't want to be just another meaningless fuck to you." I only meant to think that, but the words are out with no chance of being retracted now. His sexual past isn't any of my business, and even if I thought it was, I wouldn't want to know.

Understanding surfaces on his face, and I close my eyes, full of regret. "And there we have it," he mutters, the sound of his bare feet padding toward me.

I hate myself for saying what I did. Mainly because I sound needy and insecure, and that's the last thing I want to portray. Even to Jake. Even if I really do feel like I need him.

His fingertip meets my chin and he applies the lightest of pressure, encouraging me to lift my head. "Look at me."

I reluctantly open my eyes, finding Jake's dark gaze soft and reassuring. It only serves to make me feel worse, because he understands me so well.

He smiles. "I'm not going to tell you that it isn't true. I'm not proud of it. I screwed women. Nothing more, nothing less."

"Stop." I look away from him, hating the thought of anyone taking the pleasure I get from him.

"No, I won't." He fully grabs my chin, a silent but firm indication of what he wants. It kills me, but I comply, looking him in the eyes. "When I couldn't distract myself with work, that's all I had. They were faceless women, angel." Dipping, he pushes his scratchy cheek into mine and whispers in my ear. "I see you."

His sincerity can't be mistaken for anything less than that. I hear it, I feel it. But what about the woman in the picture? She clearly meant more to him. And she isn't faceless. She has a face, and it's in that photograph. Yet I want her to remain faceless to me. Like she never existed.

Wearily and on a sigh, I nod and promise myself never to let my mind wander there again. I circle his waist and hug him.

"That's better." He lifts me from my feet—my towel falling from my body—and carries me into the bedroom. He takes me down to the bed and kisses his way up my body until he finds my lips. I'm indulged and worshipped, his mouth consuming mine as his fingers creep closer to my thighs, my insides quickly unfurling with anticipation.

"I think we should stay in bed all day," he mumbles around my lips, kissing his way to my ear and dipping his tongue inside.

The muffled sound, his hot breath penetrating my hearing, all do a perfect job of ridding me of the last lingering remnants of aggravation and worry. His suggestion is fine by me. The longer I have to work myself up to facing my father, the better. Until then, I'm happy to let Jake work me up, all day, all night...forever.

"Hmmmm..." I let my mind go blank and my body come alive under his attention. It's blissful, his lips all over me, his body sliding against mine. I feel his cock swell against my thigh.

"Jesus, angel, I just can't take enough of you."

Bang!

"Jake!" Lucinda's voice, followed by a loud thwack, yanks us both from our euphoria, as if we could have fallen into ice water. Jake growls and is up from the bed in a second, abandoning me.

"I thought you said she'd left," I mutter, annoyed.

"She did."

"Jake!" Lucinda's rankled yell rings out once more.

"For fuck's sake, what?" Jake shouts, stalking away.

I roll onto my side, disliking her that little bit more. If she's brought another magazine loaded with snaps of us, then I'll take great pleasure in shoving it up her arse. That's if Jake doesn't get there first.

Sighing my frustration, I drink in Jake's naked back as he paces away. But my desire immediately turns to worry when he freezes in the doorway, every muscle in his back going hard.

I'm off the bed like a shot, my legs working before my brain, running over to join him and find out what's gotten his attention. I just make it to him when he steps back without warning and I collide with his back. His arm comes up and extends behind him, keeping me back.

"What's up?" I ask, trying to see around his big body, not giving the fact that I'm naked a second thought. "Jake!" I muscle past him with some effort and make my way to his side, enough to see, but enough to still be safely concealed by his body. "Oh my God!" I gasp as I take it all in, my eyes jumping from one place to another, trying to make some sense of it.

I can't.

Jake hauls me into his side. His skin is electric, shocking me. "What the fuck is this?" he asks, his eyes fixed firmly in one place.

On my father.

He's standing by Jake's couch, looking worried but determined. He's taking me in, his eyes refusing to fall below my neck. My heart sinks as I cling to Jake, as if I fully expect my dad to physically drag me away. He'll have to. I'm not moving.

"You immoral arsehole," he says, landing Jake with a contemptuous glare. "I trusted you to keep her safe and you take advantage of her?"

I clench my eyes shut, everything inside of me deflating. "He didn't take advantage of me," I grate, feeling the anger Jake just chased away returning. I'm a grown woman. I have my own mind and my own life.

"Quiet, Cami," Jake whispers, forcing my eyes open and up. He's still staring Dad down, still unwavering in his death glare. Jake looks set to charge, and part of me is willing that he does.

Casting a look around the room, I take in the rest of the occupants. Lucinda is looking inconvenienced more than anything, flanked on each side by Grant and Pete.

"How did you find out where I live?" Jake asks, flipping a glare to Lucinda.

She shakes her head. "I've already had your gun pointed at me this morning," she mutters indignantly to Jake. "I didn't fancy being sandwiched between these two oafs." She tosses Pete and Grant a filthy look. "They must have followed me."

"Don't think you can outsmart me," my dad snaps. "Cami, get your clothes on. You're coming with me."

"No." My answer is quick and automatic. Never.

"Don't push me, young lady!"

Young lady? Like a child who can be told what to do? I stand my ground, something I've never had a problem doing with my father, except now he looks the angriest I've ever seen him. It just makes me dig my heels in more. I move behind Jake, keeping my hold of him. "You'll have to rip me away."

"Pete!" my dad orders with a gesture of his hand, and his arsehole of a bodyguard starts pacing toward me. Is he serious?

Jake steps back, taking me with him. "Touch her and I will kill you," he breathes, calm as can be, yet I can feel the rage coursing through his veins like a dangerous poison.

Pete pulls to a stop, his hesitance clear. He's wise. I've seen what Jake's hands are capable of. I've watched him spiral into a destructive madman and go apeshit all over a group of five men, all comparable in size to Dad's security. Pete isn't going to present him with much of a problem.

"Jake," Lucinda pipes in, giving him a cautious look.

"Listen to her, Sharp," Dad says, stepping forward. "Is a meaningless roll around in the sheets with a woman worth losing your job for? Your credibility? Quit while you're ahead. My Camille is too good for you, and you know it."

I gawp in shock at the words coming from my father's mouth. The malicious, selfish bastard!

"And what about your daughter's safety?" Jake asks. "Is that worth compromising because of your pathetic need to control her?"

"I know what's best for my daughter. As of now, Camille is no longer your concern. Walk away from her and I will not destroy you." Dad cocks his head and raises his brows, watching Jake closely.

"Why are you doing this?" I ask, feeling my control slipping the more my father persists with his relentless threats.

He looks at me, an edge of sympathy marring his round, crabby face. "Because I love you, Camille. Everything I do is because I love you and I want the best for you."

"How the hell would you know what's best for me?" I yell, my entire body quaking with frustration and despair. "You're on your third wife! All you want is a trophy on your arm. A good pair of tits until it all goes south and you find a replacement! Someone who won't question you and take the money you shower them with! You don't want what's best for me! You want what's best for your fucking business!"

"Do you think you're not a trophy to him!" Dad roars, flinging his arm out at Jake. "A score for a man who's clinging onto his ego after being thrown out of the SAS!"

I withdraw, staggered by my father's low tactics. He's been looking into Jake? "You know nothing about him!"

"I know enough!"

"How dare you!" I scream. "You have no right to dictate who I see. What I do!"

Jake swings around and pushes me back into his room, his hands finding my face and holding tightly.

"Shhhh," he hushes me, his lips pressing a kiss to my forehead.

The tender compassion makes me break down completely, and I'm crying uncontrollably as I cling to his forearms.

"Calm down," he whispers.

I'm staggered by his self-control. I know the agony he shoulders, the self-abhorrence and regret. His parents died at the hands of terrorists. Innocent people caught up in the war. He needed to play a part in stopping them. No one can strip away Jake's efforts or the danger he put himself in to protect his country, no matter how badly it turned out for him.

"He doesn't know what he's talking about," I sob, being pulled forward into his arms. "Don't listen to him. He's a hateful bastard."

"I want you to get dressed," he says, nuzzling down, pushing his face into mine and raining kisses all over my face. "Get dressed and I'll go talk to him."

"No." I refuse point blank. "He'll never listen. Just throw him out." I'm sniffling over my words, my breath catching constantly in my throat.

Jake grabs my face and pulls it up, gazing down at me with nothing but adoration. "Do you trust me, angel?" he asks, throwing me for a loop.

But my answer is still dead easy. "More than anything."

He nods, swallowing, and releases me. Walking over to a chair in the corner of his room, he takes some jeans off the back and yanks them on, then pulls a T-shirt over his head before slipping his feet into some leather boots. He says nothing more to me and walks out of his room, closing the door behind him. I stand there, desperately trying to fight off the dread that's engulfing me, not being able to stop myself from fearing that Jake might not come back.

Chapter 21

JAKE

I saw the look in Logan's eyes when he cocked his head at me. That look told me he knows. My military history, the shrink reports, the statements—everything is confidential and stored on a secure system somewhere in an impenetrable building. If he can get access to that, there's no telling what else he's found out. I'm not having him using it as ammo to drive a wedge between Cami and me. She knows some things, but she doesn't know everything. Not yet. I need redemption. I need to fix too many things and accept myself before I can expect Camille to accept me. All of me, every dark, dirty, sinful piece.

I leave her in my bedroom, out of earshot, and quietly lock the door behind me, for no other reason than if this turns nasty, I don't want her in the firing line. I enter my living space, taking in every inch—what's positioned where, who's standing where, while mentally plotting my moves.

I look across to Lucinda, seeing her holding her iron composure, but I've known this woman for many years, and I know when she's anxious. She's anxious now. Not because she feels threatened, but because she knows as well as I do that this pond scum has the power and influence to wreak havoc at the agency.

"She can go." I nod toward her, making sure I don't make it sound like a request. There's hesitance in Lucinda's face, but none in Logan's. He nods and she shakes her head, heading out without a word.

As soon as the door closes behind her, I speak. "There's nothing casual about my feelings for your daughter," I start, kicking plan A into action. I'll only hurt him if I absolutely have to. I hope I don't have to. Logan's many things, but he isn't stupid. Taking me on would be stupid. He might surprise me yet. Voicing whatever he might have found out about me would be stupid, and I guarantee it will tip me over the edge. That would be a shame. So far I've managed to keep a lid on the violent beast that's so desperately trying to break free. "The sooner you realize that your daughter isn't some damsel in distress, the quicker we can clear this up."

Right on cue, Cami starts banging on the door. "Hey! Why's the door locked?"

No, there's no damsel in there.

Logan keeps his narrowed stare on me and sniffs, giving me a hint of how easy and clean this is going to be. Not easy and clean at all. "Walk away and I won't tarnish her belief that you're a hero. I'll also keep the scandal of the agency's top bodyguard bedding a young subject from public knowledge."

I look at him, my head cocking. "You think you can keep me away from her with threats? I don't give a fuck about the agency. My purpose goes beyond that now."

"How much?" Logan asks, while Cami bangs relentlessly on the door.

"Are you fucking kidding me? You think you can buy me off like that lowlife drug addict?" I ask, disgusted.

Logan definitely flinches. He didn't know that I knew about the payoff. He might have shit on me, but I have shit on him, too.

I walk forward, ignoring the two fat twats moving in from both sides. I'll floor them in a fucking heartbeat. "Get the fuck out of my apartment."

"Not without my daughter." Logan moves back and looks over his shoulder to the door.

I come to a stop, because I can tell he's not gauging the distance that he's got to run and escape. Plus, a noise has just rung out from the elevator shaft. "Ah, the police," he says casually. "It was really rather brutal what you did to poor Sebastian Peters."

My frown is unavoidable, but the pieces slowly start to fall into place.

He smirks at me. "You can't see her if you're locked up."

Motherfucker!

Pete and Grant move in fast, one grabbing me on each side. I don't bother wasting energy wrestling them off. I let them seize me, let them think they've won.

"How much have you paid Sebastian Peters to press charges against me, you immoral fucker?" I ask, my lip curling. "He physically hurt her!" My anger is getting the better of me, rising fast. "He hit her!" I roar.

Logan frowns, and I remember…he doesn't know that part. To him, Sebastian Peters is simply an addict who dragged his daughter down a temporary dark path. He didn't know his daughter's ex knocked her about a few times, and Cami didn't want him to. Logan's face straightens out, quickly telling me that this news isn't going to make a bit of difference.

"Good-bye, Sharp." His tone is drenched in victory.

Pete and Grant tighten their hold of me, like they think I might start struggling.

There's no need to struggle.

My bedroom door starts jumping off its hinges from the force of Cami's bangs. "Let me out!"

I keep calm and still for a few seconds, just enough time for Logan's "security" to relax a little. Then I throw my head back, catching Pete clean across the nose. His scream comes after he's released me, the pain of his broken nose taking a few startled seconds to register in his bewildered mind.

I hear him stagger away and before Grant can react, I grab his wrist, twist it, dip and throw myself forward, hauling the lump over my back and launching him into the air. I keep hold of his wrist, watching his body twist awkwardly as he meets the ground, the clean crack of his shoulder ringing through the air.

"Whoa!" Logan stumbles back, his hands coming up in defense.

But as I'm about to claim my final prey and shred him, the sound of the elevator reminds me of the more imminent threat. The police.

Fuck!

I look at Logan, my lips twisting. "If one hair on her head is damaged before I make it back to her, I'll kill you with my bare hands."

"She's my little girl. You think I'd let anyone hurt her?"

His words stand for shit, but I haven't got time to fuck about. "Your daughter is still in danger and you know it. You haven't been telling me everything and I'm going to find out why."

The elevator doors rattle.

"You're going to wish you'd never met me, Logan." I break into a sprint and head for the only window that opens in my entire apartment.

* * *

So now I'm a wanted man, on the run from the fucking police.

Worse, I have no idea where Camille is. Her fucking phone is turned off, or it's been taken from her. If her father thinks I'll just go away, he's so wrong. I won't rest until I find out what the fuck is going on.

I go to the only place I have to go, and she'd best not give me a hard time about it. Lucinda throws the door open, her tiny frame encased in an oversized dressing gown and her petite face riddled with disdain. I push my way past her, ignoring it.

"Come right in," she says, condescending as hell.

I stomp over to her drinks cabinet and pour myself a healthy helping of Jack. "You led them to me. Quit your whining." I knock back my drink, praying for some calm in my shaking world.

"You let him take her?" The door slams and she joins me by the cabinet, placing a glass in front of me in an indication to pour.

"I didn't let him take her," I snarl. "The depraved prick paid her scumbag ex to press charges against me." I leave her glass empty and pour myself one more. Just one more. "The police turned up. I ran." I stalk away, this time sipping my drink as opposed to downing it, and put myself in front of her window.

"I'm sorry," Lucinda says, perplexed. "You've lost me. He paid her ex to press charges? For what?"

"The picture in the magazine," I breathe. "I was getting her away from her ex. I gave him a pair of black eyes. And probably broke his nose. And I might have stripped him of the ability to reproduce." I've done the world a fucking favor. I should get an award, not a sentence.

"You did *what*?" she yells, showing rare shock.

"Don't even." I turn and lift a finger to point at her. "He cornered her in the ladies' and hit her before tossing her to the ground like a piece of rubbish."

Lucinda wisely backs down, reaching for the hard stuff and pouring one for herself. "You know, none of this would have happened if you hadn't gotten emotionally involved. It's rule number one. And you're *you*, for crying out loud! Women love you for as long as it takes them to make you come. Then you piss them off and they hate you! What the fuck has changed?"

"Camille Logan," I breathe, letting my head fall back, my eyes searching for the heavens and a God I don't believe in. Someone needs to help me out. Lucinda's right. Emotion hasn't featured in my makeup for a long, *long* time. I can't blame her for being shocked. I'm Jake Sharp, for fuck's sake! Arsehole extraordinaire! I don't love, I screw.

My thoughts grind to a screeching halt and I physically recoil. Lucinda frowns at my sudden, unprovoked jerk, watching me as I rewind through my thoughts. When I find what I'm looking for, I double over and nearly throw up. Love? Camille Logan has a habit of reducing me to a pussy, and she's done it again.

Love.

Fucking love? Where the fuck did that come from? I start laughing in my bent position, while trying desperately to locate a logical reason for me using such a stupid word. I love her hair. I love her eyes. I love how she looks when she's lost in her thoughts. I love how strong, determined, and passionate she is. I love...

My amusement gets dowsed by more heaving.

I fucking love her.

"Jake?" Lucinda's hand rests on my shoulder, sending high-voltage electric shocks though my bloodstream. I straighten and jump back, away from her. There's alarm on her face and her hand hovers in midair where my shoulder was a moment ago. "You okay?"

"Fuck." I curse and slam my palms into the side of the drinks cabinet, dipping my head and fighting with my chaotic mind, trying to force it to straighten out.

You love her.

I feel so fucking stupid. And like I'm going mad. I love her—so fucking much—it's the only reason there is to explain the tatters my heart is in right now. I'm panicking, scared that I'm going to lose her.

"Jake, for fuck's sake!" Lucinda's impatient voice half pulls me from my mental breakdown.

I search her out, just so she can see the sincerity in my eyes. She's gonna need to see it. "I'm in love with her, Luce."

She gapes at me for a few moments before she finds her voice. "Oh, fucking hell," she whispers, knocking back her drink. "Oh, Jake."

Her words say it all. She's one of the only people on the planet who knows my personal history, as well as my professional one. She knows the magnitude of the situation I'm faced with. She knows what Camille must mean to me for me to put myself in this situation. "Yes," I agree. "Fucking hell."

"Does she know?" She's not talking about the fact that I love her, though I plan on making sure Camille knows how I feel the second I find her. Lucinda is talking about the thing that might stop Camille from returning my love. The thought cripples me.

"She knows I was in the SAS; she knows there was another woman and personal emotion had me relieved of duty." I find a chair and slump into it.

"But she doesn't know about..." She drifts off, knowing I can't face hearing the words.

I shake my head. How can I expect someone else to understand if I can't wrap my mind around it even now, four years later?

"Camille's father has been digging into me, too," I tell her.

"It's not censored information, Jake. If he wants to find out, he will. If he doesn't already know all about it."

"Camille's still in danger, Luce. Three days are up. They said time's up! I don't know what the fuck is going on, but I need to find out." Calm. I need to keep calm.

She nods, taking a deep breath. "Then we will," she asserts, heading for her study. "Get your arse in here, you lovesick pony."

I smile to myself and get to my feet, following her in. "Have you found out anything more?"

"Yes, and it's interesting," Lucinda pronounces, and I look over to find her lowering to see the screen of her laptop better.

"What?" I'm across the room to her before she can begin telling me.

"Logan's wife is pregnant."

"What?"

"Yep. Her GP records show a visit four weeks ago. And I bet it ain't Daddy Logan's."

"Oh, fuck."

"Indeed. She also popped in Selfridges on her way home from the doctor's office and bought a pair of Louboutins."

I look at her in utter amazement. "How the fuck do you find this shit out?"

She shrugs. "Who the fuck wears Louboutins when they're pregnant?"

I shake my head in despair, finding it hard to focus on anything except where Logan's taken Cami and what he's told her. I dread to think. He's a manipulating bastard, and though I know my angel has her own mind, the confusion she's going to be feeling now will be playing games with that. "Is any of this even fucking relevant?"

"I don't know! I'm looking into everything!"

"My relationship with Cami isn't the only reason he's sent me packing. What's he hiding? What the fuck was attached to the e-mail that was deleted?" I pull my phone from my pocket and dial Cami again.

It goes straight to voice mail and I curse my arse off. "What the fuck is going on?" I yell, getting more and more frustrated by the second as I stalk toward the door, thinking none of this shit actually matters to me. What matters is that I get Cami back and protect her from her father. He can sort the rest of the shit out himself, as long as I have Camille and she's safe. And to think he sees me as a risk to his daughter? His death is becoming more brutal by the second. "Keep an eye on that e-mail account."

"Jake, where are you going?" Lucinda chases after me, but I don't look back. Screw the agency. Screw my job. And screw the fucking police. "Don't do anything stupid, Jake!"

I laugh to myself. Stupid? I've fallen in fucking love. I couldn't be any more stupid than that.

CHAPTER 22

CAMI

I'm numb, dying slowly on the inside as I listen to my father reel off what's happened. Jake's gone. It doesn't make any sense. I was locked in that room for half an hour, banging to get free, and when Dad finally let me out, Pete and Grant looked worse for wear and Jake was nowhere to be found. What the hell happened?

"Let me take you home, my little star." Dad's arm comes up around me, and though the urge is there, I don't shrug him off. Quite honestly, I'm not sure what I should be doing. "You'll be safe with me." He starts to lead me from Jake's apartment, waving Pete and Grant ahead of us as we go.

I look at my father, my mind a mess of confusion, and see genuine concern on his face. Concern for me? He's my dad. There's no one in the world who I should feel safer with. Yet the fear in me isn't showing any signs of lessening. "Who are you keeping me safe from, Dad? Men you've bankrupted? Sebastian? Jake?"

"All of it, sweetheart." He hugs me into his side and kisses the top of my head. "I'm keeping you safe from all of it. He was no good for you, sweetheart. Too old, a quitter, and a failure. He realizes that now." We enter the elevator and Grant pulls the bars across with his good arm before turning and handing something to my father. A phone. *My* phone.

"No one is good enough for me," I murmur to myself, looking at the two large backs of the men in front of me. Jake would have them on the floor by now if he was here. He wouldn't let them take me.

So where is he?

"Give me my phone," I say to Dad as he slips it into his jacket pocket. He completely ignores my request, not even entertaining me with a fleeting glance. I frown at him as the elevator jolts and the ear-piercing screech of the sliding metal doors echoes throughout the derelict factory floor. I use my slight stagger into my father's round body to my advantage, slipping my hand into his jacket pocket and taking my phone as he steadies me.

One second I'm being escorted to my father's car, and the next I'm in a dead sprint, running toward the daylight on the other side of the factory, my phone in my fisted hand.

"Camille!" Dad roars.

I ignore him. My instincts are telling me to get away from my father—a man I should naturally feel safe with.

I burst into the daylight and quickly assess my surroundings, seeing nothing but more old factories, wasteland, and water. I look across the Thames as I run, finding the city too far away for comfort. It's only just across the water, but too far nevertheless.

"Damn it!" I curse, glancing over my shoulder when I hear the thunderous pounding of Pete and Grant following. Neither are built for speed, even when they're uninjured. But that comfort doesn't slow my pace. I keep running, feeling like my life is depending on it.

* * *

My lungs are burning by the time I make it to a river bus on the pier. The journey across the Thames feels like it lasts a year, but the ride gives me time to try to clear my head. Or let my thoughts become even more jumbled. I turn my phone back on and scroll through my contacts, but I don't find what I'm looking for, the one thing I need. Jake's number has vanished from my phone. Gone. I curse and try to breathe some calm into me, interrupted a few times by my father attempting to ring. Rejecting a call has never been so easy.

I look up as the boat chugs into the dock, deciding there's only one place I can go. For the first time in as long as I can remember, I need my mum.

I dial her number and hold my breath as I disembark from the river bus, my bag dangling from my hand. "Camille?"

"Mum," I exhale, detecting concern in her voice.

"What's going on? Why would your father be calling me?"

I shrink on the spot. I can only imagine how desperate he is to find me if he resorted to calling my mother. "Mum, can you come and get me?" I refrain from feeding her need for information. It's neither the time nor the place, and I'm worried Pete and Grant could appear at any moment and manhandle me into Dad's car.

"Where are you?"

"Canary Wharf Pier."

"What in good heavens are you doing there?"

"It's a long story, Mum. I'll tell you, but please just come and get me."

"I'll send my driver this moment," she says, making me sag in relief. I've never known her to back down with such ease. "Wait outside the Hilton, sweetie pie."

"Thanks." I hang up, unable to help myself from constantly looking around me, checking that the coast is clear. I must look like a jumpy, paranoid waif, standing here all disheveled, my eyes darting. The paps would have a field day.

Feeling a little more at ease with the knowledge that Mum's driver is on his way, I walk over to a nearby café to get a coffee. The caffeine is a welcome hit to my tired brain as I wander around the pier toward the Hilton, still remaining super alert.

All kinds of scenarios are rolling through my mind—what I'll do if I see Dad or either of his two minions, what they'll do, what any of the passersby will do if I scream bloody murder if one of them tries to force me into Dad's car. I didn't bargain for this. He's always tried to control me and I've managed to keep his strong will at bay, but this time is different. He's never taken things this far. Following me? Digging into the background of who I choose to see? The sense of intrusion is infuriating, but that's nothing compared to the devastation of thinking he's possibly succeeded in chasing Jake away. I know Jake's struggles. His flashbacks, his anxiety attacks. My dad using his knowledge of Jake's problems as ammo will play havoc with Jake's frame of mind. It'll make him question himself. Question *us*.

After half an hour, keeping myself as concealed as possible while I wait for my ride, the Bentley pulls up and Mum's regular driver gets out and opens the back door for me.

"Miss," he says, nodding as I hurry over and slip into the backseat.

I'm not surprised my mother hasn't come along for the ride. She needs a good couple of hours to primp and preen herself before she'd even *think* about letting herself be seen in public. My request was too urgent and she sensed it, yet her distressed daughter on the end of the line still isn't enough for her to brave the outside world without her lippy and her hair styled. And here's me in last night's clothes, no makeup, and my hair tangled haphazardly into a loose braid. She'll be horrified.

I smile my thanks to my mum's driver as he shuts the door, and once again return to my phone, staring down at the screen. Why hasn't Jake called me? I feel like I'm clutching at straws, clinging to something that's fading fast.

Not many people in the world would take on my father, but I thought Jake was one of them. Unaffected, unbothered, and unimpressed by my dad's status. My head meets the glass of the window and I watch the bustle of London pass me by, wondering where the hell I go from here.

* * *

My mother doesn't greet me at the door in a rush to comfort me. Sighing, telling myself I shouldn't have expected anything less, I wander down the entrance hall of her obscenely plush apartment in Kensington, the only thing she has left from my father. It's lined with elaborate gold-gilded frames, all displaying intense oil paintings of various English countryside landscapes. So over the top. *So* my mother. I enter the even more elaborate lounge and sigh. A giant rug takes up the center of the room with two roll-top couches perched precisely opposite each other, both with gold, intricately calved legs and two fringed velvet cushions sitting neatly at each end. The vivid colors of the room—royal blues, greens, and reds—have always given me a headache. Today is no different.

"She thinks she's the bloody queen," I mutter, hearing the chink of china coming from the kitchen. Don't even get me started on the kitchen. It's a busy mess of designer utensils, gadgets, and deep carved wood. She doesn't even cook.

"This way, Maria," Mum calls, entering the room, followed by her housekeeper, who's carrying a tray of tea. "Camille!"

"Mum," I say, the strangest feeling coming over me. I feel all tearful all of a sudden, but I put it down to the familiarity of her face. She looks as perfect as ever in a pale blue skirt and cream blouse.

"Well, look at the state of you!" she cries, looking me up and down, her face a picture of alarm. "You look like a homeless stray!" She points for Maria to place the tray on the gold-plated coffee table and then shoos her away.

I burst into tears, the gravity of my situation suddenly hitting me like a kettlebell to my face. He's gone. Just gone, and I have no explanation to help me try to come to terms with it. My arse hits the firm seat of mum's couch, my face landing in my palms.

"Camille!" Mum cries, her court shoes padding across the rug to me.

She lowers next to me and puts an arm around my jerking body, patting at my shoulder. "Now, now, sweetie pie. Has this got anything to do with that strapping man who was photographed carrying you out of The Picturedrome?"

I shrink into her half-embrace and mumble my confirmation, sniffling constantly. "Dad hired him." I hiccup over my words. There's no holding back now. Mum can shred my father with her words all she likes, and I hope she goes all out. I hate him.

"Hired him?"

"As a bodyguard. Dad received a threat."

She scoffs, for good reason. "Your father receives those weekly, darling."

"It was directed at me this time. He said Jake was a precautionary measure, but I didn't want a man following me around. Sebastian's back in town. I thought Dad was being underhanded. So I tried to give Jake the slip a few times."

Mum smiles knowingly. "My sassy little Cami."

I return her smile. "Then some photographs were delivered to my apartment—photographs of me."

She frowns, so I go on.

"Like proof I was being watched. It made it all very real." I shrug, watching her beat down the curses she wants to fire off that my father would no doubt hear from the other side of town. "Jake and I got...close," I add quietly.

Mum's face softens in an instant, and her hand comes down to my knee and squeezes lightly. "He's a very handsome, strong man, Camille," she says. I study her, knowing there's more to come. "And a little older."

"He's thirty-five. Just ten years older than me. Dad's twenty years older than you."

Mum ignores my defensive retort. "So Daddy Dearest has laid down his demands, I expect." She can't mention my father without a bucket load of venom in her tone.

"He says Jake's no good for me. He thinks that because he was re-lieved of duty in the SAS, he's a failure."

Mum hisses. "Ooh, your father is immune to failure." Every word is laced with sarcasm. "Where's Jake now?"

I'm unwilling to admit that I don't know, so I explain everything that happened at Jake's apartment instead. The sympathy on her face when I finish is too much to bear. Tears pinch at the back of my eyes. "Why is he doing this?" I whisper hopelessly.

She sighs and leans forward, pouring each of us a cup of tea in her posh china. "Because he is a narcissistic control freak. That's why, sweetie pie."

"Why did you marry him, Mum?" I ask the question outright for the first time ever. It's a desperate search for something to redeem him. Something to make him less ugly to me right now. But I know I'm searching in vain.

"I was young." She says it wistfully, but for the first time I see true regret lingering beyond the mask she wears. Not regret for marrying such an arsehole, but regret because her life has passed her by and, besides me, all she has to show for it is a posh apartment in Kensing-ton. She's hasn't found another love. She's as bitter and twisted as the rest of the divorcees she keeps company with. "Plus TJ was just a boy, his mother gone after your father forced the poor girl back to Russia. Someone needed to instill some humanity into him before he turned into his father completely."

I smile at my mum's rare display of a maternal side.

"And look what thanks I got." She laughs. "Disposed of for that child-wife of his! And the moment I remarry, your father will cease all spousal payments. I barely survive on the peanuts he throws my way now."

I could laugh. Peanuts in Mum's eyes would probably keep a small village alive for a lifetime. "You don't have to remarry," I point out. "Just date."

"There's not a man on earth who could survive me." She chucks my chin and stands, brushing her skirt down. "Now, let's get you cleaned up. You're making the place look untidy."

I laugh lightly, not in disbelief because of her cheek, but because this is my mum, and despite her being overbearing and a total snob, I love her dearly. "What am I going to do?" I ask, rising to my feet as I set the china cup down.

"Well, before you do anything you're going to clean yourself up." She looks at me and tuts her dismay. "No woman can conquer the world if she isn't looking her best." Reaching forward, she brushes a stray tendril of my hair away. "I'll have my driver pop over to your apartment and collect some things for you."

"No!" I blurt, making her recoil. "Dad might be there. He'll know I'm here if he sees your driver dropping by."

"Then what am I supposed to do with you?" She indicates up and down my tatty form. "I can't leave you looking like this."

"I don't know," I admit, immune to the offense I should be feeling.

She huffs and wanders out to the hallway. "I'll call Harvey Nic's and have them pick out some things for you. My driver can pick them up. Use the pink guest room, sweetie pie. There's a robe on the back of the door."

She disappears and I let my whole body deflate a little, exhausted after a particularly strong dose of my mother. God, I feel even more drained.

Once I've taken a moment to muster the energy, I make my way to the pink guest room, wincing at the chintzy décor as I pass through to the bathroom. And then I'm shielding my eyes when I arrive in the en suite. It's like King Midas has been let loose. Everywhere I turn, there's gold glaring at me—the bath, the taps, the shower frame, the toilet seat. This is the spare bathroom. It's ridiculously ostentatious, and completely my mother.

After showering and wrapping my hair and body in a towel, I

wander into the pink room and see a Harvey Nic's bag waiting on the bed for me. With a little trepidation, I pad over and take a cautious peek inside. My mother ordered these clothes. This could be disastrous. The first thing I spot are some lacy knickers and a matching bra and, pleasantly surprised, I pull them out and smile when I see the brand. I modeled for this range. Mum knows this.

"Perfect," I say, now not afraid to delve deeper. I get a rush of warmth knowing Mother keeps up with my career, next pulling out an oversized black T-shirt dress, totally me, followed by a pair of cute Dune ballet flats. Collecting it all up, I pivot...

And walk face-first into someone. Everything held in my hands tumbles to my feet, and my lungs balloon from my shocked inhalation, ready to rush out on a frightened scream.

CHAPTER 23

JAKE

I only just get my hand over her mouth before she lets loose with what I knew would be a scream that would probably stretch from here to Manchester. Her eyes are wide and frightened as I seize her and carry her into the bathroom, squinting as I enter to avoid being blinded by the offensive amount of gold.

I push the door closed with my foot and set her on her feet, being sure to get my face in her field of vision before I release her mouth. It takes her a few seconds to focus, and I see the moment she realizes it's me. Her whole body softens in my arms, her dull eyes sparking back to life. Oh God, the feel of her, the sight of her. The past few hours have been pure hell.

I gently peel my palm away from her mouth. "I'll always find you, angel."

"Oh God!" She launches herself at me, throwing her arms over my shoulders and burying her face in my neck. "I thought you'd left me!" She sounds freaked . . . and totally amazing.

"Don't be daft." I meld into her and hug her with a force that could probably break a bone. "Does your father know you're here?" I ask.

"No. I ran away. I didn't know what to do."

I smile at her instinct. "I had no choice but to leave, Cami." The thought of her thinking I would just abandon her is crippling.

"Why?" She starts to kiss my neck—quick, constant pecks across my skin.

"Your father's paid your ex to press charges against me. The police turned up."

Her mouth stops moving across my skin, and she's out of my neck a split second later. "What?"

She heard me just fine. Her request for a repeat is simply because she's shocked. Fuck me, she hasn't heard anything yet. "You must have seen the police at my apartment."

"No! I was locked in your room for...ever!"

I shake my head in disbelief, though the extent of Logan's ruthlessness shouldn't be a surprise. There's no way a bunch of cops would ignore the screams of a woman coming from my bedroom, which tells me Logan has more than one corrupt cop in his pocket. Fucker!

I take her cheeks in my hands, bringing my face closer to hers. "He really, *really* doesn't want me to have you, angel." I say it with a light, almost humorous edge, but her jaw still tightens.

"How did you find me?"

"Your phone," I tell her, seeing her frown. "You switched it on an hour ago. I tracked it via GPS." I can't help but smile at her astonishment. It's simple tracking technology, though I'm seriously considering having her microchipped so I don't have to go to hell and back again should her phone ever be switched off when she's out of my sight.

She withdraws and jabs me in the shoulder with surprising force, her face going from astounded to annoyed in a nanosecond. "Then why didn't you call me and tell me where you were? I've been going out of my mind!"

"I didn't know who was with you," I grate, unreasonably thinking that she has no idea what it feels like to be going out of your mind.

Fuck me, every artery I have is blocked with stress. I feel like I could have a heart attack at any moment. "Your father could have taken your phone. How the hell was I supposed to know?"

"He did take my phone, but I got it back. And he deleted your number so I couldn't contact you. But even if you didn't want to risk calling me, you should have contacted me somehow!" she argues.

"How?" I'm truly flummoxed.

"I don't know! You're the stealth ninja in this relationship!" Her gorgeous face twists with frustration that's heavily mixed with relief.

"Sure." I laugh. "Next time I lose you, I'll have a satellite signal sent to your lipgloss."

She gasps her disgust as her arm flies out again, except this time I block her swing with ease, making her stagger forward a little on another disgruntled gasp. She quickly finds her composure, the nostrils of her cute button nose flaring. I keep my lips straight, but there's nothing I can do to stop my cock lunging behind my fly. How easy it would be to bend her over that gold-plated bath and smash into her from behind. Lord knows, I need to let off some steam.

I see every muscle in her go lax, despite her raging eyes. She's playing it cool. Her willowy body wrapped tightly in that little towel is one of the most gratifying things I've ever seen.

But then the tiniest of movements from her right arm catches my eye and tells me her intention. My hand comes up between our bodies and her wrist lands in my waiting palm. She grunts her annoyance, bringing the other up in quick succession. I catch that one, too, now unable to hold back my victorious smirk. She yanks, incensed, and battles with my hold. And I let her, unmoving, working out the distance to that gold tub.

"Jake!" She flips her body, sending her towel tumbling to the floor. She freezes. I smile.

Then I lock her in my hold and push her toward the tub, placing her hands on the edge. "Hold on, angel."

"Jake…" Her voice is now pure lust as I bend her over in front of me, my mouth lax as I drink in the expanse of her back, my palm stroking the entire length slowly. Good God, I need to be inside her. I pull my fly open and push my jeans down a little, letting my cock spring free.

Widening my stance to level me up, I take her hips and inch forward, no need to hold myself to guide my cock to her pussy. It knows where it wants to be. I nudge at her opening, teasing a little, wanting her to beg.

"Please, Jake." She says it softly, desperately. "Please."

I smile and sink into her, gasping and freezing when she constricts all of her muscles, hauling me in the rest of the way. "Ohhhh, fuck," I breathe, clenching my eyes shut. "Cami, today I need to take you hard."

"I don't care!" She rams back onto me, her arse hitting my lower stomach, prompting my eyes to spring open and watch.

"Fuck!" I dig my fingers into her flesh and retreat, watching with rapt attention as my cock, slick with her arousal, slides from her passage. "Angel, I can't tell you how fucking good you look." Her back stretched before me, her head bowed, her arse firm and round, all within my sights. "Fucking amazing."

She groans, her wet golden hair cascading onto the side of the gold bath, her arms ramrod straight against it. The urge I have to pound into her can't be contained. My relief at having her back is too great. I let rip, yanking her back onto me hard and fast, needing to possess her, needing to surrender to my body's demand to demonstrate my need for her, to show her in the best possible way that I'm here and I'm going nowhere.

I throw my head back on a suppressed roar, feeling the blood in my cock begin to bubble. I'm mumbling mindlessly. I'm starting to shake, my knees going weak. I can't hold back any longer.

"Cami." I choke her name through my mind-bending pleasure, trying to tell her that I'm tipping the edge.

"Go!" she shouts, ramming back onto my groin with a force that nearly knocks me to my arse.

"Fuck!" I can't even find the decency through my pleasure to ensure she's nearly there, too. I let go, tingles penetrating my skin and ripping through me, shaking me to the core.

"I'm coming!" she yelps.

I force a few more strokes, gritting my teeth, the sensitivity almost too much to bear. I know the moment she comes. She slams her fist on the side of the bath, and I tug her back, holding her tightly against me as my cock rolls out its release and my body starts to tremble uncontrollably.

"Ohhhhhh..." Cami breathes, going limp against me, her arms giving against the tub. "Oh, fucking hell, that's powerful."

I find some energy from nowhere and pull her up, holding her naked back against me while I fight my way through the furious attack of my climax. My breathing is all over the place, my heart beating for the first time since I fled my apartment. I'm alive again.

She mumbles something, exhausted. I can't make it out. "What, angel?"

She drags in air, and I lower my face into her neck, getting close to her mouth. "Muuuuu," she breathes.

I frown, slipping free of her, making sure I keep hold of her body. She feels like she could crumble to the floor. "Cami, I can't hear you."

"Mum."

"Sweetie pie!"

I fire a look toward the door, hearing the shuffle of some shoes across the carpet.

"Camille, sweetie, I'm popping out."

"Oh, shit!" I yank my trousers up with one hand while holding Cami up in my other, willing her to come back to life. "Cami, for Christ's sake!" I reach down and grab the towel, pulling it up her body. She doesn't help. She's bloody useless.

The door flies open and I'm confronted with her overbearing, preened, perfectly coifed mother. She freezes when she clocks the scene, her manicured hand poised on the gold doorknob.

"Hi." I cough, arranging Cami's towel around her useless body. I wish she'd fucking snap out of it!

"Well, hello." She looks to Cami, eyebrows raised, then to me. I'm just relieved as fuck that I was too desperate to be inside Cami to think about removing any of my clothes.

Cami seems to come round, taking the towel from my grasp and holding it up herself. "Mum, this is Jake," she blurts without warning, startling me.

I feel like a delinquent. Fucking my girl in her mother's bathroom? And being caught? I'm fucking mortified.

There's no escaping the condemnation on Camille's mother's face and for the first time in my life, it bothers me. For the first time in my life, I care what someone thinks of me. I really am a pussy. I step forward, all chivalrously, and extend my hand. "Pleasure to meet you, Ms. Logan."

She eyes me with caution. "It's Ms. *Bell*." She raises an indignant nose and I die on the spot. I knew that. I knew she'd reverted back to her maiden name after Logan dumped her for a younger model. What's gotten into me? I'm all nervous.

"Of course." I mentally shoot my brains out and smile sincerely. Camille Logan is unearthing all kinds of chivalrous behavior from me. "Pleasure."

Her hand finally puts me out of my twitchy misery and takes mine. "So you're the man causing all this trouble?" she asks, a roving eye skating up and down my disheveled frame.

Again, I scoff, but only on the inside. There's a man causing trouble all right, but it isn't me. I pull myself together and release her hand, trying to stand tall when I feel like a midget before this woman who is a foot shorter than me. "I'm trying not to." I take an out, not knowing what other angle to take. She's one of the good guys. I don't usually bow to anyone, but I have an overwhelming need to bow to this woman. She's the epitome of everything I hate in a female, but she's Cami's mum. "I realize Cami's father isn't so keen—"

She snorts, interrupting me. "You could be Prince Harry and he still wouldn't approve if he hadn't set up the date, or wasn't set to get some financial perk from it." She looks at her daughter, a little twinkle in her eye. "Why don't you get dressed, sweetie pie? I'll take Jake into the lounge. We'll have tea."

I look down at Cami and see her frown as she drags her towel close, like she hadn't realized she was half-naked until her mother pointed it out. "I thought you were going out."

Ms. Bell purses her lips and flicks an eye to me. "It can wait." She spins on her polished shoes and sashays out, and the moment her back disappears I stagger toward the wall, feeling a pressure like no other. The irony of it doesn't escape me. Approval isn't something I care for. Cami's mother might have changed that.

"You okay?" Cami asks, her forehead creasing.

I need to pull myself together. "Yeah, I'm fine." Pushing myself away from the wall, I approach her and slip my arm around her neck, pulling her into me. Then I go in for the kill. She needs to know how I feel. All her fears, the thoughts that I'd deserted her, hurt like fucking hell. I just have to say it. With spoken words. Loud and clear.

Yet when I open my mouth, nothing materializes. The words are there. They're everywhere. "I . . ." My throat closes up, and I start to tremble under the weight of my intended confession.

"Jake?"

"I . . ."

"What's the matter?"

"Shit, Camille." I cup her cheeks with my big palms, leveling my face with hers. The wideness of her eyes kicks me into touch. She's worried. "I love you," I say, searching her blue eyes. "I love you so fucking much and I need you to know that."

She moves back, making my hands drop from her face. She's shocked, her eyes clouding over. I don't know what I expected her to say or do, but I wasn't prepared for this reaction. She looks ready to bolt.

After what feels like a lifetime—a torturous, painful lifetime—she finally speaks, her lovely lips trembling over her words. "I love you, too," she blubbers, hiding her face in her hands.

Her reply brands itself on my heart and brings another small part of me back to life. I breathe out, not realizing I was holding my breath until that moment, and move in to claim her quaking body, lifting her from her feet and constricting her in my hold. She loves me, too, and I can only pray that it's enough to see us through the dark days ahead.

I spend not nearly enough time holding her in my arms, reinforcing my declaration with the force of my squeeze, before detaching her from me. The light I catch in her eyes floors me. So bright and hopeful. I'm the reason for that, and it's both deeply gratifying and equally guilt in- ducing. She doesn't even really know me. But she will. Once this shit is all cleared up, I'll take the steps I've been avoiding for so long. Just the thought of what needs to be done makes my heartbeat slow.

Dropping a kiss to her head, I walk her back to the shower and flip it on. "Get showered," I order softly. Then I rip myself from the bath- room to join her mother.

After I've located Camille's phone and switched it off, I wander through the palatial apartment, taking in all of the surroundings, try- ing to ignore the garish décor as I mentally calculate the distance I'm putting between Cami and me. I pop my head around the few doors I pass to check for windows and possible ways of entry, and once I'm satisfied that there's no chance of anyone getting in or past me without being detected, I wander into the lounge.

Ms. Bell is perched on one of the couches, which are definitely there for show rather than comfort. She looks up at me as I lower to the one opposite her. I don't try to get comfortable. It'd be impossible. She hands me a tiny china cup, and I pass it between my hands a few times, the thing feeling like a thimble in my big grasp. I give up trying to hold it delicately and place it on the glowing gold table in front of me. "Thank you," I say, feeling her studying me.

My main objective these past few unbearable hours has been to find Cami. I haven't given much thought to what I'd do beyond that. Now's the time to figure all that out.

"How did you get into my house?" she asks, her eyes running up and down my frame suspiciously.

She *should* be suspicious. I think it best to avoid the details of how I slipped the locks, crept through the apartment, and sniffed her daughter out like I could be a bloodhound hunting a fox. "Cami let me in," I reply smoothly instead. I can't quite tell whether she believes me, so I decide it's best to change the subject as quickly as possible. "Were you aware that your ex-husband paid off Cami's ex-boyfriend and funded his rehab?"

She laughs under her breath, stirring her tea. "It doesn't surprise me. Does Camille know?"

"I haven't told her yet. There's a lot I need to figure out."

"Like what?"

"Like the true threat to your daughter. Something wasn't sitting right from the day Logan hired me. He kept information from me and when I questioned him, he pulled my protection. I don't think his disapproval of my relationship with Cami is the only reason he wants me gone. He's hiding something, and I intend to find out what it is."

Her eyebrows jump up, surprised, but then she laughs. "He must really dislike you, Jake."

My cheeks puff on a little huff. That's confirmed. He's paid Cami's scumbag ex to press charges against me. The one who's slapped her around a few times. Anything to get me out of the picture, since I won't be taking his payoff.

There's more to this than a simple disapproval of me. He's worried I might find out something he doesn't want found.

"The feeling's mutual," I say. "I *will* find out what's going on. She'll be safe with me until then."

She smiles, telling me all I need to know. She approves. It's a relief, even if I don't give a shit in what capacity that is, whether she's relishing the knowledge that her manipulating ex-husband has finally met his match, or whether she's genuinely happy that I clearly feel so strongly for her daughter. Something tells me it's both.

"I have no doubt," she says quietly.

Looking past her, I see Cami entering the room.

"Hey." She pads over, looking like a beacon of glowing gorgeousness in a simple black dress. Her hair is cascading over one shoulder as she combs through it with her fingers, her face free from any makeup.

"Sweetie pie," her mother sings, joining me as I stand. Her sickly pet name for my angel is over the top and grating, and I can tell Cami feels the same about it. "Would you like some tea?"

Cami shakes her head and homes in on me, tucking herself into my side. "Thanks for the clothes." She indicates her dress, prompting me to take another appreciative peek.

"You're welcome. Now, I should be going," Ms. Bell announces. "I'm already late." She comes over, giving Cami a fond smile before taking her from my side and cuddling her. "You are more than welcome to stay here, sweetie pie."

"No need," I say without thought or consideration for her mother's feelings. That's not happening.

Cami looks up at me in question as her mother releases her. "Really?" she asks, her worry obvious.

"Really," I affirm, knowing exactly where I'm taking her until I sort this mess out. I ignore Cami's evident curiosity and turn to her mother. "It was a pleasure."

She laughs and surprises me when she reaches up and forces me into her embrace. My arms remain by my sides, my whole body tense. "Don't underestimate my ex-husband," she whispers in my ear. "And don't you dare break my baby's heart."

I keep my mouth firmly closed. I'm not deluded. I'm not ignorant to the fact that I could hurt her more than anything else. More than her ex. More than her father. The way she sees me, the pedestal she's put me on, I don't deserve it. I don't deserve *her*. If I were her father, I'd try to keep me away as well.

But I'm too far gone now. I'm in too deep with this addictively gorgeous woman. My despair of the past few hours when she was taken from me was enough of a reality check, not that I needed one. I love her too much to give up. So fucking much, it hurts. I just hope she loves me enough to get past the shock when she finds out I'm not the man she thinks I am.

CHAPTER 24

CAMI

Jake is agitated and tense as he guides me to his Range Rover, which is tucked away in a nearby alleyway. He doesn't even settle once I'm safely in his car. He's alert, scanning everywhere as he weaves through the back streets toward the outskirts of the city.

His suspicion is rubbing off on me, my eyes darting also, keeping an eye out for any police cars. My father has reached an all-time low. The knowledge of his stunt, of the fact that he paid Sebastian to press charges against Jake, makes me sick to my stomach. It also makes me question what further lengths he'll go to in order to keep Jake away from me. I'm trying to understand his reasoning, trying to locate a scrap of compassion for my dad that'll dilute the hatred I feel for him now, but there's none to be found. He'll never succeed in tearing us apart. I swear, if he continues with this craziness, I will never speak to him again. He'll be dead to me.

I turn in my seat a little to face Jake. "What are we going to do about my father?"

"Let me worry about that," he replies coolly, completely together. Calm, even. Why doesn't he seem as concerned by this as I am?

"Jake, he's trying to get you thrown in jail to keep you away from me!"

"That's not going to happen."

My mouth drops open in disbelief. Has he forgotten what my father is capable of? "How can you be so sure?"

"Trust me," he says, reaching over and taking my knee gently. "He isn't going to win, Cami."

I look down at Jake's big hand holding my knee, his touch warm and comforting, yet it doesn't eliminate all of my worry. "You're an ex-soldier." I murmur. "You wanted to save the world, and all he wants to do is rule it." I reach over and stroke the bristle on his jaw, and he closes his eyes briefly, removing his hand from my knee and placing it over mine on his cheek. He looks despondent all of a sudden, lost in thought.

"I love you, angel," he says quietly, pulling my hand to his lips and kissing it gently. "More than anything."

I smile, wishing I could convey exactly how much he means to me. There are no words. "Snap." I return his gesture and bring his hand to my mouth, kissing his knuckles. "Where are we going?"

"I have a little place in the countryside. No one knows about it."

"So you're going to keep me holed up until when?"

"Until your father sees sense."

I could laugh. "That's never, then," I mutter, relaxing back in my seat. He turns a half-smile onto me. "Then I'll keep you there forever." I shrug, unfazed. "Fine by me."

* * *

After two hours on the road, we turn onto a tiny country lane, edged tightly with hedges. We're on the same lane twenty minutes later, the road seeming to go on forever, no end in sight, the twists and turns just coming and coming. It's wide enough for only one car, and there have been no other drivers along the way. It's a good job. No one would get past us, not even on a push bike.

All I can see are fields for as far as my gaze can reach. Empty fields—no cows, no sheep, no life. I keep quiet as Jake negotiates his Range Rover down the narrow lane with ease, seeming to know exactly where every pothole, divot, and bump is. We start to climb a steep hill, and the clouds above seem to come closer and closer until we hit the summit and start a steady decline back down to earth. I peek out of the corner of my eye to Jake, seeing him more relaxed, all evidence of his tension gone. Then he smiles to himself. I look to see what's spiked the sign of happiness. And gape.

A little place in the country? The house stands proudly in the distance, surrounded by a number of other, smaller buildings—a garage, an outhouse, some barns and stables. It's a big cream structure, with dark wood-framed windows, and a massive wooden front door.

"Little?" I ask, wondering what I was expecting. A cottage, maybe?

"It's only four bedrooms. It looks more imposing than it actually is." He takes a sharp curve in the road, forcing me to crane my neck to keep my eyes on the house. "My nearest neighbor is fifteen miles away."

"Sociable," I mutter as he takes yet another turn in the road. We are literally in the middle of nowhere. "You don't seem like the farmer type."

"I'm not."

"So why the stables, the fields, and the pig sheds?"

"It was the most obscure and isolated place I could find."

"Why would you need an obscure and isolated place?" I ask, sounding casual though on the inside I'm itching with curiosity.

He pulls to a stop and cuts the engine, then turns in his seat to face me. I can tell by the knowing smile on his face that he's sensed I'm about to burst with questions. "Because one day I knew I'd meet a beautiful princess who'd need protecting from her wicked father."

My eyes narrow. "That's not funny."

"You don't approve of my attempts to lighten our situation?"

Our situation? I hate that we're in a situation. I hate my father. "I hate that we've had to run away."

Jake jumps out, circling the car and opening my door. Taking my hand, he helps me down. "Your father has the police after me, Cami. I'm not hanging around London waiting for them to catch up with me. We stay here until I've sorted it out."

"And how do you plan on sorting it out?" I ask, reluctantly letting him push me toward the front door.

"I'm working on it." He unlocks the door and pushes it open onto a massive square hallway, with doors leading off to various rooms and a staircase to the first floor.

The realization of my *current* situation hits home. Maybe I'm not so bothered that we've been forced to run away. Me and Jake. Alone. In the middle of nowhere. Maybe he shouldn't work on fixing it, because being locked up here for the foreseeable future is suddenly very appealing.

"Is there much to do here?" I ask, wandering in, gazing around.

"I can think of plenty of things to do." His front meets my back, and I smile on the inside. "Just me and you here. No interference." He kisses my neck, sending a flurry of activity to between my thighs. I sigh into him, shuddering. "But first I'm taking you out for dinner."

I frown into the space before me. I didn't see any signs of life for miles. "Where?"

"Let me worry about that." He turns me in his arms and stares down at me, his dark eyes roaming my face, not missing a millimeter of my skin. I let him, happy to absorb him, too. He looks so content and at ease, something I've not seen very often from Jake. "For tonight we forget everything and just be together." He dips and takes my lips gently, coaxing my mouth open with light, gentle pecks. I hum and relax into his kiss, more than happy to oblige. But what about after tonight? What happens then?

* * *

Jake shows me to a bedroom, a huge space with high ceilings and detailed cornicing. A glass chandelier hangs low over the huge well-made bed, and the walls are covered in a warm mink-embossed paper. There's an open fireplace, too, loaded with logs. It's sumptuous but not over the top, so cozy and welcoming. It's a far cry from the minimal space of his factory apartment.

After he leaves me to get ready for dinner, I head into the attached bathroom, finding a familiar bag. I pull out some of the contents, discovering my clothes and random cosmetics from my bathroom. I smile. *How...?*

Looking up to the mirror, I study myself for a few moments, falling into thought. Just me, Jake, and this big country house on acres of sprawling land. I smile again, but it quickly falls when I realize I've not let Heather know where I am. She'll be worried. My phone's off, and I just know she'll be trying to call me.

"Shit!" I rush into the bedroom again, finding my phone on the bed, and as soon as I switch it on, I see endless missed calls from Heather. I ignore the ones from my father and call my best friend.

She answers on the first ring. "Cami, there's a shot of you and Jake in the magazines!" she says urgently.

This is old news to me. I'm surprised. Heather is usually more up-to-date on things happening in London. "I know."

"You do?"

"Yes, my father knows, too."

"Oh, fuck."

"Yes, he's not happy." I tell her what she'll already know, but extend it and tell her something that she definitely won't. "He's paid Sebastian to press charges against Jake."

"What?" Her volume makes me wince. "Why would he do that?"

"Because he wants Jake gone," I breathe. "And I don't."

"So, you've not fallen for your bodyguard, then?"

"Cunny funt."

"Indeed." She sighs. "Where are you?"

I look around and find a window, then wander over to look out across the fields. "I don't know," I admit.

"What do you mean?"

"I'm with Jake. The police are looking for him so we've left London until he can sort this out."

"You're on the run?"

I laugh under my breath. "I guess so." But I'm not entirely sure who I'm on the run from.

"Oh, shit, Cami," she breathes. "Why does your dad have to be such a dick?"

"I don't know." I sigh, my fingertips coming up and pressing into my forehead. "Listen, if anyone asks, you've not spoken to me, okay? Especially my dad."

"Of course!" She sounds slighted that I even need to ask.

"Thank you. I'll give you a call tomorrow."

"Make sure you do."

I hang up, turn my phone back off, and throw it onto the bed. Then I rush to the bathroom, keen to get ready as instructed and find Jake. We've been practically touching for the past few hours. Anything more than a meter between us now feels wrong.

* * *

I have no idea what to wear. He's taking me out. Where? Was there some hidden restaurant I missed along the way? I pad down the wooden steps, my black strappy wedges dangling from my fingertips, listening for Jake as I go. I have a grey parachute-style dress on, with thin straps and a band of embellishment around the hem. I figured I could dress it up or down, depending on where he plans on taking me.

"Jake," I call, rounding the bottom of the stairs and heading for the country-style kitchen. I enter and find no Jake. Frowning, I backtrack and make my way to the lounge, discovering the inviting space empty, too. "Where are you?" I ask thin air, backing up into the hall. I stand for a few moments, wondering where to search next, and deciding he might be out front, maybe waiting in his car, I turn toward the front door.

There's a piece of paper stuck to it, and, curious, I approach and read the first line.

Take this paper and follow the instructions.

I smile, pulling it down from the wood before reading on.

Head across the driveway. There's a gap between two oak trees. Follow the trail until you reach the huge trunk of a fallen tree. Your next instruction is there.
Jake x

A silly, excited thrill courses through me at the thought of going on a treasure hunt. Because Jake is the treasure.

I drop my shoes to the floor and slip my feet into the ballet flats by the door. I waste no time letting myself out of his house. I see the two oak trees at the far end of the drive like he said I would.

I run, an unstoppable grin on my face, and once I pass through the middle of the trees, I find myself in an overgrown woodland, but there's evidence of a trail. I hurry down the path, being sure to avoid the larger branches that are scattered here and there.

I feel like I'm in a fairy tale. The canopy of trees above me is allowing only a sliver of low evening sunlight to break through as I hurry along, eventually finding myself in a huge round clearing with a massive tree trunk laying across the center, its bark falling off. It looks like it's been here for a hundred years. There's a piece of paper pinned to the top.

My excitement lurching, because I'm closer to Jake, I dash forward and snatch it up.

One day I'm going to fuck you on this ancient tree trunk.
Look to your right. There's a silver birch. Pass it and follow the new path until you reach a red rosebush. You'll find your next instruction there. Watch the thorns.
Jake, x

I bring the paper up to my mouth and bite the corner, resisting running off toward the silver birch that I've already located. Maybe if I stay right here he'll get fed up waiting, wherever he is, and come find me. Then he can make "one day" today and fuck me on this old tree trunk.

Circling slowly, I take in my surroundings, floored by how beautiful it all is. A lost woodland, swamped by huge trees, some of them hundreds and hundreds of years old. It's quiet and peaceful. The only sounds are of nature—pure, untouched nature. No cars, no buildings, no pollution. I could stay here forever. Why can't we just stay here forever? Get married, have children, and bring them up in this peaceful sanctuary, away from the big city and outside world? I bite my lip, thinking I'm getting way ahead of myself. Or am I?

I rush over to the silver birch and pass it, finding myself on another clear pathway. The crunching and breaking of twigs under my feet barely register. I'm desperate to see him, desperate to fling myself in his arms and disappear into an oblivion of Jake. Nothing but Jake. His strength, his passion—all of him.

I see the rosebush up ahead, the burst of bright red pulling me in like a magnet. It's huge, a picture of English beauty amid the overgrowth of the woodland. Slowing my pace, I see the crisp white of a

piece of paper nestled amid the thorns and flowers, waiting for me. I
come to a stop, taking a minute to wonder what this note might say.
The blooming scarlet blossoms are ripe with an intoxicating scent that
makes the urge to caress one and bring it to my nose too hard to resist.
I inhale and breathe out, closing my eyes. I'm warm through, calm and
serene. Releasing the rose, I reach for the paper, being sure to watch
for thorns. The note catches on a few as I tentatively pull it from the
foliage until I can read his words.

> *This place is my safe haven. Now it's yours, too. Everything I have is*
> *yours.*
> *I love you. More than I imagined I could ever love someone.*
> *Take a rose and put it in your hair. Then follow the trail until you find*
> *the beautiful red Acer tree.*
> *Jake. x*

I bring the paper to my nose and inhale deeply, like I could breathe
his written words into me. He loves me. Everything he has is mine,
but the only thing I truly need and want is his heart. His peace.

I carefully reach forward and gently pick the biggest rose I can find.
It comes away from the stem with ease, as if wanting to help me out.
Tucking some loose strands of blonde around my braid, I push the
bubble of ruby petals behind my ear.

Then I circle to find the trail and begin to follow it, smiling the
whole way. I weave through trees, sometimes even coming back on
myself a bit, but I stick to his order and keep to the path. The huge red
tree it leads me to takes my breath away, the leaves as red as the rose
tucked behind my ear. Pinned to the trunk is another note, and for the
first time, I wonder how many notes there are. I'm growing impatient.
I hurry over and detach the paper.

> *Whatever you decided to wear, take it off. Take everything off.*

A quiet hitch of breath spills, my body tingling with life.

There's an opening past this Acer tree that will lead you to me. Hurry.
  Jake. x

I swallow and drop my bag, releasing the paper, too. Then I check around me as I kick off my shoes and reach for the hem of my dress. It's a crazy thing to do. There's no one here. No one can see me. It doesn't make Jake's demand feel any less forbidden, though. It's warm, the evening sun still low and bold beyond the treetops, and the night time chill hasn't yet spiked the air.

But my nipples still harden as I pull my dress over my head. Letting it tumble to the ground, I bite my lip as I start pushing my knickers down my thighs, instinctively looking around as if someone could be watching me. I giggle to myself. I bet the squirrels and the birds are wondering what the hell is going on. Who's this human stripping in our woodland?

Stepping out of my knickers, I leave them at my feet and look beyond the Acer tree for the opening through the mass of bushes and trees. I see it and smile. Re-securing the rose behind my ear, I start toward the clearing, my breathing quickening with each step.

I'm sure to be careful as I breach the gap, the green foliage around me still dense and threatening to scrape my naked skin as I pass through. I shimmy and skirt past bushes and branches, until I see sunlight, not just scattered now, but bursting more freely up ahead. My pace quickens, and I hold my breath until I break free of the woodland that's held me in its enchanted clutches for too long.

"Oh my God," I whisper as I move into the clearing. I'm still in woodland, except it's more open. The trunks of the trees are thinner, smooth, and spaced generously in neat rows. I look down and smile, absolutely mesmerized by the sight. The ground before me is a sea of blue. English bluebells. I take it all in. Or I try to. It's beyond beautiful, this hidden haven.

Something stirs behind me, and I spin, forgetting momentarily why I'm here. My hand comes up to my chest on a small whimper when I find Jake.

He's standing behind me, his lean body naked, too, a smile on his handsome face.

CHAPTER 25

JAKE

She's like a mirage. Like something that only your wildest imagination could dream up. I feel like I've been waiting here for eons, my temptation to go hunt her down nearly getting the better of me. I've imagined this all afternoon, from the moment I drove her down the long lane to my safe haven. This part of my land is like something out of a picture book. It matches my angel perfectly and seems to have come alive, like it's been waiting all this time for her to arrive.

The light wind stirs the leaves, the sunlight more obvious in this section of the dense woodland that backs onto my home. The carpet of bluebells surrounding me is vibrant and mesmerizing. Not unlike Camille. Her blue eyes are sparkling brightly, in wonder and awe, her slender body still but alive.

Taking one step forward, I tilt my head a little, trying to coax my body to relax, my hard muscles beginning to ache from tension. I'm not sure why I'm tense. She's safe here. She can roam free on my land and putter around my home without me trailing ten paces behind her all the time. Yet that knowledge didn't make it any easier to wait here for her to find me. I felt anxious, and the reason is deeper than a fear for her well-being.

As long as she's away from my sight, the deep ache within me will never leave. I need to have her close by for my own selfish reasons. Because I feel incomplete when we're apart.

Her flawless skin is glowing, the mounds of her small breasts pert and calling for me. She has a single red rose tucked behind her ear, just like I asked. She's a vision of pure, exquisite beauty.

I go to her, loving the sight of her chest pulsing more visibly the closer I get, her eyes never straying from mine. I've never felt so alive. My heart has never pounded so hard. My cock has never longed for release so desperately. She's mine for the whole of the night, all of my fears forgotten for now. Until tomorrow. Tomorrow I fix everything. Not just with her father, but with myself, too. And I'm praying that if Camille Logan doesn't already know the extent of my feelings for her, she will after tonight. And she'll forgive me for keeping so much from her.

She's looking up at me, keeping quiet as I absorb her face, drinking in every tiny piece of her. "You found me," I say, my voice unavoidably hoarse. I slide my palm onto her hip and round to her bum.

"I'll always find you." Cami's voice is equally rough as she mimics my words, her hand coming up to rest on my heart. It fucking sings with happiness. "This place is beautiful."

"It's yours, too. Everything is yours." I dip my head and capture her mouth, pulling her in closer to me. I don't close my eyes, unwilling to sacrifice the striking vibrancy of her blues. I'm gentle, nibbling and pecking my way across her lips, and then plunging my tongue deep, swallowing down her groans. My cock is jerking, shouting at me to give it what it wants. But it'll have to wait. I have other plans, and they don't involve diving into her just yet.

Slowing our kiss, I gently pull away, having to be more forceful when Cami's hand comes to the back of my head and tries to push me to her. "Patience, angel," I murmur, smiling when she grumbles under her breath.

"You're waiting here for me naked, and you're asking me to be patient?" She sounds totally exasperated, and I love it.

I look down at her, my hand smoothing across her cheek. "I want to make this last." Pushing her away until we're completely disconnected, I point over her shoulder to where I've laid down a blanket in a small circular clearing.

Giving me a sideways, curious smile, she turns slowly to find what I'm pointing to. I hear the slight hitch of her breath. "A picnic?" she breathes, swinging back to face me, the loose strands of her hair whipping her face.

For reasons unbeknownst to me, I feel my cheeks heat. Am I blushing? "Yes, a picnic." I move in and sweep her from her feet, my ears invaded by her surprised squeal. "I'm going to feed you, feel you, lick every inch of you, and then I'm going to make mad sweet love to you."

Her hands cling around my shoulders, her face a picture of delight. "Are you blushing, Jake Sharp?"

"I don't blush." Let's get that straight before she clings on and runs with it. "It'll be *you* blushing soon."

I drop to my knees, still with Cami draped across my arms, and find a clear space by the basket, which is loaded with champagne, strawberries, and cold meats. A picnic. In my bluebell woodland? Fuck me, who would have thought?

But I needed to take her off to a faraway land where no one and nothing could disturb us. And I need to show her how much she means to me.

Laying her gently on the blanket, I guide her arms to above her head, my eyes traveling the length of her long body stretched out before me. This might be more difficult than I thought. Every part of her is calling me, and my body is reacting, making it imperative that I lock down my focus and resist it. She's not trying to make this hard for me. She's just lying there, looking up at me as I fight the urge to take her breasts instead of the champagne. I rest on my haunches and pull the foil from the lid, glimpsing down at her every now and then to see where she's focused. As suspected, each time, she's skating greedy eyes across my torso, nibbling on her lip.

"I didn't see any glasses," she observes when I pop the cork, slipping my thumb into the bottle neck to avoid losing too much.

"We don't need glasses." I tip the bottle and let a splash of the liquid hit her tummy. She gasps, her body bowing sharply with shock. The move has her nipples pushed up high, the buds erect. I swallow down my control and maneuver so I'm stretched out beside her, on my side. Flicking one last look up to her, I lower my head and catch the trickling champagne that's running down her side, licking it up until I find myself on her abdomen.

"Oh, shit!" She slams her palms into the blanket at her sides, cracking her body further into an arch.

"Feel good, angel?" I ask, circling her belly button with my firm, slick tongue.

"Yes!"

It feels *so* good, the warmth of her skin and the cold of the champagne creating a delicious mix of hot and cool in my mouth. Tipping the bottle again, this time more carefully, I start dripping the liquid across her breasts, working my way down her body until I'm at the apex of her thighs. She starts to shake, mumbling incoherent words to the treetops above.

She's felt nothing yet. I take a swig and hold it in my mouth, then resting the bottle to the side, I push myself up and straddle her, bracing my upper body on my arms. I wait for her to open her eyes, my hardness jutting from my hips, brushing across her ribs. I can't tell her to open, so I dip my hips, pushing my cock into her tummy. It works in an instant. Her eyes open on a desperate yelp, landing on mine with a bang. I release a little liquid from my mouth, letting it trickle across her lips. Her eyes widen with knowing delight, her hand lifting from the ground. I shake my head, and she pouts. It's adorable, and it very nearly has me spitting out the rest of the champagne and ravishing her.

Damn, keep your control, Jake!

She licks her lips. She fucking licks her lips, slowly, purposefully, and with one hundred percent intention. The little fucking minx. I let a few more drops escape and plummet to her lips again, except this time she opens her mouth, capturing the flow. And once she's swallowed slowly, she performs the same calculated string of movements, licking her lips. The vision is arresting. My heart kicks in my chest and my erection begs for some relief. I'm a fool. I don't know how I thought I'd get through this, teasing her, tempting her, making her wait for me. It's completely backfired. I swallow down the remaining champagne and shake my head to myself, silently amazed by this woman's ability to send my self-discipline to shit.

"Taste nice?" she whispers, tilting her hips up and pushing into my groin.

I drop my head, my body concaving in a ridiculous attempt to escape her. "Stop it, angel," I warn, clenching my eyes shut.

"Stop me," she counters, egging me on, her voice silky and enticing.

"Fuck." I give in to the magnetism that's pulling my body down to hers. Our skin meets, my arms come up to lie upon hers above her head, and I swivel my hips, finding her slick opening and pushing a tiny way in. The little bit of penetration steals my breath.

She moans, arching beneath me deliciously. "Jake."

I'm in only a tiny bit, but her muscles tighten powerfully, trying to pull me in further. I grab air, drinking it in urgently as I break out in a sweat.

"All the way," she begs, fighting against my arms holding her down. "Jake, please!"

The sound of her begging so desperately breaks me, and I surrender to my body's need, pushing forward until I hit her deep. "Oh Jesus," I pant, my forehead meeting hers. "Camille..." My whole fucking body is buzzing with a need so profound, I don't know what to fucking do with it.

"You're shaking," she pants, looking deeply into my eyes. So deep, I'm sure she's found my dark soul.

I swallow down the sudden lump in my throat and start to gently rock into her, gliding smooth and slow, thriving on the constant moans and cries she's releasing. Her sounds of pleasure are the most potent aphrodisiac, spurring on my craving. But I try to keep my rhythm cool and consistent.

"I just..." My words evaporate. I feel so fucking overwhelmed, more so than I've ever felt when indulging in her. Maybe it's because I'm here, in my peaceful place. Or maybe it's because I've finally accepted what I need to do. What I've wanted to do for so long but doubted I had the strength I know I need. Doubted *myself*. Cami has given me that strength. Given me clarity. I have so much to mend.

"You just what?" she asks, her voice a breathy whisper, her hips matching my sway, pressing us together perfectly.

"I just love you so fucking much." I can't begin to comprehend it. I can't wrap my mind around the intensity of my feelings for her. My building emotion is getting the better of me, stabbing at my heart with relentless force, physically hurting it. Releasing her arms, I cradle her head, feeling her legs coming up around my waist and gripping me.

"Snap." She threads her fingers through my hair and tugs a little, reinforcing her cute counter. She's showing all the signs of an imminent orgasm, her eyes bright and almost frantic. She starts nodding, like she's read my thoughts, telling me she's on her way.

Shit, the sight of her unraveling under me beats anything I've experienced. And knowing I'm the cause of her condition just makes it all the more gratifying. I nod, too, my eyes stuck to hers, needing to see the moment she lets go. My strokes become faster, my instinct searching for the release we both need, and which only I can find for us.

I'm nearly there, every muscle stretching, my jaw tightening. The blood is pounding in my solid cock, driving me on.

Her round eyes are panicked, her legs squeezing around me viciously. "Put your legs down," I order, knowing that will tip us both.

She screams, launching her legs down my body, her teeth gritting. I cough, our new position stripping me of the ability to breathe. "Oh God." I feel the rush of pleasure start to seize me. Cami's lids snap closed, denying me the vision of her eyes. "Open," I order harshly.

She growls but obeys.

"I need to see you."

She whimpers and groans, her hands on a feeling frenzy all over my head before moving to my back. "I see you," she whispers, and then convulses violently, losing control of herself.

Those words, her reactions. They take me with her. I hiss, my cock undulating in waves, spilling everything I have to give into her. My body surrenders to the power of my pleasure, falling into her curves, molding to her. The sensations taking over my body blank my mind and shrink my lungs. I feel helpless, but the strongest I've ever felt. I feel hijacked by a force too powerful to keep back.

I feel her go slack and manage to lift my face a fraction to get her in my view, seeing her eyes closed, her head fallen to the side in exhaustion. Her arms are no longer clinging to me, her long, slender limbs splayed out at her sides. The only signs of life are her heartbeat, currently thumping against my chest, and the constriction of her internal muscles, milking me dry. I study her for a few moments, feeling so fucking emotional. She's turned me into an emotional pussy. I hate her for it. But I mostly love her for it.

She's made me feel again, which scares me to fucking death, because feeling again means I can hurt again.

On a content and disturbed sigh, I lower my face into her sweaty neck and settle above her, keeping her caged in. She's not going anywhere. Not now. But what about tomorrow? What about when I reveal my ghosts?

Chapter 26

CAMI

Moving isn't an option. Neither is speaking. All I can do is feel, and somewhere amid my exhaustion, I can find the energy to enjoy it. I've been lost in semiconsciousness for... I don't know how long. It doesn't matter, because I can still feel him spread all over me, breathing into my neck.

I'm not sure what just happened. All of the usual crushing feelings and pleasure were there, but this time there was something else. I can't put my finger on it. Jake seemed so absolutely together, cool and controlled, stable and with it. Then something switched in him. His desperation spiraled, taking me with it. He made love to me like he thought he would never get the chance again.

"Does it swallow you up like it does me?" he asks quietly, unmoving above me. "Does it consume you so much you think you might never break free?" He rises to his elbows, taking his time, until he's gazing down at me, looking almost confused. His handsome face is clear, his gorgeous eyes twinkling. "Tell me you feel the same. Tell me I'm not alone."

If he needs the words, then I'll give them to him. If that's what it'll take every day, then I'll repeat them until he finally knows without the need for me to voice it. I bend my arms and bring them

under my head, using them as a pillow to lift my head a little.
"You're not alone," I say, watching for his reaction. He doesn't lose
the hint of perplexity from his features, but he does smile a little.
"Can we stay here?" I ask.

"In the bluebell woods?"

"At your house," I correct him. I'd happily remain right in this exact spot forever, but that would be a silly dream. My actual request
isn't silly. There's no reason why we can't just hide here forever; just
me and him.

He looks off into the distance as if considering my request. "We
have things to deal with," he says, but more to himself than to me.

Nevertheless, I still answer him. "We don't have to deal with them."
I sound sure of that, but Jake's fleeting look of sympathy tells me I
shouldn't be. He's looking down at me, seeming torn. "No one knows
we're here. They don't have to," I say quietly.

"You want to live with unfinished business threatening to catch up
with you?"

"It's finished," I retort, more snappily than I meant. If I never see
my father again, it'll be too soon. Mum can visit me here. Or I'll Skype
her. And I can't help but imagine Heather and me poring over our designs at Jake's huge kitchen table, or maybe even converting one of the
outbuildings into a work studio. It would be perfect. *So* perfect. London is only a couple of hours away. It's doable.

Jake sighs, heavily and despondently. "The police are looking for
me, Cami. I don't want anything to hold us back. I want a clear path,
angel. I want you to pursue your career. I want us to be together. I
want us to be happy. No holding back."

"What if the path is never clear?" My father is a relentless bastard.
I know him. He doesn't know how to lose.

"It will be." He sounds adamant, but it doesn't lessen my trepidation. I might be suggesting the most cowardly option, but it's also the
easiest. "It's going to be okay."

Jake doesn't sound so resolute this time. He averts his eyes from mine, only emphasizing it.

I feel incredibly protected here, but catching these occasional signs of uncertainty in him, seeing him have these internal battles, makes me question my peace. It makes me feel very *unprotected*. I fall into thought. I realize the situation with my father isn't cause for us to be dancing on the ceiling, but why do I think there's something else? Something more.

My mind is quickly bombarded with flashbacks of that silver picture frame and Jake's happy face. "Who is she?"

He doesn't ask me what on earth I'm talking about, despite my question being vague. I start chewing my lip nervously.

He stiffens above me, his face remaining straight, but his dark eyes darken. He shakes his head.

"Jake, who is she?" I repeat, ignoring all the signs that are telling me to drop it.

He's up and off me in the blink of an eye, leaving me bare and now chilly on the woodland ground. "Everything isn't always as it seems, Cami," he says through a tight jaw. "Don't believe everything you see." He paces over to his pile of clothes and yanks his jeans up, pulling them on aggressively.

Sitting up, I wrap my arms around my legs, feeling small and stupid. I watch warily as he wrenches and yanks at the buttons of his fly, trying to fasten them. His hands are shaking. "Then tell me what to believe," I plead tentatively.

He breathes in deeply and turns to me. "I'm not ready to share that part of me with you."

Hurt slices me, and I drop my gaze to the ground, not wanting him to see it. So there's something to tell, but he doesn't want to tell me? He knows everything there is to know about me. It doesn't seem fair. He knows what Sebastian did to me. I confided in him when I'd never breathed a word of Sebastian's violent outbursts to anyone except Heather. No one could know I'd been that weak. Never.

I could get up and walk away from Jake. I could demand to know and refuse to let it rest until he tells me.

I could.

But I won't.

Perhaps my subconscious is telling me I actually don't want to know. It's painful to him, therefore it means something. Anyone who's caused him to behave so hurt and damaged hurts me also. Not because Jake feels that way but, selfishly, because someone else had that power over him. Someone else had that effect on him, and they still have.

"Angel?"

I show him my face. It's not streaming with tears, nor is it hurt or slighted. It's just me. "I understand," I tell him, even though I don't.

But my reasons for not wanting to know go way deeper than Jake could ever comprehend. I don't want to believe he ever existed before I found him—that he was a soldier or, most significantly, that he was someone else's. I want to believe that he was just a shadow. Or that he's always been mine.

I'm huddled on the ground, feeling a little lost amid my thoughts, as Jake comes over and takes my arms, pulling me to my feet. "We haven't eaten," he says, taking us off track to issues that are far more trivial, yet much more appealing, despite my appetite having run for the hills.

I don't tell him that, though. It'll hint to the sick feeling I have rolling round in my tummy, and of which I'm trying my hardest to ignore. "Then let's eat." I force a smile and cherish the one I get in return.

"Sit." He pulls me down to the blanket and starts rummaging through the basket, eventually pulling out a platter of cold meats and a basket of bread rolls.

"Where did all of this come from?" I ask.

"I have someone who stocks the cupboards for me. A local farmer based about thirty miles that way." He nods past me, but I don't look. I won't see a farm thirty miles away even if I wasn't surrounded by trees. "He has a little farmers' shop."

"And he delivers from thirty miles?"

"For me, yes." Jake smiles, offering me the plate and a fork. "The beef has been hung for thirty days. It's divine."

I help myself to the beef. "Does he know you?"

He gives me a look as he loads his own plate. "He knows me but he doesn't *know* me," he says, making me laugh on the inside. That makes two of us.

We eat in relative silence. It doesn't bother me, because it gives me the opportunity to discreetly watch him. This place isn't the kind of house or location that I would have matched up to Jake. It doesn't suit him, but then, it does, in a weird kind of way. It's secluded. Just like he is. What's certain, though, is his peace. He's mellow. Calm. And the longer I watch him, the more relaxed and serene he appears.

I force myself to eat what I've put on my plate. There's no signs of any green or salad, and I'm wondering if that was consciously chosen on his part. I shouldn't care. I haven't got another shoot until a week from Friday. Plenty of time to worry about avoiding carbs. I've gone without them for so long, that tiny roll has stuffed me. I feel fit to burst.

Moving my plate to the side, I fall to my back and stare up at the sky. "I love it here," I declare to the clouds, hearing Jake's light laugh as he clears my plate.

"So do I." He appears above my naked body, towering high. With a gun in his hand.

My eyes stick to it, the black weapon resting easily in his grasp, pointing at the ground.

"Is it loaded?" I ask, pushing myself up onto my elbows.

"It's always loaded." A slight shift of his grip has a chamber falling out of the handle into his spare hand. "Want to try?"

My eyes bug. "Try firing a gun?"

"Yes." He grins wickedly. "It's a massive rush."

"Okay!" I'm up like lightning, weirdly excited by the prospect. "What do I need to do?"

He's delighting in my enthusiasm. "This here is the magazine." He holds up the black rectangular thing.

I frown at him. "Magazine?"

"Not your kind of magazine." He rolls his eyes on a mild chuckle. "It holds the bullets." He slips it into the bottom of the handle and smacks it, locking it into place on a thrilling sound of metal on metal.

The sound isn't the only thrilling thing. Jake looks hot as fuck handling it in only his jeans. I swallow, trying to moisten my suddenly dry mouth.

"Here." He hands me the gun, handle first, and I reach forward tentatively, taking it from his grasp as I hold my breath, feeling all kinds of forbidden resting in my hand.

"It's heavy," I muse, flexing my grip.

"It's one of the lightest handguns on the market." He circles and comes in behind me, pushing his back close to mine. "You're a true vision, bollock naked and with my gun in your hand."

He pushes his groin into my lower back, making me jerk. The gun starts to shake lightly in my grasp, and my breasts are pushing forward as my back lengthens. "You shouldn't do that when I'm holding a loaded weapon."

"Easy now." He laughs, reaching round me and steadying my wrist. "I want you to aim for that tree over there."

"I can't shoot a tree!" I object, horrified. "They're living, breathing things!"

"In that case, they've just got the show of their lives." He laughs again, the sound so lovely I can't possibly scowl at his quick quip. "It's already dead, angel." Jake releases me and points to some branches above. I follow his pointing hand and spot the signs of hollows in the trunk. "Has been for years."

"Oh." I shrug my shoulders and lift the gun, pointing it at the center of the trunk, one eye closing as I try to aim. I feel my lips twist in concentration, determined to hit my target. "Do I just pull the trigger?"

"Not so fast, angel." His palms push into my shoulders. "Keep your shoulders square, your arms relaxed, and your thumbs away from the slide at the back. It pinches like a bitch if it catches you."

I nod, despite being a bit overwhelmed by the onslaught of instructions. I check my that thumbs are clear, square my shoulders, and force my arms to soften. "Right."

"The power will shock you at first. Be prepared for the kickback."

"Okay," I say, widening my stance a little.

Jake comes in closer to my side and indicates the back of the gun. "Pull the slide back." He points to the top of the gun, and I do as I'm bid, pulling it back as I pull in breath. "The red light here tells you the gun is uncocked and you're ready to fire.'

I move my eyes to where Jake is indicating at the back of the gun, seeing the red light. "So I'm ready? Just squeeze the trigger?"

"Just squeeze the trigger."

My teeth grit and I close one eye as I squeeze the trigger.

Bang!

"Holy shit!" I jump a mile into the air, vibrations rippling up my arms, the gun flailing as I swing around.

Jake's quick to move in and seize it from me, obviously prepared. "You missed by a mile," he says, amused, pointing toward my target.

"It wasn't a mile!" I protest. "And how would you know? Those things fire bullets at stupid-miles-per-hour."

"Ooh, is my angel competitive?"

"No." I snort, ignoring his smirk. "Give me that gun!" I know better than to snatch it back, so I hold my hand out and give him an expectant look.

He's enjoying this. And I can't deny it, so am I. Laying the gun in my palm, he gestures toward the tree, all gentlemanly. Piss-taking arsehole.

I secure my grip, then aim once again, following all of Jake's previous instructions. I don't miss his small sound of praise. I'm going to hit it with this shot. Just watch me. Keeping both eyes open this time, I squeeze.

Bang!

My arms don't fly around this time, and I manage to remain in position, which is how I know the bullet missed the tree by a long shot. Not a mile, but still. "How do I reload?" I ask, keeping my focus on the bark of the trunk.

"It's semiautomatic."

I sigh. "Which means what?"

"Which means it loads itself each time a bullet is fired. One pull of the trigger, one shot. As soon as you release the trigger, it's ready to go again."

"Right. So I just keep firing?"

"Just keep firing," he confirms.

I pull again, sending another bullet zooming toward the tree. And past it. "Damn!" I release and squeeze, but again I miss by a mile. I growl under my breath and realign my focus.

Bang!

Bang!

Both miss. "Shit!" I keep firing, each time failing to hit my target, until the slide atop the gun doesn't retract to allow me to fire anymore.

"You're out of bullets, angel." He sounds smug.

"I don't like this game," I mutter, dropping the gun to my side. It's much harder than it looks.

Jake moves in and takes the gun from my hand. "Practice makes perfect," he quips, releasing the magazine thingy.

"How perfect a shot are you?"

He tucks the weapon under his arm and goes to his pocket, pulling out some bullets and feeding them into the chamber of the magazine. "Shall we see?"

"You're perfect, aren't you?" He was a sniper. Of course he's perfect.

He waggles a cocky eyebrow and locks the magazine in place. "What am I aiming for?" he asks seriously.

Oh, I'm going to make this as tricky as possible. I turn toward the tree and search for an obvious distinguishable mark, something small and precise. I smile when I find it. "About two meters up from the ground, just to the right. There's a black circular mark."

Jake searches it out. I know when he finds what I'm pointing at because he smiles that beautiful smile. "There?"

"*Exactly* there," I say, standing back.

"Whatever my angel wants." He pulls the slide back, raises his arm, aims, and fires with hardly a second to line up his shot.

The dead wood of the tree bursts, sending scraps of bark flying in every direction. "No way!" I yell, running toward the tree. I reach the base and look up to the exact spot I indicated, finding a perfect bullet hole. He couldn't have got it more perfect if he was at point-blank range.

"Jesus, Jake!" I swing around and find him directly behind me, looking up at the tree, too.

"I think I hit it." He shrugs nonchalantly.

I gasp and jab him in his hard stomach, punching a chuckle from him. "That's unreal!"

With a smirk, he lifts the barrel toward his mouth and gently blows across the end. The playful move has all kinds of pricks, stabs, and tickles happening all over my naked skin. Oh fuck, he looks unreasonably gorgeous, bare-chested and armed with a gun. I bite my lip and transfer my line of sight from his lush, pouting lips to his sparkling dark eyes. My condition is clear. His awareness to it is clear, too, in the form of a mild, knowing grin.

"Okay there, angel?" he murmurs, slowly bending and placing his gun on the ground before rising back to his full height. He reaches forward with the tip of his finger and drags it from my shoulder down to my breast. I convulse, backing up into the tree. I try to talk, to match his poise, but it's in vain. I'm so turned on. He smiles and steps forward, not allowing me to escape him. Then he follows through with the same action, letting his fingertip meet my shoulder again and trail lightly down to my breast. His eyes follow its path carefully. This time, he circles my nipple, and I bang my head against the tree, my eyes closing, a moan breaking free on a puff of wispy air. "Naughty girl," he whispers, his touch dragging across my stomach, heading to the apex of my thighs. My desire gushes south, leaking from my core. I'm so fucking wet.

"Jake," I whimper, running my hands across the rough bark of the dead tree.

He hums and slips his hand between my thighs, my wetness making his caressing fingers slide with ease. I buck against the tree, hearing Jake expel a burst of breath. His hand is suddenly gone and he's pressed up against my chest. I open my eyes and find him breathing down on me. He smirks and attacks my mouth with brute force, kissing me punishingly, fisting my hair. His fingers slip between my legs again and rub, slipping and sliding around my swollen clit. I grab him, ravishing his mouth as he growls and works me furiously toward where I need to be. I start to shake, I start to sweat, and then the pressure explodes without much warning, sending my knees bandy. I collapse forward into his body and shudder through my release, my mouth coming to a grinding stop, though Jake makes sure our lips remain connected, slowing the strokes of his fingers when I cry into his mouth. He gives me the time I need to recover, holding me up, breathing in my ear.

"Time for a bath, angel," he whispers, victory and satisfaction rampant as he collects my limp body into his arms and carries me out of his enchanted woodland.

Chapter 27

JAKE

I ran the bath, tested the temperature, made sure it was fluffy with bubbles, and then lowered her into the water, melting under the sound of her contented sigh as she slipped beneath the foam. It's up there at the top of my list of favorite times with Cami. It wasn't premeditated, but I somehow managed to get the depth of the water just right, so the peaks of her breasts just broke the surface. I could have stayed there all night squeezing the sponge over her shoulders as she hummed happily, her eyes closed.

But the water started to get cold, and I started to see goose bumps appearing over her exposed skin. After coaxing her from the tepid water, I wrapped her up and put her in bed. Being here, hidden away at my safe haven, I should have had no problem snuggling up to her and sleeping deeply all night.

But I couldn't sleep. I did, however, climb in behind her, spooning her deliciously, her body curving perfectly into mine. My mind was too busy to shut down. Still is.

Once she'd drifted off to sleep, I gently detached myself from her warmth and sat on the edge of the bed. All damn night. My thoughts were so loud in my head, I was convinced they would wake her.

I hate myself with a vengeance for reacting like I did when Cami gently pressed me on the photograph again. It was my perfect opportunity to spill, but it's still too soon. I have things I need to do first. Today is the day I fix everything. Find Abbie and put my darkness to rest. And then I'll tell Cami everything. I'll give her all the missing pieces. Today I'll know whether I can have a life with Cami, or whether I'll be falling over the edge of the dark hole I've balanced on for so long.

I rise from the bed and pull on some boxer shorts, then make my way down to the kitchen, leaving her sleeping. I'll make her breakfast. Something stodgy and filling.

I fill the frying pan with bacon and whip up some scrambled eggs, before loading the toaster. The smell is soon permeating the kitchen, and I don't hold back on noise, knowing it'll be traveling through the house along with the smell, and hopefully stirring her from her dreams. Flipping the bacon, I look over my shoulder when my phone starts ringing on the counter behind me. I can see from here who it is. I had planned on calling him as soon as I had tended to his daughter. So, he's beaten me to it.

"Logan," I say, resting my arse against the worktop, keeping my eye on the door for any sign of Cami.

"We need to talk."

"You don't say," I quip dryly, not exactly building the trust I'd planned on. "Get the charges from Sebastian Peters dropped and I'll talk to you."

"How?"

How? Did he really just say that? "Just like you do everything else, Logan. Ruthlessly. Pay him. Bribe the cops that are in your pocket. I don't care how. Just get it done." I walk over to the pan and poke the sizzling bacon around.

"What about my girl?"

Hearing this lowlife refer to my angel as his girl not only makes my skin physically crawl, it makes my blood boil. "Cami isn't exactly holding you in high esteem right now."

"That's because you've brainwashed her! You've manipulated her into bed and taken advantage of her. I can see to it that you never work again!"

"I couldn't give a fuck if I never worked again. Don't think I need the cash, Logan. I don't. I need the focus, that's all. Your daughter is providing me with that these days." I didn't plan on stooping to those levels. Honestly, I didn't.

"You sick bastard!"

"Don't call me sick when you're playing Russian roulette with your daughter's safety." The metal spatula in my hand is being squeezed to the point it's bending. I swear, if Logan was in front of me now, it would be wrapped around his fat head.

"My daughter is perfectly safe."

"She is when she's with me. But I've been doing a little digging myself, Logan. You've probably guessed. I know there's an e-mail file you've been keeping from me, and I'm guessing it's part of the reason you want me gone."

His silence speaks volumes.

"Get the charges dropped." I hang up and drop my phone and the spatula to the counter, bracing my hands on the side and breathing through my fury.

I'm at fucking war with the father of the woman I love. And worse still, I'm prepared to take him out if he gets in my way. I almost laugh at the irony. Logan brought me in to protect Cami from the enemy. Bet he never thought the tables would turn against him. I bet he never bargained for me. I close my eyes and let my strung muscles work their way down until they're soft again.

I can't waste time anymore. Grabbing my phone, I do what I should have done a long time ago. I call the number that's been haunting me for years. It's time to lay some ghosts to rest. It's time to make things right.

Each ring gets my heart racing faster and faster, until it's shuddering in my chest, making my breathing erratic and sharp.

"Hello?" Abbie's voice makes my heart slam to a stop just like that. I open my mouth to speak, but nothing comes. "Hello?" she repeats.

There's air, waiting to be expelled with some words, but nothing forms. I can't speak. The silence stretches, as I search for the capability to talk, to say anything, to tell her it's me. My determination has been flattened by the sound of her voice. Memories are thundering forward, pounding in my head. Her face. That beautiful, angelic face.

I can't do it.

I go to disconnect.

"Jake? Jake, is that you?"

I freeze, my whole body arrested by shock. How did she know?

"It's me." I spit the words out before I can convince myself otherwise, and wait for her reaction.

It comes instantly. "Oh my God..." she breathes, the words disjointed and threatened by tears. "Jake, talk to me."

I search far and wide for anything to say, but there's nothing to be found.

"Jake, please." She's starting to cry now, her desperation cutting through me like acid. I look up to the ceiling, feeling hopeless and so fucking guilty.

"I'm here," I say, gulping down some strength and vehemently denying my hand's desire to cut the call.

"Where are you?" she asks, panic rampant.

I swallow hard. "I need to see you."

The brief silence is filled with unspoken words. *Need*. I need to see her. Not *want* to or *have* to. I *need* to. "Okay," she agrees. "When?"

"I don't know. Tomorrow, maybe."

"I'll be here." There's no hesitation whatsoever.

"Good."

"How have you been?" She's trying to keep me on the line, trying to gauge what she might be faced with.

I can't feed that need in her. Not now. "I'll call you tomorrow." I hang up and throw my phone across the worktop, trembling like a fucking pussy.

How can a grown man be so terrified of a female? How can she reduce me to this? It's the exact reason I've stayed away. It's the reason I'm dead to her. I try to stabilize my chaotic breathing, collapsing to a nearby chair. It's done now. No going back. I can't have a future if I can't put my past to rest. I never wanted a future before Camille. I was happy residing in my fucked-up limbo, beating myself up day after day.

"Hey, you okay?"

I shoot a look across the kitchen, finding Cami in the doorway, her body concealed by that white T-shirt I just love. I AM NOT TO BE IGNORED.

I never knew how apt that statement would be. Her hair is a tangled mess atop her head, her eyes sleepy but still bright. And her legs—the most perfect legs I've ever seen. Her face, her presence, her voice. They realign my focus and kick me into gear. Standing from the table, I wander over and seize her aggressively, soaking up the startled yelp she sounds off. I can do this. For Cami, I can do anything.

"I'm just about fucking perfect," I say, ravaging her neck, growling as I do.

She giggles, holding onto me as I recline her back in my arms, going to town, getting everything I can from her. I need it. "Jake!"

"How did you sleep?" I return her to vertical and make a fuss of straightening her out. I don't need to. She's flawless.

She frowns at me, a bit bemused. "Fine. You?"

"Perfectly," I lie, taking her hand and leading her to the table. I push her down in the chair before tucking her in and rushing to the pan to take it off the heat. "I made you breakfast."

"You did?"

"Yes. Eggs and bacon." I throw the eggs in a clean pan and grab some plates.

"But I'm—"

I swing around and wave a wooden spoon at her, shutting her up before she goes on to tell me that she's not up for breakfast beyond spinach. "You're not leaving the table until it's gone."

She recoils, her head tilting in amusement. "Like I'm a child?"

"No," I counter quickly, stirring up the eggs. "Like you're a woman with healthy eating habits." So there.

"Right," she says from behind me. I can picture her face. It'll be affronted. She can argue all she likes. She's eating this breakfast.

I stir the eggs and get the toast from the toaster. "And guess what?"

"What?"

I turn and slap the toast on the chopping board, grabbing a knife. She watches me with interest. "You get real butter." I hold up the slab of pure fat and grin like an idiot.

"I prefer dry toast." She gets up and wanders over to the cupboard, pulling a mug down blindly, keeping scornful eyes on me.

"No you don't. Your *agent* prefers dry toast." I scoop a huge helping from the tub and hold it up for her to see. Her eyes narrow, and I grin some more. "Yum." I lick my lips and then slap it on the toast, smearing it liberally.

"It's my job, Jake," she sighs, turning toward the kettle. "You don't see me taking bullets out of your gun."

I consider what she's said . . . for a second. "It's my job to make sure you eat decently."

"That's not decent. It's a heart attack on a plate."

"Doesn't hurt once in a while." I serve it all up and slide it onto the table, then sit and wait for her to finish making the tea.

I'm hungry. I could dive into my breakfast, but watching her putter around my kitchen is far more fulfilling. I sit back in my chair and get comfy, studying her every movement. She reaches up on tippy-toes to get the teapot from the top shelf, making her T-shirt ride up to her pert arse as she does. I smile, and she starts to hum, jiggling her shoulders as she moves around my kitchen, oblivious to the observation she's under. She opens the door to the fridge and bends to get the milk, and then she's reaching across the counter to open the drawer and grab a spoon.

She's sex on legs, and she isn't even trying. My arms come up across my chest, my arse slipping down the seat a little as I relax. The smile on my face is glued into position. Always will be if I get the pleasure of this every day. Compelled to touch her, I get up from my chair and walk silently over to her as she waits for the kettle to boil. Her hands are resting on the counter, her fingers strumming as she continues to hum. I'm keeping her forever. Resolution courses through me like an elucidating lightning bolt. Everything falls into perfect place.

I'm as close to her as I can be without touching her, virtually breathing down her neck. "Angel."

Her humming stops and she stills before me.

"Turn around."

She holds her unmoving position for a few seconds, the kettle bubbling in front of her.

And the moment it clicks off, she slowly turns to me, her profile coming into perfect view, her eyes round and unsure as she searches me out. She holds onto the counter for as long as her turning body will allow, finally releasing it and facing me.

She looks down at me.

Down at me?

I'm six foot four inches fucking tall. How is *she* looking down at *me*?

Then I realize.

I'm kneeling.

Her chest expands sharply above me, her hand coming to her mouth.

"Marry me." I've no idea where that came from, and by the look on Cami's face, neither does she.

"Jake?" She says my name as a question, like I might be someone else in disguise.

"Marry me." The demand just tumbles right out again, my hand lifting and taking hers. Deep down, I know I shouldn't be doing this. I shouldn't be asking her to make a lifetime commitment to a man who is pretty much deceiving her. Keeping her in the dark. But I can't take it back now, and more than that, I don't want to. I'm a desperate man, willing to do anything to reinforce how much she means to me. So when I share the horrors of my past with her, I stand the best chance of keeping her. It's tactical, I realize that, but my devotion to her is all I have. It's the only weapon I possess that can win me this battle.

Her round eyes look like they could explode with tears. And then they do, with little notice and not a hint of whether they're happy or sad tears. "What are you talking about?"

"Me and you," I begin, a little panicked by her reaction. I tug her down until she's kneeling with me, perseverance running through my body like quicksilver. "I want you to be mine, Camille. Wholly. I don't know how else to express that."

She drops her eyes a little, but not so much that I can't see them darting with uncertainty. I swear, if you were to stick a knife through my heart, I wouldn't feel a thing. Doesn't she want me? Has this been some exciting game, some way to defy her father? All kinds of stupid thoughts plague my mind as I wait for her to say something, my senses being questioned. I'm not alone in this. I can't be.

"Yes."

I barely hear the word, my screaming mind too loud. "What did you say?"

She looks at me. Her expression now is clear and certain. "I said yes."

"Yes?" I need clarification. I need to know I'm not hearing things.

"Yes," she affirms, nodding as she does. "Yes." Tears start to trickle from her eyes, forming a river down her cheeks. "Yes. I don't know how else to say it." She drops to her haunches, as if exhausted by the whole emotional episode. She shrugs, cute and on a half-smile. "Yes, I'll marry you. Right now if I could. I can't begin to imagine my life without you in it." She winces, as do I. It fucking hurts. Like hell. "I don't need anyone else." She goes on. "Just you. So yes, I will marry you."

My internal organs all turn to mush and when I try to express my gratitude, I only manage a pathetic whimper. My arse drops to my heels, too, and I swallow repeatedly, forcing the lump down my throat. I'm feeling a bit emotional. How the fuck does she do this to me?

"You've taken everything manly in me and pulverized it." It's the stupidest thing to say, but with a lack of anything else coming to me, I just mumble on like an idiot. "I flat-refused this job when Lucinda first e-mailed me the details. I looked at your picture and laughed at my laptop." I bumble on, and she smiles knowingly. "I pride myself on being impenetrable. I don't like myself, Cami, but *that* bit I loved. No one got close. I wouldn't let them. But you..." I trail off, dropping my gaze to her lap and exhaling on a shaky breath. "You changed all that." I meet her eyes again. I'm still at a loss for how, when, why, and where. "You calm me, regardless of the fact that you've actually made my life the most chaotic it's ever been. You've found me, despite the fact that I never wanted to be found." I grab her hands and squeeze, desperate for her to understand the depth of impact she's had on me. She looks stunned but calm. "You're the missing piece I wasn't looking for, angel. And now I'm scared of being incomplete again. I'm so scared of being without you."

She sags before me, her lips trembling. "I said yes." She hiccups over her words, her throat pulsating from her gulps. "And I kind of knew all of that." Her voice breaks and her breath stutters, her eyes dropping, like she's ashamed of crying.

She shouldn't be. I'm a hot mess.

I grab her shoulders and haul her into me, clinging to her like my life depends on it. Scarily, I realize now that it does. No Cami, no me.

I just hold her, our bodies a mess of tangled limbs on the kitchen floor, my hands working constant strokes over her head as she sobs into my chest. "You're not to be ignored, Miss Logan," I say into her hair, kissing the back of her head.

"My dad," she croaks, making no attempt to break free from me.

"It's all going to be fine." I don't hold back, and she doesn't question it, because she depends on me. Her faith in me is fierce. I can't let her down, but at the same time I realize that there's far more than her father that she should be afraid of. "I don't have a ring." I say the words with amusement that's probably a little inappropriate.

"I don't care," she declares, pulling out of my clinch. "Draw one on."

She shouldn't put ideas in my head. Looking up onto the counter, I spot a ballpoint pen. I can just reach it without getting to my feet. Bringing the pen to my mouth, I pull off the cap and grab her left hand.

She doesn't even flinch. I position the pen on the top of her ring ringer and start to draw a neat line around the circumference, dragging it across her flesh lightly. I'm sure to be as neat as I can, which is fucking easier said than done when you're shaking with happiness. She keeps still as a statue, watching me pen an engagement ring on her finger. I add another band, and then fill in the gap, before tracing a circle atop, representing what I intend to be a huge fucking diamond. "There," I declare, pulling back and inspecting my handiwork. "I guarantee you'll not see another like it."

She pulls her hand away and flattens her palm, straightening her fingers, her head tilting from side to side as she studies it. "It's beautiful." She grins, and clenches her fist, bringing her knuckles to her mouth and blowing it dry. "I'll never take it off."

I laugh, so fucking happy as I chuck the pen aside. "Just come here, woman."

She throws herself into my arms and crushes me, eating my neck, so over the top, but so welcome. "I love you, Jake Sharp."

"Snap," I whisper, smiling into her embrace.

This is the proverbial *fuck you* to her father. He might see it as tactical. Maybe it is a little. But what it is above everything is the ultimate sign of my devotion. It was impulsive, but above that, it was natural. I love her with a merciless power that's rooted in the deepest part of me—a part I never knew was there. I never knew I was capable of such possessiveness. She'll never know how much she's helped me. She's straightened out my fucked-up head. I will do whatever it takes to keep her. If that means facing my past head-on, then I'll do it. If that means eliminating her father, then I'll do it. The purpose burning through my bloodstream is potent.

"Is that your phone?" Cami shifts in my arms, waking me from my inner thoughts. I hear the light buzzing of my mobile and get to my feet, pulling Cami up with me.

"Finish your tea," I order softly, pushing my lips against her temple as I cast my eyes across the kitchen to where my phone is sitting on the worktop.

"Okay," she agrees easily and lets me release her, returning to the kettle and flicking it on again.

I stalk over to my phone and snatch it up, surprised to see Lucinda's name glowing at me. I was expecting Logan. Either way, this isn't a conversation I want Cami hearing. I connect and wander from the kitchen. "What do you have?"

"Logan's wife has filed for divorce."

My steps stutter before I make it from the kitchen. Taking a quick peek over my shoulder, I find Cami busy pouring boiling water into the teapot. I carry on my way, out of earshot. "Does he know yet?" I make my way into my study and shut the door behind me.

"No. The papers were filed yesterday. I guess he'll receive them soon enough."

"I'd love to be a fly on the wall," I muse. "Something tells me he'll need to get another divorce lawyer."

Lucinda laughs loudly. "Oh, he will. You know Logan's officially called off your protection, right?"

"Shame I'm not going anywhere," I mutter. "But he's not told the agency about me and Camille?"

"Not yet."

"He won't," I say, sure of that.

"How d' you know?"

"Because he knows I know he's hiding something, and it's something more damaging to him than my relationship with his daughter." I drop into my office chair, trying to unravel everything in my head. "I plan on seeing him tomorrow and I *don't* plan on leaving his office until he tells me what's going on." I'll hold a gun to his head if I have to.

"What about the police and the fact they want your arse?"

"He's rectifying that little issue."

"And the other little issue? Or a *massive* issue for Logan? Like the fact that you're in love with his precious daughter."

I laugh under my breath. "And the fact that I've asked her to marry me."

"You did what now?"

"You heard."

"And what about..." Her words fade to nothing, though I still hear them, loud and clear, deafening me.

"I'm working on it. I've called Abbie."

"Fuck me, Jake."

"Thanks, but you've never been my cup of tea."

"Fuck you."

I smile. "Original."

"I like to keep things simple and to the point." She sniffs.

"I have something I need you to do for me."

"What's that?"

"I need you to watch Cami for me when we're back in town. I have a few things to do."

"I'm not a babysitter, Jake. That's *your* job, remember?"

"You're the only person I trust, Luce. Don't be a bitch about it."

"Fine!" she huffs, probably throwing me evils over the phone.

"Thanks. I'll call you later." I hang up and slide my phone down my cheek, nibbling on the edge in thought.

It vibrates and chimes against my lip, notifying me of the arrival of an e-mail, and I open to find a voice recording from Logan. Interested, I play it, hearing a conversation between Logan and another younger man, who I recognize as Sebastian. The conversation is short and sweet. Logan offers him money. Sebastian accepts, agreeing to drop the charges against me immediately. That kid must have cost Logan hundreds of thousands.

It'll do. He works fast; I'll give him that. Anyone would think he's a desperate man.

Time to go sort out this mess.

CHAPTER 28

CAMI

The dread that engulfs me as we drive down Edgeware Road into the city the next morning is bordering crippling. I'm constantly glancing down at my fading makeshift ring to remind myself everything is going to be fine. Jake has said so, and I'm clinging onto his words with all I have.

I just want all this awful, bad feeling to be over. I want everyone to get along and be happy. It's a big hope.

Jake has been quietly pensive for most of the journey. I can tell by the way he smiles at me each time he catches me studying him that he's trying to fill me with ease. I don't have the heart to tell him that he's failing.

"Where are we going?" I ask, trying to sound casual when on the inside I'm begging him to take me back to the bluebell woodland.

"To your place." He says it with an ease that should probably chase away my apprehension. Yet it doesn't.

"My place?"

"Yes, unless you want to go to my place?" He looks across the car at me, waiting for my answer.

I don't know. Where do I want to go? "My place," I answer without giving it too much thought.

"Then I'll take you to your place." Jake reaches over and takes my hand, threading his fingers through mine. "Call Heather. She can keep you company."

I can't hide my rising panic. "Why, where will you be?"

"I have a few things to sort out."

I shrink in my seat. "Dad."

He looks out the corner of his eye to me, his Adam's apple protruding on a hard swallow. He suddenly looks nervous, and that makes me feel *really* nervous. "Your dad," he confirms, shifting in his chair.

"What about the charges?"

"Your father's seen sense."

I recoil in my seat, gawking at him. My father's seen sense? That's the most ridiculous claim I've ever heard. "He's had the charges dropped?"

"That's right."

"He told you that?"

"Yes."

"And you believe him?"

"I told you this would all be sorted out, angel. I meant it." He looks across the car to me again, his eyes full of reassurance that I'm in no position to appreciate. "Trust me." He has a lot more faith in my flesh and blood than I do.

What else can I do? I have to trust him. I *do* trust him. But my father? There's only a fraction of guilt attacking me when I decide on the spot that I don't trust *him*. My own father.

* * *

After Jake takes my bag to my room, he comes back through the lounge and heads toward his own room. I smile to myself a little, thinking it funny that I automatically think of it as *his* room. I follow him and push through the door, finding him sitting on the end of his bed, pushing bullets into the magazine of his gun.

My mouth drops open, but Jake doesn't flinch, just continues loading his weapon. He's going to see my dad and he's loading his gun? I raise my arm, pointing at his working hands, unable to locate the words I'm looking for.

"Just a precaution," he tells me, standing and locking the magazine in place before shoving the gun down the back of his jeans. "Don't panic. I always carry it."

"Forgive me." I laugh sardonically. "For a moment there I thought you might be planning on killing my dad."

Jake doesn't laugh. Nor does he acknowledge my curt quip. He walks right past me without another look. My body turns as he passes, my eyes following his path. No answer.

"Hey!" I go after him, the lingering panic bubbling. Snatching his arm, I yank him to a stop, but I don't have the strength to spin him to face me. So I circle him and hit him with the most serious stare I can muster. "Tell me you're not going to shoot my dad," I demand, placing my palm on his chest, my hint to him that I'm not letting him pass until he's obeyed my demand.

His face softens a little, his eyes closing briefly. He's gathering patience. Or is it strength? "I'm not going to shoot your father, angel."

My eyes scan the floor at his feet. I feel so lost. Here, but lost. "I just want to be with you." I look up at him, seeing the hopelessness in him, too. "Why all this hate and obstruction?"

He smiles sadly and moves into me, coiling his arm around my neck and settling in for a cuddle. I need it. "Because your father thinks I'm not the man for you." He nestles his lips into my hair and breathes in, long and deep. "I need to convince him that I am."

"By putting a gun to his head?" I ask into his shoulder, wondering, maybe, if it's the only way.

Jake frees me and bends, looking me directly in the eyes. His thumb draws a line across my eyebrow and down my cheek. "I'm not prepared to lose you, Cami. Your father needs to get used to that fact." He raises his eyebrows, waiting for me to agree.

I nod, reluctantly and slowly, because regardless of this being extreme and dramatic, I know he's right. "Okay."

"Besides," he goes on, clearly seeing I need more reassurance. "I've carried a loaded weapon every time I've met your father. I've managed to avoid shooting him so far."

"That's not funny." I scowl and he smiles, dropping a chaste kiss onto my forehead. "Please don't tell him about this." I raise my hand and flash him my inked ring. Jesus, one step at a time.

Jake glances down at my finger, smiling as he takes my hand and slips the pad of his thumb across the top. "Just one more reason for him to disapprove. We need to fix this."

We seriously do. I'm quite fond of my makeshift ring, for no other reason than Jake lovingly and meticulously having put it there. My dad, on the other hand, would see it as an insult. Lord, he's not going to be happy. About any of this. Jake's proposal *or* the inked ring. It breaks my heart. "We'll tell him when the dust settles."

"Whatever you want, angel." He kisses my ring and straightens, taking on an edge of resolution. "What time will Heather be here?"

"About—" Right on cue, there's a loud, forceful knock at the door. "Now," I breathe, looking over my shoulder to ensure it's still on its hinges. "Can I tell Heather we're engaged?"

"Can she keep her mouth shut?"

I ponder that for a second, pouting. I expect the whole of London will hear her squeal of surprise when I tell her. "Yes," I conclude. I'll gag her as need be. I need to tell someone.

Jake pulls me back around and pushes the hair from my face. "Relax. Look for a ring on the Internet. Plan where you want to marry me, when, and who you want there. Have fun, angel."

He drops a loving kiss on my nose before making his way to the door. The prospect of planning my wedding should excite me, but I feel unable to embrace his enthusiasm until I know what's next. Right now, his encouragement just feels like an attempt to pacify me.

He looks through the peephole—instinct, I guess—before he swings the door open and Heather virtually falls through it, her auburn hair swishing, a bottle of Prosecco in her grasp. She gives Jake the once-over as she straightens herself out, her eyes smiling. "Hey, big man."

"Afternoon." He strides past my best friend and disappears down the corridor. I breathe some strength into me. God knows I'm going to need it.

"I love how he pulls the broody sexy persona with such ease," Heather jokes, shutting the door before turning and waving the bottle at me. "I came prepared. I want to know everything." She points to the sofa and I comply, leaving her to fetch the glasses from the kitchen.

* * *

An hour later, Heather is up to speed on the chaos that is my life. She's swigged her drink in between the odd stunned gasp, and listened carefully. Honestly, I wasn't particularly looking forward to relaying every tiny detail to her, but it's been a great time killer. Jake's been gone an hour. I'm expecting a call any minute to tell me that everything is settled, my dad has graciously admitted he was wrong and accepted Jake with open arms, and we can all live happily ever after. Then I fall back down to earth and remember who my dad is.

"No disrespect, but your dad is being an arsehole," Heather declares, finishing the last of her Prosecco. "I mean, come on! He's on wife number three! What position is he in to pass judgment on what love is? And besides, if he didn't upset so many people, he wouldn't have got that threat against you and hired Jake to protect you." She smiles a little. "The irony is really quite beautiful."

I hum my agreement, looking up at the clock.

"Hey, what's that on your finger?" She makes a grab for my hand, and I pull away on impulse, looking as guilty as I feel. There's one thing I haven't told her yet, mainly because what I've already shared is a lot to take in.

"Camille?"

I look away, evading her questioning eyes.

"Is that a penned-on engagement ring?"

"It was just a joke." I don't know why I'm behaving like I'm ashamed. Perhaps the absurdity of this has just filtered into my over-loaded brain. I've agreed to marry a man I've known a matter of weeks. Maybe so, but I feel like I know him like no other person I've ever met. I dive into my glass of fizz, feeling like I'm under interrogation.

"Cami, has he asked you to marry him?"

"Yes!" I spit, waving my glass in the air, making Heather sit back, wary. "I know it sounds mad. I don't need you to tell me so."

She purses her lips, looking like a duck, and I wait for the squeal of shock that I predicted. It's a long few seconds before I conclude that it isn't going to come. I give her an expectant look, rushing her along.

She shrugs, and I frown.

"Have you anything to say?" I ask.

"Apart from the fact that he should have bought you an actual ring?"

I toss her a filthy glare. "Yes."

Cocking her head to the side, she stares into her glass, contemplating my question. She has to be shitting me. Nothing?

She eventually looks at me, and I see it. The bubbling scream working its way up from her toes. I bite my lip and move back, waiting to be blasted by the force. "Oh my God!" she screeches, her face reddening from the drain of air from her lungs, "Oh my God, Cami!" She puts her glass down and throws herself across the couch, tackle-hugging me. "Tell me I'll be your maid of honor. Tell me the budget is colossal. Tell me we can have the hen party in St. Tropez!" she squeals in my ear, making my head ring.

"I've not thought about it," I admit, taking my finger to my ear and rubbing away the aftereffect of the ringing there as Heather detaches herself from me. "Kind of finding it hard to think beyond the thought of Dad and Jake at each other's throats."

Heather laughs lightly, rubbing my arm in a sign of support. "I love how Jake isn't afraid to stand up to your dad."

I nod, agreeing. It's doesn't make our situation any less extreme, though. Glancing at the clock again, I see another fifteen minutes have passed. At what point do I check up on him? Check to see if everyone is alive? This is painful.

"Let's look at dresses," I blurt, taking drastic action in an attempt to distract myself.

"Yay!" Heather's totally on board. "Get the laptop. Oh God, Vera Wang has some beauties this season!"

I grab my laptop and load Google, trying to match Heather's enthusiasm. I don't even get to load the first page. My phone rings from the table and I scramble to my feet, virtually throwing the laptop at Heather in my rush to answer.

When I see Dad's number, I freeze, unsure as to whether that's a good sign. He's still alive. It has to be good. I connect the call. "Dad?"

"My little star!" he sings, immediately making me feel a million times better. The tension deflates out of my body like it's sprung a puncture. "Darling, the last thing I wanted to do was hurt you."

I could cry with relief. "I love him, Dad." I cut straight to the chase, feeling the need to enforce that. "I know it's a shock for you, but he's a good man." I feel like the weight of the world has been lifted from my tired shoulders.

"Camille, I need to make you understand." His voice is less jovial now, more serious. It's what I would from expect from a man who has never apologized in his life. This is a huge step for him.

"It's fine, Dad," I assure him. I know he never meant to hurt me to the extent he has. I may not like how he's conducted himself, but I understand why he did it. He needs to let go. Accept that I'm a grown woman with my own mind and my own decisions to make.

"It's not fine." He sighs. "It's not fine at all. I've failed you."

"No, Dad, you—"

"He has a wife, Camille."

The room starts spinning and I reach for a chair to steady myself. "What?" I whisper, every drop of moisture in my mouth sucked up in a second.

"Darling, he's married," he reiterates solemnly, punching the words into the crevice forming in my heart. "The bastard has been lying to you all along."

Stop saying that!

I fumble for the chair and drop to the seat, staring blankly across the room. The woman in the picture. Jake's happy face. I hate that what my father is telling me fits into place. Jake evading the question when I asked about the photo. Of course he would. But *married?* It doesn't seem possible.

"Camille?" Dad's worried tone punches through my daze.

"How do you know this?" I ask, needing details to try and process the shock. "Where's Jake now? He said he was coming to see you. To sort things out."

"Well, he needn't bother," he scoffs, full of repulsion. "I'll have him destroyed for hurting you, Camille."

I shake my head, frustration and hurt gripping me. "Tell me how you know this for sure."

"I had Grant follow him. He went to a woman's house. His wife's house. Grant just called to confirm it."

I shoot up from my chair. "He's there now?" I'm on my way to the door before I get my answer. "Where, Dad? Where is he?"

"Darling, I'm not having you go there alone."

I stutter to a stop. "You're lying," I goad him, knowing he'll prove it if it's true.

"18A First Street." He gives up the address easily. He's not bluffing. My heart squeezes. "Wait for me, darling. I have something to see to and I'll come and get you."

"Okay," I lie and hang up.

I'm not waiting for anyone. I grab my bag and swing the door open, forgetting that Heather is probably wondering what the fuck is going on.

"Cami!" she calls, sounding totally perplexed.

I skid to a stop halfway down the corridor, not because Heather is coming after me, but because someone is blocking my path.

"And where do you think you're going?" Lucinda looks like a stern headmistress, arms folded over her chest, her foot tapping the carpet.

"He's got you watching me?" I ask, somewhere between amusement and disbelief.

"I'm not enjoying it," she sniffs, looking past me to Heather. I don't have to turn around and find my friend to know that she'll be looking a bit blank, wondering what the hell is going on. This is just brilliant.

"Am I to assume that your duty is to stop me from leaving?" I ask, my frustration converting into boiling rage.

"You've got it." She winks, and I want to punch her face in.

"Why?" I ask. "The threats are redundant. My father told me it was all resolved."

She blanks on me. It tells me too much and not enough. "Jake's simply taking precautions."

I nod, choosing not to argue *or* raise her suspicions. Precaution? Yeah, like guarding me while he pays a visit to his wife. I turn on my heels, wandering back to the apartment, Heather looking at me, all *what the hell?* But I just shake my head, my way of telling her not to ask. What would I say, anyway? She's in there searching for wedding dresses and I've just found out my fiancé has a wife.

As I enter my apartment I look over my shoulder, seeing Lucinda hasn't budged and doesn't look like she's going to. Bitch.

Shutting the door behind me, I shove my face straight into the wood, looking through the peek hole. She looks tiny. I pull away, thinking as I pivot, scanning my apartment for an escape. I run to the window and look out. I'm too high. "Damn," I mutter, looking to my front door again. The fire escape is on the other side of the corridor. There's no way past Lucinda.

"What's going on?" Heather asks from behind, and I turn to face her, chewing my lip, fighting down the emotion that's threatening to break free and hamper my clear thinking. She takes a step back, studying me with caution. "I don't like that face," she declares. She shouldn't like it. It's my determined face.

I race to the kitchen and grab the only thing that can work, before dashing back to my lounge.

"Why the fuck are you holding a frying pan?" Heather asks as I run past her. "Cami, will you fucking speak!"

I quickly check the peek hole again and see Lucinda still keeping guard. I can't believe this is what I'm resorting to! I turn to face my bemused friend. "I need you to do something for me."

She's looking at me like I might be mad. I could well be. "What?"

"That woman out there works with Jake."

"Why is she here?"

"To stop me from going anywhere. Jake's told her to watch me."

"Why would he do that?"

Her question hampers my flow, and I pull up, realizing I'm not going to get away with vagueness, especially since I'm about to ask her to be my accomplice. I close my eyes and breathe some strength into my lungs, preparing to hear it out loud. "Dad told me Jake has a wife."

"What!" The decibel level of her yell knocks me back a few paces.

"Shhhh!" I hiss, jumping forward and slapping my palm over her mouth.

Her eyes go like saucers and she mumbles something against my hand. I have not a clue what it is, so I take my hand away, bringing my finger to my mouth in a sign to keep it down. "Do you believe him?" she asks.

I swallow down my pride and admit what I've been thinking. "It makes sense. I saw a picture of him and a woman and asked him about it. He wouldn't tell."

"It could just be another attempt by your father to tear you apart, Cami."

"He's not stupid. He wouldn't make shit like that up. Not unless he could back it up, and I doubt he'd go to the extreme of paying a woman to pose as Jake's wife." I laugh hysterically on the inside. Yeah, because *that* would be going too far. This is all adding up perfectly, and it's tearing out my heart.

"Oh, shit, Cami." Heather's sympathy could break me. "I'm sorry."

I smile. I don't know why I'm smiling. On the inside, I'm dying. "I need to find out what's going on."

"Of course." She nods, understanding, but then her eyes drop to the frying pan I've almost forgotten I'm armed with. "What are you going to do with that?"

"I'm going to knock out my replacement bodyguard." I don't beat around the bush. I haven't got time.

"I had a feeling you were going to say that." Heather shakes her head in despair. "I don't want to piss on your bonfire or anything, but I doubt the bulldog out there is going to let you walk right up to her and smack her around the head. And you can hardly tuck that thing down your knickers to conceal it."

"That's where you come in." I grab her hand and drag her over to the door.

She comes, but I feel the reluctance traveling through her limbs into mine. "I had a feeling you'd say that, too." She sighs.

"How are your acting skills?" I ask, peeking through the hole again and spotting Lucinda holding position.

"The last time I acted was in the school pantomime."

I smile, rather inappropriately, given our situation, remembering Heather playing Cinderella. "You're going to open the door and throw yourself into the corridor. Look panicked."

"I can do that."

"Tell her I'm climbing out the window."

"I can do that, too." She rolls her shoulders, readying herself, then drops her eyes to the frying pan again. "And as soon as she barrels through the door to stop you . . ."

I smile and raise the pan. "I'm going to whack her over the head."

"Fabulous," Heather mutters, putting her hand on the knob. "I only came over for wine and a chat," she reminds me grimly. Then she opens the door and starts screaming like a deranged nut job.

CHAPTER 29

JAKE

I've been sitting in my car across the road for . . . I don't know how long. Time has slowed to nothing. My heart is slowing to nothing, too. All of the purpose I'd found slipped away the moment I left Cami in her apartment. The moment I left *her*. The urge to go straight to Logan Tower to sort *that* mess first was a constant challenge. But Camille is safe under Lucinda's watch while I deal with this. Whatever Logan throws at me, I need to have made the first step to put things right. I can't move on if I have this noose around my neck. I need to face my demons and find forgiveness. Then maybe Cami can forgive me for deceiving her. Cami. I close my eyes and start rolling through the endless mental images of her face, her smile, her eyes. She's the clarity I've needed all these years. She's the trigger I needed to pull myself together and do what I've been delaying.

I reach for the car door and let myself out, shutting it softly behind me. My steps start slow as I cross the road, but get faster, more determined, the closer I get to the familiar house. It's exactly how I remember. My heart starts to beat faster, and I'm quickly flooded with the memories of this place.

I move up the path, my legs wanting nothing more than to turn and sprint away.

I don't have a chance to knock. The door swings open and I freeze.

Tears burst from Abbie's eyes the second she sees me, and she comes forward, but I move back. No touching. I can't have her touching me.

I look to the ground, escaping the desperation in her tear-filled eyes. I can't speak through the bad memories attacking my mind. I can't look at her. I haven't planned what I'm going to say. I'm totally unprepared.

"Come in, please," she says, and I see her feet move back from my dropped vision, opening the way for me.

Walking into this house could finish me off, but thinking of Cami, I step over the threshold and put myself in the closest place I can imagine to hell. The hallway walls are lined with photographs. Endless fucking photographs on both sides, caging me in. I don't look at any of them. My gaze remains downward, claustrophobia overwhelming me, making every muscle tense.

"Come through," Abbie says, inching past me in the narrow space. I practically pin myself to the wall to avoid the risk of her accidentally brushing past me, my eyes remaining on my feet as I follow her toward the kitchen at the back of the house.

"Please, sit," she says, indicating one of the chairs at the table. "Tea?"

I resist asking if she has any Jack and nod instead, lowering to the chair. She busies herself preparing tea, leaving a long fucking awful silence lingering between us.

"How have you been?" She turns with a tray and makes her way over, resting it on the table before taking a seat.

"Alive," I mutter, short of anything else coming to mind.

"I can see that." She offers a small smile that no matter how hard I try, I can't return. "Why are you here, Jake? Why now, after all these years?"

"I've met someone." The confession fires from my mouth without warning, and her face drops as a result. That was so fucking heartless, but I'm in fucking turmoil here. I don't know what the fuck I'm supposed to say.

"I guess it was only a matter of time," she says mindlessly, stirring an empty mug. "Can't say I blame you."

"I didn't plan on it," I begin, wondering why the fuck I'm explaining myself. I don't need to justify it, but I can't seem to stop myself. "It took me by surprise, trust me. I wasn't looking."

"So did you just come to tell me that?" she asks, looking up at me. "All this time I've been waiting for you to get in touch, to at least let me know you're alive. Nothing, Jake. I didn't stop caring about you."

"I can't move on with my life with all these regrets hanging around my neck." I push the words through my clenched teeth, needing some level of understanding from her. "I love this woman. I need to tell her everything there is to know about me. I can't have a life with her without that. It'd be a lie."

"Oh." She laughs sardonically, stripping away any hope I had left of her understanding. "As long as *you're* okay. As long as *you* have peace and *you* can get on with *your* life, Jake."

"I haven't got on with my life for four years, Abbie!" I yell, slamming my fist down on the table in temper. She jumps, stunned, and I immediately feel terrible for it. Her bottom lip is quivering. My elbows meet the table and my palms hide my face.

Silence falls again, yet my brain is screaming at me, making me want to get my gun from the back of my trousers and blow my brains out. Put myself out of my misery, as well as everyone else affected by this.

"You're not the only one who hasn't been able to get on with their life, Jake," she whispers. "I've been raising your daughter on my own."

Everything inside of me dies a long, painful death, my fingers clawing into my face. "I'm going to make things right," I vow, so meaning it. Cami has clarified so much for me. I just don't know where to start and how.

"Daddy?"

The sweet voice has me up from my chair and backing up, trying to escape my reality. I throw a shocked look at Abbie. "You said she wouldn't be here." She'd agreed. One step at a time!

I can't believe she's done this to me! This is emotional blackmail at its worst. I chance a quick look to the little girl and immediately regret it. She's the spitting image of her mother. Her mother. The deceiving, manipulating bitch. Abbie rushes over and kneels before the little girl, but she doesn't get her attention. Her curious eyes are nailed to me, judgment all over her little face. I look away, unable to bear it.

"Charlotte, darling, I told you to stay in your room and play."

"He looks like my daddy."

I turn away, facing the wall, my vision blurring from tears that I can no longer hold back.

"Why did you come down? Do you want a drink?"

"No. There's a lady at the door."

I whirl around on impulse. It's not only Charlotte's announcement that drives me. I can feel her close by.

Cami is standing in the doorway, her face stained with tears. The crevice in my heart cracks, splitting in two. "Cami." I move forward carefully.

She turns and runs.

"Cami!" I bolt out of the kitchen and fly down the hallway like a bullet, seeing her disappear past the front door. "Cami!"

"Stay away from me!" she screams, sprinting down the street and jumping into her car.

"No!" I keep going, my legs nearly numb from the force I'm injecting into them. "Cami, please!"

Her car roars to life and she speeds off down the road, swerving all over the place. She's going to fucking kill herself! "Fuck!" I pelt to my car and slam it into drive, pulling out and wheel-spinning after her. She's gained some distance with her head start, but she's just in my view. She takes a left at the bottom of the street, barely stopping to check for oncoming cars. "For fuck's sake, angel!" I put my foot down, prepared to slam my way through any vehicles that get in my way. I turn the wheel hard, the back end of my car swinging out, but I pull it back into line, narrowly missing a black cab.

I lose count of the number of turns I make, following her. She's five cars ahead, her driving erratic and clumsy as she tries to escape me. I won't let her. She's going nowhere. I'll *make* her understand.

My hopes of catching her build when I register Charing Cross Road up ahead. No matter which way she goes, left or right, it's going to be rammed busy with traffic. She'll have no choice but to stop.

She does a left. I wipe the sheen of sweat away from my brow and grip the steering wheel, racing to make it past the lights before they turn red. "Fuck!" They flick to amber, and I see a million pedestrians on the side of the pavement, waiting to flood the road once the green man illuminates. I'm not going to make it. I slam on my brakes, just screeching to a halt before I hit a group of tourists, bracing my arms against the wheel and heaving in my seat. They're all frozen in the middle of the road, looking at me with cameras poised in their grasps.

I exhale loudly when I see they're all still in one piece. "Shit!" I jump out of my car and run around the corner, praying for the first time in my life for bumper-to-bumper traffic.

I see her. Her red Mercedes is in the distance, caught up in the traffic. I break into a sprint, running up the center of the road, being shouted and beeped at. The other side of the road is clear, and I see the nose of her car start to jut out. She's going to make a turn. I pump my legs with more energy, gaining on her. And then the door to her car swings open and she appears, looking down the road at me. "Don't run, Cami!" I yell.

"Stop!" she screams, and like a button has been pressed, my legs come to a screaming halt. "Don't come near me, Jake!"

I hold my palms up to her in surrender, blowing out my arse from exhaustion. "Just let me explain," I call, not liking the fifty meters between us. I need to touch her, hold her while I tell her.

"You're married!" Her voice breaks, her accusing words fading into devastation. "You have a daughter! You've lied to me!"

"No!" I shake my head, taking a step forward but stopping when she moves back. "I *was* married, Cami. Not anymore."

"You're lying!"

"I'm not fucking lying!" I clench my fists, knowing I need to spit the words out before I lose her forever. "She's dead, Camille. My wife is fucking dead."

She blanks on me, making me go on.

"That woman is my wife's sister. I came back from tour and found my wife in bed with my best mate!"

"What?"

The mental flashbacks nearly have me approaching the nearest wall and smashing my head against it to crush them. But I need to persevere. I need to go on.

"We had a baby, angel. While I was on tour, she had our baby. I was coming home to be a father and a husband. I was a week early. Thought I'd surprise her. I found her in bed with my best friend." My fist comes up to my head and bangs against my forehead. "They'd been having an affair while I was fighting the fucking world!" I face her, physically shaking with returned anger and pure, raw fear. "I told myself the child wasn't mine."

Cami looks like she's in a state of shock. I can relate. My world ended on that one day. I died for four long years and I've only just come back to life.

"I found them in bed and walked out." I force myself on. "My wife came after me. Got in her car and chased me. She oversteered." I clench my eyes shut and look to the heavens. She's up there somewhere, probably looking down on me and thinking I'm getting what I deserve. "A bus took the car out. She was confirmed dead on the scene."

The whole horrific event I watched in slow motion in my rearview mirror is fresh again. Clear and vivid. I die on the inside all over again.

"Oh my God." I lip-read her sobbed words, just before her hand comes up to her mouth and covers it.

"I went back to war." I fight through my agony, reliving every second of my past. "I felt it was all I had left. I lost all sense of respect for my safety. For the safety of others. I didn't want to be here anymore. Alive. They dismissed me after medical reports deemed me unstable. Being alive became a form of continuous torture." I give into the swelling lump in my throat. I don't swallow it down. I let the tears form and my voice crack. "Then I met you."

She grabs the side of her car to steady herself. The horns are blaring now, constant and piercing, and I look to see the traffic is moving on, slowly progressing around Cami's car blocking the road. "Why didn't you tell me?" she asks, oblivious to the chaos around her.

I'm honest. "I was too bitter and twisted to face it. My wife betrayed me. I couldn't even find it within myself to forgive her when she was dead. I left. Walked away. Shut down. I turned into a hateful, bitter bastard, Camille. My daughter was better off without me. I didn't want to poison her with my blackness."

She wipes at her eyes, looking around her like the crowds of people can offer her some advice of what to do.

"Cami, I love you!" I shout it, just to be sure she hears it, my arms swinging up in front of me before dropping to my sides. She looks at me, the tears still coming. "Nothing about the time we've had together has been a lie. Not one second."

"You should have told me."

"I had every intention of telling you. I just needed to find my own clarity before I could offer you yours. I needed to see my daughter, start to make things right. I *want* to make things right. You've made me see that I can do that."

She drops her gaze, nodding, and my hope is revived as she lifts a foot from the ground. She's coming to me. I silently spur her on. I've never needed to hold her more than I do now. She takes a step, and not prepared to delay the comfort we both need, I begin toward her, too.

I ignore the continued sounds of car horns screaming around us, my focus set only on getting her back where she belongs. In my arms. She wipes at her eyes again, her face lifting as she comes to me, her eyes alive with relief and hope.

But then the loud screeching of tires adds a new ringing to my ears, and I find myself abandoning the comfort of her coming closer, searching out the source.

The rest happens in slow motion.

A van.

A white van. The same white van that sped away from me when I approached it outside Cami's agent's office. It speeds toward Cami, and her attention is immediately grabbed by how close it's come. I don't realize I'm running until the soles of my feet start burning through my boots, my legs spinning in a sprint. I see her smile drop away. I see her body lock up. But she doesn't seem to be getting any closer to me, no matter how fast I run toward her.

I watch as the van pulls to a screaming stop next to her. I see the door on the side slide open.

"No!" I bellow, the roar echoing through the streets of London. A pair of arms appear, covered in black material, and seize her, pulling her into the van. Screeching rings out through the air again, and the smell of burning rubber invades my nose. The van heads straight for me, forcing me to dive from its path. My body crashes into the tarmac with force and I roll, springing to my feet, sweating and heaving, watching as the van slams into Cami's Merc and forces it into a nearby wall on an ear-piercing smash. I'm sprinting again, trying to make it to the van as it reverses. "No!" I bellow again. It speeds off, taking a corner fast, the door pulled shut as it goes. And I lose sight of it, my legs slowing until I come a gradual stop.

Numb.

I'm numb, cold...dying.

The world is happening around me—people staring, taking a wide berth as they pass, cars moving. I feel as though everyone's looking at me like I might have broken out of an asylum. No one asks if I'm okay. No one approaches me to see if they can help.

I'm beyond help. I glance around, circling on the spot, the madness of London a blur of color and noise. She's gone. I throw my head back to the sky and roar her name.

CHAPTER 30

CAMI

I don't know where I am. I haven't seen a thing since I looked into the blackness of his eyes past the balaclava. I screamed and wrestled with him until exhaustion rendered me immobile. My brain isn't working. My body is shutting down. The blackness is now constant, my eyes covered, and my ability to scream has been taken away by the rough gag strapped in my mouth. There has been no talking. I don't know how many of them there are. I'm cold, too. Strangely, I'm not crying anymore. I'm scared, but I'm not crying. If I had the ability to think, I might wonder why.

But I don't.

So I remain silent and unmoving on the hard floor, praying.

Chapter 31

JAKE

My body is sore, my eyes are sore, my heart is sore.

She'll be frightened. She'll be calling for me.

I run back to my car, calling Lucinda on my way. "Hello?"

It's not Lucinda's voice. "Heather?"

"Oh…"

I frown down the line. "Where's Lucinda?"

"Um, she's waking up."

It falls into place very quickly. Lucinda wouldn't have let Cami leave her apartment if she could physically stop her. Which means she couldn't physically stop her. "What did you two do?"

"What did *you* do, you arsehole?" she counters scathingly, making me drink in patience before I lose the plot. "Camille's dad told her you're married!"

"Shut up, Heather," I hiss, damning Cami's determined little arse to hell. She didn't know about Charlotte. Heather doesn't mention that monumental point, and I could see by the shock in Camille's eyes. Logan dug only deep enough to find out about my wife, Monica, and didn't go any deeper, happy enough with the information he'd found to turn his daughter against me. "Cami's been taken."

"What?"

"She's been fucking kidnapped! Put Lucinda on!" I jump into my car and waste no time running the red light, smacking my horn to startle the pedestrians crossing. "Move!"

"Jake?" Lucinda sounds weary, and for a fleeting second I wonder again what the fuck Cami did, but I don't have time to go into that now.

"Cami's been taken." I swing a hard right, knowing exactly where I'm going. Blood is flowing through my veins like poison, threatening to turn me to a point of no return.

"Oh, shit. Where are you?" Lucinda asks, warranted worry evident in her tone.

"I'm about to go psycho on her father."

"Oh, fuck. Jake, don't do anything stupid."

"Too late."

* * *

I dump my car in a no-parking zone outside Logan Tower and race toward the building, pushing my way through the doors with force. The glass ricochets off the wall, sending a deafening crash through the lobby. Everyone falls silent and turns their attention to the doors and the murderous man steaming through them.

I keep my focus forward, seeing the X-ray machines up ahead and the old boy who keeps watch. His eyes grow wider the closer I get, his stocky frame dropping from the stool he's perched on. I don't give him a chance to try and stop me. I reach to my back and pull my gun, pointing it straight at his head as I stalk forward. There's no need to follow it up with a warning.

Smart man.

He backs up, hands raised, eyes now bulging. "Whoa, matey! Let's not be hasty."

I snarl, passing through the machine and marching on, leaving behind the alarms going wild behind me. I push the call button with the barrel of my gun and an elevator opens immediately. I walk in looking calm as can be, which defies the chaos coursing through me.

I've never been in an elevator for so long. By the time I reach the very top of Logan Tower, I'm ready to shoot my way out of the metal keeping me prisoner, delaying me from finding her.

I stride past the reception desk, where a gaggle of women are gossiping, and keep moving down the corridor to Logan's office. The women's high-pitched chatter soon dulls to silence before the panicked whispers start. But no one tries to stop me. The comfortable weight of my gun in my hand tells me why.

As soon as I reach the door I turn the handle, but it doesn't shift. I laugh wickedly and move back, bringing my knee up to my chest and throwing my foot into the wood. The crash doesn't even penetrate my fog of fury.

Logan jumps in his chair, his desk phone at his ear, and one of his minions staggers back in shock. "It's fine," Logan says down the line, obviously reassuring whoever's called up to advise him of the madman on the loose. "Everything's fine." He hangs up slowly, his eyes wide and cautious.

Fine? It's far from fine. I lift my arm and aim for Logan's head. "You have ten seconds to tell me what the fuck you've been hiding before I blow your brains out." And he'd better not question my intention. I pull back the slide of my gun.

"What are you talking about?" he asks, backing up in his chair like the pussy I know he is.

"You're wasting time, Logan." My jaw tenses, the pulse riding up into my brain. "Seven seconds."

"Where's Cami? What have you done with her?"

"She's been fucking taken!" I thunder forward, socking an elbow to Pete's head when he tries to stop me. He drops to the floor with a crash, groaning.

I round his desk and wedge the barrel of my gun against Logan's temple, pushing it in as hard as I can. He whimpers, his shakes riding up the metal of my weapon and tickling my hand. God help him, my trigger finger is twitchy enough already. "Fucking talk!"

"Okay, okay!" He cowers, his eyes clenching shut. "They've been blackmailing me for weeks! They asked for money. Said they'd expose me if I didn't pay!"

There we have it. Expose him. His something to hide. "Expose you how?"

His frightened eyes flick from me to Pete, who's currently peeling himself from the floor, rubbing at his head. "Leave us," Logan says, low and serious.

Pete doesn't question him. He doesn't even acknowledge the fact that I have a loaded weapon pointing at his boss's head. He walks out swiftly, not looking back.

The door closes and I jiggle my gun, my indication that he'd better hurry the fuck up and explain before I blow his head off. "They have photos," he mumbles, breathing heavily, nervous as shit.

"Of?" I push.

"Me."

I grab the collar at his throat and yank. "And?"

"A woman." He swallows, forcing the flesh of his throat to protrude and brush against my knuckles at my neck. "Or a girl."

I exhale, disgusted, but most of all relieved that I seem to be getting somewhere. "How old?"

His eyes close and he deflates before me, giving up. "Fifteen."

I drop him like the filth he is and relieve his temple of my gun, stepping back, repulsion invading my expression.

"I didn't know!" Logan squirms in his huge office chair, refusing to look at me. "She looked at least twenty. Tall. Blond. Well formed."

"You bastard."

"This can't get out!" His eyes dart across his desk, frantic and panicked. "I'm an ambassador for a children's charity, for Christ's sake! My reputation..." He looks at me, pure dread in his smarmy eyes. "My wife."

My lip curls, and I take the greatest of pleasure from what I'm about to say. "Your wife's leaving you, Logan. She filed for divorce yesterday."

"What? What are you talking about?"

"She's been having an affair with your divorce lawyer." I laugh under my breath, a laugh of utter disbelief. "She's pregnant with his child."

"You don't know what you're talking about! She wouldn't leave me!"

"Do you think I give a fuck?" I slam the gun into the center of his forehead, quaking with anger. "You called off my protection knowing Cami wasn't safe! What the fuck were you thinking?"

"You were digging!" He pushes himself back in his chair, eyes wide. "When I got the first threat, they demanded money and gave bank account details. They said that if I didn't pay, they would send the pictures to the newspapers. I told them to go to hell. I wasn't about to bend to their will. Besides, I keep close council with all the editors of the papers. I scratch their backs, they scratch mine. They certainly wouldn't benefit from the scandal and my ruin, trust me."

I balk at the immoral, egotistical twat, and he evades my eyes.

"The pictures ended up on the desk of the editor at the *Mirror*," he tells me quietly. "He called me and I made sure it would be worth his while to keep the pictures out of the papers."

"How much?"

"A million and a very interesting story on a member of Parliament."

I snarl. The man is more ruthless than I ever gave him credit for. "How much did the ransom demand?"

"Two million." Logan eyes me warily as my nostrils flare, my anger building.

"And the threat on Camille?"

"That came when they figured the pictures weren't going to get them the money they wanted. I thought I could take care of it. I couldn't let you see the real threat on Camille that I received. It talked about the photographs! The threat I showed you was printed by me. I just needed to protect Camille, and you're the best! I knew she'd be safe with you! Then you started digging. It was only a matter of time before you found something. You cared too much!"

"Because I fucking love your daughter! I couldn't give two fucks about you and your reputation. All I cared about was her safety, which is more than I can say for you! Her own fucking father!"

"You can't tell!" he says on a rush, sitting forward in his chair beseechingly, still only concerned for his fucking public status. "I'm not just worried about my business and reputation. I don't want my daughter to hate me!"

I scoff, truly amused by the deluded prick. "It's too fucking late, Logan." I shove my gun to his temple again and put some more weight behind it, forcing him to collapse back into his chair. His brow is a sweaty mess, his hands up in front of him like his pathetic, fat limbs can serve as some kind of protection. Nothing could protect him from me right now.

"You have a wife," he mumbles pathetically.

"She's fucking dead!"

"You still lied to my daughter! You still pretended to be someone you're not!"

"Don't make me fucking kill you before I have all the information I need to find her!" I lean in, sure I'm going to pierce his head with my gun to save me the bother of shooting him. "Your concern over me and your daughter is irrelevant right now."

He closes one eye, trying to lean back and escape my gun. It's a fruitless endeavor. "Please help me find her," he begs.

I relieve his temple of my Heckler and stalk around his desk, putting myself on the other side of him. He follows my every pace until I come to a stop. I aim, watch his eyes widen and his hands come up, and I fire.

The sound of shattering glass ricochets around his office, and he curls into a ball in his chair, making himself as small as possible. "I'm already planning on breaking your legs for putting her through this. But I swear, Logan." I load my lungs with air and let it stream out on my lethal vow. "If she has one scratch on her when I get her back from whoever's taken her, I won't aim past you next time."

He uncurls himself from the chair, shaking and sweating, his terrified eyes glassy.

"Nod!" I yell. "Give me something that tells me you fully comprehend what I'm telling you!"

He starts nodding frenziedly, sniffling like the spineless arsehole he is.

I search for the calm I need to function to my fullest and sit in the chair opposite him, laying my gun calmly on the table, while Logan hangs on nervously for me to speak.

He can wait while I talk myself down. He's a desperate man. A stupid man, thinking he could handle this alone. The only credit I can give him is calling me in to protect Camille. Then he fucked that up and called me off.

I remind myself that kidnappers rarely take their victim with the intention of hurting them. The sole purpose is to extort money from someone.

"Who could know what you've been getting up to in your spare time?" I ask, watching him closely. "Who could have taken those pictures of you and the minor?"

"I don't know!" he cries, waving frantic hands around his head. "I've looked into every possibility and come up with nothing! I can't ask my IT department to look into the e-mails! I can't show anyone!"

"Show *me*," I demand curtly.

"I deleted them."

I fly forward, my hand on my gun. "Don't push me, Logan."

He goes straight to his pocket and pulls out his keys before pointing to the wall across his office. "They're in the safe."

"Get them."

He gets up from his chair, struggling like an old man, and walks backward, his eyes dancing between my gun and me. His hands shake as he swivels the dial, left and right, and left again, before he takes the key to the lock and struggles with it for a few moments.

His whole body folds in on itself when he reaches inside, pulling out a blue file. Fingering it with nervous fingers, he brings it to me. I snatch it and fling it open, not treating the offending papers with the same care as Logan. I'm hit with a vivid image of his naked, hairy arse and the euphoric face of a young girl. Wincing, I go to the next sheet, not needing to see the debasing evidence that has thrown my world into anarchy. I force myself to breathe deeply before I retrieve my gun and relieve my twitching trigger finger.

Logan remains standing, nervous and quiet at my side as I flick through, finding an e-mail dated two days ago with all the incriminating pictures and more pictures of Cami. "I tried looking into the bank details listed," Logan murmurs, not needing to go on. I note the details. It's a Swiss bank. He'll get nowhere searching on basic search engines.

I get out my phone and type the digits into a message, but before I can click send, it rings in my hand. I answer quickly. "Luce?"

"Get online. Go to the London by Night website."

The name is familiar. "The magazine?" I've perused the glossy weekly a few times since I've been shadowing Cami.

"Yes. Do it." She sounds urgent, and I'm not about to argue.

I reach across the desk and pull Logan's iMac across, hitting Google and holding my phone to my ear while I type in what's been ordered of me. "Done," I tell her, seeing nothing but adverts and a few irrelevant shots of various celebs.

"The search bar at the top. Type in Camille's name."

I follow through on her order and hit search, immediately being presented with endless shots of Cami, the latest being me and her outside that café after her shoot. I'm holding her hand across the table.

"The first shot. Of you and Cami," Lucinda says.

"What about it?"

"Look behind you. Top left-hand corner."

My eyes dart up and locate *exactly* what Lucinda's talking about. "Motherfucker," I breathe. There's a shop window behind me in the picture, and clear as day in the reflection is the image of a white van tucked away in the alley opposite. There's an outline of a face through the windscreen. It's blurred, but nothing the right technology can't fix. "Run a face check."

"Already done. I've sent the picture to your phone. His name's Michael Scott, thirty-six. Been inside for drug running, armed robbery, and..." She pauses, and I swear I hear her swallow.

"And what, Luce?" My phone dings and I open the message, seeing a clear image of the man I'm going to hunt down and slice into pieces. I breathe in and take my phone back to my ear.

"Jake, it's..." Lucinda's voice drops to nothing, and I tense from head to toe.

"What?"

"Rape."

My blood freezes in my veins, and I look across the desk at Logan, his face a sea of questions. It's a high possibility that my heart is going to jump from my chest and land on Logan's desk. It's hammering *that* hard.

"Jake?"

I can't speak. Can't think.

"Jake, the van was stolen last week. The plates have been changed." She reels off the fake plate numbers. "I've run a check on Scott's address. He's supposedly in a halfway house in Bethnal Green being taken through rehabilitation." Lucinda gives me the address and it imprints to my brain, along with the fake plate numbers of the white van.

"Someone must be paying him to hold her but I can't trace any phones to his name. Probably using a disposable. I have no more than that. I'm sorry."

I stand and drink in air, placing my hand on the desk to hold me up. "Bank details. Swiss." I fumble for the file Logan handed to me and push the papers about haphazardly until I find what I'm looking for.

Then I reel off the bank account number and fill her in on everything I've just learned from Logan—the girl, the photo of his hairy arse, everything; hearing Lucinda inhaling shocked breaths, seeing Logan squirm on the other side of the desk. "Look into that account."

"I'm on it," she says, her voice drenched with compassion that I just can't handle.

I go to hang up, but she calls my name and I bring the phone back to my ear, lost in a haze of desolation. I give no indication that she has my attention. "Be careful," she says softly, showing rare concern. "Please."

I hang up and slide my gun from the table slowly, slipping it into the back of my trousers.

"What is it?" Logan asks. "Who was that?"

I look up at him, immune to the terror and anxiety on his face. "Do you know this man?" I ask, holding up my phone to Logan.

He looks, frowning. "No, I've never seen him before. Who is he?"

"He's the man someone hired to take your daughter. Pray she's unharmed, Logan. Pray real hard."

I turn and stride out of his office, sweating murder.

CHAPTER 32

CAMI

I play dead. It's easy when you pretty much feel it. I've been moved, carried by two men, from the van to somewhere else. I know it's two men. They were sure to keep quiet, but I felt two pairs of hands holding me. All I can think about is what Jake will do to them if he finds them. Will he find them? Can I be found?

I don't know where they've put me. It smells damp and dirty, and it's chilly. The floor is hard and cold, and I'm being kept in my darkness, the blindfold pulled too tightly. The gag is dry. My mouth is dry. I couldn't scream if I wanted to.

They left silently after binding my hands behind my back and sitting me up against a brick wall. It's funny. If I was ever to imagine myself in a situation like this, I'm sure I would have imagined myself crying and freaked.

The initial ten minutes were exactly like that. The following...however long it's been...I've been limp and unresponsive.

I'm not sure why I've chosen this way. Preservation of energy? I don't know. All I have to cling to is hope. Hope that if I think about him hard enough, he'll find me.

Chapter 33

JAKE

I'm a trained killer. It's a skill that earned me a formidable reputation in the war against terror. People feared me. The unknown, unseen threat. I never broke a sweat. I never let anger possess me. For a long time I never let my personal struggles infiltrate my mission. I missed my wife. I missed watching her baby bump blossom and the first kick. I missed the scans, the parenting classes, and the birth of my child. I missed the first few months of my baby's life. But none of those private battles affected my missions. My aim and balance were never compromised.

Until four years ago. Everything changed. My life turned upside down. My wife hadn't missed me. She hadn't mourned my absence. She'd found her comfort elsewhere. I had no purpose anymore.

Living wasn't just having the ability to breathe, a heartbeat in your chest. It was having people to live for. I lost all sight of my other purpose in life—the one spiked by my parents' deaths in the Lockerbie disaster. It didn't seem to matter anymore. I was no longer able to think straight and act on sensibility.

I became careless. Reckless. I became a danger to myself, and worst of all, I was a danger to everyone around me. I couldn't change anything, but after drowning in a sea of Jack, spending too many months lost in a haze of drunkenness and misery, balancing on the edge of the black pit to hell, I grabbed onto the only thing I could do to give myself some kind of self-purpose again. I couldn't have my life back. But I could protect others.

All my subjects were a job. A duty. A way to maintain my selfish purpose. I needed to forget everything about my previous life. My subjects gave me focus.

Camille Logan spun that on its head. She gave me a reason to confront my demons. She made me feel and love again. I had everything arranged in my mind, all of the hard truths set to be faced head-on, cushioned by a hope I couldn't let falter.

I handled it all wrong, and now I might have lost her forever.

Her face. The devastation when I looked up and found her in Abbie's kitchen. And then the understanding that came after I'd poured my heart out on the street, rushing to explain, my hope rebuilding by the second.

Then she was taken.

My phone startles me, vibrating in my hand, and I rush to answer, praying for something. Anything. "Luce?"

"Where are you?"

"Outside Scott's block of flats." I look across the car park that's littered with abandoned cars and piles of rubbish. Kids who should be in school are climbing in and out of the smashed windows of cars, some jumping from the roof of one abandoned vehicle to another. The grim high-rise apartment block has more windows boarded up than not, and grubby rags hanging at the smeared, filthy glass of the ones that are still intact. The monstrosity of a building stretches up into the sky, casting a shadow as dull as the brickwork across the landscape before it. It's the pits.

"Anything?" Lucinda asks.

"Nothing. No sign of any white van and the apartment is empty." I glance up to the apartment window that's in plain view, shuddering when my mind's eye reminds me of the squalor I found beyond the door after I kicked it down. And the stench. It's still embedded in my nostrils.

"I might have something."

I'm upright and quickly alert. "What?"

"Scott served his last sentence in Borstal. He was granted probation eight weeks ago and one of his parole conditions is to check in weekly with his parole officer in Shoreditch. Jake, today's check-in day. If he's following his parole conditions, he should be there now. I'm sending you the office address."

I start the car and race out of the car park, leaving a cloud of dust and crowds of tatty kids cheering in my wake. "He's doing well keeping himself out of trouble," I growl, not bothering to stop at the junction, forcing a beat-up old Escort to swerve from my path. "I think someone's hired Scott to take Camille. Keep an eye on Logan's e-mails. I expect he'll be hearing from whoever it is." I throw my phone onto the seat next to me and drive like a demon to Shoreditch.

* * *

The high street is busy, hampering my speed as I scan every face I pass. I drive up and down every road around the vicinity of the parole office at least ten times, my pulse dulling with each precious minute that passes. No white van. She'll be scared. It'll be another week before Scott has to sign in with his parole officer. It could be another week of waiting for something that could lead me to her.

"Come on!" I say to no one, taking a left and then an immediate right, coming to a stop at a zebra crossing when the road floods with schoolchildren, marching across the concrete like ants, all laughing, holding hands in pairs. Their little backs are covered with high-visibility waistcoats, making them unmissable to everyone around them. What age are they? Four, maybe? Charlotte's age.

She's mine. That little girl is mine. Shirking that sense of knowing was easy. Running away from my miseries was easy. Telling myself she wasn't mine was easier than taking care of her. I didn't even know her. She didn't know me. I couldn't be a dad. Didn't know how to be. Abbie could take care of her, bring her up and nurture her into a fine young lady without my toxic blackness affecting her life. That was best for her. For everyone.

My eyes follow the children across the road until they're disappearing down the park path, their teachers spread down the line evenly, keeping them safe. Making sure no one can take them.

Beep!

I jump in my seat, being brought back to my fading existence by a car honking impatiently behind me. "Fuck," I mutter, grasping my bearings before pulling off, having to round a parked car and put myself on the wrong side of the road.

It's then I see it.

A van.

A white van.

I just catch the back of it as it disappears around a corner, maybe three hundred yards up ahead. My heart shoots up to top speed and my foot slams the pedal to the floor. I fly up the high street at a dangerous speed, keeping one eye on the pedestrians, any of which could step into the road, and my other eye trained on the turn the van just took.

"Come on." I will my Range Rover to go faster and take the turn, wincing when the tires screech with the strain I'm putting them under.

Don't draw attention to yourself. Keep a safe distance.

Scott's been watching Cami. He'll know my car. He'll know *me*. I follow a few cars behind, hyper-alert. A roundabout appears on the horizon, and though the road splits into two lanes, I keep myself where I am, concealed behind the line of cars behind him. When the van pulls onto the roundabout, I get my opportunity. I reach for my glove compartment and grab my binoculars, zooming in on the plate's numbers. The rush of air that deflates my lungs could fog the screen.

It's him.

I dial Lucinda, never taking my eyes off the van, seeing it take the third exit onto the City Road. "I have him," I say when she answers. "Have there been any e-mails? Ransom requests?"

"Nothing. I'm watching," she informs me. "Jake, be careful."

I nod and hang up, unable to ease her concerns. Then I take the wheel with both hands and center my attention forward. It's the longest journey of my life.

He makes two stops on the way. One at a service station, picking up some water and a crummy sandwich, and then a few miles down the road at an industrial park, where he picks up a scrawny, scruffy man with long greasy hair and a hooked chin.

"Take me to my girl," I whisper, edging out slowly and following them. Countless turns, stops, and too many skips of my heart later, they rumble up a deserted road toward an abandoned ruin of a factory.

I pull over to the side of the broken-up lane, positioning my car amid some sad-looking evergreens, its branches dead and woody but still perfectly dense. I run the rest of the way, half-bent, keeping myself low, seeing the van circle around the back of the unit. I reach the crumbling masonry of the building's face and take a few moments to gather some air, keeping my breathing steady as I pull my phone free and turn it to silent, not leaving anything to chance. Then I replace it in my pocket and fill my hand with my Heckler, pulling back the slide.

To this point, I've had to rein myself in, hold myself back when all I wanted to do was ram Scott off the road and torture him for her whereabouts. Telling myself not to jump the gun, that she might not even be here, has been a fight like no other I've had. I walk in calm, measured steps, treading carefully, keeping my shoulder close to the flaking brickwork of the derelict factory building. My ears are hyper-sensitive. I hear the closing of the van doors, I hear one of the scumbags laugh, and I hear the scuff of their boots on the ground.

The echo of metal hitting metal invades the air, and I round the corner carefully, spotting a huge iron door. I reach up to my brow and wipe away the beads of sweat, blinking rapidly to keep my vision straight and focused.

Remaining unseen and unknown—it's built into me. I can't allow my personal desperation and attachment to affect me. Not again. Creeping to the door, I take the handle and pull gently, flinching when the iron scrapes against the rusty frame. A damp stench smacks me in the face, along with a cool gust of air and the echoes of their voices.

Once I've let the door close softly behind me, I follow the sounds of the voices coming from the throats I plan to slice. I'm surrounded by abandoned machinery, all of it ancient and resembling torture devices rather than industrial equipment. I can still hear them in the distance, the old dilapidated building carrying the sound through the musty air. I pass through room after room, my gun constantly poised to fire, my eyes surveying every inch.

Then they stop talking, and my feet stop moving. I pull in behind a huge piece of machinery and hold my breath. The sounds of moving metal rings loudly all around me, followed by the labored breaths of one of the men.

One of the men.

"What the fuck!"

I swing around, finding the snarling, scrawny man Scott picked up en route, raising an old handgun. I don't fuck about. Instinct has me aiming and firing before his finger even finds the trigger of his weapon. The noise is ear-splitting. The blast ricochets off the metal machinery around me, and I watch as the man drops like a rock.

As soon as he hits the ground, I break into a run, sprinting through the factory, trying my hardest to keep the pounding of my boots against the concrete to a minimal volume. Easier said than done when potent purpose is coursing through you, burning your veins, making your head spin. I wipe the sweat away from my forehead again before it trickles into my eyes and hampers my vision, and round corner after corner, listening carefully. Then I hear something. I slow to a stop. A distant shift of metal on metal registers in my chaotic mind, and I back up, my back pressed against a rusty metal-paneled wall. I slowly raise my gun and edge around the corner.

I know the second I find where they've been keeping her. The door is half-open, and slight sounds of a scuffle come from beyond. I pace forward quietly, cautiously, and push the door open farther. Only a little, but enough to see inside.

The scene beyond could break me. I shoulder the door open the rest of the way and fill the entrance, stance wide, gun poised.

I recognize Scott from his picture. And he has Cami held against him, her back to his chest, a blade at her throat. His hands are shaking wildly, sweat pouring from his brow. He's panicking, and that only makes him more dangerous.

Cami is quiet, her head pressed back onto the shoulder of his filthy shirt, the length of her beautiful neck extended, her face pointed toward the ceiling. Her hands are bound. Her mouth is gagged. Her eyes are covered by a scrap of ragged material. Not seeing her eyes is my only consolation. Seeing her fear would tip me. I need to maintain my composure. Now, more than ever, I need to lock down my control.

"I'll slit her throat!" Scott yells, backing away, dragging Cami with him. Her feet clumsily slip and slide along the dusty floor. "Don't think I won't do it!"

I force my eyes to his and make sure I keep them there. You can tell the most about a person from their eyes. There's evil lingering in Scott's, past the apprehension. I have no doubt this man is guilty of all of the crimes he's been accused of.

Rape.

I momentarily lose my focus, having to blink the horrors away. If the thought has even crossed his mind, I'll...

I force myself to concentrate. "Who are you working for?" I ask evenly, keeping my gun low but poised. He's an uneducated piece of shit. He wouldn't know how to mastermind a kidnap.

"I'm telling you nothing."

"How do you communicate?"

"Fuck you." He backs up some more, his face close to Cami's, breathing on her. She flinches when a spray of his spit hits her face, and my focus wavers again. She's twenty feet away from me and I can't get to her. The blade pushing into her flesh, pulsing against her throat as she breathes, is smeared with filth, the handle rusty and bent. It won't slice. It'll saw.

I gulp, my grip tightening round the handle of my gun. "You made a really stupid mistake when you took this job," I say, my voice loaded with a threat he shouldn't underestimate. I cock my head, forcing the sight of Cami into a blur of nothing, the hollows of my cheeks pulsing as I bite down on my back teeth. "Really stupid," I murmur.

His comprehension of how serious I am comes in the form of a jerky movement that pushes the knife into Cami's throat, spiking a muffled murmur and a drop of blood to appear. It trickles down her neck.

The rage. Deep, hot, raw rage.

I step forward, feeling it consume me, my blood on fire.

Keep cool.

I. Must. Keep. My. Cool.

It's hard when I'm mentally lining up the most important shot I've ever made.

"Stay back!" Scott shouts, panicked.

"Good-bye." I close one eye, raise my hand, and pull the trigger. *Bang!* I see the bullet. I watch as it travels toward my target, the accuracy frightening, and I watch as it sinks dead center into his forehead. He drops like lead as blood splatters Cami's face.

Chapter 34

CAMI

My constant praying and picturing him has worked. There wasn't a second of our time together that I didn't revisit. It was the perfect diversion, something to take me away from the cold brutality of my reality. The second I heard that distant shot, I knew he'd found me. I was manhandled up from the floor by panicked hands, and then I heard Jake's voice.

The pressure of my captor's sweaty body against mine was unbearable. I could feel his shakes rippling through me, but fought to repel the effect. I forced myself into stillness. I used the remaining scraps of my energy to keep myself frozen, hardly breathing.

Because I knew what Jake was going to do. I could hear his intention. I could see the wood of the dead tree in his bluebell woodland burst. I knew without question that my kidnapper would be dead within seconds.

The ringing in my ears is painful and the warm liquid coating my face excruciatingly unbearable, but I'm powerless to wipe it away. Without the support of my captor holding me up, my knees give out and I collapse to the concrete floor. All of my held breath tries to break free on the impact, the force of air against the gag making it impossible to catch a breath.

I know it's only Jake and me in the room now—alive, at least—but I still jump like a frightened animal when I feel his big hands grab me and pull me onto his lap.

He works fast, unbinding my wrists until my bones crack with relief and my muscles spasm back to life. I flex gingerly, pain searing up my arms as he yanks the blindfold away. I slam my eyes shut, the bombardment of dusky light too much after being kept in the dark for hours.

"Oh, Jesus, Cami," he whispers, stroking at my face, his hands working fast and frantically, feeling me. "Open your eyes, angel." He pulls away my gag, and I drink in air, my lungs burning in gratitude.

I allow my lids to peel open a tiny bit, needing to see him but still being unable to tolerate the light. His strong thighs beneath my shoulders are the only comfort I can seize and run with, my arms refusing to lift and feel him, my eyes sore, my mouth dry.

Regardless of all that, though, I still feel the most at peace I ever have. I feel safe and hopeful. I feel determined. After what we've both just been through, nothing can stop us from being together. Not Jake's hidden demons, not my dad's enemies, and not his expectations, either. Nothing.

I open my eyes and blink some focus back, squinting. He's just a blur of darkness floating above me, the outline of the man I love.

A shadow.

I become agitated, pissed off with my lack of ability to see him more clearly. My hands come up to my face in broken, jerky movements, and I find my eye sockets with my fingers, rubbing some sight back into them. Then I try again, opening my eyes and searching him out.

The blur slowly fades, and Jake slowly forms. All of his face, clear and perfect. It's the most magnificent thing I've ever seen. Swallowing, I open my mouth to speak, but my lips stick, frustrating me further. There's so much I want and need to tell him. He needs to know that I accept him. His secrets, his mistakes, his regrets. He needs to know that I'll help him to make things right. But the words refuse to come, and when he places a finger over my mouth, settling me, I give up trying to talk.

"I know," he says quietly, smoothing his hand onto my cheek and cupping it. "I already know, angel."

I can only nod. It's feeble and weak, but it's all I can manage, and when he smiles—a sad but relieved smile—I know he understands.

"I'm taking you home," he says softly, maneuvering and negotiating my weight into his arms. "Can you hold on?"

It takes everything I have, but I strain to lift my arms around his neck, clinging to him as he rises to his feet.

"Don't look," he orders softly as he turns away, my eyes just catching a glimpse of a body sprawled on the floor, arms splayed out at the sides. The horrific sight of the pool of blood growing around his head doesn't deter me. I look at his face. His eyes are wide open, his mouth lax.

"I don't know him." My confused statement comes from nowhere, my voice found.

Jake releases one hand, keeping me secure against his chest with his other, and pushes his palm into my cheek, encouraging me to rest my head against his chest. "Shhh," he hushes me, and my body begins to sway in time to his long strides as he carries me away.

I look up at his bristly neck and listen to his heart beating evenly under my ear. He's focused forward, his face straight, but his jaw is tight.

When we make it outside, I bury my face against his chest and hide from the glare, drawing in long breaths through my nose, making the most of his scent and the fresh air. The walk to his car is long but he doesn't tire. His hold of me doesn't shift, and his pace doesn't falter. He's like a machine, programmed with purpose.

He sits me in the passenger seat carefully, letting me take my time to accustom my body to my new position. Everything is suddenly aching. Pulling open the glove compartment, he takes a tissue and starts wiping at my face, ridding it of blood and dirt with painstaking care. His finger meets my chin and lifts a little, and he homes in on my neck, prompting me to lift my hand and feel.

He stops me. "Don't touch it." Pressing my hand back to my lap, he lets it settle and then pulls my seat belt across, securing me in my seat. He doesn't miss the opportunity to push his lips into my forehead as he steps away.

The door closes and he's next to me in a heartbeat, starting the car, pulling his phone from his pocket and dialing. "I've got her," he says, to Lucinda I expect. "There are two bodies in the old Warston factory off the A505." He pulls out onto the bumpy lane and turns around in two quick moves. "Let Logan know she's safe." He falls silent, listening carefully, his eyes flicking briefly to mine. "I have one of their phones."

I frown, trying to keep up with the conversation, but what I can hear is too sketchy.

"Whoever it is should be calling soon," Jake says.

I'm confused. Whoever it is? Didn't he just kill them?

"See you there." He hangs up and looks across to me. "Okay?"

"What phone? Who will be calling?" I ask, relief disappearing, replaced by anxiety.

"I don't know," Jake admits. "Your dad hasn't been entirely honest with us." He says this tentatively, like he doesn't want to tell me. "He's chosen to keep certain things to himself."

"Like?"

"Like information on the threats he received—information that would have helped us find the people who sent them."

"Why would he do that?" I ask, perplexed. "He called off your protection! Said he'd dealt with it! Why would he do that if he knew I was at risk?" This doesn't make any sense. Even his tenacity in thinking that Jake isn't good enough for me isn't a good enough reason. It's crazy that he'd behave so heedlessly.

Jake's expression takes on a frightening edge of anger, his jaw ticking violently. It's a hint that he's thinking the exact same thing. "He was a desperate man," Jake spits, and I sigh, unable to comprehend why Dad would go to such lengths to keep Jake away from me rather than accept him and take comfort in the knowledge that I'm safe with him. I feel like he's gambled recklessly with my life. How could he? My own father?

"How did you find me?"

Jake smiles now, keeping his eyes on the road. "I've told you before, angel." His hand takes mine in my lap and squeezes. "I'll always find you."

I smile and rest back in my seat, returning his squeeze. All of my life I've strived for independence. I've repelled attempts to have that taken from me. Now I would surrender it all to Jake in a heartbeat. If I had to choose, I would always choose Jake. But I know I won't need to, which makes me love him all the more. I've found someone who sees me as me. Someone who encourages me. Someone who I know will always be with me, no matter what. No judgments. No conditions. No gain to him except my love. It's his. Unconditionally. Just like I know his for me will be.

"Where are we going?" I ask.

"Home."

"Where's home?"

"Where do you want it to be?" He looks across at me, keeping his face blank, waiting for my reply.

"You're my home now," I tell him. "Wherever you are, that's my home." I don't care where that may be.

Nodding his understanding, he returns his attention to the road. I let my head fall to the side and I study him for the entire journey. He looks like he's been to hell and back, his hair askew, his stubbled face covered in a sheen of sweat, his eyes tired.

"I love you," I say to him, thinking he looks like he needs to hear it. "Whatever you need to do to make things right, I'll be here for you."

He looks across to me, but he doesn't say anything. He just smiles a little.

* * *

I don't realize where I am until Jake pulls over and cuts the engine, and I break my stare at his profile.

"Dad's office?" I ask, bewildered. "You said you were taking me home." I know I said my home was with Jake, but not here...

"Just a small detour. I'm not overly happy about bringing you here, but I'm not prepared to let you out of my sight." He gets out and rounds his car, coming to collect me. The shakes set in. I didn't anticipate this. I haven't the strength to face my father. Not now.

Jake opens the door and helps me down. "Jake, why do we have to do this now?" I ask, looking up at the building. "I can't—"

"Hey." He places a finger over my mouth and hushes me. "There will be no arguing or attempts to pry you from my arms."

How does he know that? This is my father we're talking about. Hasn't he learned a thing? "I don't—"

His palm rests over my mouth. "Trust me, angel."

Trust him. I could search far and wide for a lifetime and I'd never find a reason not to trust him. He's been protecting me the whole time. From my father, from my ex... from his secrets.

I nod and look past him to the glass doors, bracing myself to face the last man in the world I want to see right now. Everything that has happened is because of him. His selfishness. His obsession with power and victory, in every capacity.

He's lost this time, the biggest loss he'll ever suffer. He's lost me.

"Come on." Jake tucks me into his side, taking slow steps, letting me take my time. I don't need it. I decide I want to get this over with as soon as possible.

Strangely, the security guard doesn't bat an eyelid when Jake skips the machines and walks me straight through to the elevators. Barbara, dad's long-suffering PA, doesn't question my unexpected visit or the man who's with me when we pass her desk. And Jake doesn't knock on my dad's office door when we arrive, instead pushing his way in. I frown at the sight of splintered wood on the frame as Jake walks me in, his hold of me increasing as my dad's office comes into view.

My father's not sitting at his desk holding court. He's pacing, looking the most disheveled I've ever seen him. When he looks across the room and spots me, I fall into shock when he breaks down, tears streaming uncontrollably down his face.

"Thank God!" He hurries over but pulls to a sharp stop before claiming me in his arms. I'm astounded when he looks to Jake for permission. What the fuck? I silently curse Jake for releasing me and exposing me to the corrupt clutches of my father.

Dad flings his arms around me and hugs me like he's never hugged me before. I don't return it. How can I when I'm less than pleased to see him? He's lied to me. He's tried everything to convince me Jake was bad for me, and when those efforts failed he manipulated the truth, told me Jake had a wife. He neglected to mention that Jake's wife was dead. On top of all that, he paid Sebastian to press charges against Jake to get him away from me. I always knew my dad was ruthless, but this? This I'll never understand. I never want to see him again.

"Camille, I'm so sorry."

I look at Jake and sense his inner battle to reclaim me. I want him to. I'm his. "I want to go home," I say, uncomfortable with Dad's guilt and his over-the-top attention.

Dad pulls away and swallows, scanning me up and down. I remain still and let him absorb my state. The state that he's responsible for.

"I'm so glad you're safe," he says.

"No thanks to you," I retort mechanically, shutting down completely. I need to leave. Not give him the opportunity to offload his reasoning on me. It won't wash. None of it.

Dad flinches, wounded, but I have no sympathy for him. I've turned into a cold-hearted cow. "My little star, please just—"

"Don't!" I yell, stunning myself with the decibel level of my voice, moving back. Jake seizes and hushes me, tucking my face into his chest and stroking my hair. "Take me home," I beg, feeling his chest expand. "Please."

"Camille, please. I must explain."

I turn my most disdainful look onto my father, but before I can hit him with my scathing words, Lucinda comes flying in the door, looking grave. She claps eyes on me, assessing me up and down, and gives me a small smile. I return it, feeling so fucking remorseful for clouting her over the head and running.

She turns her focus to Jake, her face serious again. "I might have something," she declares.

Jake goes rigid against me. "What?"

Lucinda's eyes bat between us. I know why. It's sensitive. Maybe not for my ears. I couldn't suffer any more than I already have.

"Go on," Jake prompts, and I look up, finding him staring at my father. He looks . . . apologetic?

Dad shifts, nervous and uncomfortable. "Go on," he breathes, walking over to his desk and dropping onto the chair heavily. "It's too late, now."

Lucinda marches over to the desk, pulling her laptop out as she goes. "I have a contact who tells me Scott had an unusual friendship in prison."

She's talking gibberish. I haven't the first idea what she's going on about.

"'Unusual' usually means 'significant,'" Jake says, turning us toward Dad's desk. My father holds my attention. He looks like a broken man sitting in his chair, a far cry from the man I know.

"He shared a cell with Vladimir Sochinsky."

I draw a total blank, the name meaning nothing to me. At least, it doesn't for a few seconds.

Dad's eyes enlarge. "Sochinsky?" he questions. "Sochinsky was TJ's mother's maiden name. Vladimir was her eldest brother."

And like an omen or something, TJ bursts into the office. "Oh God, you're safe!" He launches himself at me, knocking me back with the force of his hug. "Jesus, Cami, I've been so worried."

One minute I'm warm in my brother's hold, the next I'm not. Jake's claimed me and pulled me in, giving TJ a murderous glare. "Where have you been? How did you know Cami was missing?" Jake asks suspiciously.

"Dad called me." TJ frowns, taking in everyone in the office. I know what's running through Jake's head right now, and I have to put it to rest. Never. TJ loves me!

"No, Jake," I warn, wriggling free of him.

"Don't you dare throw your accusations around!" Dad's disgusted boom comes from behind, and I'm suddenly facing him again, courtesy of Jake moving us. "TJ is loyal through and through!"

"Forgive me," Jake grates, beginning to twitch, his potent anger making a swift return, "but I have little faith in your family's integrity."

Dad backs down in a second, his eyes flicking to mine. "TJ wouldn't do such a thing," he whispers. "He's my son. Camille's brother!"

"What?" TJ asks, truly exasperated. "Is someone suggesting I'd kidnap my own sister for a ransom from my own father? How the hell would someone come up with that stupid explanation?"

"Because," Lucinda pipes up, walking forward, eyeing TJ carefully. I don't like all this suspicion pointing at my brother. It's crazy! "The man who took Camille, and the man who is now lying on a factory floor with a bullet in his head courtesy of Jake, shared a cell in Borstal with *your* uncle."

TJ's face drops. "My uncle?" he whispers quietly, looking at me. He looks lost. A bit confused. He hasn't seen his mother since Dad divorced her and won TJ in the custody battle. She went back to Russia.

"Vladimir Sochinsky. Your mother's eldest brother." Lucinda goes on, looking for TJ's reaction. "He's been blackmailing your father."

"She tried to connect with me," TJ breathes, his hand coming up to his chest and applying pressure. "I told her I didn't need her." He looks to Dad, his idol, and deflates. "I told her that Dad and I were fine and she wasn't wanted. I haven't heard from her since."

"When was that?" Jake asks.

TJ shakes his head, confused. "I don't know . . . three months ago?"

"When did you get the first threat?" Jake asks my dad.

"Two months ago," he says. "Her brother's always hated me. But I have no idea how they got those pictures."

"They were obviously following you, Logan. Looking for something, anything to use against you. Probably even set you up." Jake gives my father an accusing look. "And you gave them what they wanted."

What they wanted? What did they want?

TJ looks at me, sorrow drenching his eyes. "This is all my fault."

Dad's up from his chair and racing to his son, taking him in his arms and hugging him. It's a strange sight. I've never seen my father hug my brother. It's always been hard love. Cruel to be kind. "It's not your fault, son. It's all me. My choices. My mistakes. I've made some terrible mistakes."

I could pass out with shock. My dad has admitted to making mistakes? "What mistakes, Dad?" I ask. "What did you give them to use against you?"

He stops comforting my brother and kisses the top of his head before facing Jake. "You've not told her?"

"I won't turn her against you. You've done that yourself," Jake says quietly.

"What?" I push, looking between them.

"I made a poor decision that gave them ammunition against me," Dad mumbles, defeated.

"Poor decision?" I ask, looking up at Jake when he moves in and places himself next to me. Why do I get the impression that he's got so close because he thinks I might need the support?

"There are some photographs." Dad sighs, his body squirming with discomfort. "Some compromising photographs."

"Of what?" I look around me to the other people in the room, noticing Jake looks uncomfortable; Lucinda, too. TJ looks totally bewildered.

"Me. And a woman." He's holding back. The sweat on his forehead and his refusal to look at me are making it obvious.

"What woman?" I grate, my anger working up without the need for the whole truth.

"A young woman."

"Just tell me!" I scream, batting Jake away when he tries to calm me down. "Stop fucking about and tell me!"

"She was fifteen," he whispers, ashamed. "I didn't know!"

TJ gasps, looking at his hero with disgust, and I fold.

"I was being blackmailed. It ran away with me. I thought I could handle it on my own. I got Sharp in to protect you. That's all that mattered, my little star! Your safety! He started digging, getting closer to the truth. I didn't want anyone to know!"

And there we have it. I was all that mattered? My safety? Then why the fuck did he call Jake off? He's a joke! All he cares about is his reputation. His business and his money. "I need to go." I look up to Jake, making sure he sees my desperation. I've heard enough. "Please," I beg. He knew. Jake knew, but I can't be mad with him. I can't hold him responsible for keeping me in the dark. He was protecting me. Even now, after everything my father has put us through, he didn't want me to have the extended burden of my father's shameful exploits.

Jake nods, but is distracted from coming to me when a phone starts ringing. He frowns and rummages through his pocket, pulling out a cheap, unfamiliar phone. "Unknown number," he says, looking up at Lucinda.

"Not for long." She takes the phone and accepts the call, but she says nothing, indicating with a held-up finger that everyone should remain quiet. She listens. And listens, and then she smiles, mouthing *Russian accent* to Jake. She hurries over to her laptop and plugs the phone in, holding up a silencing hand.

Jake opens the door and motions everyone out of the office, leaving Lucinda to it. Once he's closed the door, he strides past my father and lifts me so my legs wrap around his waist, then walks down the corridor toward the elevator, not even faltering when my father is suddenly at our side, trying to pull me away. He fails. My grip on Jake is as tight as his on me. He shakes my dad off with ease and determination as I cling onto him like he's all I have. Because I feel like he is.

Strong.

Dependable.

My protector.

CHAPTER 35

JAKE

It was too late to save Logan. I didn't want Cami to know the depths of his betrayal, but in the end I was powerless to stop it. He'd gone too far. I wanted to protect her from the hurt, but I also wanted to protect her from him.

Logan was beyond help. The man who's always been pissed-up on power was powerless. He was finished. Those pictures were never going to go away, not for all the money or contacts in the world.

Lucinda traced the call from the disposable phone I retrieved from Scott's body to a townhouse in North London. They found Vladimir Sochinsky and Logan's first wife, TJ's mum, and a mountain of evidence that will put them away for a long time, including details that matched the Swiss account mentioned in the messages to Logan. His first wife was broke. Logan didn't have much to give, back when they'd divorced, and the bitterness, her lost son, and Logan's obscene wealth today made a very tempting proposition for a twisted woman. She felt wronged, good for an heir and nothing more. Logan had always had it coming.

I virtually carried Camille to hospital to have her checked out, even after she refused to go. That knife. I shudder every time I think of it: filthy and cutting into my girl's flesh. She sulked, but she didn't try to stop me. Not even when the police turned up. Watching my angel relay every moment of her time in captivity was the worst few hours of my life. Her strength and conviction staggered me. She's a fighter. My little fighter.

Her mother showed up, large as life, shouting orders to staff left, right, and center. Her mother. Oh, her mother. Endearing but testing. She has basked in the glory of being the only one of Logan's wives' that hasn't turned on him. A ridiculous thing to be proud of, since I know for sure she'd love nothing more than to kick him in the balls and finish him off. The fact that her spousal payments might cease seems inconsequential, however. She'd rather have Logan's arse on a plate than his money.

The share prices of Logan's companies dropped like stones once the pictures surfaced, and the papers all printed them. Whatever immoral relationship he had with the press was doomed. He was arrested for sex with a minor. His third wife left him, pregnant with another man's child, and his first wife tried to extort money from him. He's ruined.

TJ is still in a state of shock. His integrity was questioned. He didn't have a clue what was going on. He hadn't seen his mother since he was three and had no idea what she was up to. The poor bloke is in tatters, feeling guilty, though he has nothing to feel guilty for. None of what happened was his doing; it was their father's doing. That megalomaniac of a man has lost everything.

The media have picked at the story like vultures, adding bits here and there, sensationalizing something that was already sensational enough. And through it all, Cami hasn't shed a tear. She's remained dignified, not speaking to the press and not voicing her opinions on her father. She was kidnapped and everyone wants a piece of her, but they can't have it.

The comfort I have knowing she's not been mentally scarred by her ordeal is beyond explanation. All of the reasons why I fell in love with her hit me between the eyes every time I look at her. So fucking strong. And I feed off that strength. It drives me, makes me want to be the man I always should have been. The only reason I'm here now is because of her. I'll never be able to repay her. But I'll try.

Just two days after the showdown at Logan's office, Cami's agent was on the phone, calling her about a meeting the next day with a new potential investor for her and Heather's clothing line. I thought maybe it was too soon, though I kept that thought to myself. Cami was too excited for me to dampen it. Then the next day came and I wasn't at all surprised when she was up and ready to head to her agent's office, armed with files and files of designs, fabric swatches, and her best friend and partner. I offered them a lift. Camille politely declined with a knowing smile. After shadowing her for so long, I'm struggling to let go, have to keep reminding myself that she's no longer in danger.

While she was gone, I paced her apartment until I'd worn a track in the carpet. And the moment she got home, I knew by the twinkle in her eyes that she'd nailed it. Not that I had much doubt. They offered a diamond of a deal on Cami's and Heather's clothing line, and I got a blow-by-blow account of the meeting from beginning to end. Camille and her friend didn't have to compromise on a thing. They got everything they had hoped for and worked so hard for. I'm so fucking proud of her. Of both of them, actually.

I haven't seen Abbie and Charlotte yet. We've talked on the phone, Abbie has kept up to speed on the crazy events, and she's been understanding. She's a good woman. I always knew it. I should have had more faith in that. She's nothing like her sister. My dead wife. Abbie is compassionate and resilient. I'm grateful. Any lesser woman would have given up on me by now.

I can't wait to try to make it up to Charlotte, to be there, be a dad, but I need to do it the right way. I've been planning how to go about this since the moment I walked out of Logan's office with

Cami wrapped around me like a blanket. This will be a barrage of shit Charlotte's little head might not be able to get around. But I pray she does. I pray she gives me the chance to explain my absence. I pray her four-year-old mind understands.

It's a week on and as I sit on the couch in Cami's lounge, listening to her chat with her mum on the phone, her head on my lap, I try to psych myself up for the afternoon ahead. It's been arranged, carefully thought out by me and Abbie. Cami knows what's keeping me quiet and apprehensive, but she hasn't made a huge deal of it. She's simply told me that she's ready when I am.

I'm ready now.

I wait patiently for her to wrap up her call to her mother, my eyes falling the length of her body and taking in the T-shirt I love so much as my fingers comb her hair. She's looking up at me, her eyes alive with happiness.

"What?" I ask, my eyebrow raised curiously. She's trying to conceal a grin.

Her shoulders shift on my thighs from a little shrug. "Nothing."

"Sure doesn't look like nothing from where I'm sitting."

She loses the fight to restrain her grin. "Mum wants to know when we're going out for dinner."

That's it? "You can go out whenever you like." The words sound far more sincere than I actually feel. Letting go is a challenge I've underestimated. Constantly telling myself that she's safe is easier than believing it.

Her grin widens. "She means *all* of us."

Oh. Like socializing? "All of us?" I mutter feebly, twisting her blond locks around my fist until my hand is a ball of hair. "I'm not sure that's my thing."

"What is your *thing*?"

"You." That's easy. "You are my thing."

"Will you think about it?" she asks, hope rife in her topaz eyes.

How can I refuse? I've been alone for so long, I don't know how to be sociable. To make normal conversation. "Yes," I agree, nudging her to lift as I sit forward. For her, I'll do anything. "Up you get."

"Why? Where are you going?"

I get to my feet and look down at her huddled on the couch, looking unprepared to move. "*We're* going out for the afternoon."

"We are?"

"Yes, we are." I take her hand and pull her to her feet, making sure I put enough force behind my tug to land her against my chest. Her tiny exhale of breath hits my neck and sends my knees weak. A lifetime of this makes every heart attack I've had since meeting Camille Logan worth the agony.

"Get dressed." I kiss her but push her away at the same time, mindful that if my pelvis captures a skimming touch of hers, I'm done for. We can't be late.

She grumbles, relenting and detaching her mouth from mine, narrowing her eyes on me as she backs away. "I don't know where we're going. What should I wear?"

"Something pretty. Girlie." I wave a hand to her head. "And braid your hair down one side," I order, meaning to be as demanding as I sound. I love her hair like that. Tousled and cute.

"Makeup?" she asks, knowing damn well what the correct answer is to that silly question.

"Are you trying me?"

"Yes. I like it when you're all bossy." She blows me a kiss and pivots, heading for the bedroom, a tactical sway to her arse. That T-shirt. Simple and sexy. Camille Logan is not to be ignored. And I never plan to. I need to find out where she got it from. She needs at least seven of them on rotation.

She likes it when I'm bossy? I can fully comprehend the weight of her admission. Cami Logan, miss headstrong and independent, loves me being bossy. It's just as well. That isn't going to change. She'll never lose her feistiness, and I hope she doesn't. It makes for good bouncing off when the time calls for it.

Smiling, I head for the shower to get myself ready.

* * *

I'm waiting for the treacherous shakes to make themselves known. I've got out of the car, I've walked down the street, and I've been standing at the end of the pathway to the house for at least two minutes. Two silent minutes, with Cami on my arm. I feel too calm for such a monumental moment. What's going on?

"Okay?" Cami looks up at me, her arm linked through mine. My hand rests in my jeans pocket.

"Yeah," I answer, because I am. Calm, stable, and resolute. It's the woman attached to my arm that's helping. I glimpse down at her and siphon off some more of the purpose that she feeds me. "I never imagined I could do this."

She reaches up on her tiptoes and pushes her lips against my jaw. "You can do anything."

Closing my eyes, I push into her kiss and slip an arm around her tiny waist. "Only because you're here," I tell her, leading her on.

Abbie is expecting us, so I'm not surprised when the door opens and she appears before we make it all the way up the path. She looks more nervous now than she did on that awful day when it all went so horribly wrong. She smiles and motions us in, giving Cami a reassuring rub on the arm as we pass. The gesture doesn't go unnoticed by my angel. She swallows and glances up at me, tears forming in her eyes. She doesn't let them take hold, though, shaking them away like the brave girl she is.

"We're in the garden," Abbie says, gesturing toward the dining room off the hall. "It's a lovely day. Thought it would be nice to make the most of it."

I nod, and Cami drops my arm, making my steadiness waver for a moment. I shoot her a look but she just tilts her head toward the door that leads into the dining room, her way of telling me I can do this.

I *can* do this. Taking in plenty of oxygen, I clear my throat and slowly make my way through, feeling able to face the photographs lining the walls of the hallway this time. My little girl. She's everywhere—posing, captured playing, dancing. I've never seen such a perfect little thing.

My pace stutters when I come face to face with a picture of my dead wife, her expression bright and happy. Again, I wait for the shakes to attack me, but they don't come.

All the hatred and bitterness that's weighed me down for all these years has vanished. Gone like it was never there. I'm looking into the eyes of the woman who destroyed me, and I feel nothing but sadness and sorrow. We both made mistakes. We both let our little girl down. But I'm the only one left who can make things right. Or as right as they can be. I pass a silent message to her, looking straight into her dark eyes.

I'm sorry, Monica.

I don't know if she'll hear it. Whether it would mean anything if she does. But I *am* sorry. I'm sorry for abandoning my little girl. I sniff, ripping my eyes away from the image of my wife. The sound of a child's squeal floats into the house, and I peek my head around the door to the dining room, seeing the patio doors flung open. I'm aware that Abbie and Cami are hovering behind me, probably silently willing me on. Taking one hesitant step, I put myself in the room, bringing part of the garden into view. I don't see Charlotte, but I can hear her. She's chatting away buoyantly, and I turn to ask who's out there with her.

Abbie chuckles. "She's having a tea party with her teddy bears."

"Oh." I show acceptance and understanding, when what I'm actually thinking is, *Huh? She's talking to her teddy bears? Having a tea party?* My silent bewilderment speaks volumes. I haven't got a fucking clue how to humor or entertain children, least of all a little girl who talks to her toys. I'm suddenly very nervous, but I bully myself to move forward before I chicken out and run for the hills.

When I round the corner, I can't help but stare, a little taken aback. It's not a tea party, it's a banquet. The garden table is set and platters of fruit and cakes are positioned in the middle. A few bottles of water are scattered, and two of the six chairs have teddy bears perched on them. Charlotte, dressed in an adorable lemon cotton sundress, her dark hair in a high ponytail, is dishing up some grapes on the plates laid before her bears.

"One or two, Mr. Piggles?" she asks seriously, holding up a spoon with two red grapes perched atop. "Two?" she asks, and I look to the bear like a twat, waiting for his confirmation. "Greedy!" she giggles, tipping the spoon onto the plate. The grapes roll around, one finding its way to the edge and toppling off the side. She tuts, grabbing it with her hand and tossing it back on the plate. "No, you may not leave the table." She waves the spoon in the bear's face. "Only when you've eaten all your supper."

I'm speechless. Turning, feeling a little lost and stupid, I find Cami and give her a pained look. I have no idea what to do, and she knows it, but instead of coming over and helping me out, she flips her eyes to Charlotte's back and gives me an encouraging smile. Then Cami looks at Abbie and she nods, understanding, and they both turn and wander back into the house. I watch, mouth hanging open in stunned silence, as they abandon me, leaving me to fend for myself.

Talk about throwing me to the fucking wolves! They disappear, not even flinging me a backward glance to check whether I'm still alive. I come over all stressed, my forehead prickling with sweat beads. I didn't bargain for this.

"Hello."

The sweet little voice has me swinging around more violently than I should, my expression undoubtedly panicked. She's looking up at me, her tiny chin lifted high to get my towering frame in view. I feel like a giant. This little thing, she can't hurt me. Coughing over my thick tongue, I yell at myself for being such a pussy. "Hello," I reply—short, sweet, and simple, praying she takes the lead and gives me a heads-up on where our first ever conversation will go.

But she says nothing. Just stares up at me, making me fidget and avoid her dark eyes. She's inspecting me. I can't help but wonder what her tiny mind is concluding. The silence becomes painful. At least, it does for me. Charlotte seems quite happy studying me.

I cough again and offer my hand, not knowing what the hell I'm doing. "I'm Jake." I keep my voice low and as soft as I can. I don't want to frighten her. I'm terrified enough for the both of us.

Her little face twists in amusement, her rosy lips tipping at the corners. "I know who you are." She almost chuckles, but holds onto it as though she realizes it might make me feel a little stupid.

"You do?" I retract my hand a little, cocking my head.

"Yes. You're my daddy." She says it so matter-of-factly, with no hint of accusation or discontent.

Fucking hell, I'm flummoxed. Just like that? My heart constricts in my chest, twisting painfully over and over, until I feel the need to push the side of my fist into my pecs in an attempt to ease it.

She places her little hand in mine and I look down, seeing it looking like it could be the most delicate of birds perched there. Those beads of liquid that were forming on my forehead have somehow made their way to the backs of my eyes. I blink the sting away and look at her, amazed. She smiles. It's the most beautiful sight I've ever seen.

"Nice to meet you, Daddy. My name is Charlotte. I'm your little girl."

My aching heart explodes in my fucking chest, shattering into tiny fragments that are all heavily weighted down with guilt, remorse, and so much sorrow. "Nice to meet you, too," I reply, my voice broken as I smile through my emotion.

I deserve to be hanged. After everything I've done—for abandoning this little girl to wallow in my pit of misery—I deserve to be sliced to pieces and left out for the vultures. I realize now that Charlotte would have helped me. We would have muddled through. She would have brought light into my dark world and given me determination to find my way. This tiny creature, so alive and resilient, is putting me to shame.

I wrap my huge palm around her little one and apply a little pressure, hoping she reads into it as I want her to. I'm struck dumb for words.

Giggling a little, she shifts her hand so she's holding mine and starts pulling me toward the table. "We're having a party."

I look at the table, reminded of what I first walked in on. Oh heck, she's not going to make me talk to her stuffed toys, is she?

"Looks fun," I muse, trying to swallow down the lasting overwhelming feelings that Charlotte has stirred. It's no good. It's all wedged securely in my throat with no chance of going anywhere.

"Sit." She releases my hand and points to where she wants me to be, and I obey quickly, waiting for my next instruction.

She looks delighted by my willingness, and my chest actually swells a little, proud that I've pleased her. "I have a table and chairs, too." She points to the bottom of the garden, to a minuscule table and chair set. My foot is bigger than the seats of the chairs. "Aunty Abbie said you might be too big and break them."

Thank God for Aunty Abbie. I'm already frightened of breaking this fragile little girl. I don't want to risk damaging her toys. "I think Aunty Abbie is right."

Charlotte pushes herself up onto a chair, looking even smaller as she shuffles her bum forward to the edge so she can reach the table, the long, dark strands of her ponytail jumping across her little shoulders. She takes a little teapot and pours some water into a thimble of a teacup.

"Have some tea." She passes the cup over and I grip it between my thumb and forefinger awkwardly, trying not to look like a big clumsy oaf.

"Thank you." I give up on the tiny cup and place it down, reaching for my inside pocket. "Can I show you something?"

Her excitement is instant. "What?"

"I'd like to show you a photograph of your mummy, if you'd like?"

"I've seen lots of photographs of my mummy."

Her reply gives me pause. Of course she has. The hallway is lined with reams of them. But not like this one. This is the only picture of me and Monica together. "This one is a little different."

Her hairline drops as her little forehead furrows deeply. "Why?"

Fingering the picture inside my pocket, I momentarily question if this is the right thing to do. "Well, because I'm in the picture, too." I blurt the words, nervous, and pull it out before I can convince myself it's a bad move. "Here." I hand it over, trying not to take a peek myself.

I don't know why I've kept it all this time. Personal torture, perhaps? Seems like a reasonable explanation. I've been hell-bent on it the past few years. Or maybe I knew deep down, beneath all of the twisted bitterness, that I'd one day see sense and do anything to get my little girl back. I prefer that conclusion.

I watch, fascinated, as her eyes shine like diamonds, seeing her mummy and daddy together for the first time. She studies the image for a long time, her gaze roaming every inch of the photograph.

"Did you know my mummy?" she finally asks, looking up at me.

"Yes." I point to the picture, but she doesn't look again, keeping her curious eyes on me.

"What was she like?"

What was she like? I know Abbie has filled her little head with an abundance of information that will shine her mother in the best possible light. And so she should. "Aunty Abbie has told you all about her."

"I want *you* to tell me." She places the picture down and continues to watch me, waiting.

What can I say? Monica broke me. Made me want to kill someone every day for the rest of my life. The reason I've been missing from my little girl's life is because she screwed me over and made me a hateful, selfish bastard and I wanted to shelter my baby girl from that?

"She was wonderful and beautiful, just like you." My answer fights past all of the nasty shit with ease as I bully myself into remembering the better times. Like how we met. Like how fast we fell in love. It's the first time in years that I've allowed my mind to venture that far back into my past—to the times before the shit and anger and hurt. They were buried too deep. The memories were too hard to find. Somehow, it seems easy to locate them now.

She giggles, her long lashes fluttering. "Have you finished fighting the bad men now, Daddy?"

Her curveball question has me looking up, startled. "Huh?"

"Aunty Abbie said you would be home one day, when you finish fighting the bad men." Her little head cocks in question. "Have you finished fighting the bad men now?"

I could crumble. Good God, I'm on the verge of pooling into a huge blubbering mess. "Yes." I clear my throat and take the photo off the table, tucking it back in my pocket. "All the bad men are gone."

They aren't. Never will be. But they are from *my* life, and that's what matters for now. I haven't got the heart to dash that notion. Her innocence is infectious. I want in on it.

"Does that mean you can start being my daddy now?"

That's it. I can't hold them off anymore. There are too many and nowhere for them to go but down my cheek. I wipe them away furiously, sniffling like a fool. I nod, the emotion strangling me.

"Why are you crying, Daddy?" She reaches over and places her hand on mine.

"I'm crying because I'm happy," I tell her. "I'm really happy that I can be your daddy now."

I have no fucking clue how this is going to work. My sense of possession toward her is growing with every second that I sit here. I've fallen in love with her. Madly. So fucking madly. This smart, sweet, vivacious little girl is mine. I realize we need to do this slowly. Get to know each other. Form a bond. I have no right or claim on her, but as I look across the table to her, I find her big brown eyes alive.

And I realize...

She's made a claim on me.

CHAPTER 36

CAMI

Watching him from the kitchen window handling the spirited little girl has me all choked up, wrestling down the lump in my throat. He looked so terrified. Leaving him to it was one of the hardest things I've ever done. But I have every faith in him. He needs to do this, take that final step into his past and make it right. The past week has been spent quietly, me coming to terms with my father's betrayal, and Jake wrapping his mind around his future. A future with me, and hopefully, with that little girl, who is currently introducing Jake to her teddy bears. I smile as I watch him gingerly reach forward and shake a limp paw. God love him, he looks petrified of the tiny girl and her collection of stuffed bears.

"He's doing okay." Abbie appears beside me at the window, smiling fondly. "She's a character. No nonsense and matter-of-fact."

I laugh a little, thinking of someone else with similar qualities. "She's adorable."

"Yes, she is."

"How have you coped?"

"You just do, don't you? I always lived in hope that Jake would come back. She knows Mummy is in heaven, and she thinks Daddy has been fighting all the baddies." She laughs, and I join her.

"It's true, I guess."

"Yes," Abbie agrees, nodding to herself. "I didn't know Jake for very long, but I know a good man when I see one. It's a shame my sister toyed with that."

"What was she like?" I ask, feeling comfortable. I've been in the kitchen with Abbie for less than half an hour and feel so relaxed. She has a serene, calming aura surrounding her that you can't help being affected by.

She folds her arms across her chest. Her dark hair is tied up loosely, and she's dressed in a tie-dye shirt and jeans that have paint splattered up the pockets.

"We were very different from each other," she says wistfully, gazing out into the garden. "Monica was bold, highly strung, and daring. I often wondered how we came from the same parents."

"My brother and I are very different, but we have different mothers."

She looks at me and smiles. "I know."

I feel a blush creep up on my cheeks. Of course she knows. Everyone in London knows.

"Monica and Jake's romance was a bit of a whirlwind," she goes on, surprising me. I had no intention to ask or pry about that part of Jake's life. Silly as it sounds and despite it all ending so horribly, I can't help but feel a smidgen of jealousy. There's also a bit of resentment, coupled with a hint of gratitude. It's a strange mix of feelings toward a woman who is dead. I resent her for destroying Jake, but I'm grateful that her bad choices meant I could one day fix him. I'm jealous that she had that effect on him.

"They met when Jake was home on leave," she continues, pulling me from my thoughts. Then she laughs. "They were married before he returned to Afghanistan. She found out she was pregnant soon after and that was that." Abbie sighs and collects her mug, sipping thoughtfully. "I knew she was making a mistake. Monica was a demanding woman, craved attention, and Jake couldn't very well meet those demands from the Middle East."

Step in his best mate, I think to myself, joining Abbie and having some tea myself.

"I loved my sister dearly, but she was a selfish girl." She looks at me, a sad smile on her face. "She was so caught up in lust, she didn't consider being a wife and a mother at home alone."

I don't know what to say, so I go with the only thing that I have. "Thank you."

She looks at me, interested. "For what?"

I feel a bit silly, wondering if it's my place to say, but I kind of feel like I should. "For looking after Charlotte. She's a credit to you." This woman didn't ask for any of this. She picked up the pieces and got on with things, and has kept Jake alive in his daughter's eyes. She's a sincere, good woman. Jake will never be able to repay her for what she's done.

"I love her." I can hear the quiver in her voice, and compelled to try and ease her sadness, I place a hand on her arm. She laughs, chasing away the emotion. "I'm being silly. I've wished for this day all her life, and now that it's here I feel a little overwhelmed. I wanted him to see what an amazing little girl she is. I knew he'd fall for her the moment he saw her."

Her faith and empathy is beyond my comprehension, and I look out of the window again, seeing Jake now with a bear on his lap, feeding it a strawberry, and Charlotte showing him how it should be done. I laugh, savoring the beautiful scene. Jake's smiling, his eyes bright and happy, but there's pure wonder on his face, as if he just can't fathom how that little girl has him doing such a pansy thing.

"I think he's fallen," I muse to myself.

"It was a given." Abbie places her mug down. "Oh, they're coming back." She turns laughing eyes onto me. "Shall I get him something stronger than tea?"

"Yes!" I giggle, just as Charlotte marches into the kitchen dragging Jake along behind her. I purse my lips and take him in, finding a far more relaxed Jake than when I left him to go into the garden on his own.

Charlotte puts herself in front of me, keeping hold of Jake's hand. "My daddy said you're his angel."

I dart a surprised look to Jake, and he shrugs nonchalantly. Wow. I wasn't expecting that. "Um...I..." I stutter like a fool.

"Like my mummy?" she questions with an innocence that melts my heart. "Are you an angel like my mummy?"

"Well...I'm..." I search for what to say to her in language she'll understand, turning into a nervous wreck.

"Not quite like your mummy." Abbie steps in, detecting my struggle. "Mummy is an angel because she has gone to heaven. Cami is an angel because she's Daddy's savior."

I inhale sharply, looking to Jake. He looks a little shocked, too.

"What's a savior?" Charlotte asks.

Abbie, oblivious to my and Jake's stunned faces, bends a little and rests her palms on her knees, getting closer to her niece. She smiles at Charlotte, content and calm. "A savior is someone who makes another person happy when they have been sad." She reels off the simple explanation like she's practiced it, handling the little girl's inquiry with ease and calm, whereas Jake and I have disintegrated under the pressure. Christ, I'm getting more nervous about this by the minute. How is this even going to work? We haven't spoken about the logistics or what will happen.

"Why was Daddy sad?" she asks, sounding so sad herself at the notion.

"Because he wanted to be here with you and he couldn't be," Abbie says gently, pacifying her.

My gaze shoots to Jake, finding his eyes fixed on the little girl, emotion pooling in them. I don't know if I can hold myself together for much longer.

Charlotte seems quite satisfied with the answer, turning away from her aunty and back to me. "Thank you for making my Daddy happy!" she sings, beaming up at me. "Now I can help you make him happy, too! Because he's fought all the baddies! And now he can be my daddy!"

Oh my God. I swallow repeatedly, forcing a smile before I have a quick peek at Jake to gauge what's going through his mind. I can't tell. He looks lost between wonder and confusion. "You're welcome," I whisper.

"Daddy asked me to help him with something," she declares, her little chest puffing out proudly.

My recoil is mild. "He has?"

She nods, taking Jake's hand in both of hers, hanging from him. "You have to come into the garden."

I throw Jake a questioning look that goes right over his head. "I guess we should go in the garden," he says, coughing his throat clear, gesturing for us to lead on.

I look to Abbie and she shrugs, a hint of a smile on her face. "The garden," she affirms, placing a hand on my back to encourage me onward.

With nothing left to do except as I'm bid by all three of them, I follow Charlotte until I'm in the lush green space that boasts a vegetable patch as well as a shed that has had each panel of wood painted a different color. The mix of colors between each plank tells me Charlotte may have helped out.

"Would you like to sit?" Jake asks, circling me and pointing to an empty chair.

"I don't know. Do I need to?"

"Yes!" Charlotte squeals, excitement building, pushing me on with a strength that defies her little frame. I plop down into the chair and she assesses my position, then looks up at Jake. "You're tall, Daddy. You need to kneel or you won't be able to kiss her."

I sit up straight and Jake laughs, bringing a finger to his lips. "Shhhh."

Charlotte's eyes go all round and she slaps a hand over her mouth. "Oops!"

"What's going on?" I ask, not liking being in the dark *or* the center of attention.

Jake's happy smile turns shy as Charlotte pushes into his hip, forcing him closer to me. I look up at him, and it takes me a few blank moments to realize that his face is coming closer.

Because he's dropping to his knee.

I sit back in my chair, anxious. Oh my goodness, what is he doing?

He lands on his knee and takes my hand, pulling me forward. I make it as hard as possible for him. Cocking his head curiously, he tugs so I jerk forward. "When I told Charlotte that we were going to get married," Jakes begins quietly, "she asked me how I'd asked you." He looks at his grinning daughter and laughs a little, raking a hand through his hair nervously. "She wasn't very impressed."

She wasn't? But it was perfect. I don't say that, though, because Charlotte is nodding her agreement, her little head bobbing fast. Abbie laughs from behind.

"She said it wasn't like the fairy tales," Jake goes on, his voice breaking a little, but he fights his way through it and pulls in air.

"Why?" I look to Charlotte and her little eyes roll impatiently.

"Because he didn't give you a ring!" she cries. "All the princes have a ring for their princess!"

"Ohhh," I breathe, thinking it best not to tell her that I did, in fact, have a ring. Until it washed off in the shower.

"Now he has a ring!" She's virtually shaking with excitement. "Give it to her, Daddy!"

He does?

I bite my lip, feeling Jake flexing his fingers around mine.

"Do you mind if we do this again?" he asks, a little embarrassed.

I could cry. I'm about to tell him that he doesn't need to, but I'm interrupted by Charlotte crawling up the side of my chair, pushing something onto my head. "Now you're a proper princess," she declares, climbing down.

I reach up and feel the plastic of a tiara resting in my hair.

"It was Cinderella's," she tells me, all matter-of-fact.

I laugh nervously. "Thank you." She looks so proud of herself.

Jake looks to his daughter for permission to go on, and she nods her agreement, grinning. Then he turns to me and pulls out a ring— a beautifully simple diamond ring. "Camille Logan," he breathes, and I choke up, straightening my lips to prevent showing myself up and blubbering like a fool. I'm certain Charlotte wouldn't be impressed. Cinderella didn't cry. Jake smiles, so dazzling and happy. I swear he'd give Prince Charming a run for his money. He squeezes my hand. "Will you have me forever?"

"That's not how you do it!" Charlotte jumps in, annoyed.

"Okay!" Jake laughs, giving me sorry eyes. He breathes in deeply. "Will you please do me the honor of becoming my wife, Camille Logan?" His hand constricts around mine, his smile shy. "I can't imagine my life without you. I want to be by your side for the rest of our days on this earth. I want to see your beautiful smile, hear your voice, watch you work. And I want to share my happiness with you. Every day for the rest of our lives." He reaches forward and strokes my cheek tenderly. "Will you marry me?"

I swallow, choking up, forcing my lips to remain locked tight so my emotion can't escape. Then I start to slowly nod.

"You have to say yes!" Charlotte sings, and I chuckle along with Abbie and Jake, while Charlotte waits for me to follow her instructions. I don't bother telling her that we've been through all of this. It'll hold no importance to her, since Jake screwed it all up in her eyes.

I pull away, smiling through my overwhelming emotion. "Yes," I say clearly, accepting the ring as Jake slips it on my finger. "You're my home now." I'm done for, a wreck, tears streaming down my cheeks.

Screw Cinderella. She must have been a hard bitch. "You're my every-thing, Jake Sharp."

"Yay!" Charlotte squeals, and I laugh over my tears, seeing her pirouetting on the spot.

Jake rubs a thumb across the gem, sighing. "Thank you," he mur-murs quietly.

"You have to kiss now!" Charlotte starts bouncing to the side of us, clapping her hands.

I don't waste time. No one will ever need to tell me twice to kiss him. I throw myself into his arms and slam my mouth to his, push-ing him back to the grass, losing all of my inhibitions. I'm lost in a haze of happiness, optimism, and undying love, while Charlotte dances around our sprawled bodies, clapping her hands and cheering.

I only come up for air once she's demanded that we stop kissing. Crouching by her daddy's head, her little hands joined and resting in her lap, she looks at me, while Jake looks up at her. "Daddy gave me a ring, too," she announces proudly, holding her chubby hand out in front of me. "He said it is superspecial."

I look down and see a replica of the penned engagement ring that Jake drew onto my finger at his country hideaway. My lips stretch into a massive smile, my gaze flicking to Jake.

He looks a little shy and awkward. "You're lucky," he says on a shrug. "She wanted *that* one." He nods down to my ring finger where my diamond sits perfectly.

I laugh loudly, thinking something I never thought I would. I think about how willing and excited I am to share Jake. To share him with this spirited, gorgeous little girl. *His* little girl. Everything he has is mine. And Charlotte is now mine, too.

I breathe in the fresh air and the overpowering scent of love sur-rounding me, closing my eyes and burrowing down into Jake's chest. "What happens now?" I ask quietly.

"What do you want to happen?"

"I'd like to live in your enchanted land and have my happily ever after."

I feel him smile against my neck. "Anything you want."

Charlotte squeals, and we both look up at her. "I want to live in an enchanted land, too! Can I, Daddy? Can I, can I?" She looks almost panicked by the possibility of being refused, and I look at Jake, wondering how he might handle her. I'm not deluded. I realize we're not going to be sweeping Charlotte up and whisking her off to the countryside to join us in our happily ever after. This is going to take time and deep consideration. Jake's lips straighten as he looks at his daughter's hopeful face, clearly wondering how he should approach this without upsetting her, or, most importantly, stepping on Abbie's toes. She's raised his daughter for four years. She needs to be considered here, too.

Abbie steps forward and drops to her haunches, getting Charlotte's attention. "Maybe you can visit on the weekends for a little while. Just until Daddy and Camille get everything fixed up for you. I'm sure they have a lot to do to get ready for your arrival." She smiles a small smile that is strained, and I see the effort it's taking her to speak, her voice a little wobbly.

Jake starts to sit up, taking me with him. I move to the side, seeing his intention. He reaches for Abbie's hand and squeezes comfortingly. "Thank you," he says quietly.

Abbie swallows and shakes her head. "And, of course, they need to fix my bedroom up, too, for when I come visit you."

"I'll be a princess in Daddy's enchanted land!" Charlotte jumps on the spot excitedly before launching herself at Jake, tackling him to the ground. He laughs, letting her sit astride of his chest. She looks down at him seriously. "I'm glad you're home now, Daddy."

The hollows of his cheeks pulse, emotion threatening to wrack his body as he reaches for her chubby cheek and strokes it gently. "Me too, baby. Me too. I'm never leaving you again."

Charlotte drops to her daddy's chest, looping her small arms around his big body. "You can be my king, Daddy."

Jake's face disappears into his little girl's small neck, and he crushes her to his chest. He's hiding his overwhelmed tears, whereas I let mine stream down my face, so happy, feeling Jake's peace reaching me.

My shadow has his own shadow now.

About the Author

Jodi was born and raised in the Midlands town of Northampton, England, where she lives with her two boys and a beagle. She is a self-professed daydreamer, a Converse and mojito addict, and has a terrible weak spot for Alpha Males.

Writing powerful love stories and creating addictive characters have become her passion—a passion she now shares with her devoted readers.

She's a proud #1 *New York Times* bestselling author, and all six of her published novels were *New York Times* bestsellers, in addition to being international and *Sunday Times* bestsellers. Her work is published in more than twenty languages across the world.

You can learn more at:

JodiEllenMalpas.co.uk

Twitter @JodiEllenMalpas

facebook.com/jodiellenmalpas